FINDING A HERO

BAYTOWN HEROES

MARYANN JORDAN

Finding a Hero (Baytown Heroes) Copyright 2022

All rights reserved. No part of this book may be reproduced or transmitted in any form or by any means, electronic or mechanical, including photocopying, recording, or by any information storage and retrieval system without the written permission of the author, except where permitted by law.

If you are reading this book and did not purchase it, then you are reading an illegal pirated copy. If you would be concerned about working for no pay, then please respect the author's work! Make sure that you are only reading a copy that has been officially released by the author.

This book is a work of fiction. Names, characters, places, and incidents are either products of the author's imagination or are used fictitiously. Any resemblance to actual persons, living or dead, events, or locales is entirely coincidental.

Cover: Graphics by Stacy

ISBN ebook: 978-1-956588-17-0

ISBN print: 978-1-956588-18-7

❀ Created with Vellum

Author's Note

Please remember that this is a work of fiction. I have lived in numerous states as well as overseas, but for the last thirty years have called Virginia my home. I often choose to use fictional city names with some geographical accuracies.

These fictionally named cities allow me to use my creativity and not feel constricted by attempting to accurately portray the areas.

It is my hope that my readers will allow me this creative license and understand my fictional world.

I also do quite a bit of research on my books and try to write on subjects with accuracy. There will always be points where creative license will be used in order to create scenes or plots.

1

TWENTY-TWO YEARS AGO

Joseph (Eastern Shore of Virginia)

"I d…d…don't feel so g…g…good." Scuffing the toe of his shoe on the floor, Joseph Newman stood in the nurse's office, wishing he could just call his mom to come get him without explaining why he wanted to go home.

"She's not home right now," the nurse said, barely looking at him as she bustled around the clinic. "But you can stay here for a little while until your stomach feels better."

He nodded, sitting on the hard, plastic chair, his legs swinging since they didn't touch the floor. The clinic's door was open, and he could see into the hall. Recognizing his brother walking past the door, he felt his heart leap when Wyatt popped back around the doorframe, his eyes wide. "Joseph? Are you sick?"

Joseph looked over at the nurse, who was busy dispensing medication to several others who'd come in. Wyatt sat in the chair next to him, and Joseph noticed it was easier to breathe just by having him close. Shrugging, he mumbled, "J…J… Just don't feel g…g…good."

Wyatt didn't say anything for a moment but put his arm around Joseph's shoulders. "You want to tell me what's really going on?"

He shrugged again, not surprised that Wyatt knew he wasn't really sick. Wyatt had just turned ten years old, two years older than Joseph, and he was lucky because Wyatt was also his best friend.

"Stevie making fun of you again?"

He nodded, looking down at his worn jeans where his knee almost showed through the threadbare material. They had been bought as used at the thrift shop when Wyatt was eight, and now that he'd outgrown them, they'd come to Joseph. He didn't mind hand-me-downs—it seemed that most kids he knew wore them. But when their dad lost his job, it was harder to replace the clothes when they were worn out. Stevie and his bully friends made sure to point out when Joseph's clothes had holes in them. And the speech problems he'd overcome with speech therapy in first grade came back when he became nervous.

"I'll find him after school and make sure he knows not to bother you," Wyatt promised.

Joseph jerked around and shook his head. "N…N… No, Wyatt. You c…c… can't. I d…d…don't want you to g…get in trouble." Wyatt was never in trouble. He always did his homework. Always helped their parents.

And always helped him and their little sister, Betsy. Joseph didn't want Wyatt to get in trouble as much as he wanted Stevie to have to take back his mean words. "Anyway, it's not j...just me. He m...m...makes fun of others, t...too. I t...told him to leave S...Susie alone, but then he m...made fun of m...me." More than anything, he wanted to be brave like Wyatt and make Stevie stop making some of the other poor kids cry.

Wyatt nodded, sighing heavily. "Stevie thinks his poop doesn't stink because his family has money."

He snort-giggled and covered his mouth with his hand before nodding for Wyatt to go on.

"But deep down inside, he knows his poop does stink. He's just trying to keep everyone from looking too hard at him. You're the nicest kid in third grade. That's what matters."

The two sat for a moment, then the nurse turned around, her eyes widening. "Wyatt, I didn't see you there. Are you sick, too?"

"No, ma'am. I just came in to check on my little brother." Looking down at Joseph, he asked, "Are you feeling better now?"

He nodded. Nothing was quite like having his big brother around to make the world seem less worrisome. Looking up at the nurse, he said, "I think I can g...go back to c...class now."

As the two Newman boys walked down the hall, they first came to Joseph's classroom. Turning toward Wyatt, he grinned, then worked hard to get the words out. "Thanks, Wyatt. I'll be okay n...now."

"You've got this, Joseph." Wyatt smiled in return.

"Remember, whenever Stevie starts running his mouth, you just hold your head up high. And then you tell me, and I'll kick his ass!"

Stifling a grin, he nodded, then walked back into the classroom, lifting his head even though his stomach still flip-flopped a little. More than anything, he longed for the day when things would change, and he'd be able to protect others.

Shiloh (Pennsylvania)

Shiloh walked along the path that led from her tiny school toward home with the others from her community. The mountains were thick on either side of the road, and she loved to jump between the rays of sunlight that streaked through the limbs.

"Come on," Rebecca called. "You know this is bread-making day, and Mama wants our help."

Shiloh's eyes widened with anticipation. She loved freshly made bread, especially when their mama would let her make her own small loaves for her pretend tea parties. "I'm coming!" she called out, racing after her older sister. Her dress was a little long since it was a hand-me-down from Rebecca, but their mama had stitched it so that it fit Shiloh's thin body as though it were made just for her.

Rebecca was already eleven, four years older than

Shiloh, and so much more grown up. Rebecca walked when Shiloh ran. Rebecca listened quietly when Shiloh loved to talk. And Rebecca didn't wiggle in church when Shiloh wanted to dance.

"My girls are different, but they're just the way God meant them to be," their dad would say with a smile.

Hurrying after Rebecca, she raced up the lane, deeper into the mountains surrounding their little community. Many of the families in their town would homeschool their children rather than have them make the long walk to the closest school. Their parents insisted their girls attend public school, even with the walk. Although when the weather was rainy or snowy, her dad would take them in the old farm truck. But on days like today, Shiloh felt as though she could walk forever, loving the fresh air, the scent of the pine trees, and the glory of the surrounding mountains.

Sometimes she would look at books and wonder about the people who lived on the other side of the mountains. Big cities. Fancy clothes. Cars and buses and trains and planes. *The ocean!* She thought perhaps that was what she might like to see the most.

"Hey, Rebecca. If you could go anywhere, where would you want to go?"

Her sister looked over with an indulgent smile on her face. "We play this game all the time. You know my answer... I'm happy right here." Rebecca waited a few seconds and then sighed. "Okay, Shiloh, if you could go anywhere, where would you go?"

"The ocean!"

Rebecca pretended surprise as her head whipped

around, causing her long braid to fly over her shoulder. Laughing, she replied, "You always say the ocean."

"I know, but don't the pictures in our books make it look so big with waves and sand and crabs and shells?" Her imaginings came to a halt now that they had rounded a curve in the road. The woods fell away, and she could see a field in the distance. Their dad was on his tractor and spied them as well, lifting his hat off his head and waving it in the air. Shiloh looked around at the beauty before her. "I want to see the ocean, but then I don't want to leave this."

Rebecca reached for her hand as they crossed the field. "Stay here with me, Mama, and Papa. Then nothing will ever change."

Shiloh liked that idea and raced her sister toward home.

2

TWELVE YEARS AGO

Joseph (Eastern Shore of Virginia)

Joseph stared at Maggie and couldn't believe the words coming from her mouth.

"He makes me feel special... He brings me roses, not picked wildflowers... He has his own car... His daddy works at the bank."

On and on, each explanation for why she was breaking up with him was like a lash against his bare skin. Or another piercing of his heart.

"You can't mean that, Mags. How could you go from 'I love you' to 'I'm breaking up with you' in a day?"

Her face contorted as she shot her glance to the side. "It hasn't been just a day."

He jerked as though hit in the gut. "You've seen him while seeing me?" He couldn't imagine how that happened, and no one told him. A hot flame of embarrassment hit him.

"He doesn't go to our high school. I met him when I visited my aunt in Maryland last month."

"S... So, these *family trips* you've been taking each weekend have been to see someone else?"

"I'm sorry, Joseph. I just need someone who'll be here for me after graduation and not on a ship somewhere far away." She glanced over his shoulder toward his house. Pressing her lips together, she said, "Your family probably hates me."

He didn't need to look behind him to know that his family gathered for his birthday celebration could hear them. His parents now had air-conditioning, but to save money, they mostly kept the windows open to let in the fresh breeze. He wanted to beg and plead for her not to leave but instead lifted his chin, working to hold on to his pride.

"So, um... well, have a happy birthday. I'll see you around, Joseph," she tossed out, almost as an afterthought, before she hurried to her car.

He'd stood on his lawn, battling tears, his heart ripped open, and wondering how the hell he could have been so wrong. He was barely aware of the front door opening, but Wyatt soon stood next to him.

"I'm sorry, bro," Wyatt said, placing his hand on his shoulder.

His nod was the only acknowledgment he could manage. Wyatt had always been the responsible one. And in truth, he was both Joseph's idol and a source of envy. Wyatt was the serious one who looked out for him and his sister. The two brothers had always been close, although it had sometimes chafed when teachers would roll their eyes and purse their lips at his laid-back attitude and easygoing wit. They'd remind him that Wyatt had always taken his studies seriously. Growing up, he battled the desire between wanting to be his own person and wanting to emulate his older brother.

He supposed that if their parents had always made unfavorable comparisons or if Wyatt had been sanctimonious, he probably would have hated being around him. As it was, they became closer as they grew older.

"You don't want to hear this, but honest to God, if she wants to be with someone because of the material things they offer in place of being with you, then she's not the right one."

The right one. Swallowing deeply, he winced. "But I thought she was."

"I get it. But you're young. You've got a career ahead of you. You've got a world to explore. You've got a lot of years to see what's out there before settling down."

"I don't know if I'll ever find them. Or even know when I do." He swiped at his eyes, the pain in his chest almost unbearable.

"I know, and I'm sorry as fuck." Wyatt sighed. "The truth is, I've got no real good advice, so I probably should just shut up."

He looked over, sucking in a breath that felt like molasses instead of air. His brother had given up a day of leave that he could have spent anywhere but chose to spend it with family for Joseph's birthday. Wyatt joined the Navy after graduation, and Joseph couldn't wait to follow in his brother's footsteps. With only one more month to go until graduation and then heading off for Navy boot camp, he'd been on top of the world.

His heart ached, but he was also pissed. The girl he loved and thought loved him had chosen a shitty-ass time to break up with him. All that told him was that she really wasn't the right one.

Like his brother, Joseph had gained height, muscles, thick, dark blond hair that lightened in the sun, blue eyes, and what the girls called a *killer smile*. And for the first three years of high school, he'd used those to his advantage. He'd dated, never going steady with anyone until Maggie. Meeting her on the first day of their senior year in English class had made a one-woman man out of him.

The *right* one. Joseph had been sure he'd found the right one, sure that he and Maggie would stay together forever. He loved that they could have a good time on a walk doing nothing more than picking wildflowers by the side of the road. Or going out in his dad's old truck to sit on the little pier nearby. He thought she liked the simple pleasures, too.

He'd even considered not joining the Navy just to stay on the Eastern Shore for her, but his family convinced him that he needed to follow his dreams. They'd also reminded him that as soon as he was stationed somewhere, Maggie could join him.

He wasn't stupid enough to think he would get over her quickly, but reaching over to place his hand on Wyatt's shoulder, he said, "I'll be okay. It might take a while, but I'll be okay. Hell, I'll soon be going to boot camp, and she'll become a distant memory." He wasn't too sure about the "distant memory" comment but figured if he started saying it now and said it often, it might come true.

Wyatt grinned. "Let's go get more of the leftover birthday cake."

Agreeing, the two brothers walked inside the house where his anxious family wanted to make sure he was taken care of.

Lying in bed that night, he gave way to a few tears before rolling on his side and letting the night breeze blow through his window.

If he knew one thing, it was that his parents had met the *right* one. No matter how tight money had been over the years, his parents pulled together to make sure the family had what they needed. They gave unconditional love not only to him, Wyatt, and Betsy but to each other as well. He'd overheard Betsy ask their parents one time how they knew they were right for each other, and while he'd thought that it was a *girlie* question, he couldn't deny that he was curious about the answer.

"You just know," his dad had said. "You'll feel something. It might be a tingle. It might be a kick in the gut. But you'll look into their eyes and feel something you've never felt before. And it'll hit you that you want to keep looking into that person's eyes forever."

He tried to remember if he'd felt something when looking into Maggie's eyes but had to admit that he'd mostly loved the way she filled out her clothes. Rolling to his back, he tossed his hand over his head and sighed.

One day. One day I'll look into someone's eyes and just know. And until then, no one gets my heart.

Shiloh (Pennsylvania)

Shiloh looked into the mirror at the dress her mother had sewn. White cotton with a bit of lace for the short sleeves and around the scoop neck and hem. It was beautiful. Fit for a bride. It had been Rebecca's wedding dress four years ago when she married the man of her dreams, Thomas. They now had a little girl who was the center of the family's world.

Blowing out a breath, she continued to stare at her reflection as she thought of what would happen in a few months when she turned eighteen and married Edward. Edward Wallen. He was three years older and had just been given land by his father close to her parents' farm. She'd known him for years but had never felt anything other than friendship for the reserved young man. He was handsome enough with his dark hair and hazel eyes. He was tall and lean— certainly not like the muscles she'd seen on the covers of a few romance novels her mother had hidden away. Her mother always called the books her guilty pleasure, and considering they weren't on the shelves in their living room for visitors to take note of, Shiloh assumed they were also her mother's secret. But Shiloh had read a couple of them and loved the idea of a forever, passionate love with a man who would take her breath away. And she'd look at him and just know she'd found the one... the hero who would come in and sweep her off her feet.

Unfortunately, that wasn't reality. Edward was friendly and had always been polite to her. But he didn't take her breath away.

At least he wasn't Isaiah. Now there was a man who made her uneasy. He was the nephew of their pastor but couldn't be more different. Whereas Pastor Aaron was jovial, giving, and preaching God's love, Isaiah was becoming more vocal in their community about needing to shun outsiders, ruling the residents with what he called God's dictates, and demeaning the place of women. And what was disturbing was that he seemed to have gathered others around him who agreed. She had been sheltered from much of this but heard her parents talking after they thought she'd gone to sleep. And from what she understood, Isaiah had just started casting his eye her way about the same time that Edward had. Since her parents were friends with the Wallens, they encouraged her to accept Edward's proposal.

She agreed quickly. After all, it was the way in their little community. Marry early, have a family, and contribute to their somewhat isolated society. A sigh escaped. There was only one thing she'd hoped to be able to do before she'd settled—and that was to see the ocean. *Well, unless Edward wants to take me there, I guess I never will.* As soon as that thought hit her, she grimaced.

It's my place to become a dutiful wife and stop with childish wishes.

"What do you think, Shiloh?"

Looking at her mother's hopeful expression, she smiled. Reaching over, she took her mother's hand and squeezed. "I think it's the most beautiful dress I've ever seen."

"And I think you make the most beautiful bride. Edward is a lucky man."

As her mother helped her take the dress off carefully to hang it in the closet until the wedding, she remained quiet. Her parents had been lucky. They'd ended up with the partner that completed them, gave them happiness, and brought them joy as well as love. And she wished she could have what her parents had but wasn't sure it would happen for her.

3

FOURTEEN MONTHS AGO

(Joseph - Eastern Shore of Virginia)

"Good to have you home, Joseph!"

"Glad you're back safe!"

"You look good, sailor!"

"The first beer is on me!"

As the family gathered at Finn's Pub, Joseph was surrounded by heartfelt congratulations, pride swelling in his chest, and a wide grin on his face. After twelve years in the Navy, he was home. He scrubbed his hand over his short, dark blond hair, ready to have it grow longer than regulations allowed. As he cast his gaze around the pub, it appeared exactly the same as it did the night before he headed off to boot camp. Sure, he'd been home for visits in the past twelve years, but mostly to visit his family who lived north of Baytown.

The brick building had once been a bank, a cornerstone of Baytown on the Eastern Shore of Virginia. The bar extended along the right side, complete with tall, mismatched bar stools. The wooden floor was scuffed with age, as were some of the tables and booths. Growing up, he'd never entered the establishment considering money had always been tight, and a trip to a restaurant was an extravagance his family couldn't afford. But just before he'd left for boot camp, his parents told him he could pick anywhere for a family dinner, and he'd chosen the pub because it seemed to be the most adult restaurant in the area.

He'd been surprised that the restaurant was tame on the inside, filled with families and some of the local fishermen at the bar. Somehow he'd always imagined it being rougher... the kind of establishment that would offer a rowdy send-off. He remembered they'd come the night before he shipped out—tears in his mom's eyes, a worried look on his dad's face, and only his younger sister with them since Wyatt was already in the military.

Now, after all the years of living on ships and in different ports, he'd spent plenty of time in rowdy bars. While he wasn't old at thirty, he no longer felt the desire to bend elbows with the eighteen-year-olds. He'd come full circle. A lot of people didn't want to go back to wherever home was, but for him, the Eastern Shore of Virginia was the best place to live.

His grandfather clapped him on the shoulder, jerking him back to the present as the older man reminisced about his time in the Navy. His parents, sitting on one side of him, beamed as others stopped by their table to welcome him home. His sister, Betsy, winked at him as she and her husband kept an eye on their rambunctious kids, who were bouncing in their seats with excitement at having the whole family out at a restaurant.

And on the other side of him was Wyatt. They'd always looked like brothers, even more so now with their similar, just over six feet height, lean but muscular bodies, and thick, short-trimmed dark blond hair. Wyatt now sported a trimmed beard, and Joseph was still clean-shaven. And would be for another year until he finished his training at the Virginia Law Enforcement Training Academy. That was another way the two brothers were alike. Wyatt had completed the training when he'd left the military several years ago and was now the police chief of Manteague, another local town. Joseph had completed the application and received his acceptance but had a few weeks before the training classes began.

"I hate to leave, but we've got to get home," Betsy said, managing a smile toward him while lifting a warning brow toward her eldest son, busy shoving in the last of his fries.

"Really?" Joseph asked, jolted back to the present.

She pushed her chair back and stood next to her husband. "If I don't get these monkeys home, bathed, and in bed, they'll fall asleep in school tomorrow."

"I don't know what's wrong with that," Joseph quipped, jumping to his feet to offer hugs. Ruffling the hair of his nephew, he grinned. "I fell asleep a lot of times in school."

The little boy looked up and scrunched his nose.

"Then how did you pass your tests if you were sleeping?"

Bending low, he winked. "I always found a pretty girl who'd help me out."

"Joseph!" his mother and Betsy exclaimed at the same time.

Laughing, Wyatt shook his head. "He's telling the truth."

Dodging his sister's attempt to slap his shoulder, he wrapped his arms around her and kissed the top of her head. She leaned back and sighed. "You're incorrigible, and I'm not sure having you home all the time will be a good influence on my kids!"

"Come on, Betsy. Their Uncle Wyatt can be the stern influence, and I can be the fun uncle!"

Her nose scrunched, much like her son's had. "Although, once you go to the academy, we won't have you around as often. At least if you promise to come back to the Shore to stay, then I'll let you be the fun uncle."

Laughing, he hugged her again before letting her go. His parents, grandfather, and stepgrandmother stood as well. More hugs ensued before the rest of the family headed home. As Joseph watched them leave, Wyatt grinned and jerked his head toward the bar. "I figure you're not ready to shut down this evening yet, so I'll buy you a drink."

"Appreciate it." With his hand on his brother's shoulder, they hefted up onto the barstools. His smile widened as he spied two old friends behind the bar. Aiden and Brogan McFarlane. They'd all been in high school about the same time, although he'd been a couple of years younger. Most had played baseball for the high school, earning the moniker of Baytown Boys.

Joseph had heard through his mom that Brogan was now married and had a little girl, and Aiden was married to a woman who had a daughter. Joseph figured that accounted for the smile.

"Joseph!" Aiden called out from the far end of the bar, his hand lifted in the air.

"You can walk down here and greet the man properly without yelling across the place!" Brogan called back, offering a lowered-brow scowl aimed toward his brother.

Joseph chuckled and shook his head, remembering the two brothers always fighting until someone insulted the other one, and then with fists flying, they defended the MacFarlane name. Looking toward Wyatt, he said, "Looks like some things never change."

"You got that right, bro."

The two McFarlanes made it to their end of the bar, welcoming handshakes along with setting two more beers in front of Joseph and Wyatt. It didn't take long for them to be surrounded by more good friends, many who had joined the service and then came back to Baytown, finding the world less welcoming than their little corner of the Chesapeake Bay. It also didn't miss his attention that a number of them were first responders like Wyatt and what he wanted to be.

Soon surrounded by former friends who were now police chiefs, officers, deputies, sheriffs, and rescue workers, he felt like it was a true Baytown homecoming.

Listening to them talk, it quickly became evident that the former high school *hotties*, as the cheerleaders used to call them, were now married with children. *Better them than me!* He didn't mind the idea of one day settling down, but having just left the chains of military service, he wasn't ready to be tied down. In fact, one of the servers had caught his eye, and she'd managed to lean close every time she passed by.

"Joseph, good to see you."

He jumped, dragging his attention away from the server as he felt another clap on the shoulder. Twisting around to lay eyes on Callan Ward, a latecomer to the party, he grinned. "Damn, Callan, good to see you, too." Digging into his memory, he shook his head. "I remember you joined the Coast Guard. You still with them?"

"I was. My last assignment was stationed right here in Baytown, believe it or not. Got married a couple of years ago, and I left the Coast Guard and joined the Virginia Marine Police."

Having grown up on the bay, he knew about the VMP but had never had any dealings with them. An inkling of interest moved through him, but the thoughts were pushed below the idea of a few weeks of no responsibility, no early morning calls, and no duty. At least until the law enforcement academy started their classes. He was also focused on catching the eye of the server again, hopeful for a night of horizontal bliss.

The group slowly dispersed as most of the men said their goodbyes, heading home to their wives and children. The evening crowd beginning to surround him came from some of the younger people in the area who'd remembered him from high school and offered to buy more drinks for his homecoming. He looked to the side to see Wyatt tossing money onto the bar and sliding off the stool.

"Man, you're not leaving me, are you?" Then looking around, he wondered who'd caught his brother's eye. "Oh, got some action already lined up? I'll make sure to come home late." He was glad that Wyatt had offered to let him crash at his place until he headed to Virginia Beach for training but didn't want to stifle his brother's plans.

"Nah." Wyatt shook his head and chuckled.

Incredulous, he jerked his head back. "Seriously? You always used to go home with someone."

"My days of shutting down a bar are over. Anyway, it's been a while since I've had a one-nighter that could bite me in the ass."

"No kidding? Don't tell me you're settling down, too."

Hefting his shoulders, his brother said, "Not yet, but I wouldn't mind finding someone special. Anyway, I've got an early shift tomorrow."

"Damn, you're the police chief— the man in charge. You could go in late."

"No can do. Being in charge means the opposite. I'm the one who sets the tone for my department." Leaning closer, Wyatt held his gaze. "And since you've been accepted at the law enforcement training, you better get used to early mornings just like in the Navy."

"Fuck, that's a few weeks down the road. Now, I just want to celebrate my freedom!"

Wyatt glanced down at the empty bottles in front of Joseph. "Don't fuck up by trying to drive."

Clasping his hand over his heart, he shook his head. "Damn, you wound me thinking I'd be so irresponsible. But don't worry, I've got my eye on someone, and I hope she has a place close by."

Wyatt rolled his eyes and grinned. Clasping hands, they pulled each other in for a back-slapping hug. "I'm proud of you, Joseph. Always have been. And it's fuckin' good to have you home."

"It's good to be back together, bro." As the words slipped from his lips, he felt them deep inside.

Still grinning as he threw up a two-fingered salute, Wyatt walked out of the pub. Joseph found his gaze lingering on the closed door after his brother had left. They had been close growing up, and their years in the military had only allowed them to cross paths during coordinated leaves to spend time with the family. But now, the ability to reconnect as adults sent a slow smile over his face.

"Joseph! Christ, man, I thought you were off to sea somewhere!"

His attention snagged on a newcomer, recognizing someone from his high school days, but he couldn't remember the man's name. A few others in the past joined them, and even though they were not people he'd ever been close to, the drinks kept flowing. *Hell, a celebration is a celebration no matter who's around!*

It didn't take long for the server who'd been giving

him the eye to finally come in closer, offering a perfect view of her cleavage in her tight, low T-shirt. Blond hair with dark roots, waving over her shoulders. Brown eyes, heavily lined, and lashes thick with mascara. Bubblegum-pink lipstick, slick with gloss. Painted on blue jeans. Cowboy boots on her feet. Grinning, he shifted around on his barstool. "Damn, darlin'. You're a sight for sore eyes."

"I didn't think I'd get a chance to give you my number while having a drink with you. I'm finally officially off the clock," she said, her eyes filled with both a spark of interest and expectation. Sliding a napkin over with her phone number and name printed clearly, she bit her bottom lip, waiting.

"Vicki," he stated. She'd drawn little hearts over the two i's, and he tried not to roll his eyes as he jerked his gaze back to her, making sure she was of legal age. Knowing Aiden and Brogan wouldn't hire a teenager to serve alcohol, nor would they allow her to drink if she wasn't of age. He thought the embellishment was ridiculous but lied nonetheless. "The hearts are cute, just like you."

She giggled. "I did that so that my name stands out." She leaned closer, rubbing her breasts against his arm.

"Got to say, darlin', that's not the only thing about you that stands out."

Giggling again, she said, "I've got a place nearby. How would you like to really celebrate getting out of the Navy?"

For an instant, he hesitated, something he hadn't expected to do. It was one thing to pick up a woman in a bar when he was in the service, knowing the odds of seeing them again were almost nil. Having a one-nighter near his home with a woman who worked in a place he knew he'd frequent might prove to be awkward. She shifted again, her breasts now pressing tighter, and he decided to throw caution to the wind. *I'm free, single, and have time for the next phase of my life.*

"As long as we're on the same page… one night, that's all."

She nodded with enthusiasm. "Sure. Whatever you say."

Throwing his arm around her, he tossed a wad of bills onto the counter and waved toward Brogan. Guiding her outside, he could feel the effects of all the alcohol, glad when she offered to drive.

Hours later, when the sun blasted through the uncovered windows, he managed to peel his eyelids open, squinting as the light stabbed his brain. His dry mouth tasted like he had sucked on an acrid cotton ball. Licking his lips didn't help but seemed only to increase the nasty smell coming from his mouth. The desire to pull the covers over his head and go back to sleep was strong, but the desire to piss was even stronger.

Forcing his limbs to move, he sat up and ground the heels of his palms against his forehead in an attempt to alleviate some of the pain. He couldn't remember the last time he'd had such a hangover, and, God knows, he'd had plenty of bar nights when he'd been on shore leave in the Navy. Glancing around, he didn't recognize the room, but when the mattress shifted, he turned, spying the woman sleeping next to him, the sheet only partially covering her naked body. The blond hair was matted on one side. Eyeliner and mascara had smeared dark, raccoon circles around her eyes. And her mouth, no longer bubblegum pink, was slack as she snored, and her breath was as rancid as his.

He wasn't judging, knowing he didn't smell any better, and figured he didn't look any better either. Swinging his legs over the side of the bed, he stepped out of the small bedroom and found the bathroom. After taking the long-awaited and much-needed piss, he washed his hands. While staring into the mirror, the proof that he didn't look any better than she did stared back. Grabbing a tube of toothpaste, he squirted some on his finger and tried to scrub his teeth. Slurping water from the faucet, he swished around and spit. It wasn't a great effort at oral hygiene, but it sure as fuck was better than nothing.

Walking back into the bedroom, he bent to pick up his clothes off the floor. He wasn't quite the horndog some of his Navy buddies had been, but his one-and-done rules were never broken. Make sure the woman was of legal age and wasn't inebriated before giving consent. Make sure the woman knew it was for one night only. And for him, kissing was kept to a minimum, cuddling afterward was rarely engaged in, and he usually left as soon as he woke. He didn't feel guilty that he wasn't around the next morning, not wanting meaningless conversation over breakfast, giving the impression that what had occurred might be more than simple physical pleasure. Those rules were easy when he stuck to bars around the ports of their shore leave.

Once dressed, he slipped out of her trailer, glad he was within walking distance of the pub in Baytown where he'd left his vehicle. Climbing inside, he drove toward Wyatt's house on the beach just north of the small town of Manteague, knowing his brother had already left to go to the police station. Before getting there, he jerked into the parking lot of the coffee shop and bakery after the scent of freshly ground coffee beans wafted past.

After ordering coffee and a sausage, egg, and cheese biscuit, he flirted with the young woman behind the counter. She blushed and smiled as he winked while shoving money into the tip jar. Walking back out to his vehicle, he noticed her phone number written on the cardboard sleeve around his coffee cup.

Still grinning by the time he got home, he finished his breakfast. He tossed the refuse in the trash can but kept the cardboard sleeve, placing it on top of the dresser in Wyatt's guest bedroom. Climbing into the shower, he washed away the beer-scented sweat from his body, scrubbing from head to toe. Once feeling and smelling a helluva lot better, he wandered out of the bedroom, through Wyatt's living room, and out onto the back deck.

He stared out over the long pier from Wyatt's backyard that led to the water. The sun was still rising in the sky, the perfect backdrop for the seagulls flying over the waves as they searched for their breakfast. He sucked in a deep breath, letting it out slowly. He'd been raised near here, and even though he'd enjoyed seeing the world in the Navy, he'd never considered settling elsewhere. Something about the Chesapeake Bay called to him.

Remembering what Callan had said about the Virginia Marine Police, he was determined to find out more about them. *After all, what else am I going to do with the weeks before I start the academy?* Grinning to himself, he chuckled as he thought about the woman's phone number written on the sleeve of the coffee cup. *Well, maybe I've got a few things I can do besides check in to the VMP.*

Plopping into one of the old Adirondack chairs on Wyatt's deck, he stretched his long legs out in front of them, rested his hands over his stomach, and leaned back. The summer sun warmed him, filling him with peace. For now, he had no worries and time to enjoy himself.

4

SHILOH (PENNSYLVANIA)

It was a summer day in the mountains of Pennsylvania — the kind of day that used to fill her with peace, but now Shiloh felt nothing but worry. She lifted her hand to smooth any wayward strands of hair back into the tight bun. At least the black scarf tied around her head and knotted under her chin helped to keep the breeze from pulling more tendrils loose. Her thick, dark brown hair with auburn highlights always had a mind of its own, but the last thing she wanted to do was draw any attention to herself as she walked to the community market.

Sweat trickled down her back, worse from the long-sleeved black dress that hung below her knees.

It was essential to keep her eyes down as befitting a woman in mourning, but she'd learned it was even more important to be aware of her surroundings. Or, more accurately, aware of *who* was in her surroundings. Glancing to the side where her similarly dressed niece walked next to her, she tightened her grip around the thirteen-year-old's hand. Rachel's dark-brown hair and blue-gray eyes matched her own, giving the appearance that they could be mother and daughter. *Please, God, let us get to the market and back home without any problems.*

She believed in God, but not the heavy-handed, unyielding, punishment-loving deity that was shouted each week by their leader. Not pastor... no, that title was no longer used. Leader was the position he'd filled. But she didn't dare voice an opinion. Not just about God, but about anything.

Reaching the market, she breathed a sigh of relief, hearing the same escape from Rachel's lips. She hated that her niece was filled with the same worry as she. Offering a smile of encouragement, she picked up a woven basket, and they quickly made their way around the small store, gathering a few staples and milk. It wasn't much cooler inside the store, but the fan running near the front and the refrigerated cases offered a slight respite.

Not sensing Rachel right beside her, she turned and observed the young girl staring at the candy. She shook her head as Rachel looked over her shoulder toward Shiloh. Being the sweet, obedient girl she was, Rachel moved back to Shiloh's side, not voicing her desire for the sweet treat.

Handing her basket to the cashier, Shiloh counted out her money carefully to pay for their purchases. She hated to deny Rachel anything but held tight to her secret. To everyone in the small community, she was simply the poor widow, meek and mild. If anyone thought differently, her punishment would be severe.

Once outside with their few bags in their hands, they began the walk back home. Neither she nor Rachel spoke along the way, not wanting others to think they weren't observing the rites of mourning. She did miss Edward. After ten years of marriage to a man who had become her best friend, it was impossible not to mourn his passing. She missed his calm way of speaking. The way his eyes sparkled when they walked along the river. His strong singing voice when she stood next to him in church. In truth, though, they were more roommates than actual spouses.

Rachel's feet stumbled, jerking Shiloh from her musings. Looking up, she kept her expression blank, making sure not to show the unease that moved through her. Wishing she'd asked God not only to let them get to the store without any problems but also to get home, she stopped in front of the men blocking their progress. Or rather, the one man in charge with his entourage of three other men following close.

She was never sure why he needed them other than to make himself appear powerful. He was tall and wiry, with black hair slicked to the side. His white shirt starkly contrasted with his black pants and jacket. She waited until he spoke first, giving him the deference he demanded.

"Mistress Shiloh. Rachel. I see you've been to the store."

"Master Isaiah," she said, dipping her chin. "Yes. It's our first outing of the week."

"I just came from your house. I wanted to speak with you."

Her throat tightened, but she managed to keep her breathing steady. "How may I help you, Master Isaiah?"

"Rachel, you may take the groceries home by yourself. Your aunt will be along presently."

Shiloh held her breath, but Rachel obediently nodded as she accepted the bags and walked around the community's leader and through the other men at his side. Once she was behind his back, she looked over her shoulder, worry in her eyes, but Shiloh could only offer a silent prayer that Rachel would do as asked and that she'd quickly be able to join her.

With her hands no longer encumbered with a bag, she clasped them in front of her and waited.

"You have been well?"

"Yes. The community has been generous."

"It seems that not only just those in our select community have been generous."

More sweat trickled down her back, and she prayed the oversized dress covered the movements of her chest as she tried to draw more air into her lungs. Uncertain if she was expected to speak or to remain silent, she knew she could suffer with either choice. Torn between wanting to stand firm and wanting to hide, she remained quiet.

After a moment of silence, Isaiah continued. "Your farmland is being tended to by someone outside our community. As a woman, you do not have that right. It belongs with us. Your family."

Her mouth was dry as she tried to swallow. "It was Edward. He made the arrangements long ago." She hated to throw Edward under the bus, but he was gone, and there was nothing the community leaders could do to him now.

"I will check into this. But nonetheless, the land is still yours. And you get the rent money each month?"

"No, Master Isaiah." Her heart threatened to beat out of her chest. "He arranged for it to be rented for a year if anything happened to him. The community would be paid at the end of my grief period." Silence hung between them again. She lifted her gaze, but after spying his intense, dark-eyed stare, she wished she had kept her eyes down.

"It has been one month since Edward died," he announced as though she had not felt to her very core every moment of his loss.

His words gave life to the slithering of unease growing with each second she was in his presence. "Yes, it has."

"You have eleven more months of mourning before it will be time for you to take another husband."

She hated the direction of the community leader's conversation. Everything about the man had always brought out suspicion to Shiloh, but she never gave voice to those thoughts except to Edward, who'd privately mentioned his own doubts about their new leader when they lay in bed at night. But now, with no family to protect her and Rachel, she had no choice but to fill the expected role. Managing a polite nod, she replied, "Yes, I do."

"I'll be waiting."

The air threatened to escape her lungs in a rush as her stomach threatened to empty the toast she'd had for breakfast. Forcing her expression and her body to remain still, she dropped her gaze back to her clasped hands.

"Do you understand what I'm saying?" he asked, stepping closer, his oily voice slicking over her.

"I'm sorry, Master Isaiah, but I'm still… um… still grieving…"

He placed his hand on her shoulder. "Of course you are. And that is right for you to do so. But, in time, when the year is up, I'll be waiting for you once you are free to take another. And the farm will no longer need to be rented. The land will belong to us—to the community. After all, it is God's, not yours. You cannot take what belongs to Him."

His hand lingered before his forefinger dragged along her neck. Swallowing, she prayed he would leave before she gave in to the almost uncontrollable need to shudder. He stepped backward, and she lifted her gaze just long enough to dip her chin again.

"Good day, Mistress Shiloh."

"Goodbye, Master Isaiah." As he stepped around her and his footsteps moved down the lane, she hurried the rest of the way toward her house.

Once inside, she closed the door, finally letting out the heaving breath she'd been holding. "Rachel!"

The tapping of light footsteps racing down the hall barely gave her time to throw open her arms as Rachel slammed into her body, forcing her back against the door.

"Oh, Shiloh, I was scared."

"Shhh, it's okay. I'm fine," she assured, her hand

gently rubbing Rachel's back. In truth, she was anything but fine. Squeezing her eyes shut tightly, she wondered how her life had come to this point. No parents. No sister. No husband. And guardian to a beautiful niece who needed to be protected. *I can't defend myself... how can I protect her?*

"I don't... I don't like him," Rachel whispered, fear lacing her voice.

Shiloh nodded but said nothing. She wanted to allay her niece's fears but had few words of comfort.

Rachel leaned back, her young gaze searching. "Are you safe?"

Shiloh knew what she was asking and hated that Rachel even had to ask. "Yes. I'm officially in mourning, so I have no need to fear having to take another husband."

Rachel pressed her lips together. "It wasn't always like this. I remember... before..."

"What do you remember, Rachel?" she prodded.

Rachel's eyes widened, and she sucked in a quick breath. "Oh, Shiloh, I shouldn't have said that. Master Isaiah says it's wicked to think about the past. He says it causes us to doubt God's plan for the future."

Anger slammed into her, overtaking her caution. "Hogwash!"

Rachel's eyes bugged before darting around as though to ascertain if anyone could possibly hear them before peering up again. A smile peeked out. "Oh, Aunt Shiloh!"

"Well, it's true." Sighing, she jerked off her scarf and then pulled the bobby pins from her bun, letting her fingers comb through her hair, her scalp glad for the freedom of the tightly pulled hair.

She offered a gentle smile, leading Rachel over to the kitchen table. As her niece sat down, Shiloh noted the groceries had been put away, and her heart went out to the young teen who had dutifully completed the task while terrified at what her aunt was facing out on the lane. Pouring a glass of milk, she set it on the table in front of Rachel, along with a small bowl of blueberries.

Sitting down next to her, she nodded for Rachel to eat, then shook her head when Rachel offered to share. She leaned back in the hard-backed chair and waited until the snack was finished, wanting Rachel to enjoy the treat. "Honey, I don't know why he says that, but I believe it's the remembrance of the past, especially the ones we loved and the good times, that allows us to continue praising God even when things are tough."

Rachel nodded slowly. "I know that when I think of Mom, Dad, Grandma, and Grandpa, I feel sad until I remember the fun times, and then I'm not so upset."

"Exactly." Shiloh patted Rachel's hand, wanting to choose her words carefully. "You're right to remember them. You're also right about things being different when you were younger."

"Why did things change?"

Shiloh looked out the window over the fields, remembering when her father used to plow the land with Edward's father and then later when Edward would do the same. Their small community was almost geographically shut off from others, with mountains on two sides and a river on the third. Only one road moved through the area, and it was rarely traveled by strangers. Most residents shunned the more modern conveniences, preferring a simple life.

Everyone knew everyone else. Most of the children were educated at the small school in the next county or homeschooled. There was one market and one church. Pastor Aaron had been the community leader since she was a little girl. He was well-loved and kind but getting older. It had been ripe for a new leader to take over.

"Master Isaiah isn't like his uncle. Pastor Aaron was much kinder. Much easier to talk to and listen to. Back when he was alive, we were all…" She sighed, trying to find the right word and then giving up. "We were all just happier."

"I was a little girl then, but I do remember. I remember we got to wear pants, and our hair could be in a ponytail. And we could sing when we wanted."

"Well, you keep remembering." Sucking in a deep breath, she added a warning. "But when talking to anyone but me, make sure you never question Master Isaiah. He is very powerful."

Rachel nodded, her smile fleeing her face. "I know, and I promise, Shiloh. I won't say anything to anyone. Not that I ever see anyone anyway."

The year of mourning extended to all females in the home, according to Master Isaiah. Shiloh felt sure it was a way to dominate the women and keep the younger girls from their education. She hated that her niece spent almost no time with anyone her age, but she knew it was better under the circumstances. At least for now. At least until she could figure out how to make their lives better. *Like before... before tragedies began piling up, and their lives had been irrevocably altered.*

That evening after Rachel had finished her studies and had gone to bed, Shiloh sat in the backyard. She stretched her legs out in front of the chair and rested her hands over her stomach, leaning back. The summer sun warmed her, but she wasn't filled with peace. For now, the worries overshadowed any joy. A forbidden magazine lay open on her lap, her hand resting on the glossy pages filled with pictures of places she'd love to see.

She remembered the romances her mother used to read and the idea of a handsome hero riding to the rescue. Snorting, she shook her head. *No hero is coming for me.*

The next day, she looked over the fields, her gaze seeking and finding the man who leased her land, sitting on his tractor. He and his wife lived in the next county, close to but not part of their community. He and Edward had struck up a friendship even though Master Isaiah warned against outsiders. Staring at him, she startled when Rachel touched her arm.

"Shiloh, you've been standing here staring at Mr. Kendall for half an hour."

"Oh, I must have been lost in thought." Pressing her lips together, she turned toward Rachel. "I think I'll take him some water."

Minutes later, walking over the farmland, she breathed in deeply, settling her nerves and steeling her resolve.

The older man sitting on the tractor cut the engine as she approached. "Good morning, Mrs. Wallen."

She smiled in return and handed him the glass. "Mr. Kendall. I hoped we might talk for a moment if you can spare the time."

He nodded and climbed down from his seat, standing in front of her. "I always have time for you, Mrs. Wallen. What can I do for you?"

Willing the dryness in her mouth to disappear, she pressed her lips together and pushed forward. Lifting her shaking hand, she held out an envelope. "I wondered if you would be so kind as to post this for me?"

His gaze lingered on the envelope in her hand before his eyes met hers, understanding passing over his weathered face. Nodding slowly, he took the missive from her. "Yes, ma'am. I'll be glad to."

"I'd be so grateful." Hating to push her luck, she knew she had no choice. "And if you could put your address down as the sender. Then if a reply comes, it… it won't come here."

Now compassion filled his expression, and he continued to nod. "Yes, ma'am. I can do that."

Their silent gazes held for another moment, and then she turned and began the trek back across the fields. For better or worse, she'd put her plan in motion.

5

THREE MONTHS AGO

Shiloh stood in the small living room and peeked out the window. Her stomach was in knots as she waited. Yesterday had been a year to the day since Edward had been killed in a farming accident. It hadn't been an easy year, but she'd been determined to take care of everything the way Edward would have wanted her to. She continued to rent their small fields to Mr. Kendall to farm. She and Rachel raised chickens and enough of a garden that, with the land rent, chickens and eggs sold, and the vegetables they grew, they had enough to earn a meager living. Other families in the community made sure they were taken care of when they dropped off extra food or material for making clothes once she was no longer wearing all black. She'd dutifully worn her widow's clothes for a year, not giving anyone in the community the opportunity to think she wasn't grieving properly.

In truth, she had grieved privately. She mourned for her husband, whom she'd befriended as a child. She wept for the friendship they'd shared. And even if the marriage bed had been chiefly for sleep or simply lying together and talking, she grieved that she no longer had her partner.

She rubbed her forehead, willing the pain to ease. Out of habit, she smoothed her hair back but found no tresses out of place. A noise to her side caused her to jerk her head around, seeing Rachel at the bottom of the narrow steps that led to the second-floor bedrooms. Her niece, now fourteen years old, was a beauty, so like her mother, Shiloh's sister.

Their walls had no pictures of family members, but she'd been determined to keep Rachel's parents alive in the young girl's mind. Despite their leader's insistence that photographs were selfish and prideful, she'd kept all the ones they'd had and shared them with Rachel often. Photographs of Rebecca and her husband, Thomas. Photographs of Rachel when she was younger. Photographs of Shiloh's parents. Photographs of Shiloh and Edward, both when they were younger and after they gained custody of Rachel when she was orphaned.

Her gaze roved over Rachel's expression, filled with tension, worry evident in her eyes. "You need to go back upstairs, sweetheart."

Rachel's eyes lit, then filled with tears at the sound of the endearment. Shiloh fought back a grimace. Endearments should be spoken often but were another prideful example of Master Isaiah's dictates that they should not be offered.

"I just wanted to see if you were okay."

In truth, Shiloh wanted to shake her head and

scream that she was anything but okay, but she simply nodded. "We don't know for sure what Master Isaiah wants, but I need to hear what he has to say. And it needs to be between adults and not for you to worry about."

Rachel's statue posture didn't move for a moment, and then the air left her lungs like a balloon deflating. Nodding, she turned and placed her hand on the railing and started up the stairs. Looking over her shoulder, she whispered, "I love you, Aunt Shiloh."

Swallowing past the lump in her throat, she nodded. "I love you, too." She watched as Rachel disappeared up the stairs and heard the click of the bedroom door close. Turning back toward the window, her breath caught in her throat as she watched the tall, black-garbed man striding toward her house. His entourage now included several of the large, younger men who had joined their community. Stern faces and hard fists. Master Isaiah ruled with fear and intimidation, all cloaked under the guise of God's word. Yet their community had grown. She swallowed again, this time hoping to keep down the bile that threatened to come up.

She moved to the door but halted as her hand gripped the knob. Glancing around the room, she saw that it was neat and stark with nothing out of place. Waiting until the rap of his knuckles sent shudders throughout her body, she opened the door and stepped back, allowing him entrance.

"Mistress Shiloh," he greeted, walking straight into the living room and turning to face her.

Dipping her chin in deference, she replied, "Master Isaiah. Welcome. May I offer you some refreshment?"

"Yes. That would be nice."

He moved to the small sofa and sat down, smoothing his hands down the front of his jacket. Hoping to avoid eye contact as much as possible, she quickly walked to the kitchen, where she already had slices of buttered bread and cups of tea ready on a tray. With her back still to him, she silently pulled in a deep breath and let it out slowly, trying to settle the nerves jolting through her body. Picking up the tray, she walked with more confidence than she felt and placed it on the small table in front of the sofa. Pouring the unsweetened tea into a cup, she handed it to Isaiah before taking a seat in the chair across from him.

He sipped from the cup, and not for the first time, he reminded her of a hawk with his beak-like, pointed nose and beady eyes that didn't seem to miss anything. She had no doubt he was hunting, and she was the prey.

Setting the cup back onto the table, he placed his hands on his thighs and held her gaze. "I trust you observed the final day of your year of mourning yesterday."

Nodding, she gripped her cup tighter. While he hadn't asked a question, she responded as she knew she was expected. "Yes, I did. I visited the cemetery and spent the day in quiet reflection."

Her answer seemed to please him as he nodded. "Excellent. And now it is time for you to look to the future. As you know, I have not taken a wife. After my uncle died, and I became the leader of our community, I was needed by so many that I put my own needs to the side."

Again, he hadn't asked a question, but she nodded. Forcing her fingers to slightly loosen before the porcelain teacup cracked, she sat perfectly still.

"But now, I am ready for marriage. I require a woman of impeccable background. Quiet. Calm. Respectful."

"I'm sure many women in our community would suit your requirements, Master Isaiah."

"Perhaps, but ever since Edward died, I have had my eye on you, Mistress Shiloh. Although, the fact that you were married for ten years and never had children has given me concern. But considering Edward's *delicate* constitution, I feel that the fault lay with him."

Shiloh was shocked that she managed not to show the anger that raged through her. Deeply defensive of any criticism of Edward, she knew that to speak of why they never had children to anyone in the community would be a betrayal of her husband's trust, something she would never do.

As though she had no say in the conversation, Isaiah continued. "I have come today to let you know that I have chosen you to be my wife. The community will honor you and respect you as the leader's spouse. You will be expected to be everything I need you to be. If so, you will be rewarded. If not, you will be punished as any disobedient wife should be."

Punishments were something that Isaiah felt strongly about and instituted in the community once he became the leader. It had never been the norm when his uncle was alive and never anything her parents had ascribed to. She had no doubt that Isaiah would take pleasure in meting out punishment. The idea of being his wife was so abhorrent that every cell in her body felt the tremors.

Swallowing deeply, she dipped her chin. "Master Isaiah, I am honored, of course. But I do not feel I am the right person for you. My heart still aches for Edward. And I cannot be certain that I am not barren. It would not be right to saddle you with a woman who cannot bear children."

There. The words were out. She prayed they were as softly spoken and respectful as she could have made them. And more importantly, that he would accept them.

"Mistress Shiloh, I'm afraid you do not understand. You do not have a choice in the matter. I have decided on you, and we will be married. If you disagree, then perhaps I will extend my right as leader of this community to take Rachel into my care." His lips curved ever so slightly, his voice as oily slick as ever. "I believe she is fourteen years old now. In our community, that makes her old enough to become my wife. Or perhaps I will simply take you and, if you do not please me, have her as well. One way or the other, you and the land you possess will be mine."

The shivers that had moved through her body turned into full-blown shakes, and the teacup in her hands began to rattle, threatening to spill the tea. Unable to keep the gasp from her lips, she noticed her reaction only caused him to smile wider. "No, you wouldn't. You couldn't."

"I think you know better than that. I have the power as leader of this community to do anything I want." He stood suddenly, looking down at her. "This discussion is now over. I will give you two days alone to consider your answer. At the end of that time, I'll come back. By then, you will have decided if you will be my wife, and Rachel will be protected in our home, or she will become mine."

She jumped to her feet, unheeding the spilled tea, but he had already walked to the door and pulled it open. Without looking back at her, he said, "Two days, Mistress Shiloh."

She watched him leave, then rushed to close the door, collapsing on the floor as she leaned against the wood. The sound of running footsteps down the stairs met her ears, but Shiloh could barely lift her head before Rachel rushed into the room and dropped onto the floor next to her.

Throwing her arms around her, she cried, "Shiloh! Shiloh! What happened? What did he say?"

The desire to protect Rachel was strong, giving Shiloh pause for just a moment. But she knew she could no longer keep the situation from her niece. Dragging in a deep breath, she felt her lungs burn before the air rushed from her lips. "We need to talk, sweetheart. Help me up, and we'll talk." Not trusting her legs to hold her, she leaned against Rachel as they both stood. With arms still wrapped around each other, they hugged in silence for a long moment.

Pulling back, she said, "Let's get some tea and sit down. There are some things I need to tell you that are too important to hide anymore. You're only fourteen years old, but I need to—"

"I might only be fourteen, but I'm not a child! Whatever you need to tell me, I want to hear."

She walked into the living room and gathered the tray, leading Rachel into the kitchen. Not one to waste food, she still tossed the buttered bread out into the yard for the chickens, not wanting to handle anything that Isaiah may have touched. Looking down at the cup his lips had sipped from, she dropped it into the garbage. Seeing Rachel's wide eyes at her actions, she simply pulled down a new cup from the cupboard and poured tea for her niece, sweetening it with a bit of sugar that she'd saved. Leading Rachel over to the table, they both sat.

How often had she and Edward sat at the table with friendly and compassionate conversation moving between them? He'd loved her cooking, and she'd loved watching him enjoy the meal. Those times reminded her of so many when she watched her sister and brother-in-law and baby Rachel enjoy a meal or her parents' loving relationship with each other. But those days were gone. When their community leader, Pastor Aaron, died and his nephew took over, everything changed.

Looking at Rachel's expectant face, she knew it was time. "There's so much I want to tell you. So much I want to explain. But we don't have much time, so you need to trust me to give you only the information I need you to know right now." The earnest expression on Rachel's face sparked courage in Shiloh's heart.

"I trust you, Shiloh."

"Good. Remember that your memories are important, Rachel. Always keep them. They will remind you of the time when this community was warmer, more loving, more trusting."

"You're talking about before Master Isaiah, aren't you?"

"Yes, I am. He has brought mean-spiritedness to our community and rules with an iron fist. He has those that back him, giving him the power to do what he wants, take what he wants, and make threats."

"Did he threaten you?"

Sighing, she replied, "He has decided that he wants me to marry him."

Rachel gasped, a look of displeasure crossing her face.

"And I don't want to marry him."

Eyes wide, Rachel asked, "He can't make you, can he?"

It was hard to know how much information to give. "He will not take no for an answer, but if I don't marry him, he's threatened to take you away from me."

"No!" Rachel started to rise from the chair.

Her hand snapped out, her fingers closing over Rachel's arm. "Don't worry, sweetheart. I'll never let that happen."

"But how? What do we do?"

"This is where you will have to trust me with all your heart and mind."

Rachel jerked her head up and down with emphasis. "I do. I will."

Holding Rachel's gaze, seeing nothing but a resolute expression of determination, Shiloh nodded. Standing, she walked over to the counter and pulled open a drawer. Feeling around on the underside, her fingers closed over the envelope she had taped to the bottom. Sitting back at the kitchen table, she smoothed her hand over the papers.

Looking back at Rachel, she explained, "I've made plans. Actually, I've been making plans since Edward died, and I knew that Isaiah was overly interested in me. This community is no longer the loving and peaceful place where our parents and grandparents wanted us to live. A place where we could make our own choices, worship God in freedom, and live a simple life. Isaiah has turned it into a..." She hesitated, afraid to use the word that sent shivers through her. "Well, a place that is run by himself. I've known for a while that we might need to leave. And I've planned for us to escape, knowing that as soon as my year of grieving was over, we would have run out of time to stay here."

Eyes still wide, Rachel whispered, "Escape?"

"We can't stay here, sweetheart."

Rachel was quiet, thoughts working behind her eyes before she nodded slowly. "You're right, Shiloh. And I don't want to. I don't like being afraid. I only want to be with you."

"What if I told you that it could be an adventure? A whole new life?"

A smile slipped over Rachel's face. "Like the ones in the books you let me read?"

In the past, books were not banned in their community. Families were free to read what they wanted, and the church had a small library in the basement. Their community had not been closed to the outside world but simply chose to live a life that moved a little slower. But now, under Isaiah's regime, he had banned books, ordering the families to destroy anything other than their Bibles. And even those were to be interpreted by him.

But Edward had refused to follow the edict and privately stashed the books they owned under the floorboards of one of their closets. At night, when he was still alive, they would pull them out and read. During the last year that Rachel had been homeschooled by her, she shared them with her young niece, making sure her vision of the world was not just what Isaiah wanted them to know.

A spark of excitement filled Rachel's face, and for the first time since she'd woken up after Edward died, the same spark filled Shiloh.

Glancing down at the envelope on the table, Rachel asked, "What is that?"

Opening the envelope, she pulled out a letter. The print at the top in a swirly script was clearly visible and memorized. The Sea Glass Inn. And underneath was the name Tori Evans. "I found a place in Virginia that sounded amazing in a magazine. There was a picture of a beautiful historic inn, and I wrote a letter to the woman who owns it. I gave it to Mr. Kendall to mail for me. I simply told the owner that I'd seen a picture of the inn and thought it was beautiful. I asked if the town was as nice to live in as it seemed. She replied, and over the past several months, we've corresponded."

"How did you keep the letters a secret?"

"Mr. Kendall is not a follower of Isaiah, and he's… well, he's helped me. He agreed to take and bring the letters to me."

Rachel's brow scrunched. "So how is this our escape?"

"Mrs. Evans needs a housekeeper for her inn. She said there was an attic room that would be big enough for both of us. You could go to school and earn money by helping at the inn. There's even a restaurant in town that always needs servers where I could work at part-time."

Rachel's hands snaked over the table, and the two women clutched each other, both bouncing on the knife blade precipice between hope and fear.

"So we just leave?"

Nodding, Shiloh explained, "This is where you have to trust me. Mr. Kendall knows and will take care of the chickens and farm." She knew there was more but kept the rest secret, afraid to overburden her niece. Because when Isaiah discovered what she had done, she had no doubt he might try to find her. And she had left a hidden missive for him in case he considered trying.

"When? How?"

"Tonight, sweetheart. We'll pack what we can carry and then walk the five miles to Mr. Kendall's place in the next county. He'll take us to the bus station."

Rachel began to shake, her whole body seeming to vibrate with excitement. Barely whispering, the awe was still heard in her words. "School. A job. Maybe friends. Oh, Aunt Shiloh, we get a new life."

"Yes. But be prepared because we'll have to leave this place behind. Remember, though— no one can take our memories away from us."

Rachel threw her arms around Shiloh, hugging her tightly, then just as quickly jumped from her chair and raced upstairs, calling out that she needed to pack.

Following, she moved to the closet and lifted the board to Edward's secret hiding place. Pulling out handwritten papers, documents, saved money, her favorite books, and a bag, she settled the boards back.

Hours later, under cover of darkness, Shiloh led her niece down the moonlit lane away from the place she'd called home for her entire life. The trees on either side of the road created dark shadows that moved with the breeze. The rustling sent fears that someone was in the shadows, ready to pounce. She wanted to hold Rachel's hand, but they both carried everything they could in an old satchel and cloth bags stuffed to overflowing.

She thought she'd be filled with nothing but excitement, but nerves tinged with a touch of sadness moved through her.

There were things she had not spoken about with Rachel and prayed she never had to. Things that had not been voiced since Edward died. Suspicions. Doubts. Bone-curdling fears. Life was uncertain, and no knight on a white horse would appear. Other than her niece, she was very alone.

6

Two days later, Shiloh sat in the passenger side of a large SUV, glancing toward the woman behind the wheel. Tori Evans had met her and Rachel at the bus station in Virginia Beach and was driving them to Baytown. Tori was beautiful, with red hair pulled back with a green headband. A green shirt was paired with blue jeans that made her look casual, comfortable, and elegant all at the same time.

When they had made the long walk to Mr. Kendall's house, they'd continually looked over their shoulders, terrified that Isaiah and his obedient minions would swoop in and halt their progress. Mrs. Kendall had welcomed them, offered them breakfast, and packed some of their shopping bags into a suitcase that she claimed she had never used. Mr. Kendall drove them to the bus station and made sure they had their tickets to Virginia Beach.

Shiloh had tamped down her fear of traveling by bus, trying to show excitement for Rachel. But once they were on the road, she no longer had to pretend. They'd both sat with their faces close to the window, watching as towns, farms, and big cities moved past.

Now, Shiloh's attention was bouncing from one scene to another. First, toward the animated Tori as she talked with enthusiasm about the Eastern Shore of Virginia, the Sea Glass Inn that had been left to her by her grandparents, and the many friends that couldn't wait to meet Shiloh and Rachel. It was the last statement that had her stomach in knots. But before she could focus on that, Rachel would exclaim and send Shiloh's attention toward the window where the seagulls flew past over the water. Neither she nor Rachel had ever seen the ocean, and even though this was just the Chesapeake Bay, she still felt as though the water extended forever.

As she looked over her shoulder toward Rachel's wide-eyed expression, happiness for being able to offer her niece this experience was mixed with sadness that she'd been forced to take her away from all she'd known. *But here, she'll be safe. And so will I.*

"We've now crossed over to the peninsula of the Eastern Shore," Tori announced.

Shiloh looked out over the farmland that reminded her of where they'd come from, and a sense of nostalgia passed over her. As Tori turned off the main highway, they soon came to Baytown, and she was struck by the quaint, homey feel of the little town.

"Over there is Jillian's Coffee Shop and Galleria. She's one of my oldest and dearest friends and supplies the pastries delivered every morning for our inn guests.

She can't wait to meet you and Rachel. And on that corner is the library. Across from that is the pub. It's a restaurant owned by three siblings, all friends of mine as well. Katelyn is also one of my oldest friends." Pointing in the other direction, Tori added, "And on that side is the town harbor. The Seafood Shack is there. It's the restaurant I told you about. They always need reliable servers, and the manager said you can come in anytime if you'd like a second job."

Busy swinging her head back and forth, trying to keep up with Tori's running commentary, Shiloh glanced back at Rachel again, observing a wide-eyed but smiling expression.

"You've done so much for us... for two strangers," Shiloh said, suddenly wondering how on earth she could ever repay Tori's kindness.

Tori waved her hand dismissively. "When I first got your correspondence, I felt that something was special about you. After we wrote back and forth and you were able to tell me a bit about yourself, I was sure this was the place for you. Even Mitch agreed!"

"Your husband?"

Tori nodded, the smile on her face giving evidence of the love she obviously had for her husband. It struck Shiloh that as fond of Edward as she had been, she'd never had a starry, lovestruck expression for him.

"Oh yes. See, when Mitch came back to Baytown to serve as the police chief after working for the FBI—"

"Police? He's with the police?"

"Yes, did I not ever mention that? Well, anyway, he also started the local chapter of the American Legion.

The others he'd grown up with and had also returned after military service knew it was a great place to live. They extended the invitation to former military, who didn't have a good place to call home, to come live here. We've had a number of people come to Baytown, finding just what you need here also. A home... good friends... a place to start over."

It was hard to focus on Tori's words as Shiloh was still stuck on the cold moving through her that Tori's husband was a policeman. While she hadn't done anything illegal, she had to tamp down the fear that he might find her actions suspicious. *After all, Isaiah might...*

Before she had time to think through her options in case she needed to run again, they turned at the end of the street onto another road that held stately homes on one side and the town beach and bay on the other. Gasping at the beauty of the sight, all other thoughts and the idea of moving away from this place fled her mind. After driving a few blocks, Tori turned the vehicle into the drive of a large, brick, three-story house. A sign on the front proclaimed The Sea Glass Inn.

"Oh my!" Rachel exclaimed from the back seat.

Shiloh simply stared, a kernel of hope blooming in her chest.

They grabbed their luggage and walked up the wide front steps that led to a wraparound porch that could easily hold an entire gathering. The beveled glass flanking the front door sent slivers of light onto the wooden floor as they moved into the inn. Oriental rugs led the way to the large formal living room and dining room on either side of the foyer. A staircase bisected the middle of the house next to a hall that led to the back rooms and kitchen. She felt a touch on her hand and curled her fingers around Rachel's, holding tight.

"Shiloh, I know you and Rachel are exhausted. Let me show you to your room, and you can rest. Tomorrow, we can go over your duties here, and I'll have some friends over to meet you two."

Shiloh's gaze dropped to her simple clothes, suddenly feeling frumpy next to the stylish Tori. When she and Rachel left in the middle of the night, they'd worn their black mourning clothes but had changed at the Kendalls' farm before boarding the bus. She still wore the knee-length black skirt but paired it with a white button-up blouse. Her clothes had been made for comfort, not style. And Rachel had outgrown her premourning clothes and was wearing an older skirt and blouse of Shiloh's, the fit slightly large on her frame.

"Hey," Tori said softly, drawing Shiloh's attention. "My friends come from all walks of life and different backgrounds. You won't find anyone judging you here. In fact, you'll think they're some of the best people to get to know."

Embarrassed to be thinking of her clothing when she'd been given so much, she nodded, a smile replacing the worry. "You're right. There will just be a lot to get used to, but we are so grateful."

They walked up the main staircase to the second floor. "This is where the four guest rooms are, each with its own bathroom." Continuing to the third floor, Tori added, "This was the room my grandmother let me stay in when I was younger. Then it became my room when I inherited the inn. Now, it's used for live-in help when I can get it. I'm so glad you agreed to come."

At the top of the stairs, Tori ushered them into a large room that encompassed the whole attic. The gasp that Shiloh heard came from both her own lips and Rachel's at the same time.

The walls were painted a soft blue with white wood trim. The lace curtains matched the white comforter on the queen bed, a twin bed nearby. A dresser and chest of drawers were painted distressed white as well, and a small window overlooked the back of the property. Underneath the window sat a desk, perfect for Rachel to use for homework when she started school in the fall.

A large bathroom was connected to the attic bedroom. But it was the French doors covered in lace curtains that grabbed her attention and sent Rachel squealing with glee. The doors led to a balcony that overlooked the town beach and the beautiful water of the bay.

"Tori, this is more than we could have ever imagined," she said, battling the tears that threatened to fall.

"I'm just glad you sent that first letter to me, and we had a chance to write to each other." Tori looked over at Rachel and added, "I'm glad you got here in the summer and have time to get acclimated before school starts. I hope you don't mind, but I have a friend with a stepdaughter about your age. I asked them to come to meet you."

"Oh…" Rachel breathed, her eyes wide. "Thank you."

"That would be lovely," Shiloh agreed. "I have a lot to do to enroll her and take care of things."

"Just take this week to get settled in, and then you can start work next week."

Hating to put off working, Shiloh knew Tori was right. There was a lot to take care of first. Tori left after reminding them that the food in the kitchen was for them and to make themselves at home.

Not knowing which way to turn first, she swiped her hand over her face, fatigue finally overtaking her nerves about the escape, the travel, and their arrival. Knowing Rachel must be feeling it too, she said, "How about I get us something to eat while you take a bath? Then I'll get ready for bed afterward."

"But it's so early," Rachel said in the middle of a yawn.

Laughing, she hugged her niece. "It doesn't matter. We're exhausted." She made her way back down to the kitchen, where she found the making of sandwiches. Carrying them upstairs with some fruit, she was pleased to see Rachel already in her gown. They ate, then she left Rachel to sit outside to enjoy the view as she luxuriated in the bathtub, using the lavender bath oil. She remembered the last time she'd had something so decadent— right before her parents died, and she'd used the lemongrass bath salts that her mother used to make and sell. It wasn't long after that Isaiah declared all frivolous things to be against God's teachings.

She'd never believed all he'd said, but fear and loneliness could make anything sound right. And for now, she didn't care. Climbing from the tub, she avoided looking in the mirror, afraid of what she might see. *Defiance or terror? Or maybe both.*

She moved to the balcony and smiled at Rachel, who could barely hold her eyes open but didn't seem to want to let go of the sight of the sun setting over the water. They watched in silence as the sky turned orange, streaked with red, pink, and yellow. It was the most amazing panoramic scene she'd ever witnessed. She had to press her lips tightly together to hold back the sob that threatened to erupt. *God, who paints the sky with so many brilliant colors, can't possibly want us to live in darkness and fear.* It was this thought that she held tightly to her heart.

Finally, she turned to Rachel and held out her hand. "Come on. We need our rest. We'll have a busy day tomorrow and lots of new things to learn."

Once they'd gone to bed, it didn't take long for Rachel's breathing to steady, and a light snore could be heard. Grateful the overwhelmed teenager had fallen asleep so easily, Shiloh couldn't resist slipping outside to the balcony again to cast her gaze over the bay, now sparkling with the reflection of the moonlight. As she looked heavenward, the twinkling stars held her gaze. *"Silently, one by one, in the infinite meadows of heaven, Blossomed the lovely stars, the forget-me-nots of the angels."* She blinked as the words poured forth, surprised that she'd remembered how her mother would quote Henry Wadsworth Longfellow when she was a little girl. They would lie in the grass on a summer evening and stare up into the sky, watching as each star appeared.

A smile curved her lips at the memory, delighted at

the thought that more happy memories would come back to the forefront of her mind. Tiptoeing back inside, she crawled into bed. Smoothing her hands over the soft sheets, she found it hard to believe their change in circumstances.

The image of Tori's expression as she talked about her husband stayed with Shiloh. She wondered if she would ever meet someone who would cause the same starry-eyed bliss to cross her face. Rolling over, she shook her head. *Don't be ridiculous. I had my chance at love. Now I just need to focus on living.*

The next afternoon, Shiloh stood in the kitchen and looked at the shaded stone patio behind the inn. That morning, she had risen early and carefully listened to everything Tori showed her.

Across from the living room was a formal dining room, but the inn guests had their breakfast in the glassed-in sunroom on the side of the house with the double doors leading from the dining room.

The duties were light compared to what Shiloh was used to. Each morning, she would make a hearty breakfast of scrambled eggs, bacon, sausage, and muffins, along with juice and coffee, for the guests. During the rest of the morning, Shiloh would then clean the rooms and, if they were checking out, wash the guest room linens. Tori assured her again that she could also fit in a part-time job at the restaurant if she wanted.

Now, the patio was filled with a large gathering of

women, all Tori's friends from Baytown and the surrounding area who'd come to meet her and Rachel. Children ran around the fenced yard and gardens. It felt overwhelming at first, but Tori had been right... she'd felt no judgment from any of them.

She was wearing another skirt, but at least it was dark blue and not black. Maybe there was little distinction to some, but the color difference was exciting to her. Her white blouse managed not to appear too frumpy, with the sleeves rolled up to her elbows. Rachel had exuded a mixture of nerves and anticipation as they'd gotten ready that morning. She'd chosen to stick with a blue skirt, but with Shiloh's encouragement, paired it with a pale-blue T-shirt that had been one of Shiloh's from years before.

Leaning to the side as she looked out the door, a sight caught her eye, and she smiled. One of the women was a doctor in the area, and Judith had brought her fourteen-year-old stepdaughter, Cindy. The soft-spoken young woman was perfect for Rachel, and the two girls immediately began chatting.

"It's nice to see, isn't it?" Tori said, walking up next to her.

Nodding, she blinked back the tears that threatened to fall. Swallowing, she said, "I feel as though I've been dropped into a dream and am afraid to wake."

"I hope one day you can tell me more about your circumstances, but if not, Maddie, the friend standing next to Judith, is a counselor. If you or Rachel ever need someone to talk to, please don't hesitate to call her."

"I'm sure we'll be fine," she murmured. She'd been on her own too much to imagine sharing with a stranger.

"And there's lots to do in the community. The American Legion Auxiliary, numerous church services to choose from, the library, and various interest groups, just to name a few. I really do hope you'll be happy here and make Baytown your home."

With a cleansing breath whooshing out to still her nerves, Shiloh nodded, and the two women walked back outside to meet more of the friends who gathered, wondering if she would ever truly feel at home. *Or stop looking over my shoulder.*

7

PRESENT DAY

Joseph sat at a high-top table with Wyatt and one of his best friends, Luke. This time, the family celebration had started at the Seafood Shack on the Baytown Harbor. The gathering had also included Millie, Wyatt's new girlfriend. The beauty had been a Hollywood actress until an accident ended her career, and she'd ended up as Wyatt's next-door neighbor. She'd already left with his parents and grandparents, and Wyatt had walked her to her vehicle before returning. As close as the two of them were, Joseph was surprised that Wyatt was staying longer and then grinned when Wyatt admitted that Millie had insisted they have "brother time." Her parents were deceased, and she had no siblings, so she and Wyatt spent as much time with his family as possible.

Celebrating his graduation from the Virginia Law Enforcement Academy, Joseph was ready for his dream job — becoming employed with the Baytown Station of the Virginia Marine Police. After researching his various options after graduating from VLEA, spending time with Callan, and being introduced to Ryan Coates, the VMP captain, he knew exactly what he wanted to do. He had a month of special training for the VMP but had already been accepted for a position as soon as he received his final certificate.

Draining his beer, he signaled to the server to bring another pitcher to the table. Grinning toward Wyatt, he said, "This one is on me."

"It's about time," his brother joked. "You've been in training and volunteering for the past year. Sure hope your savings from the Navy isn't about to run out."

"Don't worry about me," he assured. "I not only put a down payment on a small house on the outskirts of town, but I can still afford a pitcher of beer."

Luke filled their glasses once the pitcher arrived. Not originally from the Eastern Shore, he'd been a medic in the Army and then accepted a job with the North Heron Regional Jail as their medic. Joseph met him at a local American Legion meeting. While opposite in personalities, Joseph formed a tight friendship with the stoic Luke, glad for the company of another single man who didn't have to run home to their wife or girlfriend. Although, it hadn't escaped his notice that a pretty elementary school teacher in the area had caught Luke's eye. *Might be another one biting the dust.*

"Why do you need a house?" Luke asked. "I've got an apartment in town that suits me just fine."

"Man, I need a view," he replied. "Gotta admit that my view isn't as good as Wyatt's, but it still has a small pier over one of the inlets. I'm not too far from the bay, so I'm happy with it."

The door to the restaurant opened, and he looked up to see Callan and Ryan enter along with Jarod and Andy, two other VMP officers. They walked straight to him to offer their congratulations, and the celebration group grew to include even more of their friends in law enforcement. Leaning back in his chair, he reveled in the notion that he was not alone, surrounded by good friends, good food, and good beer.

Excusing himself from the group, he headed to the men's room. As he left, a server darted into the hall, approaching him. She glanced around as though to see if her boss was nearby, then smiled widely.

Black hair pulled up in a sloppy bun. A little heavy on the makeup. A tight T-shirt with the restaurant logo, S-Shack, emblazoned across her chest. And booty shorts that the manager had probably warned her not to wear. The Seafood Shack was a family restaurant and bar, and while the manager liked to hire young, pretty waitresses who had no problem showing off their figures, Joseph figured that this woman was pushing the limit. But considering her legs and ass looked good, he wasn't about to complain.

"Hey, Joseph. I was hoping to get a chance to throw my congratulations out with everyone else. I work here now. Brogan was being a real prick about how I dressed over at the pub." She stepped closer, dragging her fingernail over his chest.

She looked vaguely familiar, and he wondered if they'd once been in school together. Glancing at the name tag stuck over her chest, he recognized the little hearts she'd written as her dotted i's. *Oh yeah...* He battled a sigh as he offered his habitual charm. "Vicki, nice to see you."

She giggled. "I wasn't sure you'd remember me. I was shocked when I woke up, and you were gone the last time we were together." She bit her lip, and her coy glance raked over him. "I had such a crush. Never thought I'd get a chance for a repeat performance."

Training and volunteering had left him little time off, so it had been a while since he'd been with someone. But he didn't do repeat performances, knowing that implied some kind of relationship. "Well—"

His attention was diverted when the door opened from the back stockroom, and a woman walked out. She wore a skirt that hung to just above her knees and a short-sleeved blouse. If it wasn't for the fact that she'd come from the stock room, he would never have assumed she was an employee. Her dark hair with red highlights glistened and was pulled back into a low ponytail. Her pale complexion was as smooth as porcelain, unlike the other women who hit the beach as often as possible to work on their tan.

It didn't appear that she wore any makeup, but when she turned her gaze toward him, it was apparent that she didn't need any. He stared into her blue-gray eyes, his attention wholly captured. The color wasn't like any he'd seen before. Not like the bright blue hue that was in his own reflection— the same blue eye color that ran in his family. Instead, a light shone from their depths in her eyes, reminding him of the color of the water when the sun started to peek from behind a cloud.

Completely forgetting about Vicki, he felt the air he'd been holding rush from his lungs as he stared. He beamed his high-watt smile toward the new woman, wanting to see how her eyes would light when she smiled in return. Instead of the reaction he hoped for, her cheeks pinkened with blush, and she dropped her eyes down toward the floor, no smile on her lips.

"I said," Vicki emphasized loudly, one hand on her hip and the other tapping his chest. "Are you interested in coming back to my place tonight for a repeat performance?"

The new woman's gaze jumped back up to his, the blush deepening before she hurried past them, disappearing around the corner.

"Who is that?"

"What? Seriously, Joseph?" Vicki bit out, her eyes narrowing. "You're making plans with me for tonight, and you're asking about someone else?"

Even though he hadn't made plans with Vicki, he wasn't in the habit of scoping out other women when standing with another. "Sorry. I just thought I recognized her, that's all."

Vicki huffed, throwing her hand out to the side. "I don't see how. She's new. Not like just new *here*, you know, at the Shack, but new to the area. She just got hired a few weeks ago." Leaning closer, she whispered loudly, "A real weirdo, if you ask me."

He hated the derogatory description, remembering

when he was a child and others called him names because of his speech difficulties and poverty.

He started to point out that he didn't ask her, but curiosity got the better of him, so he did. "What do you mean?"

"You saw her clothes! She dresses like a nun! She's super shy and very quiet. Right now, the manager has her working lunch shifts." She snorted. "Dressed like that, she'll never make any money in tips."

It crossed Joseph's mind that the beautiful woman could be wearing a potato sack and would still outshine any of the women he'd seen. Hell, growing up poor, he remembered wearing hand-me-downs from Wyatt, and then his sister would get them next. He knew more than most that what someone might be forced to wear on the outside had little to do with who they were on the inside.

Vicki pressed up close, her breasts laying on his forearm as she cupped his cheek to aim his gaze back at her. "I get off in an hour."

Holding her gaze, he knew there was nothing there but lust. She was a repeat version of the same kind of woman he'd been spending time with since he'd become an adult— easy, no expectations, no demands, just sex. The woman he'd just seen was different— the type of woman who would make a man want to hand her the world as he drowned in the deep waters reflecting in her eyes. As quickly as that thought hit him, he immediately pushed it to the side.

Offering Vicki a patented smile, he hoped it would

soften his words. "I'm hanging out with my friends tonight—"

A predatory gleam flashed through her eyes, shooting unease through him. "Well, it's a good thing that I'm a friend."

Clarifying his intent, he added, "I'm not up for anything tonight. And I have to let you know that now that I'm back here to live, I don't plan on starting anything new right away."

She hefted her shoulders and shrugged. "Fine by me. But then, most men tell me that one night isn't enough. I'm sure I can change your mind." She blew him a kiss and called out over her shoulder as she darted away, "I'll get you back in my bed again."

He sighed, then turned toward his table, spying the beautiful woman standing nearby, her eyes pinned on him. Now the blue-gray reminded him of a stormy evening over the bay, where the clouds were swirling and casting shadows on the undulating water below.

Staring into them, he had the strangest feeling that this woman had weathered more than her share of storms. Whatever light he'd seen in them before, they darkened before she turned and walked away. Feeling chastised as though he'd disappointed her, he couldn't help but feel as though he'd disappointed himself.

"Hey, Joseph! Someone's buying another round for you!"

Turning to see that the VMP group had ordered more beer and wings, he slapped the practiced grin back on his face and jogged over, determined to have a good night with friends. He regretted having slept with

Vicki a year ago, having a feeling she would be a constant irritant... and because he couldn't get the blue-gray eyes out of his mind.

Shiloh walked into the manager's office, clocking off on the computer the employees used for keeping their time and attendance.

Mark Friedberg looked up and smiled at her. "How are you settling in, Shiloh?"

"I'm good, thank you. Everybody's been very nice and helpful."

His gaze dropped to her clothes and then back to her face. "How are things going on the lunch shift? Tips okay?"

"It's fine. I've served for years, just not officially in a restaurant, so it wasn't too hard to pick up what I needed to do." She smoothed her hands over her skirt, knowing she didn't dress like the other servers. She had taken Rachel to buy some new clothes, including jeans and shorts that weren't too short. Rachel had talked her into buying a few things for herself, but she often wore her former clothes, just happy not to have to wear black. While they might not be fashionable, they were serviceable. She hadn't wanted to spend too much money on anything new, at least not until she was sure they were staying. "I want to thank you for giving me this opportunity. I know Tori recommended me, but I realize you took a chance on me."

He waved his hand to the side. "Honestly, Shiloh, I

go through a lot of servers here. I never expect anyone to stay long-term because I know the pay isn't always great, and the work can be hard. So it was easy to take a chance on you." He glanced down at her clothes again. "I also appreciate you dressing modestly since this is a family restaurant. I'd like you to wear a restaurant logo T-shirt sometimes, but I'll let you pick out the size because I'd like it to be something you're comfortable in."

She smiled and nodded. "Thank you, I'd like that. I'll be sure to get one on my next shift."

"Next week is also payday, so if you're not on the schedule for Wednesday, make sure you stop by."

She offered her thanks and stepped back into the hall. Going out the back door, she unlocked her bicycle and climbed on. Pedaling out of the parking lot, she looked over to see the handsome man who'd been flirting with Vicki walk out and lean against a parked SUV.

Her bicycle bounced over a large rock in the path, and she wobbled, pitching to the side, sprawling onto the ground. Embarrassed, she pushed upward to stand, wincing.

"Hey! Are you okay?"

The deep voice sounded close, and she jerked her head around to see the man running toward her. *Joseph. That's what Vicki called him.* Heat from her blush moved from her cheeks and filled her, and she wished he hadn't witnessed her ungraceful tumble.

He reached her side, his face full of concern. As his

gaze lowered, his brows snapped together. "You're hurt!"

She looked down and spied a trickle of blood running down her leg. "Oh… well, it's not bad. Just a scratch."

"You're bleeding." He whipped out a crumpled napkin from his pants pocket and bent, pressing it to her leg.

She startled, mortification filling her. She was still embarrassed to have fallen off her bicycle, but more so because he was the first man to touch her since Edward. A simple touch— one of care, not desire. But the tingle she felt must surely be from the minor injury because she'd never felt that with her husband.

"Please don't worry about it. It's f-fine… I'm… I'm… uh… fine."

He looked up, the napkin still held against the cut. The dim light from the lamppost caught the blue in his eyes, and she was mesmerized by the color that so resembled the water on a sunny day.

He dropped his gaze as he patted her leg a few more times before standing. "It seems to have stopped bleeding. You should get that cleaned when you get home."

"Yes. Of course. Uh… thank you." She reached out to take the napkin with her blood drops on it and then spied a phone number written in the corner. "Oh. You… might need this."

His gaze dropped, and he jerked slightly. His eyes met hers again, and she could have sworn his cheeks reddened even though the evening had descended and they were shrouded in shadows. He opened his mouth, but a whiny call from the parking lot cut whatever he was going to say off.

"Joseph! I just got off if you're interested!"

Shiloh glanced over at the same time he did to see Vicki standing under the outside light near the restaurant door. She was looking down at her chest, adjusting her top so that her boobs were pushed up higher.

No longer wanting to continue to stand on the path, Shiloh bent and grabbed the handlebars of her bicycle, mounting the seat again. With one foot on a pedal, she was ready to push off when he reached out and grabbed her arm gently, a look of concern on his face.

"Are you okay? It's dark, and I could see you home—"

"Thank you, but that won't be necessary." Inclining her head toward Vicki, she said, "I think she's waiting for you."

"No. I don't… it's not…"

"It's okay. I have to go. Thank you for your help." She looked away as she pushed off. Continuing along the gravel road that was a pedestrian-bicycle-golf cart shortcut from the harbor to Main Street, she refused to look over her shoulder to see if he was still there or had left with Vicki. She soon turned the corner onto Bay Road that ran on the western side of Baytown, along the shores of the Chesapeake Bay, and heaved a long sigh.

Once in the driveway of the Sea Glass Inn, she pedaled around to the back, where she stored her bicycle in the small shed. Moving through the back door into the large kitchen, she pushed all thoughts of

Joseph from her mind and smiled. She still had to pinch herself to believe that her new life was real.

Just like Tori had promised, the work at the inn still gave her plenty of time for a part-time job at the restaurant. Mark had promised that she would not usually need to work an evening shift like tonight, but he'd wanted to make sure she understood all the workings of the restaurant.

Slipping into the bedroom, Shiloh could see that Rachel was already asleep in the twin bed. Tiptoeing into the bathroom, she washed her face, brushed her hair, and changed into her nightgown. Applying a bandage to her small cut, she sucked in a quick breath at the memory of Joseph's touch.

Still restless, she slipped through the French doors and sat on one of the chairs on the balcony. From there, she and Rachel had witnessed the most beautiful sunsets either of them had ever seen in their lives. And she never grew tired of the ever-changing view.

The bay was dark, but the few lights from the town sent diamond sparkles over the water. Allowing the sound of the surf to ease her mind, she thought back over the past month.

When they arrived, Tori had given her complete confidence that they would fit easily into the life of the little coastal town. And she'd been right. They'd already been welcomed into the community. In truth, it reminded her of the way she'd been raised, where strangers were treated as friends. At first, she felt as though perhaps they just wanted to stare at the newcomers and gossip about why they came. But slowly, she began to see that the women in Baytown were genuinely kind.

Closing her eyes, she sucked in a deep breath and let it out slowly. The image of the man from the restaurant now moved to the forefront of her mind. Tall, well-built, with an engaging smile and a twinkle in his eyes. She'd certainly met other handsome men in town, most of the husbands of the women she befriended.

But there was something about his eyes... something that pulled her in and made her want to keep staring into their depths. She could only imagine that having his full attention would be a heady feeling indeed.

She opened her eyes and snorted. Joseph was definitely a charmer. *If he knew my sheltered past, I doubt he'd try to charm me!* But he was also kind. His eyes had held concern and his touch was gentle. *And I felt—*

The sound of the door opening behind her had her twist her head around, smiling as Rachel walked out. "I'm sorry, sweetheart. Did I wake you when I came in?"

Her niece rubbed her eyes and then sat in the chair next to her, shaking her head. "No, I just woke up and thought I saw you out here. I'm sorry you had to work so late tonight."

"Oh, it wasn't too bad. The manager promises I'll be on the lunch shifts when I work. He thought I'd get some good experience tonight to see how the evening crowds were handled."

Rachel looked out toward the water, a sweet smile settling on her face.

"Are you happy?" Shiloh asked. Rachel had given every indication that she was, but Shiloh still worried. "I know with school starting soon, it will be a big adjustment."

A giggle slipped out as Rachel looked back toward her. "Are you serious? Sometimes I feel like we went to sleep and woke up in the middle of a fairy tale."

Laughing, she reached over and squeezed her hand. "It's not a fairy tale, but I know what you mean." They were silent another minute, then sighed. "I was worried about all of this."

"About leaving?"

"About leaving the home we knew. About taking you away from your comfort zone. About sending you to a new school after the small school in the community and then homeschooling you this past year. Afraid that you would hate it all and hate me for bringing you here."

Rachel shifted in her seat, clutching Shiloh's hands in her own while shaking her head. "No, no! I would never hate you for anything, especially not for everything you've done for me. You and Edward took me in when my parents died. You protected me when Master... I mean, Isaiah wanted to take me from you. Oh, Shiloh, I would never hate you." She looked back toward the water and waved her hand out over the beautiful nighttime scene. "And just look at this! We get to live in a beautiful inn right on the bay. I love helping you with the guests. It's true that I'm still a little terrified of the idea of going to a big school, but you made sure I had a friend right away."

Cindy had become Rachel's best friend, and it appeared that Cindy's older brother, Trevor, had let it be known that if anyone messed with his sister or her friends, they'd answer to him.

Not finished, Rachel continued as she held Shiloh's gaze. "So I know while coming here was frightening, I'm so glad we escaped together."

Standing, she pulled Rachel up, wrapping her arms around her. Holding tight, she whispered, "Me, too."

Walking back into the room, she secured the door behind her, and they crawled into their beds. She and Edward had shared a double bed, and the queen-size one in the large room seemed too big for just her. She'd explained that she and Rachel could share, but Tori was more than happy to provide a twin bed just for her niece. Now, spread out in the middle of the bed, her hand smoothed over the soft cotton sheets, and she smiled.

A new life. A new chance. She felt sure her parents, sister and brother-in-law, and Edward would be pleased.

With that thought, she closed her eyes and fell asleep, but the dark memory of Isaiah that usually filled her mind was replaced with the lighter image of the handsome Joseph moving through her dreams.

8

"I think I see him!" Joseph was standing on the deck of the VMP patrol boat. "Shit, he's gone!"

A call had come in reporting a dog overboard from a local fisherman who'd taken several vacationers out onto the water. The fishermen, pissed as hell that he'd allowed one of the clients to bring his dog onto the boat with him, had barely managed to make the emergency call while keeping the owner from jumping into the water.

By the time the VMP made it to the area where the dog had gone overboard, twenty-seven minutes had passed. The water was choppy as the wind from an approaching storm whipped around, making it difficult to see the head of the brown dog. Just when Joseph thought he saw it, another swell would come, and he'd lose sight.

Andy Bergstrom was at the wheel, and Ryan, the VMP captain, was at his side, his binoculars trained in the other direction so they could cover a wider area.

"How long can this dog hold out?" he asked, already hating the answer he might hear.

"He's got to be getting tired if he's not used to swimming," Ryan replied.

"Shit," Joseph muttered quietly again. Barely blinking, he trained his binoculars slowly over the undulating surf, looking for any hint that the dog still had his head above the water. Another eleven minutes passed, but Joseph wasn't willing to throw in the towel yet.

Something moved past his view, and he jerked his gaze back, narrowing his focus on the object. "Got him!" He lifted his hand and pointed as he called out so that Andy could deftly steer the boat in the right direction.

Ryan turned his way, keeping his eye on the dog, as Joseph hustled to the side of the boat. As they got closer, he could now clearly see the dog's desperate paddling to keep his head above the water, occasionally slipping under before rising again. Coming alongside as close as they could, Joseph attempted to maneuver a flotation device to the dog, but the exhausted canine couldn't grab hold.

"Going in," he said, giving Ryan time to get to his side, as well. Jumping into the water, the slap of cold was familiar, although it always caused a jolt. He couldn't imagine that the dog had been able to survive this long. Swimming closer with the flotation device in his hand, he wrapped his arm around the dog, who, in desperation, turned to cling to Joseph. "I got you, boy. I got you."

Ryan pulled the safety rope attached to Joseph, and he and the dog were lifted over the side of the boat. He knew the dog was dehydrated as it collapsed onto the deck. Ryan ordered Andy to get them to the harbor and put in a call to Samantha, their local veterinarian. "Ask her to meet us at the harbor if she can."

The wind whipped a chill through Joseph, but he knelt next to the dog and rubbed his coat with a thick towel Ryan handed him. Andy sped back to the harbor, where the anxious owner was waiting. Joseph picked the towel-wrapped dog up and carried him along the pier and into their station, ignoring his own cold, soaked clothing.

He walked straight into the workroom, surprised to see the veterinarian walking in behind him. "Damn, Sam, you must've been close."

"Believe it or not, this is my day off, and I was in town."

She reached out and rubbed her hand over the dog's face. "What's his name?"

He knelt and laid the dog on the floor where a dry towel had been placed. "Zip." By now, Zip was looking around with interest, seeming to gain strength now that he was no longer fighting the current or waves. Another officer, Jarod, walked in with a bowl of water which the dog now immediately began lapping.

"Good," Samantha said, rocking back on her heels. "I was afraid he might need subcutaneous fluids. Where's the owner?"

"Andy will bring him in as soon as all his information is gathered for the report."

The words had barely left Joseph's mouth when Andy walked in with a man who rushed past and dropped to the floor, gathering the dog in his arms. The chill from his wet clothing was now sinking in, and Joseph stood. The dog squirmed out of his owner's arms and trotted over to Joseph, sitting on his flanks and looking up with big brown eyes that seemed full of emotion.

Kneeling again, he rubbed his hand over Zip's head and grinned. "You're pretty amazing, Zip. But from now on, how about keeping all four paws on the ground?"

Zip's tongue lolled to the side as he panted, and Joseph could have sworn it was a smile on the dog's face. With a last rub, he stood and waved toward Samantha as he walked down the hall toward the men's locker room.

Once inside, he stripped and stepped into the shower, allowing the hot water to chase the chill away. Toweling off quickly, he pulled on a new uniform and packed the wet one into a plastic bag to take home. Stepping into another workroom, he sat down at his computer to include his notes in the report. Glancing at the clock, he spied that it was only a little after eleven. His stomach rumbled, and he hoped he could get an early lunch if another call didn't come in.

And he knew just where he wanted lunch to be— The Seafood Shack. He used to bring in a sandwich several days a week to save money. When he ate out, he often divided his time between the pub, Stuart's pharmacy, which had a diner inside, and the Seafood Shack. But recently, he'd spent more time at the S-Shack just to catch a glimpse of the pretty server who had filled his thoughts... and stayed in his thoughts more than any other woman since he'd met her.

Shiloh. She didn't wear her name tag right over her breast, which is what some of the other servers did either out of habit or to draw attention to their chests. Shiloh's name tag was pinned higher, near her collarbone. But that worked for him. It allowed him to see her name without looking like some creeper whose gaze was fixed on her figure. She had finally started wearing an S-Shack T-shirt, but it was enormous, hanging down to partially cover her hips. She usually wore skirts, modest in length, pairing them with navy-blue sneakers. Not one thing about her manner of dress called attention to herself, yet his eyes always moved to where she was.

She only worked the lunch crowd and seemed to be gone when he stopped in at night, which was good considering that he tried to avoid the night shift since Vicki had trouble getting it through her mind that he wasn't there to see her.

By the time he finished his report, he hurried to the other side of the harbor, seeing Callan and Ryan already sitting at one of the tables. And damned if Shiloh wasn't taking their order. Rushing over just as she turned around, his hands snapped out to catch her as their bodies collided. He hadn't meant to run into her, and from the stunned look on her wide-eyed face, she hadn't been expecting anyone to be right behind her. He grinned widely, staring down at her beautiful face, not wanting to release her. Her face flamed red, and she ducked her head as she slipped from his grip and hurried toward the kitchen.

Callan laughed, shaking his head. "Smooth move, Joseph."

"I've been trying to get her to smile at me for weeks," Joseph said, still grinning, his heart lighter for having seen her. He couldn't explain it but just seeing her a couple of times in passing at the restaurant during a week always made his day better. He'd never managed to be there when she was getting off work and had never seen her in town now that he lived just north of Baytown.

Ryan shook his head. "Looks like she's immune to your charm."

He knew Ryan was right. He'd smiled, winked, tried to joke and flirt with her, asked about her leg and bicycle, but all he received back was a combination of a quick nod, a hasty reply that she was fine, a blush, and eyes that looked away. Not wanting to admit his failure to get her to pay attention to him, he puffed out his chest in false bravado. "No woman can be immune to my charm for long."

After a moment, she came back to the table with Ryan and Callan's drinks, looking everywhere except at Joseph. He refused to give his drink order until she settled her gaze on him. "I'll have a sweet iced tea, darlin'. The sweeter, the better. And I'll take the burger special."

She dipped her chin and turned, hurrying away once again. As he watched her leave, he swallowed the sigh that threatened to escape. It wasn't that he thought he was irresistible, but he'd never had to work so hard to get a woman to notice him. In high school, he'd found an advantage to being Wyatt's younger brother, considering they looked so much alike. To a teenager, the girls looking to make their way through the Baytown boys seemed to love claiming they'd gone out with both Newmans, at least until he'd given his heart to Maggie.

Later, the bars around the naval stations were filled with women looking for fun. Usually, tossing out a smile, flirting, or even a stupid pickup line was enough to ensure someone was willing to share a drink, a dance, and a night of horizontal fun.

But for the past weeks, since he'd first laid eyes on her, she'd definitely proven to be immune to his game. When Shiloh brought over their food, not giving him any special attention, he sighed. He could be patient, though— God knows, he'd learned that as a kid when his family had to scrimp and save just for Christmas and birthday presents.

In the past month, he tossed out the phone numbers that had made their way onto his coffee orders or napkins. In truth, he'd discovered that flirting and picking up women in his hometown was a hell of a lot different than when he'd been in the Navy, or the bars he'd visited when he'd stayed a weekend in Virginia Beach during his training. He'd grown accustomed to almost never seeing a woman he'd slept with again. Sure, sometimes he'd run into a former one-nighter, but having always made sure they were on the same page before starting anything, a nod and friendly smile was the only thing required. But back on the Eastern Shore, he discovered that hooking up with Vicki had been a colossal mistake.

He'd been out of the Navy for over a year, and training, volunteering, studying, and spending time with family had taken precedence over anything else. But having slept with Vicki, she seemed to think that every time he came into the S-Shack when she was working, he was there to see her. And when he didn't flirt or ask for a repeat performance, her narrow-eyed glare and pout rubbed him the wrong way.

As Callan and Ryan continued to talk shop, Joseph's gaze continued to follow Shiloh around the restaurant as he ate his lunch, barely tasting anything.

"What do you think, Joseph?"

Blinking, he jerked his head around to look at the two men sitting across from him. While he hated to admit he hadn't been listening, he came up blank and had no choice. "I'm sorry. What was the question?"

Callan laughed as Ryan shook his head. "Damn, you do have it bad," Ryan said. "I was asking about the new training schedule. I've got the others rotating, but you just finished, so I'll put you at the end since you don't need any new certification points at the moment."

Nodding, he agreed. "Yeah, that's fine. Although, if there's anything in the training that I need, you can bump my name up."

"You got it," Ryan said. Sliding from the stool, he tossed some bills onto the table, Callan doing the same.

"I'm paying with my card, so y'all go on, and I'll meet you back at the station."

Ryan nodded and turned away, but Callan grinned,

shaking his head slightly. "Is that the only reason you're going to take an extra minute to chat with the server?"

Out of excuses and tired of playing the flirt, he shrugged, shoving his hands into his front pockets. "I'm still trying to get her to smile at me. It'll take a while, but I'm determined."

Callan nodded and clapped him on the shoulder. "You know, when some things have been easy, it makes the reward all the sweeter when you have to work to get what you want."

"Yeah, I'm sure Sophie made you work for it!"

Callan had ended up marrying the girl next door after many years apart. "You better believe she did. Just because we'd known each other since we were young didn't mean anything when it came to us finally getting together."

Joseph held his friend's gaze for a moment, then looked to the side where Shiloh was serving customers, her quiet movements making it easy for someone not even to realize she was there. Or at least until they looked up and saw that beautiful face. "At least you and Sophie had a history. With her," he said, inclining his head toward Shiloh, "I have no idea who she is or where she came from. And damn, I really want to."

"Then do. Stop flirting and try to get to know the real her. Who knows, Charmer, it might just work." With that, Callan walked out, calling over his shoulder, "See you at the station."

With that advice ringing in his ears, he stood next to the table until she returned. Gathering the money Callan and Ryan had left, she glanced up toward him.

"Was there anything else I can get for you?"

Her soft voice and blue-gray eyes pulled him in, and he suddenly found himself tongue-tied like he'd been when he was a child. "Uh, no." As she started to turn away, he blurted, "I mean, yes." Her brow furrowed, and he felt foolish as his words continued to tumble. "I'm paying with a card. So I need the, um... check. I mean, I can just give you my card to pay. I don't actually have to see the check. But I know I need to sign... uh... the receipt."

Jesus, I haven't stumbled over my words like that since I was a kid. He felt his cheeks redden but watched in fascination as she blinked but didn't laugh at him or look away. Blowing out his breath, he forgot to inhale again as he realized it was the first time she'd held his gaze. Even if it was because he sounded like a bumbling fool, he'd take it. Before he had a chance to say anything else, she nodded and turned to move to the cash register. He sucked in air and dropped his chin, wondering what had happened to his cool persona, then lifted his head quickly, not wanting to miss a moment of seeing her.

She returned with the check and handed it to him. Taking it while keeping his eyes on her face, his fingers inadvertently touched hers, and a strange warmth moved through him. She jolted slightly, and he wondered if she'd felt it too. Her gaze darted up to his, eyes wide, and her lips parted. *Oh yeah... she felt that.* Realizing she wasn't as immune to him as she pretended, he smiled, fighting the urge to pound his chest, knowing that would really send her running away.

He gave her his card and once again watched as she walked toward the register, returning quickly with his receipt. Pocketing the card, he tried to think of anything he could say to keep her standing there another moment. He started to throw out a witty comment, then snapped his mouth shut, remembering Callan's advice. Clearing his throat, he handed the signed receipt to her and smiled. "How are you?"

She pressed her lips together for a few seconds, then nodded. "I'm fine."

"So have you been in town long?" Inwardly wincing at the lame question, he noted she didn't walk away. Answering him with only a slow headshake, he plunged ahead, blurting, "I was born and raised nearby but left to join the service. Couldn't imagine living anywhere else but the Eastern Shore, so I was anxious to come back."

She didn't respond to his proclamation, but he was stunned when she at least continued to stand in front of him, holding his gaze with intensity. For a few seconds, he knew he could drown in their clear depths. Deciding to press his luck, he asked, "So where did you come from?"

The bright light in her eyes became cloudy as she jerked slightly, her brow lowering. She glanced down and twisted her fingers in the material of her skirt. "Why do you ask?" Her quickly spoken words that seemed to radiate with unease caught him by surprise.

"I just wanted to know more about you."

Her brow scrunched as her gaze searched his. "Oh." Glancing to the side, she suddenly shook her head and said, "Um… I have to get back to work." Without giving him a chance to respond, she hurried away.

He sighed heavily and walked out of the restaurant. *I stumbled over my words. I inadvertently made her self-conscious. I've got no fucking idea how to talk to a woman I'm interested in.* As he made his way back to the station on the other side of the harbor, frustration gave way as a slow smile curved his lips. *At least I spent more time with her than before. That's got to count as progress.* He was startled at the idea that progress with Shiloh was measured in baby steps. *But I'll take it!*

9

Shiloh walked through the massive doors leading into the Baytown library, her breath catching in her throat. The red brick building was three stories tall, and the lobby extended upward for two of those stories with a loft in the back filled with bookshelves. She had loved to visit the small community library in the basement of their church when she was younger, but since it had been destroyed when Isaiah took over, she hadn't been around so many books in almost five years. And, in truth, she'd never been inside a building this large since she'd been in school many years ago.

"Aunt Shiloh, come on!"

Jerking around, she wiped the awestruck expression off her face and smiled as Rachel and Cindy rushed past her. Cindy had brought Rachel to the library several times before school started so they could use the computers, but it was the first time Shiloh had visited. She was amazed at how quickly Rachel had adapted to the changes in their lives but thanked God for the resiliency of youth. "I'm going to wander for a bit," she said, her whisper seeming to echo in the cavernous room.

As the girls headed toward the fiction section, she meandered along the tall bookshelves, her fingers trailing over the spines of so many volumes. Awed and humbled at the wealth of knowledge and creativity at her fingertips, she blinked to keep the moisture gathering in her eyes at bay.

"It's lovely to see someone appreciate the library's offerings," a soft voice came from behind her.

Turning, she observed a middle-aged woman with a pleasant smile on her face. Khaki pants and a bright red blouse fit her trim body. Her brown hair was sprinkled with gray, and she wore wire-framed glasses perched on her nose. Nodding shyly, Shiloh was uncertain what to say.

"I'm Marjorie MacElvey. The head librarian. Well"—she laughed—"actually, the only librarian, although we do have many volunteers."

"Hello. It's nice to meet you. I'm Shiloh."

Marjorie tilted her head to the side. "You must be the young woman working at The Sea Glass Inn?"

Her breath left her in a rush, hating the vulnerability she felt at the idea that she didn't fit in enough not to stand out. "How do you know?"

Marjorie laughed. "Because I saw you come in with Rachel and Cindy. They came in frequently before school started, and Cindy introduced me to your niece. Tori brings her little one for preschool story time and couldn't sing your praises enough."

"Oh," she said, her breathing easier.

"So do you have any particular favorites that you enjoy reading?" Marjorie asked.

"Um... it's been a while since I've done much reading," she murmured.

Marjorie nodded with understanding. "Oh, I know how busy life can be. But we're here anytime you want to explore! Just make yourself at home. We have computers for research or email. Books we can order. Magazines. Oh, dear, listen to me prattling on. I'm sure you know how a library works, but ask questions if you desire any assistance."

After thanking her, she continued down the aisle, her gaze drifting over the various sections. Suddenly light-headed from all that was new to her, she popped out at the end of the aisle, and her gaze searched for Rachel. Seeing her at a table in front of a computer, she gasped in surprise. She'd used a computer when she was much younger, but their community had spotty internet service, so she'd found it more useful as a word processor and hadn't missed it when Isaiah decreed the internet to be the work of the devil. Hurrying over, she moved behind the girls to see what they were looking at.

Rachel smiled up at her. "Look, Shiloh! Cindy made sure I knew everything I'd need to know about computers before I started school. Since we don't have one, I can just come here."

Shiloh knew it was true but wanted Rachel to have every opportunity to succeed in this new world she'd brought her to. "We can get a computer, Rachel. I'll just need to find out what is best. It's been a long time since I've used one, and I'm sure things have changed."

Cindy gave her a quick tutorial, and she was amazed at how fast the images popped up. Settling into the seat when the girls wandered off to look at magazines, she typed in Baytown, smiling at the pictures that appeared. Next, she looked at the other websites as ideas moved through her curious mind. She'd seen the Virginia Marine Police on Joseph's uniform and was curious to see what it meant. Reading about the men and women who patrolled the waterways of Virginia, she was awed at his job description. Patrols the waters… ensures people and marine life safety… conducts search and rescue… counterterrorism patrols… investigations… public service… the list continued.

For some reason, his easygoing smile belied the intensity of his job, and she hated that she hadn't realized how brave he had to be to go to work each day.

Suddenly, feeling like a bumpkin who'd dropped in on a much more exciting world than she'd ever known, she sighed and leaned back in her chair. A seed of a thought sprouted in her mind, and she typed in the community she'd left behind. Plineyville. Not surprised to find almost nothing besides local geographical information, a couple of articles popped up with one word blaring out at her. Quickly shutting down the search, she found her chest heaved as the air rushed out, and she squeezed her eyes closed for a moment. Isaiah's face came to her, his familiar scowl and beady-eyed stare causing her to startle.

Looking around and glad no one seemed to be

paying any attention, she took to her feet and wandered over to the fiction section, where she finally decided on a few books. She found a variety of novels, including a few romances, remembering the ones her mother read with a handsome Viking or duke on the front, calling them her guilty pleasure. Shiloh had even read a few, losing herself in the idea of a forever love with a handsome man. After she married, she gave up the novels, knowing that enjoying a cozy relationship with Edward would never be the same as the breath-stealing romances she'd read about. Grimacing, she thought of Isaiah's decree against all fiction books when he became the leader.

Pushing those thoughts to the back of her mind, she walked to Marjorie sitting at the tall counter with an older gentleman.

"Did you find what you were looking for?" Marjorie asked, then, before giving her a chance to reply, turned to the white-haired man sitting next to her. "This is Shiloh Wallen. She's new here and works at the Sea Glass Inn. Shiloh, this is George MacElvey, my brother-in-law. I'm a widow, and George and I are the only ones left in our family, so we hang out together."

Smiling widely, George stood and shook her hand. "Ms. Wallen, how lovely to meet you. We knew Tori's grandparents, who owned the inn many years ago. What a beautiful example of late-nineteenth-century colonial revival architecture."

"Yes." She nodded, having no idea what he meant with his description, but since he used the word "beautiful," she assumed she agreed with him.

He held her hand, his gaze assessing. "I've seen you at the restaurant across the harbor!"

"Yes, sir. I also work there."

"Well, now that I know, I'll make sure to stop there more often, but I also hope to see you at the library as well."

"Okay, George, stop flirting." Marjorie laughed, reaching for the books in Shiloh's hand.

She laughed, enjoying their easy repartee. After obtaining a library card and checking out the books, she stopped by the magazine section where Rachel and Cindy were poring through fashion magazines. Rachel's face lit with a broad smile as she peered at the glossy-colored pages of clothes and makeup.

Walking out of the library, Cindy waved goodbye as a handsome teenage boy drove up. "That's my brother, Trevor," Cindy called out before shouting goodbye and running to get into the car.

Watching them drive off, she decided she needed to study to get a Virginia driver's license and buy a car. But first, she needed to get Rachel a computer. They fell into step as they walked back to the inn, their arms full of books with the sun on their faces. Shiloh was filled with the feeling of new experiences on the horizon, and she smiled.

Shiloh walked down the back stairs of the inn and entered the kitchen. She relished her afternoon off. She wasn't on the schedule to work at the restaurant, and since no new guests were arriving, she didn't have to do laundry today. The days passed by quickly, but she was busy, craving even the mundane activities that were so much more interesting than her existence during her last year in the community.

Community. Her feet stumbled slightly at the word. When she'd searched the internet, another word had been used, and it frightened her. Blowing out a deep breath, she was determined to clear her mind of all negative thoughts. *We're here, and we're safe.*

With Rachel at school, she decided to take a walk along the residential streets of Baytown. The small historical town was laid out in a square grid. Deciding to avoid Main Street, she meandered along the tree-lined sidewalks, taking in the architecture of the beautifully restored homes built in the 1800s, now mostly vacation rentals or permanent residences.

Breathing deeply, she reveled in the freedom as the warm breeze caressed her skin and the shade of the tall trees kept the bright sun from burning. With each passing day, she felt more relaxed than she had in years. Further away from fear. Further away from the thought that Isaiah might come looking for her.

Several people were out in their yards, all smiling and waving as she walked by. In some ways, Baytown reminded her of the community she'd grown up in as a little girl. Friendly. Warm. Although much larger and more crowded, especially when the vacationers arrived. Even though it was fall, the weekends still bustled with activity. Women walked around in shorts, bikini tops, flip-flops, and cute sundresses. She'd been wearing the

S-Shack T-shirts to work and had even bought a couple for Rachel, although her niece hadn't asked for more new clothes. Wondering when it would be time to let go of the dictates they'd lived with completely, she was willing to take things slowly.

Stopping at the end of a block, the sound of grunting met her ears, and she looked around for the cause. She was standing in front of a brick Methodist Church, and the sound appeared to be coming from the back. Afraid someone might be in trouble, she hurried over the grassy lot and through the wrought-iron gate leading to the enclosed backyard. "Excuse me! Is everything okay?"

The grunting continued, so she called out again, raising her voice a little more this time. "Hello! Are you okay?"

Walking around the back corner, she spied a man attempting to drag a heavy branch across the yard. He looked up, a full smile on his face. Dropping the limb, he stood straighter and pulled a handkerchief from his pants, and wiped the sweat from his brow.

She stared for a second, uncertain what to say as her eyes took him in completely. Black pants. White shirt. But a black collar was tucked around the neck of his shirt, and his sleeves were rolled up. While his apparent minister's clothing gave her pause, his eyes seemed to sparkle as his smile widened.

Lifting his hand, he waved toward her. "Hello! I'm afraid you caught me trying to clean up back here from the storm we had the other night."

Approaching slowly, her gaze moved from him to a pile of smaller limbs nearby, then over to the large limb he'd been attempting to move. Instinct overtook fear, and she walked closer. "Let me help you. I'm sure between the two of us, we can manage."

They bent at the same time, and with each of them grabbing part of the limb, they were able to drag it to the pile as well. Standing, they both slapped their hands together to knock off the dirt, then smiled as their actions mirrored each other.

"Thank you so much!" he said, pushing his glasses up on his nose. "I really should've waited for one of the men in the church to come by and help me, but I'm afraid my pride got the better of me. I convinced myself that I would be able to do it without having a heart attack!"

"Then I'm so glad I came along," she said, her smile still in place.

Stepping forward, he reached out his hand. "Please forgive my rudeness. I forgot to introduce myself. I'm Pastor Parton, the minister here at the Methodist church."

She hesitated, then placed her smaller hand in his, accepting his firm handshake without feeling as though she needed to jerk her hand away. "It's nice to meet you, Pastor Parton."

He let go of her hand and leaned in, whispering as though sharing a secret. "Although sometimes the teenagers call me by my initials, which then gets the children in the church laughing because all they hear is pee-pee."

Surprised by his candor and self-deprecation, she laughed aloud, covering her mouth with her hand.

"And who do I have the pleasure of thanking?"

She hesitated for only a second. "My name is Shiloh. Shiloh Wallen."

He swiped his brow again. "Shiloh! What a beautiful name." His brow furrowed, then lifted as a thought seemed to hit him. "Are you the young woman Tori Evans hired to work at the inn?"

Self-conscious, she nodded, blurting, "Yes. She was kind enough to not only offer employment but also allow my niece and me to live there."

"Lovely! Welcome to Baytown!"

She smiled, breathing a sigh of relief, inwardly chastising herself. *Not everyone is looking for fault!* "Thank you. I was just, uh… out for a walk." *Nor is everyone looking for a reason for being out!* Dropping her gaze, she noted that there were no more limbs to assist with. "Well, I should—"

"You should join me for lemonade," he exclaimed. "The church secretary is inside typing away, but she mentioned that she'd made homemade lemonade, and it's in the refrigerator. It's a beautiful day for your walk, but I'd love to offer you some refreshment."

It was on the tip of her tongue to refuse politely and keep walking, but something about his kind face, hardy laugh, and comforting tone made her want to spend more time in his company. Nodding slowly, she agreed. "Thank you, that would be lovely." Still surprised at her acceptance, she followed him through the church's back door, immediately relishing the cool interior.

They passed by an office, and a woman typing on a laptop looked up and smiled at her before continuing with her work. Pastor Parton disappeared into another room, then came back with a pitcher of lemonade and two paper cups stacked together.

"We can sit in my office if you'd be comfortable there. My secretary will be close by if I'm needed for anything." Glancing down at the paper cups, he chuckled. "I'm sure there are nicer glasses somewhere, but these were left over from the children's party."

Taking the cups from him, she smiled. "This will be fine, thank you." She followed him through the next door, finding a small but comfortable room with a window that overlooked the grassy area they'd just been in. The walls were polished wood, and on one side were built-in bookcases. A wooden desk sat near the window, messy and piled high with books and papers and a laptop.

Several leather chairs filled the rest of the space, and after he poured the lemonade from the pitcher and set it on his desk, he said, "Sit wherever you're comfortable."

She settled into one of the chairs and took a sip. "This is delicious."

"My secretary makes wonderful lemonade and iced tea." Leaning closer, he whispered, "She struggles a bit with the coffee."

She tried to hide her smile, but it slipped out, nonetheless. Casting her gaze around the room, she was filled with the memory of her younger years in the community church she'd grown up in. "This building is beautiful."

"It's been here for over one-hundred-and-twenty years," he said, his pride evident.

Breathing easier, she sipped her lemonade as they made small talk for a few minutes about Baytown.

Suddenly filled with a memory, she blurted, "You remind me of someone I used to know." As soon as the words left her mouth, the heat of blush burned her cheeks, and she started to rise from her chair.

"Please don't leave, Shiloh," he said. "I hope that the comparison is not a bad one."

Her butt hit the seat of the chair again, and she shook her head. "No. Not at all. In fact, to be honest, you remind me of several people I knew and loved dearly."

"May I be so bold as to ask who they were?"

Her chest shuddered slightly with a deep sigh. She stared into his kind eyes, comfort surrounding her. The desire to trust someone was overwhelming. "One was the former minister... um... the town leader of our little community. He was... he was very nice." She swallowed deeply, the following words hard to speak, but they fled her lips as though unable to be held back any longer. "And the other was my father."

Pastor Parton nodded, his face holding compassion. "I take it that both men have passed?"

She breathed in deeply through her nose, letting it out slowly. "Yes. He and my parents died together."

"Oh, my dear, how horrible. I'm so sorry to hear that."

They sat in silence for a moment, thoughts long since pushed down now swirling in the forefront of her mind. She'd always told Rachel it was good to keep memories alive, but at that moment, she realized she hadn't heeded her own words.

As though reading her mind, he prodded, "I'd love to hear about your parents."

Gathering her memories around her, she sighed gently. "They were wonderful people, not just wonderful parents. We lived in a… well, it was a very small… um… community. We were fairly cut off geographically. Most of us didn't have cell phones because there was no service and no internet." Her cheeks heated. "It was lovely, but I'm sure that sounds quite backward, doesn't it?"

"Not at all. Many monks, pilgrims, and those seeking spiritual clarity will often search out less modern places. I once spent a week at a retreat with no phones, no internet, and a rule of silence. It was most contemplative."

Once started, she was unable to stem the flow as the words just tumbled out from her soul. "It had been a commune at one time… in the 1800s, I believe."

"Oh, yes!" he enthused. "Many communes popped up all over the country, especially in the East during the 1800s. Some lasted a few years, and others lasted much longer."

She nodded, emboldened by his interest. "It stopped being a commune sometime in the 1900s when people could own their own land. Neighbors helped neighbors, and my parents would lend a hand to anyone who needed it. We attended a small school that was in the county, and my parents farmed their land. There was only one church nearby, but we all attended, and I think my father used to enjoy singing the loudest even when my mother would elbow him in the ribs sometimes when he hit an off note. Pastor Aaron was funny and always made us feel as though we were so blessed to be living where we were."

"It sounds idyllic," he enthused, leaning forward, his eyes bright. "I also grew up in a small town in North Carolina, so that sounds very familiar. There wasn't a lot to do, and I used to complain I was bored. But looking back, I sometimes think God was able to speak to me because I had fewer distractions."

Her chest ached. "I know God used to speak to me, but by the time I left…" she whispered, having no idea why she trusted this stranger, but the need to unburden was so strong. "I just have no idea what He was saying."

Pastor Parton leaned closer. "Did something happen, Shiloh?"

Her brow furrowed as she swallowed audibly. Encouraged by his look of concern and not contempt, she nodded. "The community had a number of deaths about five years ago, including my sister and her husband, along with my parents and our minister. I was married by that time, and my husband and I became the guardians of my niece, Rachel." She shook her head slowly, her chest threatening to cave in on itself even after all these years. "My husband and niece were the only reason I didn't give in to complete despair. But our community changed when a new leader took charge. He made demands. Told us how to live, how to dress, how to act. Some people moved away, but Edward and I stayed because that was where home was. Where our farm was. But then my husband died, too. By this time, the community had become very cold and frightening… a dictatorial place. God was in my heart, but I certainly didn't feel his presence with our new leader."

Almost afraid to look up at Pastor Parton, she forced her gaze to lift, determined to read his emotions in his eyes. What surprised her was the fire of anger that flashed from his gaze.

"Shiloh, I'm so sorry. That sounds more like a cult than a community."

A gasp slipped from her lips. He'd just spoken the word she'd read in the library article. The word she'd once heard Edward whisper when they lay in bed after everyone had given up their books when Isaiah told them to. The word she'd hidden in her heart for years. She barely lifted her chin, but he seemed to understand her frightened nod.

He reached out and placed his warm hand over her cold one. "My dear, God was in your heart. And while the new leader does not sound like a godly man, I assure you that God was there watching over you."

"Do you think running away in the dark of night was cowardly? I devised a plan and kept it secret. Then when things became untenable, I took Rachel, and we just left." The question slipped out, her breath halting in her lungs.

"I think God led you to the decision that you needed to make for both you and Rachel. While I don't know all that you suffered, I think God was taking care of you every step of the way."

"Sometimes, I'm still frightened. I can still hear the

leader's voice trying to tell me what to do, how to act, or what to say."

"It's hard to break away from a legalistic society. But you did it. You survived, and you've now given Rachel a chance at a life filled with God's blessings."

The warmth from his hand began to move through her, loosening the icy grip of fear that she had felt the past months ever since she'd fled from Isaiah. There were still her deeper suspicions, but she kept them buried in her heart, not willing to trust them even to the kind pastor.

"Have you been able to make friends here?"

She looked down and smiled. "Tori has been wonderful and introduced me to so many wonderful women. They're always nice, but they're so accomplished. Teachers, nurses, business owners, doctors." She pressed her lips together. "I'm just... well, I'm just me."

"Oh, my dear, Shiloh. You shine with the rest of them. You have strength and courage. Fortitude and imagination. You have accomplished what many would never be able to do. Believe me, you hold your head high and continue to show the world who the real Shiloh is!"

She felt the heat of blush again, but this time it was from pleasure at his words and not embarrassment. Glancing at the clock on the wall, she realized Rachel would soon be home from school. She stood and placed her empty cup into the trash can next to his desk. "Thank you, Pastor Parton. Your words mean more to me than you'll ever know."

"I've enjoyed talking to you, Shiloh." He ushered her to the back door and stepped out into the sunshine with her. "Something I read from a young author and wordsmith, Germany Kent, struck me, and I've repeated it many times to others who are learning to move forward. *'Though no one can backtrack and create a brand new start, Everyone is capable of taking their life in a brand new direction.'*"

Her eyes filled with tears, the words burrowing deep inside. Somehow she managed to offer a tremulous nod, hoping it conveyed how much the words meant to her.

"If you ever need me, you know where to find me. If you'd ever like to visit our church, you'll always be welcome. I would say go with God, but I already know you are. And in parting, let me just say I have no doubt your parents are very proud of you."

She shook his hand and blinked back the tears threatening to fall. Nodding, she turned and made it to the gate before he called out again, and she looked over her shoulder toward him.

"Give the people in Baytown a chance to get to know the real you. Don't be afraid to tell your story. Don't be afraid to open yourself up to new experiences and offer your experiences to others. You, my dear Shiloh, are a blessing as well."

Walking back down the sidewalk, her thoughts swirled. Old fears mixed with new hopes. Previous rules combined with free decisions. Remembering the past happiness before Isaiah was in charge, she knew that future happiness was now possible.

One day at a time. Baby steps. With a lighter heart and

a smile, she walked past the inn, over the dune, and down to the beach. Slipping her shoes off, she carried them as she walked into the surf. She felt alive with the sun beaming on her face, the waves crashing on her feet, and the sight of gulls dipping into the surface. Laughing out loud, she splashed as she skipped along the edge of the water, ready for a new direction.

10

Joseph sat in the VMP motorboat as it moved back toward the station. Reports of jet skis traveling too close to the town beach had been called in, and so far, he and Jarod had already pulled over several, issuing two warnings and a citation. Now, nearly to the town pier, he shifted in his seat and looked toward the beach. Vacationers lounged on brightly colored towels, and parents chased young children racing over the sand. Teens were playing in the water, boys were trying to impress the girls as they tossed a football over the waves, and the girls in their bikinis soaked up the sun's rays.

A movement near the pier caught his eye, and he observed a woman skipping at the edge of the water, her blue skirt swishing around her knees. Lifting the binoculars to his eyes, he sucked in a quick breath at the recognition. Shiloh. The expression on her face was one of joy. A wide smile seemed to erupt from deep inside her. The air rushed from his lungs as though punched in the gut. He kept the binoculars trained on her, seeing a glimpse of the true Shiloh when she let go of whatever held her back. He wasn't sure he'd ever witnessed anything so full of pure joy in his life and now craved to have that joy beaming down on him.

The radio crackled, jerking his attention over to Jarod. "Someone called in a dangerous fishing boat situation. Heading out," Jarod radioed, turning the boat around.

Joseph nodded but looked over his shoulder one more time at the disappearing beach view and the sight of Shiloh. He lifted his hand and rubbed his chest, barely aware of the strange twinge he felt.

Twenty minutes later, Joseph latched the VMP vessel to the side of the dilapidated fishing boat, *The Fishing King*, his jaw tight with anger. "Jesus Christ," he muttered, looking at the mass of people crowded together. He looked over at Jarod and shook his head. "Call for backup and transportation."

"They're already on their way. ETA five minutes."

Grabbing the microphone of their loudspeaker, he sucked in a deep breath before he began announcing. "This vessel has been stopped due to unsafe conditions. You will all be transported to the pier that you left from—"

"I paid good money for this trip!" one of the passengers yelled, shaking his fist, his face beet red.

"Got no right to stop us!" another shouted.

With over thirty passengers crowded onto the too-small fishing boat, some scared and most angry, he knew this situation could quickly get out of hand. Turning up the volume on his microphone, he belted out, "Quiet! Anyone not cooperating with the Virginia Marine Police will be arrested and taken directly to the Baytown station for processing and transportation to the North Heron Regional Jail!"

Several mouths fell open, and others snapped shut. Continuing, he called out, "But until we can process everything and get transportation out here, we ask that everyone stay calm and quiet." Looking over his shoulder at a pinched-lip Jarod, he received a chin lift, knowing his partner would maintain the steadiness of the two vessels until the others could arrive.

"Captain Doug Rogers! Stop hiding behind your unsuspecting passengers and get over here!"

Like the parting of the Red Sea, the crowd of passengers shifted slightly, causing the fishing boat and the tethered VMP boat to rock. But in the middle, moving forward, was a barrel-chested man, his face partially hidden by the shadow of his worn and frayed ball cap and sunglasses, but the unmistakable tic of anger in his jaw was easy to discern. As the grumblings around him grew, he shoved one of the passengers as he made his way forward.

Joseph fought the urge to leap over into the fishing boat and plant his fist into the middle of the man's face.

"I demand to know what's going on!" another passenger shouted, starting another round of growing mutterings.

"As I said earlier, we need everyone to remain calm and quiet. If you cannot follow those directions, you will be arrested for obstructing, impeding, and interfering with the Virginia Marine Police in the execution of their duties." Those words finally had the desired effect, and the overcrowded boat grew quiet.

Looking down at the owner of the fishing boat, Joseph jerked his head to indicate he was to board the VMP vessel. Once there, Joseph stared him in the eye and growled, "What the fuck made you think you'd get away with this?"

"A man's got a right to make a living," Doug barked. "And you're doing nothing but harassing me."

"This boat sank over a year ago and has been sitting in dry dock with no repairs. It's been banned from operating commercially until determined seaworthy by the Coast Guard, which it hasn't. Even on your best day, it was only licensed to take out no more than twelve passengers at a time. You've got over thirty here. So right now, you're looking at operating an unlicensed fishing charter boat, endangering passengers, fishing without a license, and that's just to start. Once we check the passengers, they can each be fined for fishing without a license also, unless by some miracle you had them purchase them before sailing."

He looked over his shoulder to see Callan, Ryan, and Andy approaching, as well as three larger Coast Guard boats. Knowing they needed the stability of the larger vessels, he ordered Doug to stay aboard the VMP boat, then assured the passengers that assistance was on the way. One of the CG boats latched to the other side of

The Fishing King, and the second CG boat and VMP boat stayed nearby.

Doug was arrested and read his rights and placed in Jarod's custody as Joseph moved over to the fishing vessel. The next two hours were spent checking the identification, licenses, and information from each of the thirty-four passengers. After he scanned and typed in their information, it took almost another hour for citations to be issued for twenty-seven of them for fishing without a license. To keep the angry crowd from becoming disorderly, they transferred each passenger to two of the larger CG boats. As soon as they were headed back to the pier they left from where their vehicles would be, he and Jarod assisted the Coast Guard officers as they hooked up the fishing boat so it could be towed back to the Baytown Harbor.

Once it was en route, Joseph settled in next to Doug as the two VMP boats also headed back to their Baytown station.

Offering Doug a bottle of water, he looked over and shook his head. "What the fuck were you thinking?"

"I was thinking I needed to earn a living," he grumbled.

"Don't give me that bullshit. You charged each one of those passengers two hundred dollars to go out today. You were going to make almost seven thousand dollars just today alone. Considering you didn't bring an assistant, besides paying for the gasoline to go out, you were clear of a lot of money. So to just earn a fuckin' living, that's gross negligence."

"I can't afford to get the repairs done on the boat

without money. I can't earn money if you can't take people out to go fishing."

"You grew up in this area. You know a lot of people who would help you out, work cheap, and maybe even donate some materials. You've been fishing ever since you could hold a pole and run this charter fishing business ever since you took over when your daddy died. You've been going out, knowing full well that what you were doing was illegal."

Doug shook his head and stared out over the water. "It's only illegal if you get caught. You think I'm the only charter fisherman who's taken too many people out? The only one who don't check everybody's licenses? Hell, cast a net, and you'd get a lot more than just me."

"That's not the point, Doug. Illegal is illegal, whether you get caught or not. That's no excuse, and I'd advise you not to use that in front of the judge."

Doug barked out a grunt. "Judge. Fuckin' great. Now this will cost me more money. I can't get my boat back and can't afford to do the repairs you say I need to do. It's a vicious cycle that I can't break out of."

"Then get a job with one of the other charters. Earn some money and work to get help on getting your own boat fixed up."

"You've got all the fuckin' answers, don't you, smart boy?"

"No," Joseph bit back.

"You got no idea what it's like to be poor, so—"

"Don't go there, man. You know… You know what my family went through when Dad lost his job. Don't act like you're the only one who knows tough times. But my parents took any job they could to keep food on the table. You gotta know that sitting in jail won't do your family any good. Operating illegally isn't helping your family. And if that boat had injured or killed any of those passengers, you'd be spending time in prison, not just the county jail. Not to mention the lawsuits from their families that would take all your money for the rest of your life. So think on that if you can get past the pity party you've got going on."

Doug's gaze swung around, his eyes wide. "Lawsuits… fuck. Do you think any of those passengers will sue me since they didn't get to catch any fish?"

Joseph jumped to his feet, swiping his hand over his face. "Christ Almighty, talking to you is pointless." He walked to the wheelhouse and stood next to Jarod.

"You tried, man. You tried," Jarod consoled.

"Yeah, well, it didn't seem like enough." Joseph grabbed another water bottle and chugged half the contents, glad they were on the move toward the station so that the breeze from the bay and the boat's movement cooled his overheated body. He loved his job but grew frustrated when it didn't seem like he made a difference.

"Stop beating yourself up," Jarod advised. "Because of the report that came in, we possibly saved thirty-five lives today since you know as well as I do that boat was on its last legs and not seaworthy. He didn't have enough life jackets for two-thirds of them, and if they'd begun to sink, there would've been the loss of lives, including his own. If he's too much of a dumb fuck to consider that, then the only thing that might get through to him is a judge handing down a sentence. I commend you for even trying."

With a sigh, Joseph nodded, knowing Jarod was right. By the time they docked at the back of the station, Andy was pulling the other boat in and docking next to them. Joseph escorted Doug inside and turned him over to Ryan. He waved toward one of the Baytown police officers who'd entered the VMP station, knowing they'd accompany Doug to the county jail.

Stalking into the workroom, he sat down to get his report written before his shift was over. Looking at the list of passengers and the many citations that had been written, he knew he'd be there for the next hour. Jarod and Callan came in to assist, and between them, they finally finished the ponderous report.

"Jesus, this is the longest, most extensive report I've ever had to do," he said, hoping to keep the whine out of his voice.

He realized he hadn't been successful when Callan laughed. "Just wait till you pull in a party boat of teenagers, half of them puking their guts out, most underage, and having to deal with parents who are more pissed at us than their kids."

He shook his head. "Things are a hell of a lot different on this side, aren't they? The worst was getting caught by our parents who didn't mind doling out the punishment."

"Many parents are really good, but some just can't stand that their little darlings got caught."

"Hell, my parents would have grounded me for so long, I would have never had the chance to party again!"

The conversations rolled toward the baseball games the American Legion was hosting, most of the men in the community helping them one way or the other with coaching. By the time his reports were finished, it was the end of his shift, and he was ready for a break.

As he walked out the door, he looked to the other side of the harbor toward the Seafood Shack, immediately thinking of Shiloh. The memory from earlier in the afternoon came rushing back— the sight of her walking along the surface of the Baytown beach with a beautiful smile on her face. *What was she thinking about? What put that smile on her face?*

He reached up and rubbed his chest again before climbing into his SUV. Driving to his home, he found his mind was filled with images of her, and he wished it had been him who caused her to smile. *What is it about her?*

She was gorgeous, but he'd been around other beautiful women. In truth, that was about the only thing she had in common with the women he was used to. He'd gravitated toward loud and brassy, those who made it known quickly that they were interested in more than a drink and a dance. She was shy, quiet, and after looking someone in the eye, she'd dropped her gaze, yet he so wanted to hold her attention— to know what she was thinking.

He knew it was sexist, but he'd also gravitated toward women who confidently flaunted their assets in makeup, jewelry, tight jeans, low-cut shirts, or short skirts. Shiloh's clothes were modest, and she wore no makeup or jewelry, yet no other woman came close to the way she enraptured him. He couldn't stop thinking about her.

By the time he pulled into his driveway, he was no closer to having an answer than before. He might not know why she held his interest, but he sure as hell knew that she did. *Looks like I'll just have to keep working at it. Surely, she can't resist me forever.* As he walked into his house, he almost stumbled as another thought hit him. *Or can she?*

The following two days at work were nonstop, no-breaks days that kept him from getting to the S-Shack during lunch. Hungry, he called in takeout, determined to eat well even if he didn't get a shot at seeing her. Waiting at the bar, he winked at the bartender, a woman he'd known since elementary school. "Hey, Jules, how's it going?"

"Same old thing, Joseph. Hubby's looking for a second job because the bills just keep coming. Baby had colic, and the oldest rolled in poison ivy during church camp. Lord, it makes me wonder if God is up there just laughing at us!"

He burst out in laughter. "I'd forgotten about it, but I got in poison ivy one summer when Wyatt was looking out for us. We were playing hide and seek, and I thought I'd found the perfect hiding place in some green vines in the back of an old shed." Shaking his head, he absentmindedly scratched his arm, remembering the agony of breaking out all over.

"Kids will make you crazy, that's for sure, but I wouldn't trade them for anything."

Usually, when others talked about their family troubles, he was thankful that he was still single. But right now, he looked at the smile on her face, even with all that was going on, and could see she was happy. A flash of his own parents moved through his mind. Things had been hard when he was a kid, but there had always been good times as well, and they were happy.

"I hear Wyatt's about ready to tie the knot."

Jerking back to the present, he nodded. "Yeah. He and Millie can't wait."

"What about you?" she asked.

"I—"

"Oh, Jo-Jo isn't serious about anyone, are you?" Vicki stepped between his stool and the one next to it, plastering her body against his as she handed him the takeout bag. "But I'm thinking I might just get him to change his mind."

Jo-Jo? Oh, hell no! "Vicki," he growled, "Don't—"

"Oh, I've got customers," she said, rushing away, disappearing into the kitchen.

He grimaced, his jaw tight. *I should have never—*

The sound of laughter drew his gaze back to Jules, who was wiping a tear from the corner of her eye. "Oh God. She calls you *Jo-Jo*? Please tell me you never went out with her!"

"*Went out* would hardly describe what we did," he grumbled under his breath.

Before she had a chance to keep laughing at his expense, he caught sight of Luke walking into the restaurant. Hoping to avoid Vicki, he hustled over to the hostess station.

"Hey, man." Joseph thrust his hand out to shake. Just

then, Shiloh walked over to hand Luke a takeout bag, and Joseph was startled, not expecting to see her working this shift. Her lustrous hair was pulled back, but a few tendrils framed her heart-shaped face. Tonight she wore a pale pink skirt just to her knees and a pink S-Shack T-shirt that hid her figure. But she was gorgeous.

"Here you go," she said, her voice soft. "Enjoy."

"Shiloh!" Mark called out as he stuck his head out of his office. "You can leave anytime. Thanks for staying late."

She nodded, then glanced up toward Joseph, her gaze holding his as her shy smile wobbled ever so slightly.

Not wanting her to leave too soon, he tossed out his trademark smile and winked. "Hey, darlin'. I didn't know you were working tonight."

She nodded but then turned quickly and disappeared into the crowd.

Luke laughed. "Looks like you're losing your touch."

"Nah... she's just playing hard to get." His lips pressed together for a few seconds as he thought about his glib greeting to her. *Darlin'? Why the hell did I call her darlin'?* The word sounded flippant even to him.

He sighed and looked at Luke. "Or maybe she thinks I'm a dick." He lifted his free hand, squeezing the back of his neck. He'd never given a lot of thought to what someone else thought of him, but the idea that Shiloh wasn't just shy but was uncomfortable being around him sent an unease throughout him.

Luke started to turn away when Joseph asked, "Any

reason you're hightailing it out of here when I can plainly see Allie inside?" Allie was the teacher who had captured his friend's attention, and the last he knew, they were starting to date.

Luke shrugged. "She's with her folks. Didn't want to interrupt."

Joseph continued his narrow-eyed gaze, then finally nodded, figuring his friend had woman troubles of his own. One of the things he and Luke had in common was the difficulty of letting go of things from their past. Luke was almost out of the restaurant when Joseph suddenly called out, "Don't fuck this up, Luke. Let go of whatever shit is in your mind, and don't fuck up something this good."

Luke held Joseph's gaze, then inclined his head in the direction of where Shiloh had disappeared. "I hear you, but you might want to take your own advice."

Joseph's eyes widened, and he threw his head back and laughed. "You're probably right, man." Walking out a few minutes later, he remembered baby steps.

11

Shiloh walked out of the restaurant heading toward her bicycle. Mark had asked her to cover part of an evening shift until one of the late servers could get there. She didn't mind the extra money but was ready to spend the rest of her evening with Rachel. Lost in thought, she jumped when someone stepped out from behind an SUV in the parking lot.

"Sorry! I didn't mean to scare you!"

Her heart pounded, but she wasn't sure if it was from fright or nerves when she saw who was standing so close. "Joseph?"

He blinked, then smiled widely. "You know my name?"

Clearing her throat, she nodded. "Yes... um, your girlfriend mentioned it."

He blinked again, this time his smile dropping altogether. "M... My girlfriend?"

She pressed her lips together, uncertain what to say. "Um... yes?" Her statement came out more like a question, but then Vicki had been very specific in pointing him out as her boyfriend. Right now, in front of her, Joseph appeared genuinely perplexed.

"I'm sorry, I don't understand," he said.

"Vicki... she said that you—"

"Oh, fu—" he started to blurt, then grimaced as though trying to come up with another word. He looked down at his boots, placing his fists on his hips.

Staring at the top of his head, she noticed how the low sun in the sky made the light brown appear to have blond streaks. How thick his hair was. And the way she imagined it would curl if it were longer. A ridiculous image of him standing on the bow of a pirate ship like the romance novel she was currently reading hit her mind. Uncertain what to say, she grimaced. *The heroine in the book never had that problem.* Bending, she unlocked her bicycle and began to push it toward the oyster shell walkway. "Well, um... I need to get home."

"Wait!"

Halting, she stared wide-eyed at his sharp tone. Tilting her head to the side, she started to drop her chin, then forced her gaze to stay on his.

"I'm sorry," he said, grabbing the back of his neck, his cheeks pinkening slightly. "I didn't mean to shout. It's just that... I'm... well, for starters, Vicki isn't my girlfriend. Not at all. I don't have a girlfriend. I don't know why she said that... It's, well..."

He seemed so genuine, standing there, floundering over his words. Filled with the strange sense of seeing a nervous little boy standing in front of her, she suddenly desired to make him more comfortable. Offering a little smile, she prompted, "It's what, Joseph?"

He stepped closer, a breath leaving his lungs in a rush. "It's just that I don't want you to think I have a girlfriend."

"Oh, okay…"

"No, it's important, Shiloh."

She continued to stare into his eyes, loving the way his blue eyes seemed so bright. Opposite of the way that Isaiah's dark gaze frightened her. "Why?"

"Because… Because I'd like to ask you out."

Her chin jerked back in surprise. She opened her mouth and then closed it quickly. Giving her head a little shake, she looked down at her bicycle and mumbled, "I really need to get home."

"Shiloh…"

She sat on the seat but turned her attention back to him.

"I'd really like to take you to dinner sometime." His lips curved upward, the effect caught between a little boy who was sure he'd get a treat and a man who was now uncertain.

For a second, she loved having that smile aimed toward her. Swallowing deeply, she couldn't imagine why he'd want to ask her out. Slowly, she shook her head. "It's lovely for you to ask, but I don't think so, Joseph."

"Oh," he blurted, appearing discomfited. "Can I ask why?"

Not expecting the question, it was now her turn to feel self-conscious. Her clothes were not the widow's black that she'd left behind, but neither were they fashionable. Other than lotion, she wore nothing on her face. Her hair was thick and shiny but long and pulled back in a simple ponytail. Her nails were short and functional. She didn't look like the other women he smiled at. But most of all, she couldn't imagine what they would talk about. "Um... I don't think that I would be a good dinner companion."

He stepped closer. "I'd think you'd be perfect. Why not go out with me and see?"

Feeling the need to escape before he asked again, she was afraid she might give in against her better judgment. He was everything free and fun... everything she hadn't had in so long. But she knew her heart might start to want more. From what she'd seen, he was out for only freedom and good times, and her heart might not stand more pain than what she'd already suffered. Pushing up the kickstand, she placed one foot on the pedal with the other still on the walkway. She smiled but felt her lips quiver. "I don't think I'm what you're looking for." She tried to smile to hide the tears she felt building. With that, she pushed off and pedaled away, heading toward the inn.

She wanted to keep facing forward, but the pull to look behind her was too great. Glancing over her shoulder, she jerked the handlebars, making the bicycle wobble at the sight of him standing by his SUV, his gaze still pinned on her. He lifted his hand to wave, and she instinctively waved in return before whipping her head around to face forward again, bringing the bicycle under control. But not before she heard him call out,

"I'll keep trying!" and observed the smile on his face. And a little smile curved her lips.

"So you and Cindy seem to really get along," Shiloh said, standing behind Rachel, brushing her niece's long hair.

"She is so nice!" Rachel enthused, bouncing in the chair. "She's pretty, and she likes to read a lot. With us being in three of the same classes and having lunch together, it's wonderful." Twisting around, she added, "Oh, and guess what? She's going to teach me how to canoe and kayak!"

Her hand halted in the middle of a brushstroke, her body locking into place. "Kayaking? Rachel, honey, I don't know about that!"

"But she goes all the time. Her family goes all the time. Everyone in her family has a kayak, and they have canoes, and they can go straight from a little dock in their backyard."

Until moving to Baytown, she had never heard of a kayak, but from their view of the bay, she'd seen numerous people in canoes, kayaks, and even standing on a flat board with their paddle in the water.

"Her brother could come, too. And I'd be safe. I'd wear a life jacket and everything! Plus, they have a two-person one, so I would have someone else with me."

It was all she could do to keep from forbidding Rachel from even considering something so dangerous. Swallowing deeply, she glanced at her niece's reflection in the mirror. The bright-eyed expression of hope. Full of wonder. Losing the fear she'd grown used to. Adapting to new situations. Making new friends. Trying new things.

Lifting her gaze to her own reflection, she stared, wondering if she could see the same things, terrified of seeing doubt. Then Pastor Parton's words rang out in her head. *"Though no one can backtrack and create a brand new start, everyone is capable of taking their life in a brand new direction."*

"Well, let me talk to Judith and see what she thinks."

Rachel nodded and smiled. "Thank you! I just know that it's something I can do."

"Oh, honey, it's not a question of whether or not you can learn. I know you can do anything. It's just me figuring out how to parent in an ever-changing situation."

Rachel grew quiet, but Shiloh could still see her niece's reflection in the mirror. A little smile played about her lips.

"What has placed that secret grin on your face?" she asked, tugging slightly on Rachel's hair as she now braided it.

Rachel blushed, pressing her lips together.

Walking around to the front of Rachel, she knelt, her eyes searching. "What is it?"

"I met one of Cindy's friends. His name is Jack. Jack Hudson."

Keeping her face from showing surprise, she teased, "Jack? So that's why you have such a special little grin."

Rachel's hands reached up, her fingertips pressing against her cheeks that were already turning red. She nodded, then offered a shrug that Shiloh was sure was supposed to indicate nonchalance. "So tell me about Jack Hudson."

"Oh, Shiloh! He's so cute. Even when I was around the other boys in our community, they didn't make me feel anything."

"Well, you have been isolated with me for the past year. And before that, you were just a—"

"I know, I know! I was just a kid. But I've made friends at school in the past couple of months since we've been here."

"But Jack seems special?"

Rachel grinned widely and nodded in haste. "Oh yes! He's got dark hair and blue eyes, and I found out his dad is the sheriff of the county, and his mom works at a diner somewhere around here, and he's brilliant—"

Shiloh laughed, loving the sparkle in Rachel's eyes. "Well, it seems like you did find out a lot about him."

"Oh yeah. As I said, he's really smart. He was in the science club last year in middle school. And he plays baseball. In fact, he said I could watch him play sometime. I told him science wasn't my best subject, and he said he'd help me anytime I needed it. Cindy told him I was really good at English, and he said I could help him with that. And then he smiled at me! He even said he could teach me to swim."

Shiloh's heart filled, and she wondered if it was possible to burst from just pure happiness. Rachel had only been nine years old when her whole world imploded with the death of her parents and grandparents, and then at thirteen, it changed again when

Edward died. Rachel could still remember what life was like before Isaiah took charge of their community, but her formative years were altered during that time by his influence. Now, seeing her niece make new friends and be excited about school and friends was more than Shiloh could've hoped for.

"I met someone also." She had no idea where those words came from or why she blurted them out loud. Maybe it was the openness she'd always had with Rachel. Perhaps it was the look of excitement in Rachel's eyes when she talked about some of her friends and meeting Jack. *Maybe I'm just desperate to feel normal.*

"Shiloh! Tell me! Tell me!"

She felt her own cheeks heat as a self-conscious blush rose over her face. "I don't have very many details. I've just seen him a couple of times."

"What does he look like?"

Staring at Rachel, she could have sworn there were stars in the young teenager's eyes. Laughing, she replied, "Tall, well-built, light brown hair, and blue eyes. Oh, and before you ask—yes, he's handsome."

Rachel narrowed her eyes. "There's more to it, isn't there?"

"Well, he did ask me out tonight."

"Oh my goodness! When are you going?"

Pressing her lips together, she slowly shook her head. "I'm not. I turned him down."

Gasping, Rachel's eyes widened, staring as though Shiloh had made the biggest mistake she could think of. "Why?"

She opened her mouth to answer, then snapped it

shut. The truth was, she didn't really know. But since being honest with Rachel had always been what she tried to do, she decided to go for it. "I don't know. I guess I just wasn't looking for anyone."

"Well, that doesn't matter. You don't have to be looking for someone to find them."

"I think he's the kind of man who flirts with everyone. I certainly know I'm not the first woman at the restaurant he's asked out. I just don't think he's the serious type."

Rachel's smile faltered as the corners of her mouth dropped. "You don't have to worry about being serious, now. You could just go out and have fun. I don't want you to feel like you have to work or take care of me all the time. Anyway, Cindy says that's what she's going to do this year in high school— have fun until the right one comes along."

"But," she continued to protest. "I'm a widow."

"Shiloh… Edward died over a year ago. I know that you loved him and miss him, but I know he wouldn't expect you to stay single forever."

She nodded, her shoulders slumping. "I know, he wouldn't. When the time is right, I'm sure I'll meet someone and accept their invitation."

Rachel, sounding more grown-up than only fourteen, added, "Just make sure that something good doesn't pass you by while you're waiting for the right time."

Her niece's words struck deep as she stood and laid the brush on top of the dresser.

Rachel cleared her throat, jerking Shiloh's attention

back to her niece's face. Tilting her head to the side, she waited.

Rachel hesitated, then rushed, "I wanted to know if it was possible for me to buy a few more new clothes. Nothing fancy or expensive. It's just that until now, I was okay with what I brought with me and the things we bought when we got here. I knew I didn't look fashionable, and that was fine because it was what I was comfortable in. But now, I'd kind of like to have a few things that make me fit in with the other girls my age. And I thought I might get a swimsuit. I can use the money I get from helping here in the inn—"

"That won't be necessary," she assured. She reached for Rachel's hands and drew her upward to stand in front of her. At fourteen, she was as tall as Shiloh, and she had a flash of a very young Rachel running and playing in her backyard while Shiloh and her sister watched her. She'd tried to hide so much from her, wanting to keep her innocent and make sure the young girl didn't inadvertently say something that might endanger Shiloh's plans for getting away. *But now, there's no reason not to tell her. Or at least part of it.*

"Sweetheart, I sold the farm to Mr. Kendall. He wasn't renting from me… he was making payments, and then when we left, he took out a loan and paid me what was left. I gave him a good price, and while he and his wife protested me selling it to them so cheaply, I knew it was worth it. Worth it because we didn't need it anymore. Worth it because they had been so good to us. Worth it because I knew it was what Edward would want me to do."

She pulled Rachel in and wrapped her arms around the girl who held her heart. "So we have money from the sale of the land and from what I'm making now. So yes, we can go shopping for new clothes."

They hugged for a long moment, then Shiloh cupped Rachel's cheek, seeing tears shining in her niece's eyes. "Okay, enough for tonight. Go brush your teeth."

As Rachel fairly danced into the bathroom, Shiloh looked down at the voluminous, white nightgown she wore that covered her from neck to ankles. She thought of the way Tori and the other women dressed—classy, comfortable, fun colors and styles. And she thought of Joseph and the way he looked at her when he'd asked her out. It wasn't with the same flirty way he looked at others, nor like he was staring at her as though she was an oddity to figure out. Instead, he looked at her as though he was really interested. And even though she tried to tell herself she didn't want to encourage him, she suddenly wanted to cast off the old ways. Calling through the bathroom door, she said, "Why don't we go shopping together? I wouldn't mind getting a few new things for myself."

"Oh, Shiloh!" With toothpaste still on her mouth, Rachel rushed out and threw her arms around Shiloh's waist, pulling her in for another tight hug.

Laughing, Shiloh hugged her back. "Maybe it's time for both of us to release a few more of the chains that held us back and begin living the way I know we should."

A little later, as they both lay in their beds, thoughts swirled in Shiloh's head, threatening to pick her up, twirl her into the clouds, and drop her back to the ground like a tornado. It wasn't that she didn't believe in romance or dating, but she'd never seriously given it much thought. She and Edward were friends, and while there was genuine affection, there was very little romance. She had become resigned that it would always be that way for her. But when he died and Isaiah made his desires known, she was sure there'd be no romance there either.

Pastor Parton had said she was strong, and while she valued her self-worth, she couldn't imagine what Joseph saw in her. Certainly not compared to the other women he flirted with or the other women she'd met. All beautiful. Educated. Accomplished.

For her, life had become about survival, leaving little room for dreams. Or just going out for fun. Isaiah had certainly made sure of that.

Hearing Rachel toss and turn in her bed, she knew sleep had not come to her niece either. She assumed Rachel was thinking about her friends and possibly the new young man who had captured her attention. Just when she was ready to ask if she needed some warm milk, Rachel spoke.

"Shiloh?"

"What is it, sweetie?"

Very softly, almost in a whisper, Rachel asked, "Isaiah wasn't the voice of God, was he?"

Her breath caught in her throat as she realized how deeply Isaiah had influenced not just their actions but their thoughts. She remembered the news article and Pastor Parton using the word cult. Sucking in a deep breath, she let it out slowly, the quiet sound splitting the silence in the room. Rolling over in bed, she could see Rachel's opened eyes peering at her by the moonlight coming through the window. Shaking her head slowly, she replied, "No, Isaiah was not the voice of God. He was simply the voice of a man who liked being in charge. One who liked telling others what to do. One who liked being thought of as a leader."

"Then why did we all follow him?"

At Rachel's question, Shiloh felt a tear slide down her cheek. She and Edward had always tread carefully around Rachel, not wanting her to inadvertently talk about their doubts to others for fear of retribution. But as Rachel matured, especially during the last year when it was just the two of them together, she'd given more voice to her doubts while keeping her deepest suspicions to herself. Shiloh had known this day would come when Rachel would ask more questions and prayed that she could give her the correct answers.

"Isaiah played on people's insecurities and fears. For those of us tied to the land and the community, his way simply became the way of life, and we followed his edicts until they seemed right and natural and others were wrong. He did it in such a way that made us feel like we were following God if we followed him."

"And you don't want to ever live that way again?"

"No, Rachel, I don't. And I don't want you to either."

They were quiet for long moments in the dark, and just when she thought Rachel had finally fallen asleep, she heard her whisper call out into the night.

"Thank you."

12

Joseph walked into the basement of the Methodist church where the Baytown American Legion meeting would be held. He'd only been to a few meetings since he'd been out of the Navy, missing most of them while he was in training in Virginia Beach. But now that he was back on the Eastern Shore for good, he was welcomed with open arms and glad to be there.

The group had grown with men and women ranging in age from their early twenties and just out of the military service, all the way to members in their nineties who had tales of the Vietnam and Korean wars. For him, it was a family affair, including his grandfather, father, and brother in attendance. The meeting room was also filled with most of his friends, many of his coworkers, and even some of their family members.

An active chapter started by Mitch, they were involved in multiple community service projects, one of the most popular being the youth baseball teams they sponsored. At no cost to the parents, it allowed children of all abilities and backgrounds to have a chance to enjoy sports.

Before the meeting got started, he spied Mark alone near the coffee table and made a beeline to chat with the Seafood Shack manager without anyone else around.

Seeing him coming, Mark lifted his chin and smiled. "Hey, Joseph. How's it going?"

"Good, good. It's nice to be back, working in a job I love."

"I don't get out on the restaurant floor as often as I want until the dinner shift, but I see you getting lunch at my place several times a week. Thanks for the business!"

Laughing, he nodded. "Well, it doesn't hurt that you're right next to our station, but you do have great food." He was filled with a strange sense of nerves as he glanced around to see they were still alone. "I wanted to ask about one of your new servers. Shiloh."

"Shiloh? You haven't had a problem with her, have you? I can't imagine that anyone would have a—"

"No! No problem at all! I just haven't remembered seeing her around before," he fumbled.

Mark's face split with a wide grin. "Oh yeah… she's new to the area. She's really great. It helps that she's more mature than most of the servers I get. I mean, geez, between the teenagers who miss because they can't get a ride or the college kids who can only work summers, scheduling is really a mess sometimes. Did you know that—"

"Um… about Shiloh?" he interrupted, trying to bring Mark back to the subject he wanted to know about.

"Oh yeah, sorry. Well, she's wonderful. She shows up on time, works hard, and will stay late if needed. She's super polite, just a real sweetheart. My customers love her!" Leaning closer, he added, "I was worried about her at first."

His brow lowered. "Worried? About what?"

"I wasn't sure she could handle a crowd. She was really shy. Super soft-spoken. I mean, that's fine! Lord knows we're a family restaurant, and I don't want the girls yelling all over the place. You know how some of them—"

"Mark! We're talking about Shiloh," he huffed.

"Right, right. Sorry. Anyway, she actually fits right in. She's quiet and friendly, so she gets good tips."

It struck him that he'd be jealous of Mark's effusive praise if he didn't know Mark was happily married. But at the same time, it also struck him that he couldn't remember ever being jealous. Fighting to hide the irritation that others seemed to know more about her, he tried to figure out how to ask questions without exposing his interest.

"And I find that the men who come in alone like her, too. I think it's the whole vibe of her, you know? Just real... she's just real."

Now the desire to punch out any of the men who'd basked in her soft smile or gentle words threatened to overtake his desire to find out more.

Mark didn't seem to notice Joseph's tight jaw or fingers curling into fists at his side. He continued to sing her praise. "Honestly, I'd employ her full-time if she didn't already have another job."

Blinking, his chin jerked backward in surprise. "Another job?"

"Yeah, she works for Tori Evans at the Sea Glass Inn."

Someone else interrupted when they walked over to talk to Mark, so Joseph moved away, his mind rolling with the new information. When he glanced to the other side of the room, his gaze landed on Mitch, and he headed over to dig for more information. Walking through the others milling about before the meeting started, he hoped he looked nonchalant and not like a man on a mission. "Hey, Mitch."

Mitch looked up and smiled. "Joseph, glad you're back here with us full-time and can be at our meetings."

Nodding politely, he glanced around, then plunged ahead. "Um... listen, I was wondering about Tori's inn—"

"Have you got visitors coming into town? She's pretty booked on the weekends."

"No, sorry. It's not for me. I was just wondering about her new employee. Shiloh?"

"Yeah, Shiloh Wallen." Mitch's gaze morphed from friendly to assessing. "Why are you asking about her?"

Trying not to squirm, he replied, "I met her at the Seafood Shack and thought she was new around here. I just heard she also worked for Tori."

"Yeah, she's new to town. She and Tori had corresponded over the past year, and now that she's here, Tori has taken her under her wing."

Corresponded? "It sounds like there's a story there," he continued, fishing for more.

"Oh, there's a story there, for sure." Mitch nodded. "But I'm afraid that's Shiloh's story to tell."

Trying to keep the huff from escaping his lips, he nodded just as Ryan walked over.

Mitch inclined his head to the side. "Ryan's fiancée, Judith, also knows Shiloh."

Joseph stared dumbly at his boss, now ignoring Mitch's pointed gaze. "I didn't know you knew her, Ryan. You never mentioned that."

Ryan chuckled, shaking his head. "I wasn't aware I was supposed to report on who I do and don't know to you." Joseph blushed, but Ryan continued, "Actually, I don't know her well. Her niece is the same age as my daughter, Cindy, and they've become good friends."

She has a niece here? Jesus, does everyone know more about her than me? He wondered how to ask more without the entire group realizing how interested he was in her. When he saw the shared look between the two men, he should have known with Mitch and Ryan being excellent detectives, they didn't have a hard time figuring out his reason for the questions.

"Have you asked her out yet?" Ryan asked.

Plopping his hands on his waist, he nodded, deciding to give up the pretense of being cool, considering his attempt at secret intel gathering was shit. "Yeah, but she shot me down." Looking back at Mitch, he continued to prod. "Is there anything you can give me?"

Mitch shook his head slowly. "Normally, I'd tell you to find out for yourself, and that's still going to be my advice. I don't know a lot, but Tori has shared some. I will say that Shiloh's story is one that she'll have to share with you if she wants you to know. But she's come through a lot and is a very strong, amazing woman."

George MacElvey walked over, forcing his way into their little group. "I've found Shiloh to be a delightful patron of the library," he said, nodding as he smiled. "Amazed at her desire to read everything and made sure her niece had her own library card this summer before school started. Do you know that Shiloh has never had a library card?"

Just then, Pastor Parton walked by, then stopped, and turned back to look at the four men. "I'm so sorry to interrupt, but were you talking about Shiloh?"

Joseph blinked, his body jerking. *Fuck, everyone does know about her except me!* "You know her, too?"

"I met her when she was out for a walk and gave me some well-timed assistance. We had lemonade together, and she opened up to tell me some of her history. I was so impressed with her. She's come through great loss and has a unique situation that she escaped from. Oh, such a wonderful woman, and I hope to spend more time with her."

George, seeming to want to one-up the pastor, puffed out his chest. "Well, she asked about an author, and I helped her find a book by Germany Kent. Told her it was excellent, and I recommended it highly."

"I'm the one who told her about that author!" Pastor Parton replied in haste, his bushy brows lifting.

Mitch was called to the front of the room, and the pastor wandered off with George, both still trying to see who'd had more influence with Shiloh, leaving

Joseph standing with Ryan. "Damn, it seems like everybody knows her better than I do."

Ryan laughed. "Well, I don't know her very well, but her niece seems really nice. Cindy sings her praises, and they're now proclaimed best friends. I even think Colt's son, Jack, has been hanging out with them."

As Ryan walked away, Joseph looked toward the other side of the room to see Colt and wondered about asking if he knew anything about Shiloh. *This is getting confusing and fuckin' ridiculous!*

"What's fuckin' ridiculous?"

So lost in thought, he hadn't noticed Wyatt approaching, nor that he'd muttered aloud. No longer pretending not to be into her, he blurted, "I'm finally interested in a woman who's new in town. I asked her out, but she turned me down. I just found out it seems like other people know a lot more about her. So why not me?"

"Talk to her, dumbass," Wyatt said, shaking his head. "Don't flirt with her. Actually talk to her. Stop trying to be charming. If she's smart, she sees right through that shit and doesn't want to have anything to do with it."

Before he had a chance to reply, the meeting was called to order. He made it to a seat, but his head was so muddled that by the time the meeting was over an hour later, he couldn't remember anything anyone had said.

Driving home, he thought over all that he had learned. *A history. A story. A library card. Desire to read. Sweet. Kind. Has come through a lot. Strong and amazing. A niece she takes care of.*

Now, more than ever, he wanted to know her. And more than that, he wanted to be worthy to know her.

Joseph threw open his front door, an engaging smile on his face as he leaned forward to kiss his mom on the cheek. "Hey, Mom."

Sherrie Newman smiled as she reached up to cup his face. "So handsome, so sweet, and such a handful!"

He laughed as he stepped back to allow her to enter the living room. "You've been greeting me the same way for as long as I can remember."

"Well, the words have been true for that long!"

He caught a whiff of whatever delight she had in the plastic dish in her hands, and his stomach groaned. "Oh, Mom, you didn't have to bring any food, but I'm sure glad you did. Didn't get lunch today, and I'm starving."

Her brow lowered before she turned and walked into his kitchen, setting the dish on the counter. "Is everything all right?"

He followed, appreciating how she didn't fuss about him not eating. With both sons having served in the military and now in law enforcement, she was well aware of their odd-timed shifts and how they worked overtime and often through meals. "Yeah, Mom. Just had a rash of crab pot thefts, and it took most of the day to sort out."

She nodded and reached for a dish from his cabinets. After plating some of the cheesy chicken and rice casserole and adding sliced toasted garlic-butter bread, they sat at the table together. He hated to shovel in the food, but as soon as the delicious cheesy sauce hit his lips, he couldn't eat fast enough.

"Slow down." She laughed. "It's not like when you were a child and afraid that Wyatt or Besty might steal some of your food!"

"They only tried to take my cookies," he muttered between bites. Finally pushing the empty plate away, he leaned back and patted his stomach. "Mom, you can cook!"

"Well, if you'd settle down with a woman who could cook, too, then I wouldn't have to worry so much." As soon as the words left her lips, she shook her head. "Good grief... that was the most sexist thing I think I've ever said. Let me rephrase that— if you'd learn to cook, then I wouldn't have to worry so much. And, if you'd settle down with a woman who made you happy, then I definitely wouldn't worry so much!"

He stood and carried his plate to the sink, rinsing it off before placing it in the dishwasher. Looking over his shoulder, he caught a Cheshire-cat expression on her face. "What are you thinking about?" He poured more tea for both of them and sat back in his chair.

"Well, I just heard from a little birdie that you were interested in someone."

Shaking his head, he reached up and squeezed the back of his neck, feeling the tight muscles. "I should have known someone would start yapping. Who was it?"

"Actually, it was Wyatt. He and Millie were over last night, making their final wedding plans, and he mentioned that you had become rather infatuated with a new young woman in town." Her nose scrunched as she added, "But don't worry about him saying too much. That was all he said, so I thought I'd come over and see what information I could get from you."

"Then I'm afraid you're going to be disappointed. There's nothing much to tell." She lifted her brow, and he continued, "So far, it's taken a couple of months just to even have a conversation with her."

Laughing, she shook her head. "Oh my, someone who didn't fall at your feet?"

"Come on, Mom. I was never *that* bad." Even as he spoke the words, doubt crept in that maybe he had expected Shiloh to be like most of the other women he'd been with.

His mother leaned forward, holding his gaze. "No, I don't think you were ever *bad*. It's just since you were a teenager, you didn't seem to have a problem getting girls' attention. And as long as you were always respectful and didn't lead anyone on, I didn't think too much about it."

She pressed her lips together. "I knew Maggie wasn't right for you. Not because of your youth but because she never had the look in her eye that I knew would hold you for a lifetime. Of course, all those years you were in the Navy, I had no idea who you spent time with, but considering you're still single, I assumed you never found anyone who held your interest."

He nodded slowly but remained silent, waiting to see what else she would say.

"Can I ask who this mysterious young woman is?"

He didn't figure there was a reason to remain silent since even Wyatt knew who he'd been asking about. "Her name is Shiloh. Shiloh Wallen. She works as a part-time server for the Seafood Shack and is also Tori Evans' housekeeper at The Sea Glass Inn." Seeing his mother's lifted brows with unasked questions, he added, "I don't know what it is about her, Mom. She's… different."

"Different how, Son? Besides the fact that she didn't fawn all over you?"

He caught the sparkle in his mom's eyes and chuckled. Glancing to the side, he thought about how best to describe Shiloh as she filled his mind. "She's pretty but does nothing to show off her looks. In fact, I sometimes wonder if she doesn't try to hide them. She's timid, or at least I hope she is because if she's not, that means she's just avoiding me."

"I confess, I'm intrigued."

Shifting his gaze back to his mom, he nodded. He told her what all he'd learned from the others at the AL meeting, then added, "At first, I couldn't believe that it seemed like so many others knew her, and I was still in the dark. But then I realized how many layers there were to her. Each one is more fascinating than the one before."

"Well, it sounds like what you were told is right, and there is a story there. But Joseph, I have to ask you. For a man who's never had to work to get a woman to go out with him, are you up for trying to learn about her and her story? If she's overcome so much, I'm not sure that she would be amenable to the kind of easy, laid-back fun you usually like to have."

He jerked slightly, unable to keep the hurt off his face. "Does everyone think I'm just a player? Even my own mom?"

She shook her head emphatically. "I don't think *player* is the right word. When I think of the word *player*, I think of a man who plays with women's hearts. You know, promising them one thing and then doing another. But I do think that you're used to having an easy time gaining a woman's attention, and Shiloh sounds like someone who's not willing to give into a handsome smile and a cute pickup line."

"Yeah, I finally figured that out. But then, I'm beginning to wonder what she sees when she looks at me. Maybe I'm really not worth her getting to know."

That statement brought on a narrow-eyed glare and a loud huff from his mom. "Joseph! You've played a part for so many years that I think it's hard for you to sometimes look into the mirror and see the man I see… the man who your friends see… the man who grew from the boy your father and I raised."

Her sharp words surprised him, and he wasn't sure what she meant.

Reaching over, she placed her hand on his, giving it a little squeeze. "You were the middle child. A position that's always hard. You always followed Wyatt around, wanting to do everything he did. When you had difficulty learning to speak and got embarrassed, you'd pretend it didn't bother you. But I knew the sensitive child hiding behind the pretense."

He shifted, his lips pressed together, remembering the days when he'd try to speak like everyone else, and they made sense in his head, but the sounds never came out the way they were supposed to. It was only after a couple of years of speech therapy in elementary school that he finally was able to articulate correctly. And his mom was right… it was easier to pretend that he didn't care about the taunting names. As long as he could joke and smile, he had friends.

"When your dad lost his job for a while, Wyatt stepped up and took on a responsible role when he was just a kid himself. I hated for him to do that because I hated for you kids to know about our money troubles. Betsy, being the youngest and a girl, was babied by Wyatt and you. She was so young and didn't realize how tight things were for a while. But you knew. You went to school wearing hand-me-downs, and I think more of your embarrassment led to developing a joking, nothing-bothers-me attitude. By the time your dad was employed again and money was less tight, you were already in high school. By then, the bravado that you always tried to show the world was ingrained. But so was your integrity, your desire to protect, and your true nature of being a good man. I sometimes wonder if those early experiences made it harder for you to connect with people."

He turned his hand up as it lay on the table and held hers tightly. "I never really thought of it that way. To be honest, Mom, I guess I blocked out a lot of the more negative memories. For me, my childhood memories were always of just home and family. But you're right—

it was easier to let girls chase me to keep me from having to face rejection. Even if it is just based on looks, I didn't want to get to know them so that it wouldn't give them the green light to dig too deeply into me as well."

"That's exactly what I was talking about. But it seems like something in this woman has struck you. Something that makes you want to know more about her."

A grimace passed over his face, and he sighed. "Yeah, but I don't know that she wants to get to know me."

"Perhaps, she's just like you."

His chin jerked back. "What do you mean?"

"Joseph, honey, if she's had unpleasant experiences, then she's probably afraid of getting to know someone because that means she has to open up herself also."

They sat in silence for a moment as he thought over her words, nodding. "You may be right. But I don't know what I can do."

She patted his hand and leaned back, crossing her arms over her chest. "Well, if you give up, you'll never know. Remember, not everything in life is easy."

She stood, and he took to his feet quickly. They hugged tightly, and even though he towered over her, her embrace was strong and sure.

"I need to get home to your dad, but never forget how much we love you."

"I love you too, Mom." He walked her to her car and waved as she pulled down the driveway. Once back inside his house, he grabbed a beer and sat down on his living room sofa, propping his feet up. Thinking of all his mom had said, he knew it was true that his best memories growing up were of home and family. Outside of that, he always felt he needed to pretend everything was fine. He also knew beyond a shadow of a doubt that Shiloh was worth the effort it would take to get to know her. And if she was like him, she put those barriers up and held tight to her fears.

Smiling, he knew he was ready to fight for her.

13

"Shiloh, I'm going to sit with Cindy, okay?"

Rachel bounced on her toes, barely able to stand still as Shiloh laughed and nodded her agreement, watching as the young teen in her new shorts and T-shirt ran off with her best friend. Shiloh glanced down at what she was wearing, the lightweight khaki pants reminding her of what Marjorie had worn the day she met her in the library. She'd also been tempted to purchase a bright red T-shirt to wear, as well, but instead chose a pale pink. She knew it would be hard for most people to understand that after only five years of living under Isaiah's dictates, she would have immediately cast them off. But change was slow, and she was willing to move at her own pace.

One of the American Legion youth games had already started, and she couldn't help but look out toward the ballfield where the youngest children were playing. She recognized some of the coaches as men who she'd met in town, husbands of her friends, or others who'd come into the restaurant.

She walked toward the stands already filled with people, some faces she recognized as new friends, having met them through Tori or as customers from the restaurant. "Hello, Shiloh," someone called out, and she looked up to wave at Sophia. Her husband worked with Callan, and she'd met Sophia when he'd brought her into the restaurant. She wouldn't have minded sitting next to Sophia, but she was already in a crowded section of the stands. Sighing, she kept a smile on her face, but she felt self-conscious standing.

A pretty woman with a kind face sitting near the bottom smiled at her and patted the empty space next to her. "Would you like to sit with me? I've got room here."

Glad for the company, she agreed readily. She sat quickly, not wanting to be in anyone's way.

"I'm Sherrie."

"Hello. It's nice to meet you. I'm Shiloh."

"Grandma!"

Shiloh turned to see two little boys racing over to Sherrie as she bent and gave them a hug.

"Uncle Joseph came and got us because Dad was having car trouble. As soon as he gets it fixed, he'll bring Mom."

Before Shiloh had a chance to wonder about who their uncle Joseph was, she blinked as *her* Joseph walked toward them.

"Hey, Mom. Can you keep an eye on these guys

while I get out to the field? Betsy will be along in a little bit."

Suddenly, he looked toward Shiloh, his eyes widening along with his smile. "Shiloh, I didn't know you'd be here. It's nice to see you."

Flustered, knowing that Sherrie was watching, she smiled and nodded. "It's nice to see you, too."

"Well, I've got to get to the game. I'm supposed to be coaching. Save me a hot dog, Shiloh. I'll be back." He turned and jogged away, and she sat, rooted to the spot, her gaze following him.

"I see you know my son," Sherrie said.

"Yes. Um… he comes into the restaurant where I work. The Seafood Shack." Once again self-conscious, she turned her attention to the game.

Between the cheers, she met Sherrie's daughter, Betsy, when she arrived, playfully grumbling about their truck. Sherrie chatted amiably, putting Shiloh at ease, reminding her of earlier years when children in the community would play to the cheers of their parents.

Her gaze drifted over the field, finding Joseph standing near third base. When the next little girl hit the ball, Joseph motioned for the little boy on second base to run to him. He ran as hard as he could, grinning wildly as he landed on the base, then tripped, diving face-first into the dirt. Joseph immediately scooped the little boy up and cradled him in his arms. Her heart melted at the sight of the strong man holding the crying child, brushing the dirt off his face and the front of his uniform, making sure he wasn't hurt. As soon as the little boy's tears dried, the game continued.

"Oh, how sweet," she whispered under her breath.

"Shiloh, I have a confession to make," Sherrie said.

Twisting her head around, she waited, curiosity filling her.

Sherrie winced. "When I asked you to sit with me, it wasn't just for you, but for my son."

"I... I don't understand."

"I heard your name being called, and since it is a beautiful and unusual name, I thought it might be you. Joseph had mentioned you—"

A gasp slipped out as her hand landed on her chest. "Me?"

"Yes... please forgive my intruding," Sherrie begged. "But he talked about you in such glowing terms, and when I discovered you standing in front of me, I wanted to spend more time with you."

"I see." Although, in truth, she didn't. She couldn't imagine why he'd mentioned her to his mother.

"No, I don't think you do, my dear. What I mean is that he's never talked about a woman, and to find out that he's interested in you, well, I'm afraid I interfered by asking you to sit here today. That was underhanded for me, and I hate the idea of getting to know you under false pretenses."

"I'm not sure what to say, Sherrie. I certainly don't want you to feel bad. I'm enjoying myself, and it's always lovely to meet more people in the community. But, I'm not... well, it's just that—"

"Not everyone is what they seem to be."

Blinking, she shook her head slightly, staring at Sherrie's intense gaze.

Sherrie continued, "I have a feeling you have many layers. The same goes for Joseph. Please don't judge him before having a chance to get to know him." She patted Shiloh's leg and offered a warm smile. "Now, how about we go get some hot dogs for my grandsons before they're sold out. I heard Joseph ask you to save one for him. I know he'd like that. Betsy will save our seats."

She nodded, but her mind raced as they walked to the concession stand and then came back with hot dogs, bags of chips, and water bottles. The next hour passed pleasantly as she chatted with Sherrie and Betsy, noting the dropped little tidbits about Joseph. He'd served in the Navy. He'd always wanted to protect. He'd grown up on their farm. The more she heard, the more she wanted to know. Her gaze continually moved to the ball field, always searching for Joseph. As other friends passed by and said hello to her and Sherrie, it seemed no one was surprised to see her sitting with Joseph's mom.

Judith stopped by to ask if they could take Rachel to lunch, and she agreed readily, glad that her niece hadn't overeaten junk food at the games.

When the games were over and the crowd dispersed, Sherrie hugged her goodbye, whispering in her ear, "I'm so glad to have a chance to get to know you, Shiloh," before she walked toward the parking lot with her grandchildren.

Turning around, she took one step before bumping into someone. "Oh!"

Joseph's hands snagged her arms to keep her from falling backward. "Sorry! It seems I keep startling you."

"I wasn't watching where I was going," she admitted. "Um, I have a hot dog for you, but it's no longer hot."

"So you just have a dog for me?" he joked, reaching for the wrapped sandwich and water bottle. He opened the waxed paper and took a healthy bite. "Still good," he muttered while chewing, devouring the hot dog in four bites.

Her hand fluttered in front of her as she searched for something to say, finally blurting, "It was nice to see you coaching. You're really good with the kids."

His smile beamed toward her, and she was once again reminded that it didn't look anything like the smile he threw out casually to others.

"Do you have anywhere to be right now?"

"I was going to walk back to the inn."

"I'd like to accompany you."

She started to decline, but then staring at his face, she could swear she was looking at a little boy whose expression of hope was so sincere. "Um… sure."

He blinked, his chin jerking back slightly. "I can?"

A small giggle burst out, and she nodded. "If you want."

The smile on his face widened as his eyes lit, and they turned to walk side by side toward town as groups of kids called their goodbyes to him. She let out a long breath and hoped she knew what she was doing because if she wasn't mistaken, her heart twinged a bit with each smile he gave to the children. And to her.

14

Baytown's Main Street was crowded with visitors and residents who took the opportunity to shop after the game. Many that Joseph knew called out their greetings, and he felt as though he was a bobblehead doll with each chin lift he offered. He hoped no one would stop to chat, wanting to be alone with Shiloh. Glancing down at her, it was impossible not to notice her rich brunette hair with the auburn highlights glistening in the sun. Or the fact that she was wearing pants today. Or the way the pink shirt made her cheeks seem rosy—

"Hey, Joseph!" someone else called out, waving from across the street.

Sighing, he offered another chin lift.

"You know so many people," she said softly.

"It's just that I grew up not too far from here. And now that I work out of the harbor…" He shrugged, never minding the popularity before but now wished for a less public place. A group of vacationers piled out of one of the shops, and his hand darted out to protect

Shiloh from being bumped. With his other hand lightly on her back, he guided her around the crowds. Just like the first time he'd touched her, his fingers tingled.

By the time he and Shiloh made it to the road where the inn was located, he wanted to curse at not being able to hold much of a conversation. Now that they were on a quieter street, he glanced down at her, suddenly tongue-tied, feeling as though he was six years old again.

"Your mom is nice."

A chuckle erupted from deep in his chest at her words as he shook his head. "Yeah, she's great. But... I have a feeling that it wasn't a coincidence that you were sitting with her today. I have a confession to make. I told her I was interested in you."

The blush of her cheeks deepened, and he prayed he hadn't embarrassed her. The last thing he wanted was for her to shut down on him.

"She told me."

Blinking, he nearly stumbled. "She told you?" he squeaked, his voice sounding like a pre-teen boy to his ears.

She laughed and twisted her head to peer up at him, her eyes bright. "Yes. She said she heard my name and then asked me to sit with her."

"She's normally not so meddling. Or maybe I just haven't given her a chance to meddle." He wanted to reach down and take her hand but felt like a bumbling teenager. With most women, he could swing his arm over their shoulders, knowing they were ready to plaster themselves against him, but everything about

Shiloh threw him off his game. *That's what's different... with her. It's no game.*

"We're here."

Her softly spoken declaration had him look up, disappointed that they'd made it to the Sea Glass Inn.

"Would you like some lemonade?"

"Absolutely!" he blurted, not caring how desperate he sounded. He followed her around to the back door leading into the kitchen. She poured two tall glasses of ice-cold lemonade and handed one to him.

"We can either sit on the front porch or the back patio since there are no guests out there."

The last thing he wanted to do was take a chance on more people coming by, calling out, or possibly stopping to talk if they were on the front porch. "Back patio would be great."

Walking outside, he scanned the settees, wicker chairs, Adirondacks, and the swing. "How about the swing?"

If she was surprised by his suggestion, she didn't say anything. The swing allowed them to sit next to each other but didn't seem quite so obvious as suggesting the settee.

His legs were much longer than hers, and he placed them on the ground, giving a push. Soon, she relaxed against the back of the swing seat, allowing him to direct the rocking motion. He thought about all he'd heard about her and wanted to ask questions to get to know her better. But he preferred that she was comfortable with him, giving him her story when she was ready. "So was this your first ball game since being in town?"

She smiled with an expression of relief crossing her face. He wondered if she was glad he finally spoke first or if his question was easy for her to answer.

"Yes, and I was amazed. There were so many kids playing, and the stands were filled. Is it always like that?"

"Most of the time, yeah. The AL... um...American Legion has been sponsoring these teams for about four years, but I've only been volunteering since I got back."

"Your mom mentioned you were in the Navy."

"Yeah. Joined right after high school and did twelve years. Thought about staying in to get in for a full twenty years, but I was ready to come home. I'd seen the world. Discovered it couldn't compare to what I have here."

She cocked her head to the side in silence, and he continued. "Friends. Family. A job I love. And the chance to make a difference in the place I consider to be home."

Her lips continued to curve, and he was consumed with the idea of finding out if they were as soft as they appeared. Knowing she wasn't the kind of woman who'd appreciate him acting on instinct, he forced his gaze back to her eyes and went back to a safe topic. "Um... we don't charge the parents anything for their kids to play ball. We rely on donations and our fundraisers for the uniforms and equipment. All we ask is that the parents who are able to assist can send in snacks or water for practice. Or they can simply come here and cheer on the kids. Not everyone can, but we find that almost all the parents want to support, even if they don't have the money."

"I'm sure for the kids, it's wonderful just to see their parents cheering in the stands."

He nodded, shifting slightly to face her. "Absolutely. Every kid should feel like they've got a chance to shine."

Her breath hiccuped slightly before her lips curved wider. "That's a really sweet sentiment. I agree. I always had that with my parents."

Now it was his time to have his breath catch at the first slip of personal information she'd given. "So tell me about—"

The back door opened, and a middle-aged woman looked out and then spied them sitting on the swing. Waving, she called out, "Ms. Wallen! We are going to need clean towels. My husband dropped his bottle of aftershave, and it broke in our bathroom."

Shiloh jumped to her feet and called out, "Please don't try to clean it up! You might cut yourself! I'll be right there!"

Joseph hated the interruption but was heartened by the scrunched nose expression of disappointment on Shiloh's face.

"I'm so sorry, Joseph, but I need to go in and take care of this."

He stood and smiled, giving her shoulder a little squeeze. "That's fine. I'm just glad that you allowed me to walk you home. And thank you for the lemonade."

She took the empty glass from him, their fingers touching, and sparks grew between them.

"I'm not giving up, Shiloh. I really would like to take

you out sometime, and I'm willing to be patient." Steeling himself for her refusal, the air rushed from his lungs when she offered a little smile and nodded.

"Yes… um… yes." With that, she smiled, blushed, and turned to hurry up the back steps and into the kitchen.

He wanted to howl with joy but somehow managed to hang onto what little cool he had left. As he walked back through town to where he parked at the ballfield, his steps were much lighter.

15

"I see them," Joseph called out, pointing out over the bay as Andy steered them closer. It was days since he'd enjoyed the afternoon with Shiloh, but he'd barely had a chance to breathe with two of their staff down with the stomach flu.

Now, in the bay, not too far off the coast north of Baytown, Ryan stood next to him, his face like granite. The hard-jaw, tight-lipped expression on Ryan's face let Joseph know his boss was barely hanging on to his anger.

The single-outboard fishing boat was stalled in the bay, but the call had come from Cindy for a pickup. From what Ryan said, Cindy was out with friends in their small rowboat near the entrance to the inlet that ran from the back of the Coates' house to the bay. A motorboat had buzzed them, causing the rowboat to flip. Thank God, no one was hurt, but they were on the other side of the inlet and unable to get back.

She'd recognized the driver of the motorboat, and

instead of the VMP having to locate the vessel, they lucked out when the motorboat stalled out not too far from where they'd almost rammed the rowboat.

Callan and Jarod had made it to the shore, where they picked up Cindy and the other three stranded teenagers.

"They're fine," Callan radioed. "We'll leave the rowboat for now. I can head back to the station or—"

"I'll get it later," Ryan growled. "I want to see Cindy, so bring her here."

"Roger that," came the response.

Joseph wanted to suggest that Ryan stay in the background, but from the continued tense expression on his boss's face, he didn't want to poke the bear.

As they approached the stalled boat, Joseph could see it was an older boat but appeared to be in decent shape. What concerned him was that the driver barely looked sixteen, and three other teenagers were in the boat with him, all seeming younger than the driver.

Andy pulled back, and they gently moved to the side of the boat. Joseph lashed the two vessels together for safety. Ryan started forward, but Joseph softly said, "Easy, boss. By the book."

"I know," Ryan growled but offered a curt nod toward Joseph.

"Daddy!"

They looked over their shoulders toward the other VMP vessel, with Callan and Jarod maneuvering closer. Joseph recognized Jack Hudson, the son of Colt who was the sheriff of North Heron County, and another young teen named Brian with Cindy, along with a young woman with long dark hair. While the other girl was wearing a life jacket, her arms were crossed in front of her in a protective stance, and her shaking was visible from where he stood.

Ryan changed course and headed toward the other vessel as Joseph shared a pointed look toward Callan and breathed a sigh of relief.

"Looks like you all had some problems," Joseph called out as he turned back to the motorboat. "We need everyone to stay calm, and we'll get you transported back to the harbor."

"We don't need to be transported anywhere! I just need someone to get the motor started!"

"We'll come over and take a look and let you know what needs to happen."

The young driver pouted. "I don't know why you all had to come. I could've just called my brother!"

"Shut up, Paul!" Jack yelled. "You ran us down! If Cindy hadn't called her dad, I was getting ready to call it in myself."

"All right!" Joseph called out. "Everyone, be quiet and stay seated!"

Ryan hugged Cindy and then greeted the teens with her. "I'll have you move over to the other VMP boat. We need to deal with what's happened here. Officers Cox and Ward will take care of the boat if it needs to be towed. You'll need to come back to the station with me so we can get your statements and get ahold of your parents."

Joseph assisted Cindy onto the VMP boat along with another young teenage girl. "Hey, it's okay now."

She nodded but kept her head down as she continued to shiver. "Andy? Get a warming blanket." Looking back at her, he said, "Officer Bergstrom will get you warm in just a few minutes." It didn't miss his notice that Jack took the blanket from Andy and gently draped it over the girl's shoulders, guiding her to a seat.

Jack stepped up to Ryan, his young face tense. "I'm sorry, Chief Coates. Rachel doesn't swim, and my focus was on her. I didn't notice the motor boat coming so close, or I might have gotten us out of the way sooner."

"Not your place to monitor the actions of immature idiots behind the wheel of a motorized vessel."

Joseph watched as Jack held Ryan's gaze and then nodded, his admiration for Colt's son even higher. Even though he knew the identity of most of the teens, procedures needed to be followed. "I'm gonna need to see everyone's identification." Cindy, Brian, and Jack pulled out their school IDs since none of them had driver's licenses. The other female that Jack had referred to as Rachel sat, still shaking, eyes down. Jack moved over and whispered to her, assisting as she pulled a waterproof crossbody bag from her shoulders, then handed the ID to him. Rachel Ayers.

Taking down the information, his attention was continually drawn to Paul, who paced back and forth, his behavior antsy. Wondering if the young man took the boat out without his parents' permission, he also wondered if the young man had a boating license.

While Callan and Ryan checked out the motor, determining it was burned out and not just out of gasoline, Joseph approached Paul. "I'm gonna need to see your license."

The young man reached into his back pocket and pulled out his wallet. Opening it, he held it up so Joseph could see his driver's and boating licenses. The boating license was only three days old.

Paul shoved his hands into his front pockets, his lips pinched tightly together. "See. Everything's fine. Nothing would be wrong if it weren't for having motor problems."

Joseph handed the licenses back after scanning the information. Paul jerked his hands out of his pockets, and a small bag dropped to the deck of his boat. Paul gasped, bending quickly to snag it.

"Stop right there," Joseph ordered. Reacting faster than Paul, he jerked his hand out and kept the young man from grabbing the bag. Reaching into his back pocket, he pulled out a glove and snapped it on before picking up the plastic bag. Holding it up, he could see several pills inside. Looking up into Paul's sweaty, red face, he asked, "You want to tell me whose pills these are?"

"They're mine!"

"Looks like Percocet to me," Joseph said, recognizing the marking on the pills from when he had minor surgery in the Navy.

"They were prescribed for me," Paul argued. "I had my wisdom teeth out last week."

"It's true, sir," one of the other boys with Paul said. "He did have his wisdom teeth out."

"Then why did you get the whole prescription

dumped into this plastic bag and shoved in your pocket? If you need this medication, it clearly states that you're not to be operating any heavy machinery— such as a boat."

"Oh..." Paul muttered, looking down. "I didn't know."

Ryan stepped forward, no longer heeding Joseph's warning expression. "Are you telling me that you took a narcotic before operating this boat? This boat carrying other teenagers and driving like a madman? Endangering the lives of—"

"No, man... I mean, sir. I just had them in my pocket for... for later."

Aware of Ryan's face growing redder, Joseph stepped in. "You need to step over into the VMP boat. Your boat will be towed back to the Baytown Harbor. We'll check out the story of the Percocet, and you may be required to have a drug test to see if you were operating this vessel under the influence."

"Man, this is bullshit. I was just trying to get my motor started again. I was going to call my brother to come out and get us."

"Paul, my advice is to shut your mouth. Right now, you've got a very pissed-off dad talking to the other people you were carrying. If you don't have any drugs in your system, then good, but running your mouth right now is only gonna make things worse."

While Ryan got the contact information from the other teens, Joseph helped Callan prepare Paul's boat to be towed back to the harbor. Thirty minutes later, they walked into the VMP office, where they were met by

Ginny MacFarlane, one of the Baytown Police officers. Joseph turned Paul over to her. "He's going to need a drug test."

"I've got one with me. It's an IA test. I'll let you administer it, and then I'll check. If it's positive, then we'll have to order a blood test, but they can do that at either our jail or the juvenile detention center if that's what they decide on."

Nodding, he looked over his shoulder as Callan and Ryan took the other teens into the conference room for questioning. Jack and Cindy were angry, shooting glares toward Paul. The dark-haired girl next to Cindy appeared terrified, still shaking.

"Let's go. Men's room is right here." He clapped his hand on Paul's shoulder and inclined his head toward the closest door.

"Ah, man," Paul whined, his body tense.

Once inside, Joseph stood to the side, trying to make Paul comfortable while still witnessing the collection. Walking back outside, he handed the test to Ginny, signing the form for being the one who administered it.

"It'll take about five minutes." She looked around. "One of you can witness this as well."

Before he could agree, their attention was called to the side as Callan and Ryan walked out of the conference room. Ryan's hands were on his hips, his jaw carved out of granite. Callan spoke in a low tone to him, and then Ryan dipped his chin in haste before turning and walking into his office.

"What's going on?" Joseph asked.

"We were getting the information from these kids,

but we're hearing some things. Because Cindy is involved, we want Ryan out of the room until we finish and can get ahold of the parents."

"I'll need five minutes to witness the drug test with Ginny, and then I'll be in to assist."

"Appreciate it."

Callan stepped back into the conference room, and Joseph handed Paul off to Andy. Walking into the workroom with Ginny, he observed as she gloved, then prepared the strip test. Once it was dipped into the urine, she laid it flat on a hard board she'd brought. They watched as the five minutes passed. Twisting her head around, she said, "No opiates."

"So why did he have them in his pocket?"

Lifting a brow, Ginny shook her head. "One guess."

"Yeah, that's what I figured. Probably why Callan made Ryan leave the room." He sighed, then thanked her and headed down the hall. Stepping into the conference room, he made his way over to Callan. "What do you need?"

Callan let him know which teens he interviewed. "Jarod talked to Cindy, Jack, Brian, and the other girl, Rachel. I've just taken statements from the ones in the boat with Paul. Ryan has called Colt for Jack, and I've got our receptionist calling for Rachel's guardian and Brian's parents. Hang on 'cause it's gonna be a bumpy ride."

"Yeah?"

"So far, three of the four said Paul told them that he would have some feel-good drugs for them to try. He'd even showed those two the plastic bag with the pills.

One kid says he didn't know anything about it. Just wait until we get the parents in."

It only took another minute for Colt Hudson to stalk into the station, his face as much like granite as Ryan's had been. Joseph considered Colt a friend, and at that moment, he could see Colt was barely hanging onto his anger. "Shit," he murmured under his breath.

While Colt made a beeline to Jack, who was still being interviewed, Joseph turned to the room to see the lone girl sitting by herself, her body curled in as though trying to make herself smaller. Walking over, he said, "Hey, Rachel. I know this is scary, but it'll be fine. Your parent will be here soon."

She looked up with blue-gray eyes that hit him in the gut, making the air rush out. *Her eyes look just like—*

"Where is she? Where's Rachel?" A cry came from the hall.

Rachel leaped from her seat, crying, "Shiloh!"

He barely had a chance to move out of the way before the woman who'd filled his dreams for weeks barreled into the room and engulfed Rachel in a bear hug. He gave them a moment, then moved toward them. As Shiloh lifted her tearstained face to him, he wanted nothing more than to join in their hug to take away her fears.

"Hey, she's fine. She's not hurt—"

Shiloh cried, "She doesn't know how to swim! What if—"

Jarod stuck his head through the doorway. "Rachel? Is Shiloh your guardian?"

Shiloh nodded as she turned toward him. "Yes. I'm Rachel's aunt and guardian. Shiloh Wallen."

"Ms. Wallen. If you can come this way, we'll explain what we know, and then you'll be able to take her home."

"Yes. Um… all right." Joseph stepped closer, sensing Shiloh was filled with uncertainty, and followed as they all went into the large conference room, where Cindy immediately leaped from her seat to hug her friend. Colt was standing behind Jack's chair, but the young teen moved to pull out a seat next to him for Rachel.

"Ms. Wallen," Jack began, looking at Shiloh. "I'm so sorry. When I asked Rachel to go out today, it was supposed to be fun. I promise I would never put Rachel in danger. And if you'd allow it, I can take Rachel to the YMCA's heated pool and teach her how to swim."

Joseph held his breath, seeing Jack's earnest expression mixed with the fear that Shiloh might react angrily. He felt the nerves in his gut as though he was the young man once again having to prove himself.

Shiloh swiped at her tears and nodded, dragging in a ragged breath. "Thank you, Jack. Rachel and I will talk it over. I appreciate you watching out for her, and if she would like to have you teach her how to swim, I think that would be a good idea."

Jack let out a whoosh of air and then sat back down. Joseph shot a glance toward Colt, seeing the pride on his face. With Brian and his parents also in the room, Ryan nodded toward Callan and Jarod.

"What we've been told by these four is that they were in two rowboats owned by the Coates and were in the inlet just east of the bay entrance. They heard a motorboat coming but didn't have room to move much closer to the shore when it sped up and came within twenty feet of them, knocking over the rowboat containing Rachel and Jack. Jack managed to assist Rachel to the shore with the help of Cindy and Brian. They have identified the person driving the motorboat. It stalled nearby, and we have brought it in, and an ongoing investigation is taking place. I will also add that at least one of the young men in that motorboat corroborates the story that their vessel came too close to the rowboats and did so on purpose."

Joseph's anger rose, not only at Paul's actions in general but at the tears in Shiloh's eyes. The angry grumbling from Brian's parents grew, and while Colt and Ryan remained quiet, their anger was just as palpable. After another few minutes, Callan told them they could go home.

Before Joseph had a chance to talk to Shiloh, another sound was heard in the hall, and he could tell Paul's dad had arrived. The large man was already raising his voice about illegal searches, calling his lawyer, and police brutality.

He looked toward Callan and said, "I'm going to walk them out. I'll be back."

As soon as he'd escorted Shiloh and Rachel outside, he looked at the two women, seeing the familial similarities. They waved to Cindy as her brother opened the door for his sister, having arrived since Ryan was still needed at the station. Joseph held back a chuckle. Trevor's face was a mirror image of Ryan's, and he wondered how the young man would be kept from smashing his fist into Paul's face when he learned of the whole story.

Looking down at Shiloh, he opened his mouth, but Jack raced over to say goodbye to Rachel. Shiloh reached out to grab Jack's hand. "Thank you again, Jack. I'm so grateful for all you did." Jack blushed as he waved goodbye. Joseph caught Colt's wry grin at his son's obvious crush and the equally infatuated expression on Rachel's face.

Knowing Callan was inside dealing with Paul's dad, he rushed, "Rachel, I'm so sorry this happened to you. I know your aunt and hope I can stop by to see how you are doing sometime." Squeezing Shiloh's shoulder, he added, "I hate that I can't take you home, but I'm needed inside. I really want to talk to you. Can I call?"

She held his gaze, her blue-gray eyes shining in the sunlight. As she nodded, Rachel looked on with a small smile. Turning back to Shiloh, he prompted, "I'll need your number."

"Oh," she said, fumbling in her purse. Pulling out her phone, she handed it to him.

He typed in his number and then called. "There. Now, we're connected." As he watched them walk away from the station at the harbor and toward the town, he threw his hand upward in a wave when she looked over her shoulder at him. With a sigh, he turned to head back inside, but his mind was already on when he could call her. Grinning, he realized his expression was just like Jack's eager, teenage, not-even-trying-to-be-cool look. And that was fine with him.

16

It was hours later that evening, but Shiloh hadn't stopped shaking. By the time they'd gotten back to the inn, Rachel had given her the entire story, filled with emotion and a dash of heroism over Jack's actions. She'd talked about her initial fear of being in the rowboat but how soon she grew to love the way they glided through the water and how Jack taught her to use the oar. Then she'd heard the loud roar of the oncoming motorboat but had no idea what would happen when it came so close. As soon as the rowboat flipped over, Rachel admitted to panicking. Her life jacket kept her head above water. Jack immediately wrapped his arm around her and swam with her to shore, followed closely by Cindy and Brian in their rowboat.

Shiloh had fixed her a cup of tea while Rachel soaked in the bathtub and then listened, trying not to panic at the tale. By the time Joseph called, Rachel was already yawning.

"He can come over, Shiloh," Rachel had said. "I'm going to bed. I'm exhausted."

Shiloh had watched over Rachel as she fell asleep, having just enough time to brush her hair before Joseph indicated he was at the inn's back door. Rushing down the back stairs, she saw him at the door, and her breath caught in her throat. Her mind hadn't caught up to the fact that he'd been part of Rachel's rescue and, according to her niece, had been sweet even though he had no idea she was Shiloh's niece.

Now, staring at his endearing smile aimed at her and his sky-blue eyes, she sucked in a deep breath and let it out slowly. She had no idea why he was here with all the women he could have been out with, but she no longer wanted to fight the desire to get to know him. Swiping her sweaty palms along her skirt, she straightened her spine and threw open the door, smiling. "Hello."

His smile widened at her softly spoken greeting. "Hello to you."

Stepping back, she asked, "Would you like to come in?"

"Wherever you're comfortable, but the patio swing is fine with me."

"I'll get some lemonade." Pouring two tall glasses, she handed one to him, then followed as he led the way across the stone patio to the swing. He held it steady while she sat down, then he sat next to her.

"How's Rachel?"

"She seems fine. Thank you for asking." Chuckling, she shook her head. "The resiliency of youth. I'm still shaky, and she was telling me all about it. Now that the danger has passed, I think she was rather excited at having an adventure."

"I'm glad she's all right. It could have been so much… um… well…"

"I know what you were going to say. While I have no experience with boats, I can only imagine the horror of what could have happened." She shivered, and he scooted a little closer. His presence was comforting, and she had to battle the urge to lean into his strength. Refusing to appear stiff, she managed to stay relaxed, even with his closeness. A thought suddenly hit her, and she twisted around to peer at him. "Oh, Joseph, I just realized that you've probably seen horrible accidents. How awful for you!"

He opened and closed his mouth several times before finally shaking his head. "Yes… I have. But no one outside of family has ever mentioned how it affected me. Thank you."

She waved her hand dismissively. "Don't thank me. You're the hero."

"I'm not a hero, Shiloh. I'm just a man who gets to do the job he loves."

His words struck deep inside, and she held his gaze, the air seeming hard to draw into her lungs. "That's why you're a hero," she said, her voice barely a whisper. Suddenly aware of how her body tingled, she looked down and quickly swallowed a sip of the cool, tart lemonade. "I should have made sure she knew how to swim before ever agreeing that she could go on a boat. She was sure the water wasn't deep, and I foolishly allowed it."

"It looks like Jack will take care of that," he said, his lips curving slightly.

"I need to join the YMCA so I can learn to swim—"

"You don't know how?"

Shaking her head, she said, "No. There was never a place to swim when I was younger, and then, well, no."

"I'll teach you. It would be better than a class with a bunch of people, anyway."

"Oh… I… well. I don't have a swimsuit, but I suppose I can get one."

His gaze dropped to her skirt. "So… um…"

She looked back at him quickly, uncertainty lacing his hesitation. "Yes?"

"I…" He sighed heavily, his brow furrowed. "Shiloh, I… I'd really like to get to know you. But I don't know how to start. I don't want to ask questions that would make you uncomfortable. I've heard a little, but I'd rather hear from you."

She wondered how deep he really wanted to go. And if she took him there, would he want to keep sitting next to her? Pastor Parton had advised her to let the people of Baytown know her, but trust was hard. So was the idea of others not understanding. *But if he can't handle knowing the real me, then the tingles I feel when we're together can't be real.* Sucking in a deep breath, she plunged in. "I suppose you want to know where I came from and how I ended up here." At his nod, she looked out over the yard as the fireflies began to flicker.

"I came from a small community in the mountains of Pennsylvania. My parents discovered it when my dad came back from his time in Desert Storm. I wasn't born yet, but he always said he needed space. Fresh air. Few people. Mom said his time in the Army changed him. He wanted to work with his hands and leave the modern world behind. They found a small, isolated community that had been a commune at one time. He bought a plot of land and farmed. Our lives revolved around our farm, our church, and our community. We went to school, so we weren't completely cut off from the world. But with mountains and rivers bordering our community, spotty cell phone service, and virtually no internet, we didn't have many visitors." She shrugged, taking another sip. "As backward as it sounds, it was fun. My childhood memories of my parents and older sister and our community are good. We had Pastor Aaron, and he was so kind. Neighbors knew each other and always helped." She chanced a look toward him to see his reaction.

"I know this might sound weird," he said. "But in some ways, that reminds me of my upbringing. I was raised not too far from here, but my family didn't have a lot when my dad lost his job when I was little. We grew some of our own food. Mom used to make my sister's clothes. We had a phone in the house, but I was shipping off to the Navy before I got my first cell phone. We had the internet at school, but not in the house. The neighbors were nice, and everyone was helpful. I knew we were poor, and sometimes at school, kids could be mean. But my memories growing up with my family were really good."

Surprised at his confession, she nodded. "It never

dawned on me that there might be part of my past that you would understand."

"See, we're not so different," he said, gently bumping his shoulder to hers.

Unease moved through her, and she shook her head slowly, swallowing deeply. "I'm afraid there was little else in my past that could possibly be similar to yours."

He shifted in the swing to face her, his leg touching hers. Time passed, and she felt the tingle again and prayed that it was real and not in her imagination. "My sister was married and had Rachel. I married when I was eighteen—"

"Married?" Joseph barked out, his eyes wide.

At his near-shout, she winced, leaning farther away from him.

He immediately shook his head. "I'm sorry. I'm so sorry, Shiloh. I didn't… I shouldn't have… shit… I was just surprised. God, I'm so sorry."

His hound-dog expression was so honest that she nodded. "It's okay. I told you that my background was different." Her lemonade was finished, and she stood to place it on one of the many tables that Tori had scattered around the garden. "I really should go in. Thank you for stopping by—"

"Oh no, Shiloh. Please, I want to know more. I promise I'll sit here and not say anything."

She offered an indulgent smile. "Joseph, I don't mind talking, and you can have any reaction you want. I know my story is unusual. For you to have no reaction at all wouldn't make any sense."

He held out his hand to her. "Please."

She stared for a moment, uncertainty filling her. Finally, she lifted her hand and placed it in his, the warmth moving up her arm. Allowing him to guide her back over to the swing, she settled in, keeping a space between them. He shifted again so that he could face her but still be close.

"You were married," he prodded.

"Yes, I married a man I had grown up with. Edward was a very good man. A very good friend. We were happy, living the life we chose. We knew the outside world was filled with modern gadgets, exciting new inventions, museums, theaters, and big stores. It wasn't that we were ignorant of what was out there, but we chose to live where we were comfortable. I suppose part of that was because it was all I had known, but since I was happy with my life, it hardly mattered the why." She grew quiet. The waves on the beach on the other side of the road were heard in the background.

"Why do I get the feeling that this is where the story turns?"

She looked up to see his intense gaze pinned on her. The air caught in her throat, making it hard to breathe. What could she tell him? Never the whole story. Never her deepest suspicions. Never her fears. Letting out a shaky breath, she nodded slowly. "Because this is where everything changed."

Joseph's head was reeling as he took in everything Shiloh had revealed so far. A community that had retained much of its sheltered way of life. It was the only existence she'd known. She was... had been married. Now that she'd begun her tale, he was even more intrigued. Yet nerves slithered along his insides at the idea of what lay before him. She held his gaze and the blue-gray depths pulled him in. They were once again stormy, but no matter what the outcome, he wanted to know everything about her. "Please... go on if you can."

She nodded, looking down at her clasped hands. "It wasn't as though we never left the community. It's just that after we'd take a trip to a nearby town, we were ready to get back to our home. About six years ago, Pastor Aaron had been invited to speak at another church about our congregation." She licked her lips and hesitated. "His... well, he was a widower and had a nephew who had been trained to become a pastor, also. His nephew suggested that perhaps some members should go, as well. My parents and my sister and her husband were chosen to go with him. My husband and I kept Rachel, glad to give them a little vacation."

Stopping, she rubbed her forehead, her brow knitting as though in pain. Joseph longed to ease her distress but didn't know if it was better for her to unburden or to stop. "Shiloh, you don't have to do this. I can see it's upsetting."

She shifted, this time her knee now touching his as she faced him on the swing. "I've held things in for so long. I need this. But I could talk to Pastor Parton or—"

"No!" He winced as she jumped again at his barked-out word. He had no idea why it meant so much to him, but he longed to see the dark storm leave her eyes. "I'm sorry. Damn, I keep saying that. I just mean that I want you to talk to me."

Her lips pressed together as her gaze held his, and he fought the desire to squirm under the intensity. Finally, she nodded. "There was an accident. The van they were driving lost control on the mountain roads, and… and… they were all killed. My parents. My sister and her husband... and the pastor."

The bottom fell out of his gut. "Oh, Shiloh… I'm so sorry." No longer able to hang back, he wrapped his arm around her shoulder and gently pulled her forward so that her head tucked under his chin. He couldn't begin to imagine losing his parents and siblings. Not slowly over time, and surely not all at once. How she was still moving through life… *Christ, she's so fucking strong.*

They sat in silence for several long minutes, neither speaking. Finally, she lifted her head, her eyes searching his face. He didn't know what she was looking for—pity, strength, understanding. Pity would be easy to find, as he was filled with compassion for her. Strength would be harder, considering he felt gutted, but he wanted to be strong for her. Understanding would be almost impossible because he'd never suffered that kind of loss and couldn't imagine ever crawling out of bed if he had.

"I don't know what to say," he confessed. "My heart absolutely breaks for your loss." He startled, more thoughts finally hitting. "Oh, damn. Rachel, too. She lost everyone except you, too."

She nodded, breathing deeply through her nose

before letting it out as though to cleanse her thoughts. "If it wasn't for Rachel, I don't think I'd be here. I think the dark thoughts would've pulled me under. But Edward was my rock, and I knew that Rachel deserved to be raised by two people who loved her more than life and could keep her family memories alive for her." She hefted her thin shoulders in a shrug. "So that's why I got out of bed each morning. And I did it over and over, day after day, until tears and the ache were a little less."

Joseph wanted to know more but hated to ask. She kept mentioning her husband, Edward, yet she and Rachel were here alone.

As though she could read his mind, she shifted slightly again in the swing to face him, and their bodies were much closer than before. "I'm sure you're wondering about Edward, aren't you?"

"Yeah, I am. But, honest to God, Shiloh, I only want you to tell me what you want me to know. It wouldn't be fair for me to sit here and demand to know everything about you, but I confess, I want you to feel like you can trust me."

Her hands were fiddling with the material in her skirt, and with one hand still curled around her shoulder, he reached over with the other hand and gently placed it on top of hers. She hesitated for a moment, then turned her hand up so that their palms were clasped. The simplest of touches. Completely nonsexual. A touch to offer and receive comfort. Yet, at that moment, he felt more connected to her than he did anyone in his life outside his family.

"About a year and a half ago, Edward died from a farming accident. His injuries were too severe and…"

He held her tighter, now, more than ever, willing his strength to be enough to help her go on.

"So I spent a year in official mourning and then decided to move Rachel somewhere else."

Joseph gently pulled her back so that she was once again tucked close. He had more questions. The layers that she had lifted only made him wonder more about why she would pick up and leave everything familiar and come to a tiny town, changing her and Rachel's lives drastically in the process. But as a shuddering breath left her lungs, he felt as though she'd given all she could tonight. Pressing his lips against her forehead, they sat in silence as he held her, praying the gentle movement of the swing and the twinkling stars above offered her a sliver of peace.

17

Several days later, Shiloh sat on the edge of the YMCA swimming pool, her feet dangling into the water at the shallow end. Looking over, she watched as Rachel threw her head back and laughed as she worked with Jack on learning how to float. Rachel was beautiful, but at that moment, on the cusp of blooming into a woman, she looked so like Rebecca. And that realization made Shiloh's heart both ache and sing all at the same time.

She and Rachel had bought one-piece swimsuits, and while they were modest at the neckline, she could not help but feel exposed. Rachel had tugged self-consciously on hers when she first put it on, but now, in the pool, she appeared comfortable. She didn't know if Jack was on his best behavior because she was nearby, but she had a feeling the young man would have been a perfect gentleman even if Shiloh hadn't been watching.

Hearing a noise behind her, she twisted around and watched as Joseph stalked toward her. He reached down and pulled off his T-shirt, wearing nothing more than swim trunks. Heat flooded her, and she wouldn't pretend that it only came from the sun. Oh no, Joseph had a body worthy of pictures she'd seen in the fashion magazines. His muscles were on display, his body lean and fit. As his twinkling blue-eyed gaze landed on her, his smile widened, and once again, she felt overheated.

His gaze raked over her quickly, but she was grateful when it settled on her face making her less self-conscious about how little she wore.

"You're beautiful, Shiloh," he said as he neared. Not giving her a chance to reply, he hopped into the pool, dumped his head under the water, and rose up like a mythical god with water droplets dancing over his tanned skin.

Her chest heaved at his words. Edward had told her she was beautiful, but he'd never looked at her the way Joseph was looking at her right now. And in truth, the thoughts she'd had about her husband were nothing like what was moving through her mind as she stared at Joseph. She wanted to give voice to her thoughts, but blurting out that he was the most beautiful man she'd ever laid eyes on didn't seem like an appropriate greeting. So instead, she just smiled and said, "Hello."

The little-boy grin on his face gave evidence that he could tell there was more she would've liked to have said.

"Are you ready?"

"Honestly? I'm kind of excited and kind of terrified all at the same time."

He dropped the grin and walked through the water until he was standing with his chest almost touching her knees. Placing his hands on either side of her thighs, he said, "Don't worry. I promise I'll take care of you."

As though the world had stopped spinning, their gazes held, and his words moved through her. It would be so easy to believe they meant more than just teaching her how to swim and not letting her drown. At that moment, she could feel the strength and courage that made up everything Joseph was, everything she needed, everything she'd never had.

"I want you to tell me what you're thinking, Shiloh," he gently ordered.

Without thinking her words through, she blurted, "I'm scared and excited. I want to learn something new, and I don't want to be afraid anymore. I want you to teach me, yet I'm afraid of looking foolish in front of you."

Before she had a chance to hesitate even more, he moved closer so that he was standing just in front of her, and his hands moved to her waist. Lifting her easily, he pulled her toward him. She squealed, her arms and legs snaking around him like a monkey climbing a tree.

"Whoa, whoa." He laughed, holding her close. "I'm probably nuts for saying this, but your feet can touch the bottom of the pool at this height."

She kept hold of his shoulders but slowly lowered her feet until they were firmly planted, yet the top third of her body was above the water. Blushing, she mumbled, "Oh." Tilting her head to the side, she asked, "Why did you say you were nuts?"

Still chuckling, he ducked his head slightly before

admitting, "Because as soon as you knew you could stand, you wouldn't hold on to me so tightly. It was nice."

A blush heated her cheeks and probably the rest of her, as well. "Oh," she mumbled again.

He stared, then reached out to touch her cheek with his finger. "I like that."

Her brows lowered in uncertainty. "Like what?"

"That you blush."

"Doesn't everyone?"

He shook his head slowly and simply replied, "No. Or not nearly enough." Without giving her more, he stepped back while still holding her hands. "Okay... now we learn to float."

For the next hour, she sputtered and coughed, slipped and dipped, panicked and grasped... and had more fun than she could ever remember having. By the time he led her over to the ladder so she could climb out, she could float on her back, managing to keep her body almost level and her face above the water. She could also do a somewhat comical version of a doggie paddle, again managing not to sink. She declared the lesson a victory and loved the way he agreed, the light in his eyes shining on her with pride.

Looking over, Jack and Rachel had also climbed from the pool and were lying on lounges, talking. She hesitated, her gaze pinned on them, startling when Joseph stepped behind her and draped a towel around her shoulders.

"They'll be fine," he whispered. "Jack's a good kid."

She nodded, heaving a sigh as she looked away from

the teenagers. "I know. I could tell by how he handled himself at the station and hearing how he'd ensured she was safe. It's just hard." Looking up at him, she wiped the water drops from her face, wrapping the towel around her body. "Hard to know what to do sometimes. She's such a wonderful girl. The joy of my life, really. I just want to make sure I'm the best substitute parent I can be."

He moved closer so that he was standing just in front of her, his hands on her shoulders. "From what I can see, she could have no better parent than you. That's not saying her real parents wouldn't have done just as good a job, but you have no reason to doubt the amazing, positive effect you have on her life."

Shiloh battled the urge to cry. It had been a long time since she'd given in to the desire to break down and sob out of fear and doubt. There was so much Joseph didn't know. So much more than she hadn't shared with him.

"Hey. Where did you go?" He'd moved so that his face was very close to hers, filling her vision.

Forcing a smile on her face, she shook her head. "I'm sorry, my mind just wandered down the path I try to stay off of."

With his gaze just as intense, he said, "I hope you'll share the path with me one day. I wasn't exaggerating when I said I wanted to know all about you."

I'd like that, too. But what if I share that part of my story, and you walk away?

With his hand resting on her back, he guided her inside after calling to the teens. Once she and Rachel were inside the women's locker room, where they showered and changed, her heart grew lighter at Rachel's exuberance over her swim lesson. Admitting she had just as good a time, they walked out to see Joseph and Jack waiting for them. Outside, Jack's mom, Carrie, waved to them as he climbed into their SUV. She didn't miss the look he sent toward Rachel nor the return expression of joy on her niece's face. Once back at the inn, Rachel ran inside to call Cindy as she turned to thank Joseph once again.

"We still haven't had our dinner date," he said. "Would it be too soon to go tonight?"

She chewed on her bottom lip, then found her courage. "I'd love to. But do you know what I'd really like us to do?"

He grinned, shaking his head. "No, but I'm curious."

"I'd love to go over there," she said, inclining her head toward the beach on the other side of the road. "We could get tacos at the food truck and then walk on the beach."

Brows lifted, he laughed. "You know, that sounds perfect. Give me a couple of hours, and I'll be back."

Waving, she turned and headed inside, not surprised to see Rachel bouncing on her toes at the window.

"You're going to go out with him!" Rachel gushed.

She pressed her lips together in an effort to stifle the grin threatening to erupt but failed. With Rachel's arms wrapped around her in a hug, they hurried upstairs to find something for her to wear on her first real date.

He couldn't remember ever being on a date like this—standing in front of a food truck on the beach road, ordering tacos and sodas. But then, he'd rarely gone on an actual date. Glancing to the side, he couldn't help but grin at Shiloh's excited clap when he turned to hand her the small cardboard box filled with nachos and two tacos, along with a soda. Taking his own, they walked out onto the sandy shore to the blanket she'd already placed on the sand.

Sitting next to each other, they devoured their dinner, laughing as the sauce dripped off their chins and fingers. Her eyes shone, the dark clouds in their depths no longer visible. After eating, they wiped their hands on the little wet wipes provided, and he took the trash to the receptacle.

Plopping back down on the blanket, he made sure to sit right next to her, and with their legs stretched out in front of them, he felt the electricity move through his body as their legs touched. She was wearing jeans, and it struck him that it was the first time he'd seen her in jeans. *Other than the modest bathing suit she'd worn earlier that showed off her beautiful curves.* She'd managed to hold his attention in a way that no other woman in the skimpiest of bikinis had ever managed to do. And he knew it was all because it was her.

"You look beautiful tonight," he said. "Of course, you always look beautiful."

Her hands smoothed over the cotton of her pants. "It's been a long time since I've worn anything other than a dress or skirt. When I was little, I wore pants or shorts all the time."

"Was it a personal choice?" He wondered if her husband had demanded that his wife wear dresses.

She shook her head and sighed. "I suppose you know there's more to my story than just what I've told."

"I've said it before, Shiloh, but I truly want to know everything about you. I hope you feel like you can tell me anything."

A myriad of expressions crossed her face, and again it dawned on him how different she was from other women he'd been with. She didn't hide her emotions. She didn't throw out coy comments, attempt to be intriguing, or flirt to demand attention. As he stared, he could see doubt and fear move through her eyes, slowly replaced by a resolute determination. He held his breath, praying she'd give him more.

"When the accident occurred, our community was reeling in grief. It was a time of unbearable sorrow. Looking back, I can see how our grief made us vulnerable. Our questions made it easy to accept answers." She shifted on the blanket, crossing her legs and staring out over the bay. "It's so beautiful here. It was beautiful in the mountains, also. But not when… when things changed. There was no beauty anywhere… just bone-wearying grief. But a voice came out of that time— a voice that held answers and gave direction. It came from Pastor Aaron's nephew, Isaiah. Isaiah was older than me, but I remember him growing up. He always seemed angry. Had a pinched look on his face. I'm not sure I ever saw him smile at all. But he took over our church, taking over the leadership position of our community, and made sure his voice was heard."

Uncertain of her meaning, Joseph waited. He wanted to be able to see her eyes but wondered if she needed to face away from him and toward the water for the words to be able to come.

"He told us that our community was being punished for being so wicked. He said that the deaths from the accident were to bring us in line with what he wanted. And when I say he, I'm not referring to God. But to Isaiah. His ethics and dictates came swiftly. Parties and gatherings for anything other than church were forbidden. A part of our crops was to be turned over to the community store. And that included meat and poultry, as well. He got rid of the library in the basement of the church, saying that it was evil books that had led us astray. There were more rules for women— how we could dress and how we were to speak to the men.

"Jesus, Shiloh. That sounds…"

"Like a cult?" she asked, turning her head to stare at him.

The light was gone from her eyes, and dark and stormy clouds filled their debts.

"Yeah," he nodded. Afraid of offending her, he waited, but she offered a rueful chuckle.

"I now realize that's what was happening. But at the time, those of us who stayed in the community did what he asked because we were desperate to make sure we were living the way we were supposed to. Anything to atone for the deaths we thought we might have caused."

He searched his mind, thinking of other cults he'd read about. Unable to imagine what life must have been like for her, he grimaced.

"I really should get back," she said suddenly, starting to push up from the blanket.

"Wait, please don't. I really want to hear more."

"I don't think so. You say you do, but Joseph, the look on your face shows you were disgusted, and I can't blame you."

Realizing she'd mistaken his grimace as against her, he shook his head, his hands holding on to hers. "No, no, I'm not disgusted with you. I'm horrified for you. I'm disgusted with a man who would abuse what power he thought he had."

"Make no mistake. He had power," she assured.

For a moment, he held his breath as she seemed to waver between the desire to stand and leave or sit down and stay. She looked out over the beach, then surprised him when she asked, "Can we walk on the pier?"

Breathing easier as he jumped up, he folded the thin blanket and draped it over one arm, reaching out with the other to hold her hand. Glad when she didn't pull away, they walked to the pier and made their way along the wooden planks until they came to a bench that overlooked the bay. No one else was around, and they sat next to each other, his arm now around her shoulders again, tucking her in close. "So you were talking about Isaiah…" he prodded.

"Yes… his power. He had several other men who followed him everywhere, doling out punishments for transgressions."

"Fuck," he breathed, unable to keep the curse from his lips. Then focusing on something she'd said, he asked, "So not everyone stayed?"

Shaking her head, she sighed. "Some left. Those who had family elsewhere. Or those who were newer to our community. But for those of us who had land, who'd been raised there, we had nowhere else to go."

"And your husband?" He held his breath, searching her face for clues in her eyes. He couldn't deny that he was curious about this man who had Shiloh during that time in her life. The man who both helped her raise Rachel and with her grief but also allowed his wife to live under those circumstances. He felt torn between admiration for him, anger at him, and, surprisingly, a dose of jealousy toward him.

18

She lifted her gaze to his, a slight curve to her lips as she thought of Edward. Offering a little sigh, she wondered how to put into words what he was like.

"He was a good man." As soon as the words left her mouth, she realized how often she'd used those words to describe Edward, yet now she could hear how they didn't begin to encompass their relationship. Sighing, she shook her head. "He was so much more. He was calm, quiet, reserved, patient, didn't speak much unless he really had something to say."

Joseph's expression fell. "He sounds like the opposite of me."

She could swear there was a dejected tone to his words and immediately rushed to assure, "Only in manner, but not in integrity." Squeezing his hand, she said, "You and he shared the same sense of duty and honor. Sometimes I wish that he'd been more able to express the outrage I knew he felt at times. I find myself thinking that you would never have allowed Isaiah to rule our lives."

"Damn straight," he bit out, rubbing his thumb along her hand.

"It's hard to explain, but he... he rebelled in his own way." Seeing the puzzled expression on Joseph's face, she sighed, struggling to explain. "We didn't take our books to be destroyed. He hid them in the house, and when we were alone, we would take them out and read. We provided a portion of our crops to the community because that felt right to do even without the edict, but Edward secretly worked with a man in the next county to rent some of our farmland without telling Isaiah so that I'd be provided for in case something happened to him. He also had doubts about Isaiah but felt it was safer to only talk about those things with me."

She looked away for a moment, her memories of gentle Edward always in her heart. "We followed the edicts because..." Her voice halted as she sucked in a shaky breath. "Because there was a chance that Isaiah would take Rachel from us if he deemed us unworthy."

"Holy shit! You've got to be kidding me!"

"We were willing to do anything to make sure that didn't happen. Our livelihood was there with the farm, and as long as Edward was my husband, I would stay there, too. But then he was killed in a farm accident."

Joseph seemed no longer willing just to sit close and hold her hand. He twisted around and then pulled her to him, his arms wrapped around her. "I can't imagine your loss. I'm just reeling at everything you're telling me."

She melted in his embrace, the feel of his arms and the steady beat of his heart offering his strength that she welcomed, not remembering the last time she felt so safe. They sat in silence, the town beachgoers out to enjoy the sunset seeming far away.

After a long moment, he whispered against her hair, "So you just left and came here?"

She shook her head, loving the way her cheek moved against his chest. "No. Not right away. There was… were complications."

He shifted her back slightly so he could stare into her face. She loved seeing his eyes, but right now, she felt exposed. Talking to him was like walking on a tightrope—too much, and she was afraid of exposing things she shouldn't know. Seeing his furrowed brow, she reached up and gently ran her finger over the crinkle, loving the feel of his skin underneath her fingertip.

"I had Rachel and the farm. I had nowhere to go. I needed a plan. You see, for a year, I was expected to wear widow's black and stay mostly to myself in mourning. So I spent that year putting things in place while I was safe."

"What would happen at the end of the year that would make you unsafe?"

Licking her lips, she dragged in another shaky breath. "At the end of the year, I could be forced to take a husband of Isaiah's choosing—"

"Damnit!"

She jumped, and he rushed, "Sorry. I know I shouldn't curse around you, but everything you're saying is making me want to punch the shit out of this guy!"

A giggle slipped out, and she blinked in surprise as the sound erupted from deep inside her. Even in the middle of diverging her strange tale, he'd managed to lighten her burden. Covering her mouth to hide the smile, she stared wide-eyed at him. "Believe me, my father could curse a blue streak when he was angry."

"Guess I'm not much like Edward after all, am I?"

"Oh, Joseph, maybe not, but that just makes me like you so much!"

With those words, he grinned widely, holding her close. "You like me?"

"Oh, you know I do. It seems like all women like you, and you like them, too."

He winced and shook his head. "No… it's just that I haven't found anyone I wanted to commit to in a long time, so it's easier to play the flirt. Kind of a self-protection thing, I guess."

Observing him, she knew it must be hard for him to show vulnerability. "You said *in a long time*. Did you have someone once?"

"A very long time ago, but that's a story for another night."

"But I've done all the sharing," she said. "It's like I've just dropped everything down onto you."

"Shiloh, I wanted to know. And everything you've told me just makes me like you more, as well."

His words moved through her, warming her heart. There was so much more, but she couldn't speak her fears aloud. At least not now. But being with Joseph was filling her with a hope she hadn't had in years.

He asked no more questions as though knowing she was exhausted and at the end of what she could share.

The sun was setting behind them, and they appeared to be bathed in a golden glow. Sitting this close, she could see the reflection of the blue water in his eyes. Mesmerized, she stared, then dropped her gaze to his lips. Lifting her gaze back to his, she could tell he was staring at her mouth, as well.

Just as the words of her story had been released earlier, she no longer felt chained to the past. Not wanting the moment to pass and fall into the category of *I wish I had*, she suddenly grabbed the back of his neck and erased the distance between them. Twisting her head at the last second so their noses wouldn't bump, her mouth landed on his.

Edward was the only man she'd ever kissed, finding kissing to be a sweet way to show she cared for him. But as soon as her lips met with Joseph's, the electricity crackled between them, and for a second, she wondered if lightning had struck over the bay.

Before she could pull back to end the kiss, he gripped her back as one hand slid around to cup her cheek, taking over the kiss. His tongue slid along her mouth, tracing the curves of her lips, and her core tightened, sending shivers outward. She gasped, and his tongue took advantage, plunging inside to glide over hers. The velvet touch electrified her nerves, and her whole body felt alive. This was nothing like kissing Edward.

He pulled her tighter, shifting her so that she was on his lap. Her breasts were crushed against his chest, and she could feel his erection against her stomach. Uncertain she could catch her breath, she was equally uncertain that she cared. If she was going to drown, she wanted to drown in his embrace with his lips on hers.

Holy Fuck... If Joseph was dreaming, he never wanted to wake. He'd held her gaze as the sun set over the water, her face illuminated by the brilliant colors streaking across the sky. He'd stared at her lips, wanting to kiss her more than any other woman he'd ever been with. More than his next breath.

And after the initial shock when she crushed against him, her lips finding his, he took over the kiss, giving her everything he could as the electric current ran between them. Feeling the jolts throughout his body, his cock responded, but he tamped down that reaction, wanting to just focus on their kiss connection.

She had been married, but it seemed she'd never been kissed the way a woman should be kissed. Her closed-mouth kiss was warm but uncertain. When his tongue first touched her lips, she stiffened as though surprised even though she allowed his tongue entrance. Forcing his actions to slow, he dragged his tongue over hers, swallowing her little moans and encouraging her tongue to tangle with his.

He pulled her body close, wanting to feel every inch and allowing her to feel how affected he was by the kiss.

Slowly reason prevailed, and he pulled back, loving the tiny kitten-mewl sound of protest that came from her just before she blinked her eyes open.

Her clear blue-gray eyes reflected the light, and he thanked God he observed no regret in them.

"Oh…" she breathed, just before her cheeks pinkened.

Sweeping his thumb over her warm, petal-soft cheek, he grinned. "I've wanted to kiss you for a long time."

"Why?" she whispered, her gaze never leaving his.

It was on the tip of his tongue to say it was because she was beautiful, but he held those words back. They seemed trite… superficial. Swallowing deeply, he hesitated. Giving voice to his reasons was difficult after not wanting to show any vulnerability. But, if there was one thing he was sure of, it was that Shiloh deserved nothing but honesty.

"Because of your eyes. Because when I looked inside, it was as though I could see the sunshine and the storm, and I instinctively felt that you had come through a lot of storms." He shrugged and added, "And I wanted you to have more sunshine. And I wanted to be the one to give you that. At first, I just knew you were beautiful on the outside, but I desperately wanted to get to know you. Really know you. And everything I've learned has only made me want to be with you more."

"Oh…" She let out a long breath before her lips curved gently. "I've never heard anything sweeter in my whole life. I've never had anyone say anything so beautiful to me."

He wanted to ask about Edward, but the time wasn't right. The last thing he wanted to do was bring up any more memories. This time and this night were for them.

"I hate for this to come to an end, but I really should get back to the inn."

He nodded and smiled. Leaning forward so that his forehead touched hers, he said, "I want to see you again, Shiloh. As often as possible, as much as possible."

Her top teeth landed on her bottom lip, and she nodded. "I want that, too. Although, I can't imagine that being with me is very exciting."

"Just being around you is the best time I've had. I know there's more to your story, and there's more to mine. But we've got time to learn about each other."

"I'd like that. And I'd like more kissing," she laughed.

"Oh, yeah!" he laughed. "Definitely more kissing."

Gently placing her feet onto the wooden planks of the pier, he stood and took her hand. Linking fingers was such a simple act, yet, he hadn't walked with a woman like that in years. They made their way over the sand and then the dune, crossing the street in front of the inn. He didn't want to let go of her hand, but now that they were in view of others on the street, he wanted her to be comfortable. But when she continued to walk with her hand in his with their fingers linked, he couldn't remember the last time he'd ever been so proud to be with a woman.

Walking up the steps, they stopped outside the large wooden door at the end. Handing control over to her, he waited.

And in typical Shiloh fashion, she played no games.

Lifting on her toes, she placed her hands on his shoulders and offered a gentle goodbye kiss. He kept it G-rated, but loved the public declaration she was giving.

She turned, and with her hand on the doorknob, she stopped and looked over her shoulder, her intense gaze holding his. "Joseph?"

"Yeah?"

"I think you're wonderful. Thank you." With that, she slipped inside and closed the door.

He stood, staring at the door for a moment before turning to jog down the front steps and walking to his SUV parked on the street. On the outside, he looked the same. He has a bit of a swagger in his walk. A smile on his face. A twinkle in his eye. But inside, he was changed. Somehow that powerful and brave woman had settled deep inside, giving him a chance. He wished he could take away the storms she'd been through. He wished he could take away the pain and grief she'd suffered. And while he knew there was more for her to tell, he already knew that if given a chance, he'd slay her dragons. Especially one named Isaiah.

19

"So I happened to be on the beach last night with Sophie."

Joseph looked over at a grinning Callan, then shook his head.

Callan kept talking. "And you were walking on the beach holding hands with someone."

"I heard it was with the pretty Shiloh that he was holding hands with. And was also seen kissing her on the front porch of the inn," Jarod threw out.

"Okay, you two. You're worse than a bunch of gossiping teenage girls."

"You've got to admit that's news," Callan said. "You're not exactly known for walking around holding hands with someone."

Knowing they wouldn't shut up, he stood and crossed his arms over his chest. "I would say I don't kiss and tell, but yes, it's true. I was out with Shiloh last night."

"Good for you!" Callan said, clapping him on the shoulder. "I'm happy for you, man."

Shaking his head, Jarod said, "And here I thought you'd be my wingman for a long time. She must be something else."

"What she is, is…" he faltered, suddenly unable to describe her in a way that would make sense to someone who didn't know her story.

Callan held his gaze. "Sophie met her at one of Tori's get-togethers. While she doesn't know anything in particular, she said that Shiloh has had it rough."

"She lost her parents, and sister and brother-in-law, who were Rachel's parents, all at the same time in an accident."

"Damn," Jarod added, his expression tight.

"There are other things she's been through, but I'm just learning more about her and won't betray any confidences. But suffice it to say, she really is amazing."

"Then I can't think of a better man for her to be with," Callan said. "Sounds like she needed a hero."

A call came over the radio, taking their attention, but as they pulled out onto the bay, all he could think of was that he wanted to be her hero.

The callout was routine, checking fishing boats to make sure their catches were legal and they had the proper fishing licenses. He never minded the more mundane tasks, enjoying the chance to chat with some of the local fishermen, some he'd known since he was a boy. Many people made their living on the waters of the Chesapeake Bay, but the ecosystem was a delicate balance.

He and his fellow officers were charged with enforcing marine fisheries and habitat conservation laws and regulations, as well as laws pertaining to harvesting seafood from condemned areas. Considering the Chesapeake Bay is the country's largest estuary providing over five hundred million pounds of seafood a year, he and his fellow officers took their duties seriously.

Today was a good day, though. All the fishermen they met were supposed to be there, fishing in the areas allowed and only taking in what they were supposed to. Besides that, he had the opportunity to chat with a number of them, some almost as old as his grandfather. Still, he enjoyed seeing their sons and grandsons fishing alongside them.

On their way back to the harbor, he stood on the deck with the wind blowing his hair, the salty water spray sending a mist over his face. He'd always loved being on a boat, finding it easy to think with the expanse of water before him where the horizon met the sky. Now, he continued to ponder more of what he'd thought about the night before when lying in bed after he left Shiloh. *Isaiah. Cults. How alone she must have felt after her husband died.*

And while he wouldn't give voice to his questions about her husband to her, he wondered about the man who'd only secretly rebelled. Joseph couldn't imagine not grabbing Shiloh and Rachel and taking them far away from that place.

He was also curious about her marriage relationship after he kissed her. While he had never cared about a woman's past, he wanted to know everything about her and prayed he'd have the chance to find out.

Once they were back at the station, he was ready to head to the Seafood Shack, knowing Shiloh was there. Still, an emergency callout had them scrambling to prepare the boat to turn back around and follow Ryan and Andy into the bay.

By the time he'd made it to the end of his shift, he had managed to get a quick call off to Shiloh. He'd wanted to stop by, but she was busy with late-arriving inn guests. Promising to talk tomorrow, he disconnected. After eating dinner, he sat in his living room, listening to the rain outside. Glancing over at his laptop, he grabbed it and began searching for information on cults. He was curious about what Shiloh and Rachel had been forced to deal with.

With little to go on, he started his search with communes in the 1800s, finding several in Pennsylvania with either their beginnings based on religious beliefs or utopian society. Knowing nothing about the subject, he was soon immersed in the rabbit holes of research, discovering the differences between communes and the various types of cults.

As his head began to spin, he narrowed his focus to Plineyville. This small community was in the mountains and originated in the late-1800s by a man named Horrace Pliney. It started as a community of like-minded people looking for a peaceful, contemplative place to live after the Civil War, desiring to share responsibilities and property. By the mid-1900s, it had become a place where the modern world crept in. The community was no longer a commune in that the members could own their land, buy and purchase what they wanted, and come and go as they pleased. While they lost members, others came to enjoy a more contemplative life.

Leaning his head against the sofa, Joseph closed his eyes for a moment, trying to imagine Shiloh growing up there. She'd mentioned her father had returned from Desert Storm and wanted to get away from society, looking for a place of peace to raise his family. *Did he find what he was looking for? It sounds like he did. At least Shiloh recalls good memories of her childhood.*

Continuing to dig, he found a short newspaper article from a nearby town on the deaths of her family and pastor.

The pastor of the Plineyville church was killed, along with two other couples traveling to Sullivan County for a meeting on various communities and their needs. The pastor was being interviewed on the Plineyville community's history and development.

The single-vehicle accident resulted in the van plunging over the edge of the mountain road, killing Pastor Aaron Tolson, Carl Smithers, his wife, Karen Smithers, their daughter, Rebecca Ayers, and her husband, Thomas Ayers. Local Sheriff Matthew Bundy said it was the worst accident he'd witnessed in his career. All five were pronounced dead on arrival at the local hospital.

That was it. That was all he could find. Swiping his hand over his face, Joseph sighed. Death always seems so distant when reading it in the news—the type of thing that happens to others. But knowing he was reading of Shiloh's family, his gut clenched.

Turning his attention to cults, he wasn't surprised to see that they ran the gamut from being similar to the utopian communes or like-minded religious ideologies or because their desires weren't found through other cultural, economic, or social communities. He continued to read with wide-eyed disgust at the ones where sexual, emotional, or physical abuse was rampant. All in all, the authorities seemed to agree on one thing—the leader. The essential characteristic of a cult leader is their claim to exclusive access to knowledge, and they dispense power and punishment as they deem proper. Thinking of what she'd said about Isaiah's strong-arm tactics and his minions who enforced and punished, he had no doubt that what Shiloh escaped from was a dangerous, leader-influenced cult.

And if I ever get my hands on him...

By the end of the week, it seemed as though everyone knew he was seeing Shiloh. He'd been surprised it had taken his mom two days before she called, insisting he bring Shiloh and Rachel for dinner. Now, he knew how Wyatt must have felt when word got out about him and Millie and remembered giving Wyatt a hard time. He knew payback was a bitch, but he'd gladly put up with it to provide Shiloh and Rachel with another family to rely on.

Now, he walked into the kitchen of the inn after

Rachel invited him inside. He looked at the smiling teen dressed in shorts that came to mid-thigh and a cute T-shirt. Her long hair was curling around her shoulders, and a pair of sunglasses perched on her head. Glad to see that she appeared happy with her new life in Baytown, he greeted, "Hey, Rachel."

"Hi, Joseph! I'm so excited that we're going to dinner tonight." She bounced up and down on her toes, then stopped and looked to the side, crinkling her nose. Bringing her gaze back to him, she added, "Although, if you want to go to dinner with just Shiloh, that's fine with me!"

After asking Shiloh to dinner, he'd altered the invitation to include Rachel. "No way. It's true I like being with Shiloh, but I wanna get to know you, as well."

"Yeah, but I don't want to get in the way." She dropped her gaze as her hands clasped together.

He stepped closer and lifted her chin with his forefinger. "Rachel?" Waiting until her gaze hit him, he continued. "You're not in the way. You're part of Shiloh, and that means if I'm gonna be part of her life, I'm gonna be part of your life, too. And one thing I want you to understand... you never have to lower your eyes around me. No matter what we're talking about, or even if we disagree on something... you keep your eyes on me. You will always be safe with me." A light came back into her blue-gray eyes that reminded him so much of Shiloh's. "So we're going to have a good dinner, right?"

"Right!" She beamed, her cheeks pinkening. "I just

knew you liked her! I'm so glad. If anyone deserves to be happy, it's my aunt."

"I think she'd say the same about you," he said. "I think both of you deserve to be happy."

"I loved Uncle Edward, but I like living in Baytown so much more." She sighed and shook her head. "I know it sounds weird, but we would still be there if he were still living."

Her quicksilver conversation change nearly gave him whiplash, and he now wondered how Ryan dealt with his teenage daughter. Wanting to tread carefully, he wished Shiloh would make her appearance, but it seemed up to him to reply. "I know it's hard sometimes to figure out how we're supposed to feel about things," he admitted, nervous about being on such an emotional subject so early in his relationship with her. "From what your aunt has said, your lives were not happy for the last year. So however it had to come about, I'm glad you're both here now."

She pressed her lips together for a few seconds, then said, "She told me that she explained about the village we came from. It wasn't a nice place, Joseph. I mean, it was when I was younger. But then... it wasn't... well, after... it wasn't good at all." She winced and sighed.

"I'm sorry, Rachel," he said, his heart aching for the young woman who'd had to deal with so much change.

She nodded, her face now shyly hopeful. "If you and Aunt Shiloh stay together, will that make you my uncle, too?"

He blinked at her change in conversations again, uncertain how to answer but not unsure of the feeling moving through him. "Your aunt and I are just getting to know each other, so it's too early to put a label on what we'll become. So for now, let's just say I'm lucky to get to know you, too."

She grinned and nodded.

Shiloh stepped into the room, and his gaze shot to her, his breath halting as he tried to pick his jaw up off the floor. She was wearing a small amount of makeup, just enough to softly highlight her eye color and long lashes, a touch of blush on her cheeks, and a swipe of shine on her perfect lips. Her hair was waving down her back, and her body was draped in a simple green dress that fit her curves. It flared over her hips and swirled to her knees. And on her feet were sandals with short heels. Simple. Easy. Elegant. And utterly gorgeous.

She smiled gently and moved directly to him, lifting slightly to offer a kiss. Not a man to turn her down, he banded his arms around her and kissed her, holding back since Rachel was present but making sure Shiloh knew just how glad he was to see her. She blushed, shooting a glance toward Rachel as her heels settled back to the floor.

"Wow," Rachel blinked as she turned to get her purse, grinning widely. "That's the kind of kiss I saw in a movie Cindy and I watched."

Shiloh blushed even more but smiled as she also grabbed her purse.

"Okay, ladies, let's do dinner!" After assisting Rachel into the back seat, he made sure Shiloh was buckled before heading around the hood and climbing behind the wheel.

She turned to him with a wide grin on her face. "I need to ask you a favor, but you can say no if you want—"

"What is it?"

"Well, it has to do with what I'm doing tomorrow?"

He waited, knowing whatever it was, she was bursting to tell him.

"I'm taking my first driving lesson!"

He blinked, his chin jerking back slightly. "Driving? Like a car?"

Rachel laughed from the back seat. "Yes! Isn't that great? Then she can drive me around, and in a couple of years, I can learn to drive, too!"

Shiloh nodded. "I had a driver's license when I was a teenager, although I rarely drove our vehicle, which was a farm truck. It's been years since I was... well, since I could drive. And I want a refresher course before getting my Virginia license."

"So... what's the favor?" he asked, pulling out onto the road for the short drive to the Sunset Restaurant.

"Well, I'll need to purchase a car. I just want something small and not new, but I want you to go with me when I choose."

He looked over at her nervous yet hopeful expression and wanted to kiss the nervousness right off her face. "Yeah, Shiloh, I'll be honored to go with you. In fact, I think it's a smart idea. Salespeople can be pushy and might take advantage of someone new to the process. I'll stay in the background and only be there if you need." The idea of anyone taking advantage of her brought out the protector in him, but he wanted her to feel empowered.

Soon they were ensconced at a corner table in the upscale restaurant with a view of the sunset slowly descending over the water. Rachel's eyes were wide, and she could barely contain her excitement as she asked Joseph about each item on the menu. Shiloh smiled indulgently at her niece.

"I remember traveling with my parents to a restaurant for my mom's birthday each year. We would go to the closest town where there was a little seafood place, and I'd always get the shrimp each year. I used to think that was the best meal in the world."

The faraway smile on her face reached deep inside him, wrapping around his heart. He wanted to give her the chance to discover everything that had been taken away from her. He held her hand and moved closer, gaining her smile now on him. "Then I want you to order whatever you'd like to eat. This will just be the first of many meals together." Looking at Rachel, he nodded. "You, too. Eat until you're stuffed!"

Several people he knew stopped by the table to meet Shiloh and Rachel as their meal progressed. By the time the girls were digging into dessert, he'd leaned back to sip his coffee, his arm over the back of Shiloh with his fingers gently tracing along her shoulder. Rachel was beaming and talking about things happening at school, making Shiloh and him laugh with her stories.

And he was struck with the normalcy of the evening. He'd never experienced this before, and now that he had, he wanted to keep it. He'd told Rachel that he and Shiloh were new, and that was true. But she turned to look at him with the light shining in the depths of her eyes, and what now slammed into him, causing him to rub his chest to ease the twinge in his heart, was that he wanted them in his life forever. *How could I have fallen so hard, so fast?* He didn't have an answer. He just knew what he felt. And now was no longer afraid of what came next.

"So we need to make our plans for this weekend," he said, drawing their attention. "My parents want you two to come to dinner."

Finding both pairs of identical eyes widening as they turned to him, he almost laughed at the difference. Shiloh's expression was one of surprise and maybe tinged with a bit of hope, while Rachel's was pure joy. Both were looks he loved.

20

Rachel couldn't wait for the bell to ring, signaling the end of the school day. Especially since it was Tuesday, and the science club had their meetings. She gathered her books and walked out of the classroom with the other students, and turned toward her locker. Butterflies started in her stomach the closer she got. She'd once asked Shiloh how she would know when she met the right man. Shiloh had told her that she'd always imagined she'd get butterflies in her stomach. She never asked her aunt if she'd gotten butterflies with Uncle Edward. Even though they talked about almost everything, that seemed too personal. Maybe even too painful now that he was gone. But she could tell that Shiloh definitely felt something when she was around Joseph.

She almost stumbled as she approached her locker and saw Jack waiting there for her as he did each day. *Yep... butterflies.*

Whenever Shiloh asked how she was getting along at school, she could honestly tell her that it was fine. Sure, it had been a shock to see how large the high school was, but she immediately noticed that the school was filled with all types— poor and rich and those in the middle. Those with the best clothes and those whose clothes looked a little more worn. Sons and daughters of fishermen, farmers, bankers, and shopkeepers. There were cliques, groups that had been friends for a long time, and others that were newcomers like herself. In truth, she hadn't found it very difficult to settle in, probably a large part because she already had Cindy and Jack as friends before school started.

She smiled as Jack's face broke into a wide grin when she walked to her locker. She put away her books, only keeping out what she needed for homework that night. They walked together to the science wing, and she liked how his hand would occasionally move in front to ensure someone in the crowded hall didn't bump into her.

Once at the room, they were surprised to see one of the assistant principals waving his hands. "Sorry, everyone, but Mr. Martin had to go home right after school. Unfortunately, we didn't realize that there was no one here for the science club. Does everyone have a way home?"

As others nodded, she sighed. "I'll need to hang around until the late activity bus picks us up."

"I can call my mom," Jack said. "She can take you home, too." He pulled out his phone and, after a quick conversation, shoved his phone back into his pocket. "Mom is coming, but she's not real close. We can just wait near the parking lot."

She loved the idea of having more time with him and nodded enthusiastically.

Walking down the now-empty hall, someone came barreling around the corner and shoved Jack into the lockers.

Jack regained his balance quickly, "What the—"

"Shut up, shithead!"

Rachel gasped, seeing Paul and one of his friends standing there, glowering. Jack grabbed her hand and pulled her behind him before letting go, shielding her with his body.

"Move on, Paul."

"It's a free country. I can go wherever I want."

"What the hell is your problem?"

"Right now, you, shithead. Because y'all made that fuckin' call, I got a date in juvenile court."

"That's not my fault. Whatever you did, it's on you."

Paul sneered, fisting his hands on his hips. "I'll let you know right now, my dad said on the first offense, I'll get off easy. And when I do, I'll come looking for you."

A whimper slipped from Rachel's lips, fear squeezing her gut in a way that she hadn't felt since she and Shiloh had left Isaiah behind.

Her sound was not missed by the others, and Paul's gaze moved from Jack to her, and a grin spread across his face. "And after I take care of you, shithead, I might just have some fun with her."

Jack stepped forward, his fists clenched, but her hand snapped out, and her fingers closed around the back of his shirt. He stopped, but she could feel the tension rolling off him.

Paul snorted, then turned, throwing his middle finger up as he walked away, shouting over his shoulder, "Later, shithead."

Rachel stood, her fingers still clutching Jack's shirt, feeling his body vibrating with anger. Finally, he let out a low breath and turned, causing her fingers to lose their grip on his shirt. He reached out and linked his hand with hers.

"I'm sorry," she said, still shaking. "I just didn't want you to get hurt."

"Sometimes, the trouble is worth it. I can take it if he says things about me, but I'm not going to stand by and let him threaten you."

Her mind was caught on his words, thinking it was one of the nicest things she'd heard. Before she had a chance to let him know that, he twisted his head, glaring through the window as Paul climbed into a pickup truck and gunned it out of the parking lot.

"Christ, it sucks not being able to shut him up."

She looked at him, not understanding what he meant. Jack was already almost taller than her, and while Paul was bigger, Jack was not small by any stretch of the imagination. In fact, he was bigger than many of the ninth-grade boys. But not knowing what to say, she kept her mouth shut, just glad he continued to hold her hand as they walked toward a low wall near the end of the parking lot. She loved the feel of his palm against hers, and the butterflies flitted once again in her stomach.

Sitting, he sighed heavily. "If I was Colt, I wouldn't have to put up with someone like him."

She was silent for a moment, then asked, "Why do you call him Colt?"

He glanced at her, and something passed through his eyes, but she couldn't tell what it was. "Colt isn't my real dad."

Shocked, she wasn't sure what to say, but squeezing his hand, she hoped she conveyed that he could tell her anything.

"My real dad didn't want me. Turns out he got my mom pregnant, but she wasn't from money, so he didn't want her to even have me."

A stabbing pain hit her heart. *How could anyone not want him?* "Oh, I'm so sorry. But you know what? That makes your mom so brave."

He swung his head around and stared at her for a long moment before his lips curved. "Yeah, my mom is pretty badass."

She thought for a moment about his mom compared to herself. "I wish I was."

"Huh?"

"Then I wouldn't be so afraid. I could stand up to someone like… well, like Paul."

"I like you just the way you are," he said, gently bumping her shoulder.

She smiled, the butterflies in her stomach taking flight again. "How long have your mom and Colt been together?"

"About three years. We've known him for a while since he was the sheriff." Jack grinned. "I think he had a thing for my mom for a long time before he finally let her know."

"Did your mom have a thing for him, too?"

Chuckling, he nodded. "Yeah, I think so."

"Then you're very lucky. You not only have a mom that would do anything for you, but you have a man like the sheriff who wants to be your dad."

He grinned even wider. "You're right. Thanks."

Rachel loved this time with Jack. Time when it was just the two of them. He never made her feel self-conscious. She would see other couples in high school kissing, making out, all over each other. And as much as she liked him, she knew that wasn't what she was ready for. But she could dream, thinking of the future. She smiled, wanting him to feel good, even as a touch of sadness wormed its way through her.

He stared at her for a long moment, seeming to look straight into her. "Can I ask how you came to live with your aunt Shiloh?"

She hesitated, wondering if he would think she was weird when he learned more about her. He turned his hand upward and spread his fingers, linking with hers. She stared for a moment at the simple connection, and as the butterflies took flight, she felt as though she could tell him anything.

"Do you remember that I said I was from Pennsylvania?"

He nodded, squeezing her fingers. "I remember everything you've told me, Rachel."

She smiled, feeling encouraged and emboldened. Sucking in a deep breath, she plunged ahead. "I lived with my mom and dad, next door to my grandparents, and just down the road from Shiloh and her husband." She grew quiet, wondering how to explain to someone that her entire life had changed overnight. Thinking it might be like a Band-Aid and best ripped off quickly, she blurted, "There was a car accident, and my parents and grandparents were killed."

Jack squeezed her fingers quickly, his brows lowering as he searched her face. "Damn, Rachel! I'm so sorry!"

Time had undoubtedly eased her grief, but she wasn't sure that the Band-Aid procedure had been the right way to explain what had happened. She chewed on her bottom lip. "You're the first person besides Cindy I've ever told that to."

He blinked, his head jerking slightly. "Really?"

"Yeah. Everyone in our little community already knew. Our pastor was also killed, so everyone was grieving, although it was worse for Shiloh and me."

"And that's when she became your guardian?"

"Yes, she and her husband, Edward. I was about nine years old when they became my parents."

Jack's thumb rubbed over her knuckles. "I was eleven when mom got together with Colt. The same age that I met my dad for the first time."

She gasped. "Jack, I'm so sorry. As hard as it is to lose both parents, at least I had nine years with them raising me and loving me."

They were quiet for another moment, each lost in their thoughts, before he asked, "How come you and Shiloh left?"

"Uncle Edward died in a farm accident, leaving just Shiloh and me. We had a new community leader, and he wasn't very nice. We didn't feel like it was a place we wanted to stay anymore, so we left and came here."

He tilted his head to the side. "But why here?"

She offered a shy grin. "Shiloh saw an article about Baytown and the Chesapeake Bay in a little magazine. The article mentioned the Sea Glass Inn. So she decided to write to the owner to find out more about this place. They sent letters back and forth, and then Mrs. Evans offered Shiloh a job if she decided to come." Shrugging, she concluded, "So we came."

Jack nodded and smiled. "I'm glad you did."

She breathed a sigh of relief, smiling as the butterflies flitted again. "Me, too." Just then, an SUV pulled into the school parking lot, and she recognized Jack's mom. Thinking of what he'd said about his mom and the sheriff, she suddenly asked, "Jack? Do you think that my aunt and Joseph will get together?"

They stood, and he looked down, his hand still linked with hers. Holding her gaze, he asked, "Do you want them to?"

Nodding, she grinned widely. "Oh, yeah. If anyone deserves to be happy, it's Shiloh."

"Then that'd be cool if they do," he replied, holding open the door for her.

She greeted his mom and settled into the seat. Grinning, she hoped Joseph stayed with Shiloh and maybe, Jack would want to spend more time with her, also.

21

Shiloh had worried about Rachel's emotional and social adjustment, but it seemed her intrepid niece was a bloom-where-I'm-planted young woman. Rachel was doing well in ninth grade and having the popular Coates siblings as friends seemed to have made her transition smoother. Shiloh kept in contact with the teachers, but they all assured her that Rachel was an excellent student, on par with the rest of her grade level while being advanced in English.

Lying in bed chatting, she'd listened to Rachel talk about her classes and new friends. Rolling over to face Rachel, she asked, "Do you feel like you fit in?"

Rachel was quiet for a moment. "You mean considering where we came from."

"Yes, sweetie. I know starting a new high school for anyone would be difficult. Still, considering what you were used to, I've prayed that you would be able to make the adjustment."

"Do you think I have?"

"From what I can see and what you've said, yes. But I suppose I need to hear it from you."

Rachel sat up in bed, her knees bent with her arms wrapped around her shins. "I was scared all the time before we left. And then I was scared about coming here. I was afraid I wouldn't have any friends or that the school would be too big, or everyone would look at me like I was some kind of freak."

Shiloh sat up, mimicked Rachel's posture, and focused her attention on what her niece was divulging.

"But high school has all kinds of kids. There are some who dress kind of weird on purpose just because they like being different or they like their style. Some girls spend a lot on their clothes, hair, and makeup, but no one thinks it's weird if I don't. And there are cliques, but then kids can move between groups."

She breathed a sigh of relief. "I'm glad you feel like you fit in, sweetie."

"When others ask where I came from, I just say Pennsylvania and leave it at that. But I've told Cindy and Jack a little more. They know about my parents and grandma and grandpa. They know why I live with you. They also know I was homeschooled for the past year, and I told them that I went to a very small school before that. So far, no one has acted like they thought my situation was weird."

"That's absolutely right," Shiloh said. She and Rachel had talked about what they would tell people, and she was thrilled that Rachel was comfortable enough to be able to speak to others. "And Isaiah?"

Rachel shook her head. "No, I've said nothing about

him. I told Cindy and Jack that we had a community leader who was not very nice, so we decided to move somewhere else."

A snort erupted from Shiloh. "You certainly didn't lie about that! In fact, I think that was a perfect way to describe it."

After another moment, Shiloh said, "I'm so proud of you, Rachel. I can't imagine another young person going through what you've been through and having such a positive outlook and fitting in so well with this very different and new environment. Rebecca would be so… well, both your parents and grandparents would be so proud."

Rachel tossed back her covers and jumped from her bed, dashing over to Shiloh, who barely had time to hold up her blanket so that Rachel could slide next to her. The two hugged tightly.

"Oh, I love you," Rachel enthused, her eyes shining in the moonlight. "But you have to know, Shiloh, that I am who I am because of you."

Her chest squeezed, and she battled back tears. Holding her niece tightly, they fell asleep side by side.

Life couldn't get any better. Shiloh was sure of it. But then, she knew how fast circumstances could change and a good life could become tragic in the blink of an eye. But determined to put the past behind her, keeping her good memories and burying the bad ones, she threw herself into her new surroundings.

Over the weeks, she, Rachel, and Joseph had developed a routine. Each weekday morning, she made sure Rachel got off to school, then fixed breakfast for the guests in the inn. Three days a week, she walked over to the Seafood Shack to work the lunch crowd for a few hours, seeing Joseph when he managed to stop by for lunch. She'd then return to the inn to finish cleaning or wash the linens. By the time Rachel got home from school, she had helped with homework, fixed dinner for them, and on most days, Joseph joined them if his shift allowed.

On days when she didn't work at the restaurant, she would visit the library, stop by the church to chat with Pastor Parton, or catch up with her new friends for coffee, lunch, or a planning meeting with the AL Auxiliary, having joined right after meeting Sherrie.

And weekends were spent at the ballpark where she now volunteered in the Auxiliary concession stand, trips with Joseph where he showed off the glories of the Eastern Shore to her and Rachel, and date nights where just the two of them went out, talking, sharing, stealing kisses, and making out. She could tell he was going slow with her, but with the way he made her feel, she wanted more.

Her body burned with desires she'd never felt with Edward, but that no longer made her feel guilty. Instead, she craved Joseph's kisses and the feel of his fingertips as they glided over her skin when he'd slip his hand under the hem of her shirt or along her leg. Each day she wanted more, but they had little time alone.

Now, walking into the Seafood Shack for her shift,

she foresaw her good mood taking a dive when Vicki, who usually worked just nights, was at the bar. Vicki's eyes narrowed as she spied Shiloh walk out of the manager's office after checking in.

"Well, if it isn't Little Miss Innocent thinking she can hold on to a man with her act," Vicki sneered.

Lifting her chin, she held Vicki's gaze. Keeping her voice strong and steady, she greeted, "Hello, Vicki."

Vicki jerked slightly, surprise on her face. Recovering, she leaned in and continued. "How you think a man like Joseph could ever be satisfied with you, I'll never know. He'll dump you as soon as he's had a taste, and believe me, he's not a man who keeps coming back."

"Funny… he's still around, so he must have found something he likes," she retorted. Then waving her hand dismissively, she turned to walk away. "But then I refuse to talk about him. Go serve your customers. That topic is off the menu."

"Just remember, I've had him and can have him again with a snap of my fingers," Vicki called out.

Shiloh inwardly winced at the words. It was one thing to accept that both she and Joseph had pasts before they came together, but another to have it thrown in her face how casual his relationships had been.

"Shut up, Vicki," Jules called out from the bar. "You're doing nothing but look like a fool. You're not the first one-nighter that he's had, but all you have to do is take one look at how he's fallen for Shiloh and know you're in the past. So shut up with the nasty-ass comments and serve your customers."

Looking over her shoulder toward the bar, Shiloh caught Jules's wink in her direction and grinned. A little later, she didn't see Vicki around, which should have made her feel good, except she knew it was almost time for Joseph to come for the station's pickup order. He'd texted to say he was on his way.

After dropping off the menus at one of her tables, she walked toward the front and spied him standing near the door with Vicki in his space. *I should walk away. Just walk away.* But in spite of self-prompting, she moved closer to the nearest open window to hear what Vicki was saying.

"How could you humiliate me like this?" Vicki whined, stepping close enough to place her hand on Joseph's chest.

He stepped back, his hand lifting, palm out. "First of all, don't touch me. Second of all, I didn't humiliate you. We had one night a long time ago. Hell, it was a year and a half ago. And I turned you down for a repeat when I first came back to the area. You knew it was one night, and you knew it was sex and nothing else. So I didn't humiliate you."

"That's just it," she argued. "You just have one night. That's what you said. You don't do relationships. And now all I hear over town is how Joseph is with Shiloh. Isn't it wonderful that Joseph's with that nice Shiloh? Damnit, Joseph. She's nobody. A weirdo. Sex with her has got to bore you to tears! That's what is humiliating! You could have had me, and you go for her?"

"She's everything I could want in a woman," he said,

then shook his head slowly as he looked at Vicki. "But this conversation is over. Now excuse me."

He started to walk around her, but she called out, "Jesus, you even sound like her. That's what she said to me."

He turned back and glared. "What are you talking about?"

"When I confronted her about you and told her that you'd had me first and that you'd come back to me. She told me that the conversation was over."

"Shit," he cursed. "I'll warn you once, Vicki. Stay away from Shiloh."

Shiloh hustled away from the window. Plastering a smile on her face when she saw him walk into the restaurant, she moved toward him with the sizeable takeout order for him to take back to the station. "Hey, here you go."

She watched as his tentative smile faltered before he leaned in to kiss her lightly. He glanced around the restaurant interior. "Looks like you're busy. I need to get back, anyway. I'll be over for dinner if that's okay."

"Sure. If you want to, that would be great." She tried to keep her voice steady but wondered if he could hear the tremors.

He held her gaze for a moment, then sighed heavily. "Of course, I want to. Anyway, we need to talk."

At that, she froze, uncertain what he meant. "Oh…"

"I'll see you tonight." Bending, he kissed her again before he left.

She chewed on her bottom lip, worry now scoring through her. She wasn't sure what he wanted to talk about, but after the little scene with Vicki, she was concerned.

"We're ready for our check now."

Hearing the customer's voice, she turned around and forced a wide smile. "I'll be right there!" Finishing out her shift, she was grateful that Vicki had slunk to her side of the restaurant and stayed away. The last thing she wanted was to deal with a jealous piece of Joseph's past when she was worried about their future.

22

Joseph knew it was time. Time to come clean with Shiloh. He'd never pretended to be a Boy Scout, but he liked the way she looked at him as though he was a hero who went out and saved people every day. He figured at some point, when their relationship was further along, they could have the here's-my-past-sexual-history conversation. *Or maybe not.*

Considering the way she was raised, he had a feeling she was a virgin when she got married at eighteen. And the way she described her year of mourning, he didn't figure she'd had any relationships then, either.

Scrubbing his hand over his face, he sighed. He really didn't want to have the conversation at all, but now that Vicki had opened her mouth and he'd seen the expression on Shiloh's face, he knew he needed to talk to her. For the rest of the afternoon, he could feel the tension rising. His shoulder muscles were tight, and his stomach clenched. *Hell, I wasn't this nervous the first time I copped a feel behind the stadium seats in high school.* By the time he got off work, he knew she'd be at the inn. He only hoped that Rachel wasn't around so that he and Shiloh could get their uncomfortable conversation over with and move forward. As he sat in his vehicle, a thought hit him, and this time his chest squeezed. *What if she doesn't want to move forward?* Shit. He had no idea how to fix things if they went wrong. It wasn't like he could go back and change his past.

He leaned back in his seat and squeezed his eyes shut for a moment, wishing he could figure out a way to make this whole day go away. But short of a miracle, he came up empty. *I hardly think God grants miracles to men who weren't always discreet in the past.* No, he knew he needed to suck it up. If he and Shiloh had any hope for a future, they had to figure out a way to put the past behind them.

After driving to the inn, he walked around to the back, his feet stumbling as he spied her offering lemonade to several of the guests that were sitting in the shade. *Well, fuck. I can't get a break.*

She looked over and saw him standing near the gate, and instead of the easy smile he'd grown to expect from her, he spied doubt in the way she hesitantly walked over.

"Hi," she said. It was easy to see she was trying to force her voice to sound normal.

"Hi, yourself. Are you busy right now?"

"No, I was just serving some lemonade to the guests. I don't have to do anything, but I was just looking for something to do."

"Is Rachel around?"

She shook her head. "She's at the library getting her homework finished."

"Any chance we could talk upstairs?

Clouds moved through her eyes, and he battled the urge to grimace. She finally nodded and waved him through the gate. They walked into the kitchen, and she led him up the back stairs, past the second floor, all the way to the attic.

He looked around, surprised at the large room decorated in delicate blues and whites. He noticed the queen-size bed with a smaller twin bed tucked into the corner. It had never dawned on him that she and Rachel shared a room. *Shit. I've got a three-bedroom house, and they're sharing a room.* Guilt stabbed at him, but he felt guilty about everything right then.

She inclined her head toward the French doors. "It's not too hot outside right now. If you'd like to sit there, we can."

He followed her out and looked around in amazement. The balcony was not large, but it held two chairs and a small table comfortably with plenty of room to move around. A massive tree to the side of the house provided some shade, but the view was spectacular over the Baytown beach toward the bay. "Wow."

A smile slipped across her face as she nodded. "That's what I thought the first time I saw it when Tori brought us up here."

He looked down at her and was struck by her calm countenance. Other women might be ready to gear up for a fight or pout. Or maybe they'd be embarrassed that he was seeing she shared a room with a teenager.

But it was so evident from the look on Shiloh's face that she took nothing for granted, grateful for everything. He wanted to be a man worthy of her, but never more so than at that moment.

She sat, her hands clasped primly in her lap, and turned to face him. "So you wanted to talk."

Direct. No games. Up front. He liked that. Or at least he usually did. Now, he felt the kick in his stomach again. *Come on... man up.* Clearing his throat, he tried to pull his thoughts together, but the words seemed to tangle in his mouth, just like when he was a kid.

She reached over and placed her hand on his leg, giving him a little squeeze. "Joseph, I'm not going to bite. I can see that something is bothering you, so please, feel free to talk. It's just us. It's just me."

The air rushed from his lungs, and he nodded. "I hate that Vicki got to you." He shook his head, looking out over the bay before bringing his gaze back to her face. "I haven't had a true relationship in a very long time. There was a girl in high school that I thought I was in love with, but she threw me over for another guy whose daddy had money. So I handled my hurt by telling myself that if I didn't care about someone, then it wouldn't happen again. Same when I joined the Navy. About eight years ago, I dated another woman who lived near the naval base where I was stationed. We saw each other for a few months, but when it was time for me to ship out for a tour, she said she wasn't going to wait. Since then, I haven't been in another relationship." Reaching up to squeeze the back of his neck, he added,

"That doesn't mean I've been a monk, but it means that I just had... um..."

"Sex as a physical release but no emotions involved?"

His chin jerked slightly at her words. "Uh..."

A little giggle slipped out. "Joseph, I've heard of one-night stands. My life experiences are limited, but I'm not ignorant."

"I never thought you were!" he blurted, not wanting her to be insulted.

"I admit that Vicki caught me off guard today. It really hadn't dawned on me that someone you'd had sex with would throw it in my face, so it was hurtful just because I didn't have time to process it. And it made me wonder how many other women in the area have had sex with you and might pop up out of the blue."

"No one. There's been no one else in Baytown since I got back from the Navy. I confess that I was used to the... um... well, the ease of hooking up with someone I met at a bar near the port and then never seeing them again. I knew Baytown would be different and was an idiot to have been with her."

Shiloh looked down for a moment, her lips thin and tight. "Vicki seems to think that the two of you will... hook up again."

"No way, no how. I don't do repeats." As soon as the words left his mouth, he winced. "Shit, Shiloh," he sighed. "That sounded so much worse than I wanted it to." He waited to see what she would say, but she remained silent, her gaze steadfast on him. It struck him how she gave him the opportunity to talk without jumping in with her own conclusions or expectations.

Pulling his thoughts together again, he said, "I never kidded myself into thinking that one of the women I was with was anything more than a one-night thing. A physical release, as you said. I didn't spend the night, and I didn't want them to. But I always made sure they understood what was happening and that they agreed. I did the same with Vicki, but it seems she thought she'd be different."

"Did you ever think that you would find someone that you might want to have a relationship with?"

"Absolutely." Seeing her wait for more, he added, "You've met my parents. You've met my sister and her husband and Wyatt and Millie. You've met a lot of my friends that are now your friends. I never doubted that true love was out there. I just knew I hadn't found it. My father once told me I'd know it. He said I'd know it when I looked into their eyes. He was right. It's just I've never found it before."

"Before?"

"Before I met you."

"Oh…" she breathed, as her eyes grew wide. Her lips parted, holding a perfect O before curving upward slightly.

He smiled, his chest finally easing. Reaching over, he grasped her hands, wanting to make sure she understood exactly what he was saying. "I felt something the moment I first saw you. And you didn't make it easy, but I'm glad. You made me want to get to know you. You made me want to be the best man I could be. You made me want to be sure. And Shiloh, I'm sure of what I want for us."

"What's that, Joseph? What do you want?" she asked, her voice barely a whisper in the breeze.

"I want us to be together. A couple. I want us to keep doing whatever we need to do to discover what we can become. We can go as slow or as fast as you want. I know you have Rachel, and I don't see her as baggage but as a bonus."

She sucked in a deep breath before letting it out slowly. "You've been honest about your past… you deserve the same thing from me."

Seeing her hesitation and her knitted brow, he nodded even though his chest squeezed again. But she'd given him the space to talk, and he needed to reciprocate. "Okay, Shiloh… I'm ready." As the words left his mouth, he hoped they were true.

How on earth do I explain what needs to be said? It's not as though Shiloh had not considered the words that needed to be spoken before now, but with Joseph's succinct confession of his past that he thought would be so shocking, she discovered that hers would be harder to explain.

Her tongue darted out to lick her dry lips. Joseph cut through her tangled thoughts when he asked, "Would you like something to drink?"

She hated to put off the conversation or seem like she was prevaricating. Without answering, he seemed to know exactly what she needed. He stood and walked back through the French doors, disappearing into the bedroom. He was gone for a few minutes before he returned, two tall glasses of water in his hands. Surprised, she took the proffered one and, after a large drink, thanked him.

"Shiloh, you can tell me anything."

Suddenly afraid that if she didn't speak quickly, the words might not come. "I think it's safe to say that you are much more experienced than I am." As soon as the words left her mouth, she realized he would interpret her comment only to mean the number of partners. Shaking her head, she amended, "Things were not what you might think between Edward and me."

Joseph waited for a moment, then reached over and placed his hand over hers in her lap. "I'm ready to hear it all."

"Edward was a year older than me, and our family farms were next to each other. I think perhaps our parents talked about us getting married from the time we were younger, but they would have never forced anything. Remember, back then, our community was very laid back. A few months before I turned eighteen, he asked me out for the first time, and our families seemed excited. It was on the first date that he asked me to marry him. It didn't make a lot of sense to me, but I couldn't come up with a good reason for not agreeing. Edward was sweet but not very *into* me. I think marriage for him was a way to fulfill what our community expected."

Joseph had been nodding as she spoke, but at that, his brows lowered.

She winced, torn between loyalty and truth. "In

truth, I'm not sure he was... interested in... well, I knew our families would like to combine the farms, and that's why I think he proposed. And my acceptance of his proposal was to make everyone happy."

"Jesus, Shiloh. What about what you wanted?"

"If I'd had any true objections, I would've voiced them. But I really didn't. It just seemed to make sense. So we got married even though I never had butterflies." Seeing Joseph's chin jerk slightly, she smiled. "You said that you'd know when you looked into someone's eyes if they were the right person. I always thought that I'd get butterflies in my stomach."

They sat in silence for a moment as she finished her water, her gaze drifting over the bay in the distance. Knowing there was more details to offer, she sighed as she set her glass onto the small table nearby.

"In the ten years that I was married, Edward and I only had sex a few times." Her hand that Joseph had been holding jerked as his hand spasmed. She wasn't surprised, considering what she had just confessed. "We were friends. We talked and laughed. Shared and worked side by side. We slept next to each other every night, often talking or holding each other. And I did love him, and he loved me. I still wouldn't put a worldly label on Edward, but he really wasn't interested in me sexually. Or maybe... um... any female."

"Oh, Shiloh," Joseph said, nodding slowly, understanding dawning in his eyes.

Shaking her head quickly, she said, "Please don't pity me. In many ways, I was lucky in that I was married to a good friend and a good man. When I was rocked with grief, he helped hold me together. He became a father to Rachel. The only thing missing in our relationship was sex, and I convinced myself that with all the wonderful things that I had with Edward, it was fine if I didn't have that." Pressing her lips together for a moment, she sighed, holding tightly to Joseph's hand. Leaning forward so that her face was close, their gazes locked, she added, "I've never told anyone else about this because it would feel like such a betrayal even though he's passed. But I need to be honest with you. Whatever we have, whatever we're starting, I want it all with you. But when it comes to experience, I have very little, and that scares me."

Joseph pulled her gently, settling her on his lap and wrapping his arms around her. It felt so natural to cuddle in a chair with him. She and Edward had often held hands, or he would wrap his arms around her when she was in the kitchen fixing dinner. They would lie together in bed, his arm around her. And she always felt so comforted yet, in truth, frustrated. She knew there should be more. Could be more. But if it was her lot to have a primarily sexless marriage, then there was little she could do about it. But now, just having Joseph so close, knowing everything about her, and still wanting her on his lap while his strong arms surrounded her, her body tingled. She wound her arms around his neck and waited, caught between terrified and elated.

"Shiloh, I would never do anything to hurt you. I would never push you to do anything you weren't ready for. And when it's time, I promise we'll go at your pace. "

"I know that." She held his face with her hands. "I'm not worried that you'd hurt me."

"Then what is it?"

"You have a lot of experience with a lot of different partners. I'm terrified of disappointing you."

"There's not one thing about you that would disappoint me. You're perfect." His lips landed on hers, and unlike the other kisses they'd shared over the past weeks, with all the barriers fading into the distance, she gave herself entirely to the kiss.

The velvet touch of his tongue dragging over hers sent shock waves to her core, and she squeezed her legs together to try to ease the tingles that centered in her sex. Anchored in place with one of his arms banded around her back, she pressed her front closer, wondering how she could straddle his lap without losing his lips in the process. She wanted more. More lips. More touches. More everything. *I want it all, and I'm more than ready!*

"You know," she mumbled against his lips as his mouth continued to plunder hers. His hand brushed over her breasts, and she squirmed, searching for the ease her body longed for.

"What do I know?" he asked.

His lips were still moving over hers, stealing the memory of what she was going to say. The desire to keep his tongue in her mouth and his fingers gliding over her breasts almost made it impossible to think. But with desire pooling deep inside, she remembered. "Rachel is spending the night with Cindy."

As soon as the words left her mouth, his hand halted

against her breasts, and he lifted his head slightly, just enough that he could peer into her eyes. "What are you saying?"

"You need more than that hint?"

He shook his head slowly, his gaze never leaving hers. "I need to hear you say it, Shiloh. I don't want to take advantage of you or make any mistakes with assumptions. I told you we can go slow—"

Huffing, she cupped his face. "Joseph, I'm not a blushing virgin. I may not have had the greatest sexual experiences during all the years I was married, but neither am I a repressed, ultraconservative, afraid-of-my-own-sexuality woman! I was faithful to my husband because that's the kind of person I am, but believe me when I say that I'm more than ready to have you not only in my life but in my bed—"

A squeak left her lips as his arms banded tighter around her, and he stood. She barely had time to cling to him before he stalked through the doorway and headed directly to her bed. Once there, he hesitated as though filled with uncertainty.

Still clutching his jaws with her hands, she held his gaze. "Don't you dare back away from me now."

Laughing, he shook his head. "There's no way."

"Then why are you hesitating?"

"I was trying to decide if I should lay you on the bed, stand you next to the bed and strip you first, or just tumble onto the mattress with you and we'll figure it out from there."

Lifting a brow, she laughed. "Have you always had

trouble figuring out what to do with your previous women?"

He scowled and shook his head. "For the record, no. I didn't care much about how we went about things as long as there was an understanding of what was happening. But enough about my past. All you need to know is that you are different, I'm different, and what we have is completely different. Got it?"

She smiled and nodded slowly. "Got it. No more past between us."

23

Staring at the woman in his arms, Joseph felt like a fumbling teenager having no idea what to do or how to go about making love to a woman who had filled his mind for months. This was no fuck. No one-night stand. No one and done and then out the door. Every smooth move he'd ever made, every flirting line he'd ever tossed out, every perfunctory box that he used to check off. None of these mattered anymore. She was different because of what she meant to him, but also uncertainty ran through him. While standing in her bedroom trying to figure out what to do to make everything memorable, she pushed against his chest, and he lowered her feet to the floor.

Shiloh took a step back, and he winced. *I shouldn't have carried her in here. I should've just let us keep kissing outside. I should've told her the words that expressed how special she is—*

Her hands dropped from his shoulders as she moved

farther away. Then to his surprise, she grasped the bottom of her shirt and dragged it slowly upward, exposing her taut pale stomach before lifting it over her bra and pulling it past her head. She held the material for only a few seconds before dropping it at his feet.

His gaze snagged and held on to her breasts, covered in a plain, white cotton bra. But she could not have been any sexier if she'd been wearing a scrap of lace and satin. Her hands next moved to her jeans, and he stared dumbfounded as she pushed them to the floor, stepping out of them and kicking them slightly to the side with her foot. She sat on the edge of the bed, and it only took a few seconds for her to toe off her sneakers. Her panties were also white cotton, but fit her hips like a glove, exposing her while hiding, teasing, and tempting.

She tilted her head to the side and said, "If you're expecting fancy moves, then you'll be disappointed. But I've gone this far, so I guess now it's up to you to decide what you'll do about it."

Her words would've been shocking, but the twinkle in her eyes and the way her lips curved upward had him barking out a laugh. Faster than he'd ever stripped and with certainly less finesse, he was soon standing in only his boxers. His clothes and shoes had joined hers on the floor, and a condom had now been tossed onto the bed.

As the two stood facing each other in their underwear, he had another flash of adolescent fumbling. He wanted to do everything. Look. Touch. Caress. Kiss. He wanted to lay her on the bed and strip the rest of her clothing. He wanted to bury his face between her thighs. He wanted to taste her on his tongue, with the scent of her arousal filling him.

"I can tell from the look on your face that you're doing a lot of thinking," she said, stepping closer and placing her hands on his shoulders.

"You're so beautiful, and I want to explore every inch of you. I want to bring you pleasure and have you experience the fullness of what I feel for you."

Her brow crinkled, and she shook her head. "Then what's stopping you?"

His fingers twitched. "I guess... fear."

She reached behind her and unhooked her bra, letting it slide to the floor before hooking her thumbs into her panties and dropping them as well. Spreading her arms out to the side, she said, "Here I am, Joseph. This is me. All of me. I'm trusting you with my body. I'm trusting you to lead and guide me. Remember, there's no past between us. But please stop making me wait for our future."

Those words had the desired effect when they washed over him. His hands reached out, his fingers curling around her waist, and he pulled her close. Her naked breasts now pressed against his chest, and his hands began gliding over the globes of her ass. Her skin was pale and soft and felt like silk underneath his fingertips.

He started slow, his gaze roaming over her face before he lifted her and gently lay her on the bed. He crawled next to her and propped his head up on his hand with his elbow pressed into the mattress. His free hand skimmed over her neck, his thumb resting on her fluttering pulse. Her breasts were full, rosy-tipped, and perfect. His palm continued to skim downward until it rested in the middle of her chest before he slowly cupped one breast, his fingertips grazing lightly over her nipple. Her lips curved, and he leaned forward, kissing her in the middle of a smile.

He wanted to explore every curve and memorize every nuance of her body. He wanted to discover what brought her pleasure, heady with the idea that she was discovering it along with him.

His lips followed the trail blazed by his hand, down her neck to the middle of her chest before circling her breasts and sucking a nipple into his mouth. Her hips began to move, and her thighs squeezed tightly together. He recognized her need and couldn't wait to be the one to provide the relief she sought.

His mouth suckled both breasts, moving from one to the other. His hand slid farther, memorizing the dips and swells of her body. He wanted to taste her, and even though she said there was no past between them, he was still afraid to take things further than she might want to go. As though reading his mind, she placed her hand on his face and gently lifted it so that his eyes met hers.

"There are so many things I want to experience, Joseph. Please don't hold back."

It suddenly hit him that while she'd described Edward as a good man and a good husband, there was so much pleasure she deserved to feel that had not been his nature to provide for whatever reason. Joseph realized that he was not only giving her a gift but, in doing so, was receiving a gift from Shiloh as well.

Sitting up, he shifted downward so that his shoulders were between her thighs and her sex was open for his perusal. He nuzzled her soft curls, filled his nostrils with the scent of her arousal, and with her fingers moving through his hair, he dove in with his tongue. He laved and licked, sucked on her swollen bud, and inserted a finger into her tight channel. He needed her to come before his cock was buried deep inside, or he wouldn't last a moment.

Her hips continued to shift, finding her rhythm as her fingernails curled inward, dragging on his scalp. Suddenly, her body stiffened, and a cry slipped from her lips before her essence flooded, and her core tightened around his finger. He sucked her juices off his finger and licked her again as she rode out her release. Slowly, he kissed his way back up her body. By the time he was staring into her eyes again, a smile on her face had eased all of his nerves.

"I've never done that before."

Eyes wide, he tilted his head to the side in silent question.

"Had an orgasm with a partner," she explained.

"Never?"

Shaking her head as he kissed the corner of her mouth, she said, "Only by myself. Today is the first."

Grinning, he said, "Then let's add to your list of firsts."

She nodded, her smile wide just as he leaned forward and kissed her again. He wanted to give her everything. Sliding off the bed, he jerked off his boxers and snagged the condom from where he'd tossed it. He ripped the foil and rolled it on his erection, not missing how she leaned up on her arms to stare at his cock.

Her wide-eyed gaze moved slowly upward. "Wow, Joseph. You're beautiful. And big. I know you've probably heard that before—"

"No," he interrupted, placing a finger over her lips. "There was no before. There's only us now." He couldn't change his past, but there was no way he wanted her to focus on it when all he wanted was to focus on her. Focus on making love and not just sex.

She dragged in a deep breath, then nodded. Shifting over her body, he knelt between her legs, his thigh separating hers as his upper body barely grazed her with most of his weight resting on his forearms planted next to her shoulders. He dwarfed her, realizing how petite she was. Small yet the strongest person he'd ever known.

She reached up to grasp his shoulders, and he entered slowly until fully seated. She was so tight that he had to fight to maintain control, afraid of coming too soon.

"Move. Please, move," she begged, lifting her hips, her top teeth biting her bottom lip.

"With pleasure," he grinned, bucking his hips, gliding in and out, each stroke bringing him closer to the heaven he knew he would find with the woman he loved. Each pull of her tight sex on his cock was different than he'd ever felt as he discovered when emotions were involved, the physical act and the connection were bigger, bolder, and brighter. Refusing to close his eyes, he kept his gaze on her face wanting to memorize every nuance of her expression, knowing he was giving her something no one had ever given her before.

Shifting so that most of his weight was on one arm, he glided his other hand along her curves until his fingers found the bundle of nerves slick with her arousal. Pinching slightly, he watched as she arched her back, and he thrust harder and longer. A flush began at her belly and moved up over her breasts, not ending until it heated her cheeks. She shattered underneath him, the vibrations felt not only in his cock, but in his soul.

Her fingers clutched his shoulders, her short nails digging little crescents into his skin. If he was bruised, he'd consider it a badge of honor. Seeing her fly apart, his hand glided upward over her breasts to her neck, where he cupped her jaw, refusing to look away as his own release was imminent. Falling over the cliff with her, he roared as every muscle in his body tightened. Spots danced in front of his eyes as every drop was wrung from him. Crashing down, he rolled to the side and dragged her with him, her body now resting on top of his. Their lungs battled to draw in air. His hands drifted slowly up and down her back from her neck to her ass as their breathing and heartbeats began to sync.

Her silence scared him. "Are you okay? Did I hurt you?"

She lifted her head from where it had been tucked

against his neck, and her sated smile was his answer. "Is it always like that?"

He thought about his answer, then slowly shook his head. "I don't know. I've never made love with anyone before."

Her lips curved even wider, and her eyes sparkled. She shifted upward on his body enough that their lips could meet, and she kissed him. Rolling again so that they were side by side, legs tangled as arms wrapped around each other. He let her take over the kiss, giving all control and power to her. Her gentle touch made his cock stir again.

"Can you stay?" she asked.

"Do you want me to?"

Still smiling, she nodded slowly. "Yeah, I do. But only if you're comfortable with—"

"Then let me take care of the condom, and I'll be right back." It only took him a moment before he was back in bed, noting that she'd stayed naked. Crawling in next to her, he dragged the covers over their bodies before wrapping her in his arms. "I've got my alarm set. I'll leave early enough that I can run home to shower and change clothes."

She nodded, a little sigh leaving her lips. He didn't have to ask her why because he felt the same. He didn't want to leave her bed in the morning. As her breathing slowed and her body grew heavy as sleep claimed her, he found it harder to shut down his thoughts. Swimming in uncharted waters, he wasn't sure what to expect. He wanted her and Rachel in his life. He wanted to move them into his house where Rachel could have her own room. He wanted them to have a kitchen that wasn't two floors below. He wanted Shiloh in his bed. They'd gone without... hell, so had he. But now, he wanted to give them the world. At least his little corner of it.

24

Shiloh grinned as she walked down the stairs at the inn, one thought swirling through her mind— sex with Joseph was amazing! Waking up with his arms around her after the night they'd spent together had fit every dream she could have imagined. They'd made love again, and after another orgasm, she knew what she'd missed out on all those years with Edward. The first time she had that thought, she'd been hit with guilt. But she knew it wasn't his fault. Whatever Edward's nature was, he'd loved her in his own way, and she'd loved him. But she also knew he'd want her to be happy. And with Joseph, she was beyond happy. And in truth, she couldn't wait till they had a chance to be alone and have sex again. Until then, kisses and touches would have to do.

Walking into the kitchen, she moved to the sink and peered out the window into the backyard. Her smile widened at the sight. Joseph was standing in front of Rachel, showing her a few basic self-defense maneuvers.

When Rachel had come home and told them about Paul's nasty comments, Joseph had wanted to go straight over to Paul's residence. Rachel begged him not to, terrified he might retaliate against Jack, and Shiloh agreed. But when Joseph asked them if they'd ever had any experience with self-defense, they'd both stared at him in wide-eyed silence.

In private, Shiloh had told him that she had no doubt she was capable of handling a threat, but she could see he didn't believe her. And she had to admit that Rachel had no exposure to needing to defend herself.

They'd been to an AL cookout a few days ago, and Joseph had walked straight up to Jack, who was manning the grill next to Colt. Not caring who was around, he'd placed his hand on Jack's shoulder and said, "Jack, Rachel told us how you took care of her when Paul was mouthing off. I want you to know I appreciate it. From what she said, you kept your cool and made sure she was behind you and out of harm's way."

Jack had blinked, then glanced up at Colt, and Shiloh had noticed the stoic sheriff's lips curve with a smile of pride as he looked down at his stepson. Jack's mom, Carrie, was grinning ear to ear as she stood next to Shiloh. Glancing at Carrie, Shiloh said, "My niece has a good friend in Jack. Thank you for raising him to be the way he is."

She didn't think it was possible, but Carrie's smile had widened even more. Then inclining her head toward Joseph, Carrie said, "Looks like your niece isn't the only one with a good man."

She blushed and nodded as she realized they were the center of attention of most of the people around, including their friends and his family. Joseph and Colt chatted for a few more minutes, tapped beers together, and then he walked back over, slinging his arm around Rachel as he kissed her forehead, then moved straight to Shiloh. He couldn't have staked his claim louder if he'd set off fireworks. They'd spent the rest of the evening mingling with some of the best people she'd ever met and didn't feel awkward in the least. It was as though Baytown could absorb newcomers, bringing them into the fold without asking them to change. And it struck her, but even in the best of times, that was not something her former community could do even before Isaiah. And certainly not afterward.

Now, walking outside, she pulled her purse strap over her shoulder and walked to Joseph. "I'm gonna run to the grocery store to pick up a few things for the guests' breakfast." He kissed her hard and fast, and she waved to him and Rachel before moving to her small SUV parked at the back of the Inn. It was used, but Joseph had gone with her and made sure it ran well, and she'd gotten a good deal. It only took a few minutes to drive to the grocery store just outside of town, where she hurried through the aisles, grabbing fresh fruit, baking goods, eggs, dairy, and bacon and sausage. Separating those items which were paid for by Tori, she grabbed a rotisserie chicken, green beans, and potato salad from the deli, deciding to keep things simple for their dinner.

While loading the groceries into the back of her SUV, a strange tingle along the back of her neck caused her to turn around. Her gaze scanned the parking lot, seeing nothing unusual. Giving her head a quick shake at her fanciful thoughts, she rolled the cart to the return stand and walked back to her vehicle. The tingling continued, and she couldn't help but look around again. This time, her gaze landed on an older model sedan nearby, with a man sitting behind the wheel, his gaze facing toward her. While she couldn't see him clearly, she didn't have the feeling that he was familiar. Yet, he seemed to be staring straight at her.

Unnerved, she hustled into her vehicle and started it quickly. Pulling out of the parking lot, she stared into the rearview mirror, not seeing anyone follow her. Breathing a sigh of relief, she rolled her eyes. *It must be Joseph teaching Rachel self-defense that has me seeing the bogeyman!*

Parking behind the inn, she smiled as Joseph and Rachel came over, both helping to carry the groceries inside. It didn't take long to put away items for breakfast and heat what she'd bought for their dinner, glad that he was staying.

Sitting at the kitchen table, the three of them laughed and talked in a comfortable atmosphere that she'd grown accustomed to and hoped she'd never take for granted.

Rachel walked out of the library with Jack, Cindy, and Brian. "Who wants to get ice cream?" Jack asked. Giving Rachel's hand a little jiggle, he added, "My treat."

She grinned and nodded before looking over to see Cindy, whose hand was clasped in Brian's, nodding as well. A few minutes later, they stood outside Rose's Ice cream Shop and devoured their treats. It didn't take long for Brian's mother to drive up, and he and Cindy climbed into the back seat, waving at her and Jack.

"I'll walk you to the inn," Jack said.

"Who's picking you up today?" she asked.

"My dad. He's having a meeting with Chief Evans, and I'll send him a text. He can pick me up there when he's ready to go home."

Glad to have his company, they walked down Main Street, enjoying their ice cream. Just as they turned onto the beach road, Jack dumped the last of his cone into one of the trash receptacles, twisting his head around.

"Didn't you want all of it?"

"Yeah, it was good. But I keep seeing a car slow down and then circle around. I didn't want anything in my hands while I kept an eye on it."

At those words, she looked around as well but saw nothing untoward. "I don't see anything."

"I'm not surprised," he said.

His voice didn't sound insulting, but she didn't understand. "What do you mean?"

"Nothing bad, Rachel. Really. It's just that you don't seem to have a lot of stranger danger."

Blinking, she shook her head. "I don't have a lot of *what?*"

"You know, stranger danger. Knowing that any stranger could be dangerous and that you need to be on alert."

"Where I came from, you didn't have to be afraid of people. There were… well, um… there were some that made me nervous. But I already knew who they were. Anyway, we didn't really have strangers coming through."

"That's why you need to be careful," he warned.

"But, Jack, this is Baytown! What could happen here?"

He stopped suddenly, and her feet stumbled when he pulled back on her hand. Steadying her with his hand on her shoulder, he turned her slightly to face him. "Seriously?"

"Yeah. I don't know that anything happens here."

"It's a nice place, but there's always going to be crime. We've had drugs, murders, deaths, arsonists, peeping Tom, kidnappings—"

Eyes bugging, she gasped. "Are you trying to terrify me?"

He looked around and must've felt safe because he put his arm over her shoulders and guided her down the street toward the inn. "I don't want to scare you, Rachel. I just want you to be very aware so that you can be safe."

She chewed on her lip for a moment, then said, "Joseph is teaching me some self-defense. But it feels weird."

"Weird?"

"Yes. It makes me wonder if I could actually ever hit

someone. But he says it's mostly just to be able to get away."

"Absolutely! Next time he's going to teach you, let me know, and I'll be here, too. I've learned a lot from my dad, and I can teach you some things as well."

She ducked her head and grinned. "That would be nice. I honestly don't think I'll ever need it, but if there's anything you think I could learn, I'll give it a try."

"Well, you learned how to swim, didn't you?"

She nodded and looked up as they reached the inn. They sat on the front porch until the huge SUV with the word Sheriff emblazoned on the side drove up and parked out front. Jack grabbed his backpack and gave her hand a squeeze. "I can't wait to see you tomorrow." With that, he jumped down the front steps and raced to the SUV, climbing into the passenger side. She stood and waited until he looked toward her and waved, and she waved in return.

After he drove away, she sucked in a deep breath and let it out slowly, the sun casting its warm gaze upon her face. There was little traffic on the beach road, but as a dark vehicle drove slowly by, she couldn't help but feel a chill. Suddenly feeling very exposed, she turned and dashed into the inn.

25

"Mrs. Carter. Mr. Carter. I see you've had an early morning walk on the beach."

Shiloh set the platter of scrambled eggs, bacon, and sausage on the sideboard of the dining room for the guests. She'd looked over her shoulder as the front door had opened, seeing the older couple walking into the inn. Their cheeks were rosy from the vigorous walk she'd seen them leave on when Rachel had left for school.

"Oh, it was so refreshing!" Mrs. Carter said. "I'm going to dash up to the room to comb my hair and wash my hands since I've been looking for sea glass. I'll be right down for your lovely breakfast."

Mr. Carter smiled at Shiloh and said, "Well, the breakfast smells amazing, but I'd best wait for my wife. She might accuse me of taking one of the last pastries."

She laughed at Mr. Carter and shook her head. The Carters came several times a year to stay at the inn and enjoyed Baytown during the various seasons. She met them the first weekend she was working, and this was the third trip they'd made since she'd been in Baytown.

"I must say that you look like you are enjoying Baytown," he remarked. "You look much changed and much more relaxed."

Laughing, she nodded. "I'm sure I look much different than the first time you saw me."

"Well, I thought you were lovely then, but certainly, you seem much more at ease now."

She nodded, glancing down at her jeans and bright red shirt. Her hair was pulled up into a sloppy bun, tendrils hanging about her face. "I suppose I discovered that we all have to choose how to live the life we're given. It doesn't disrespect the way our parents may have chosen to live their lives if we choose a different path. And certainly, no one should try to force their way on us."

His face settled into a kind smile as he nodded. "Very well put, and I completely agree."

"What are you agreeing with?" Mrs. Carter said as she swept back into the room, a smile on her face. She walked up to her husband and winked at Shiloh.

"I was just remarking that I thought our beautiful hostess was looking exceptionally relaxed this morning."

"Well, you two had better eat breakfast so that you fuel back up after your walk. I'll bring the coffee out to you." Shiloh turned to walk back into the kitchen.

"Did you give her the letter?"

Mr. Carter startled. "Oh, my goodness. I forgot." He pulled a small envelope from his pocket and said, "We found this taped to the door when we went out this morning. It has your name on it." He handed her the small envelope, then escorted his wife to the sideboard so they could fill their plates.

Shiloh took the envelope and glanced at the front. Her handwritten name was the only thing on the front, and there was no stamp. It obviously hadn't been mailed, but someone had hand-delivered it. *Must be an invitation.* Sliding it into the back pocket of her jeans, she went into the kitchen and then returned with the coffee pot on her way to the sunroom. Greeting the few guests that were already there, she poured coffee and made small talk. The fall season gave them fewer guests, and Tori had said it would pick back up nearer the holidays. Both couples staying were checking out today.

Tori kept the inn open through the holidays but had told Shiloh that she closed the inn in January and February for upkeep and renovations. She'd assured Shiloh that she and Rachel could still live there and would be paid during that time since they would be helping with any work that needed to be done. Shiloh was glad not to have to find alternate housing but also hated to take a salary when she wasn't doing the same amount of work as during the rest of the year. She considered if she could pick up extra shifts at the restaurant but knew Mark cut back hours during the winter season also.

As she finished the breakfast service, she cleaned the dishes and scrubbed the kitchen, finding the mundane tasks to her liking. Many people hated housework, but she loved instant gratification.

By midmorning, she was finished with chores at the inn and had just walked back up to her room to change before she headed to the Seafood Shack. Her phone rang, and she spied Mark's number on the caller ID. "Hey, what's up?"

"I know you're at the inn, but is there any way you can come to the restaurant now? I just got word that a small tour bus of seniors will be here in about thirty minutes, and it's going to take us a while to get them all seated and served."

"Sure. I'll be there in ten minutes." Disconnecting, she jerked the red shirt over her head and pulled on one with a Seafood Shack logo. Running a brush through her hair, she pulled it up in a tight ponytail, then headed back down the stairs. She made it to the restaurant in time to start moving chairs and tables around to make it easier for the senior group to be seated. For the next two hours, she rushed about filling drinks, taking orders, delivering food, and chatting with the diners. Once she managed to get everyone's check taken care of, and they were loaded back onto their bus and waved away, she turned toward Mark and puffed out her cheeks. "Wow, that was quite a lunch!"

Mark was grinning from ear to ear. "For this time of year at lunchtime… that was a huge bonus!"

She laughed, knowing he was going back into his office to start adding up the receipts. Helping the bussers to clean the tables, she worked to get everything ready for the evening service. Looking at the clock, she couldn't believe it was so late. Once back at the inn, she walked out onto the balcony and stood looking out over the bay, the warm afternoon sun beaming down on the water, casting sparkling diamonds over the surface. She couldn't believe how lucky she was to have found this place to start a new life.

What she'd said to Mr. Carter this morning was true. She loved her parents and respected their desire to step away from most of the trappings of modern life. She'd never realized how much her father must have been affected by his time in the service, needing peace and tranquility. He shunned the sidewalks and parking lots whenever they would go into a larger town. It was as though too many people made him very nervous. And so, Plineyville had become his refuge as well as his home.

She was grateful for those childhood memories but now was thrilled to offer Rachel the opportunity to experience life in a beautiful small town without shunning modern conveniences and certainly without the legalistic abuse of allowing one man to dictate their lives. She was also grateful for her years with Edward, remembering their relationship with great fondness. Those memories did not hinder the relationship she now had with Joseph, knowing that with him, she could have the romance she always desired. *And maybe, one day, marriage?* It was too early to consider that, but surely, it wasn't wrong to dream.

Not ready to go in, she sat on one of the chairs, ready to kick off her shoes and wiggle her sore feet. The sound of a slight crinkle met her ears, and she remembered the envelope still in her pocket. She pulled it out and then leaned back and placed her feet up on the small table to recline. Sliding her forefinger under the flap of the envelope, it popped open easily, and she pulled out the single piece of paper. Unfolding it, she gazed at the handwritten note.

I know where you are. I know what you've stolen. The land belonged to us. Give us back what is ours, or we will take what is most dear to you, your niece. She also belongs to the community, as do you. Do what you are commanded to do, and all will be forgiven. Isaiah

She dropped the piece of paper and envelope as though her fingers were on fire, leaping up and shoving the chair backward in her haste. She stared down at the missive for a moment, her heart pounding in fear. Jerking her head upward, she looked up and down the street but saw no one suspicious yet felt utterly exposed, even on the third-floor balcony.

Rushing back through the French doors, she halted and then whirled around, racing back out to grab the letter and envelope. Slamming the door behind her, she drew the lace curtains, then walked to the middle of the room. Her hands fisted at her sides, crumpling the paper, assaulted by thoughts flying at her too quickly to sort through.

How did he find me? How could he possibly know where I am? I didn't steal from him! I own the land and sold it! Rachel — oh my God! I can't let her know! No, that's not right— I have to let her know. She could be in danger. Danger? What would he do? What can he do?

She paced the floor, unable to think through the questions racing through her mind. Suddenly the door opened, and Rachel stood before her, fresh-faced with a bright smile, dropping her backpack just inside the room. She opened her mouth to greet her niece, but no words came out. Instead, she opened and closed her mouth several more times before finally blurting, "We need to leave."

Joseph had not been off the boat for very long and had just walked into the station when his phone vibrated. Looking down, he was surprised to see Rachel's caller ID. He'd given his phone number to her when he and Shiloh started dating, encouraging her to use it if she ever needed anything, but so far, she hadn't. Curious, he answered. "Rachel? Is everything okay?"

"Joseph! You need to come! You need to come now!" her voice screeched.

His heart leaped into his throat. He immediately turned and jogged down the hall heading toward Ryan's office. "What's wrong? Is it Shiloh?"

"Something has happened! I don't understand, but she says we have to leave. She says we're not safe anymore! I don't know what to do!"

"Are you at the inn?"

"Yes!"

"Stay there. Keep her there. Give me ten minutes."

Knocking on Ryan's door, he opened it and said, "I've got to leave. Rachel called. There's something wrong with Shiloh."

Ryan jumped up from his chair and nodded. "Absolutely. Do you need assistance?"

"I don't know. I don't know what's going on, but I'll

let you know as soon as I do." Turning back down the hall, he spied Callan, Jarod, and Andy standing there, all having heard the conversation. All three gave the same assurance, "Let us know how we can help."

With a chin lift, he jogged out to his SUV, grateful it only took a few minutes to drive to the inn. Making the decision to go to the back alley, he parked behind Shiloh's vehicle. He had no idea what was happening but wanted to block her from being able to get away until he had a chance to find out why she thought she had to leave.

Racing to the back door, he took the stairs two at a time, not even breathing hard when he reached the third floor. He lifted his hand to knock, but Rachel threw open the door. Wide-eyed and pale, she stepped back and let him in.

His gaze landed on Shiloh standing in the middle of the room next to the bed, and a suitcase opened as she threw things inside. Her face was streaked with tears. Her hair was falling out of her ponytail. And her eyes were filled with swirling storm clouds.

Stepping closer, he said, "Shiloh, baby, talk to me."

She didn't acknowledge he was there but shook her head back and forth in a jerky movement that sent more hair flying about her face. "We have to go. It's not safe here. We have to go. I can't let them take her."

At those last words, his gut clenched, knowing some danger lurked, but he had no idea what it could be. Moving a little closer, he placed his hand on her shoulder, and she jumped back, her eyes still darting around the room before landing on him. Murmuring as though to a skittish animal, he said, "Shiloh, come on, honey. It's me. You're scaring Rachel. You're scaring me. Let's talk, baby." He kept saying the same soothing words over and over until she finally sucked in a deep breath, her chest shuddering with the effort.

Swiping her hand over her cheeks, dashing the tears away, she shifted her gaze toward Rachel and then back to him.

"That's it, Shiloh. Talk to me, sweetheart. I'll fix anything, I promise. I just have to know what happened."

Her tongue dragged over her chapped bottom lip, and he moved directly into her line of sight. "Breathe with me, Shiloh."

He inhaled and exhaled slowly, and she eventually began to follow his pace, calming. Finally, dragging in another ragged breath, she whispered, "There are things I haven't told you. I haven't told anyone."

Nodding slowly, he wanted her to trust him. "Okay. Can you tell me now?"

She looked toward Rachel, and he anticipated she didn't want to speak in front of her niece.

Looking over his shoulder, he called out, "Rachel? Do you think you can go downstairs for a little while?"

Rachel shook her head violently and walked closer, her gaze never leaving Shiloh's face. "No. I'm not going anywhere. I'm not a kid anymore, and if something dangerous is happening, I want to know."

He wasn't sure how this would play out, stuck between two women who might not give in. Trying to figure out how best to handle this, it appeared that Shiloh was going to capitulate.

"Okay," she barely breathed, nodding. "Okay."

He settled her on the bed with Rachel next to her and dragged the desk chair over so that he was sitting directly in front of her, their knees touching. He wanted to be closer. To be honest, he wanted to hold her tight, but she seemed ready to snap, so he settled for placing his knees on either side of hers and leaning forward so he could hold her hand.

An hour later, Joseph was on the phone with Ryan. "I need as many of the law enforcement leaders as you can get to come in. Tell them to come to the VMP station. I'm bringing Rachel and Shiloh in. Ask Colt to bring Jack and see if Judith can bring Cindy to keep Rachel company."

Disconnecting, he walked over to Shiloh, who, after having bared her soul, her fears, her suspicions, and her actions, appeared pale. She and Rachel sat together on the bed, arms around each other. He'd love nothing more than to jerk down the covers and let them curl up together, with him sitting close by to stand guard to make sure nothing ever touched them. But he knew he couldn't do that.

"Shiloh, I need you and Rachel to come with me. We're going to talk to the others. Our friends can help us. We're going to keep you and Rachel safe." He steeled his spine, expecting her to argue. Instead, she nodded slowly. He wasn't sure if she agreed or was just exhausted or a combination of both. He made sure he had possession of the letter and the envelope. Extending his hand, he wrapped his strong fingers around hers and guided her and Rachel to the stairs. He held it together in front of her, but now as they preceded him down the stairs, his lips were pressed tightly together, his gut clenched, and his fingers itched to pull into a fist, just waiting to take a swing at anyone who dared to threaten them.

26

Shiloh sat at the table, her forearms resting on top as her fingers fiddled with the label of the water bottle a kind-faced receptionist had brought to her. She stared, watching the drops of condensation roll down the side of the plastic, and occasionally swiped one with her thumb. Her entire focus zeroed on the ring of moisture gathered on the tabletop. She was barely aware that the room was filled with people. Men she knew and had become friendly with since moving to Baytown.

Mitch, the Baytown police chief. Jack's stepdad, Colt, the sheriff of North Heron County. Ryan, the VMP police chief, and Cindy's dad. Wyatt, a local police chief and a man who would become family if she and Joseph stayed together. And Callan, another officer and one of Joseph's best friends. It seemed as though Joseph had thought of everything. Rachel was down the hall in another room with Jack and Cindy, keeping her company and hopefully keeping her from freaking out.

Shiloh closed her eyes, wincing. She couldn't believe that she'd freaked out the way she had, scaring Rachel. She'd always been the calm one. Always careful not to show emotion. Always making sure that whatever was churning inside didn't show on the outside. Yet since coming to Baytown, she'd felt so much more *normal*. And all it took was one letter from Isaiah to completely obliterate everything she'd built over the last months.

Joseph's fingers curled around her hand, and she jumped slightly. Her face heated as she realized everyone was looking at her while her thoughts had wandered. She listened as he introduced everyone in the room, even though she already knew who they were. He'd also let her know that he'd only given them the essential information. Holding her gaze, he nodded slightly, and she knew it was time to speak. And suddenly, she had no idea how much to say.

As though he understood her conundrum, he said, "Shiloh, just tell them everything you can and let them sift through what's important. Don't hold back. Don't leave anything out. That's how we'll know how best to handle the situation."

She'd often considered Baytown to be very much like Plineyville. People wanting to help. People sticking together. Yet, at that moment, she was struck with another thought. It was almost as though nothing bad ever happened in her former community. Things were hushed up. Uncomfortable things were swept away. No one talked about the dangers or evils in the world. They were simply pushed aside. Then when tragedy struck, the community was ripe for someone like Isaiah to step in and take over.

Joseph gently rubbed his fingers over her arm again, and she dragged in a deep breath, knowing it was time.

"It's not a secret that I came from a small community in the mountains of Pennsylvania. It was a commune for a hundred years or so before becoming a community where people could own their property. It wasn't that Plineyville pushed out the modern world. It's just that the modern world didn't really press in. Poor cell phone service. No internet. It was easy to live there and go to school nearby and appreciate the simple way of life. No one told us how to dress or act, but with most families working as farmers with a few shopkeepers, everything about our lives was practical. I was married at the age of eighteen, and by then, my sister was already married with a daughter. My parents and my husband had farmland together. It wasn't perfect. It wasn't an idealistic way to live. It was simply all I knew."

She swallowed, her throat feeling like cotton. Pushing on, she continued. "I know that Joseph shared with you what happened with my parents, my sister and her husband, and our pastor. The tragedy not only rocked the community but, as you can imagine, it gutted me. It was only the fact that Rachel needed me and the support of my husband, Edward, that I managed to get through that time."

"Our pastor's nephew took over leadership of the community. Insisting that he was called Master Isaiah. He'd been a bully in school, that much I remember, even though he'd been several years ahead of me. Now, as an adult, he walked around and still bullied, even though he wrapped himself in a cloak of pious godliness. He also started having several men who followed him around, and I always thought they were almost comical until I realized that they were his minions, willing to force people into doing Isaiah's will.

"My mother-in-law had already passed, and my father-in-law was still working the farm with my husband. One night, I woke up, and Edward wasn't in bed. I heard voices in the kitchen below. I didn't mean to eavesdrop, but when I went to the top of the stairs, I could hear their conversation. My father-in-law preferred to work on engines. He kept everyone's farm equipment and cars running. And he was telling Edward that the sheriff from the county where the accident had occurred had asked him if he wanted the van for parts. It was then that he discovered what may have caused the accident. He said something about the brakes looking like they'd been tampered with. I must have made a noise because suddenly Edward was standing at the bottom of the stairs looking up, his face pale and frightened. He walked up the steps and took my hand, guiding me down. My father-in-law was horrified that I had heard, and they were both scared of what I might say or do." She lifted her head and held the gazes of each man around the table. "Because, essentially, what I heard, was that my parents and my sister and her husband had been murdered."

Joseph released her arm, now sliding his hand over her shoulders to pull her close. "I'm so sorry, babe. I'm so sorry."

She looked down at the shredded label that she'd

peeled off the water bottle. She reached for it with shaky hands. He took the bottle from her and unscrewed the top, handing it back. She lifted it to her lips, dribbling some, unable to stop the shaking. As she looked around the room again, she spied the tight-jawed, hardened expression of the men sitting around the table. A strange sensation hit her, thinking of how angry Isaiah would get sometimes and how frightened she'd feel when he had that expression. But this was different. Each of these men, including Joseph, was angry, but she felt nothing but security in their presence.

Mitch nodded for her to continue, and she took another swig of the cold water, letting it ease her parched throat.

"We sat up late that night and talked about everything. There was no proof. And the only people who knew were us. But we had no idea who might have wanted to do something like that. It made no sense." She shrugged. "My father-in-law died a year later from a heart attack. Edward made me promise never to say or do anything to indicate we might think that someone could have successfully tampered with the brakes. Several years passed, but life was getting worse. Isaiah was putting pressure on families who owned land to give it up to the community."

She snorted, adding, "Isaiah would say we needed to give the land to the church and therefore give it to God. Looking back, it's hard to understand how our community fell under his spell. I was lost in grief at the beginning and simply didn't realize what was happening around me. By the time I was more aware, others had moved away, and those who stayed seemed to be giving in. Whether they believed he was speaking for God or just afraid of his minions, I don't know."

Shifting in her seat, she wasn't sure how much longer she could go as exhaustion pulled at her.

"Shiloh?" Joseph said softly, next to her.

She twisted her head and looked at him, drawing strength from his solidness, warmth from his embrace, encouraged by his expression.

"Babe, I know you're ready to drop. But you're the strongest person I've ever met. You can do this."

Emboldened by his words, she nodded and took another sip of water. "One day, after Rachel had gotten home from school, I walked out to the fields to take Edward's water to him. I was in the shadows at the edge of the field when I realized that Isaiah had come with his *companions* to talk to Edward. They had not noticed me, but I could hear the raised voices. You see, Edward had refused to give up his land, saying that he would give a portion of the proceeds in the crops as he always did to the community, but the land had been in his family for many years. He wasn't going to give it up. Even from where I was, I could tell that Isaiah was furious. My husband was not a strong man. Not physically. Isaiah commented that he needed to think of his family and make the right decision or face the consequences. I stayed hidden until they left and ran home.

"That night, Edward and I talked. He was resolute that he was not giving the family land up, but he wanted me to know how everything was laid out. We had a will drawn up after Rachel came to live with us. If he died, everything he owned came to me. We had a strong box hidden in the house where we kept some of the books that we were not supposed to keep, and in it was the deed to the land, the deed to the farm, and the will. There were also notes that he'd written after he and his father had talked about their suspicions."

Squeezing her eyes tightly shut, she brought Edward's face back to mind. It was hard to explain, considering he was so very different from Joseph. Yet she'd once told Joseph that they were alike in integrity. Keeping her eyes shut, she said, "A week later, Edward died in a farm accident. A farm accident that I do not believe was an accident. His body was found near the tractor, and his neck was broken. They said he must have fallen off."

The tension in the room skyrocketed, as well as the temperature. She lifted the bottle of water to her forehead, needing the coolness against her skin. If the other people in the room thought what she told them was terrible, she wondered what their reaction would be when she continued with the next part of her story.

"There's more, isn't there?" Mitch asked.

She shifted her gaze over to him, but it was Joseph who replied. "Yeah, there is."

She closed her eyes for a moment, casting her mind back. "With all the dictates that Isaiah had put in place, he forced many of them onto women. Especially women who weren't protected. I can look back and now see that's what he played on. Fear. Confusion. Uncertainty. It was dictated that widows would spend a year observing morning in a very old-fashioned, somewhat archaic way. I was to wear black dresses and only go out for basic shopping. Neighbors would bring in food and check on me, but our contact with others was limited. Rachel was also not allowed to go to school, so I homeschooled her that year."

She rubbed her forehead, a headache blooming behind her eyes. She hated to look at the others, knowing the questions and censure she might see in their eyes. "You're wondering how people can become so cowed in a modern world."

"Please don't think that, Shiloh," Colt said.

She lifted her gaze and looked at the large, dark-haired man with a strong jaw and intense expression. "I grew up in this area and remember a man coming through during a tent revival. My grandma took me, and it wasn't just that he was a hellfire preacher, but he had folks convinced that if they didn't pray a certain way or act a certain way, they weren't doing God's work. I was lucky. When I got home, I was scared silly, but my grandma was mad. She didn't believe him and didn't mind saying it. But I remember for at least a year after that, she was questioned by a lot of her old friends who didn't think she was following God in the right way."

Shiloh nodded slowly, more grateful for Colt's words than she knew how to express. "Grief isn't something we just get used to. It's not something we move through and then pop out on the other side and say, 'look, I did it.' After losing my parents, my sister and her husband, and then Edward, I was so beat down. The only reason I got out of bed each morning was because I had Rachel. We leaned on each other. It was simply easier not to make waves even though I clung to everything Edward and I had discussed."

"How did you get away from that?" Wyatt asked. She cast her gaze to the other side of Joseph and looked at the man who so resembled his brother. "Before Edward died, the farm had become too much for him to handle on his own, so he had a man outside our community working it. Edward had made arrangements in case something happened, but he told me all about them. Isaiah wasn't happy because he thought I was getting rent money. But I told him that Edward and Mr. Kendall had an arrangement that would last for a year during my mourning. It bought me a year to figure out what to do. One day, Mr. Kendall brought some magazines to me that his wife was finished with. One was on coastal towns on the Chesapeake, and there was an article about Baytown. There was a beautiful picture of the Sea Glass Inn, and I thought it was the most magical place in the world."

Mitch smiled and nodded. "I remember when the magazine interviewed Tori for that article."

"I wrote a letter and had Mr. Kendall post it for me. I just felt compelled to let her know that seeing the inn gave me hope during a dark time. We began corresponding, and she told me that if I ever wanted to come with Rachel to live here, she'd make sure I had work. From that moment on, I had a plan. You see, Mr. Kendall wasn't renting the land. It had already been sold to him, and he was holding the money for me. Part of me was terrified of what I had to do. I wasn't sure I was strong enough. I wasn't sure if it was the right thing to take Rachel away from the only place we'd ever known. But then, Isaiah made sure I had no choice."

She felt Joseph tense next to her, knowing he was struggling with what she'd told him in her room. "This was the part that I kept from Rachel, but I needed to make sure she understood what was happening, so she was in the room when I told Joseph. You see, Isaiah told me that at the end of my year of mourning, he was coming for me. He wanted me because he wanted the land. When I told him that I wasn't ready to take another husband, he told me that if I didn't give in to him, he would take Rachel as his wife even though she was only fourteen—"

The room erupted around her in cursing and anger. She jumped, not surprised that the others were upset but surprised at how quickly they gave voice to their fury. Joseph held her hand, but she wasn't sure who held on more tightly. She was so tired. The men mumbled their apologies, each leaning forward with their gaze pinned on her. From the expressions on their faces, she wasn't sure how much more they could take before moving out as a vigilante group. She almost laughed at the idea of those men storming out to confront the threat she faced.

"I had things arranged but didn't know when we would need to put them in place. Suddenly on that day, when Isaiah said he would take Rachel or simply marry me and have both of us and the land, I was ready. We waited until the middle of the night and took our money, what clothes we could carry with us, and anything of personal value. We hiked to the next county to Mr. Kendall's house, where he and his wife were waiting. He and his wife had bought bus tickets, and we arranged for Tori to meet us at the bus station in Virginia Beach."

She lifted her shoulders in a shrug. "From there, you know everything else. Rachel and I settled into Baytown, making this our home. We've worked to integrate into a lifestyle that was very different from what we came from, and it wasn't always an easy transition. But Rachel is doing wonderfully in school, thanks in great part to Jack and Cindy and her teachers, who understand a little about her previous situation. I'm working, earning money, and taking care of our lives the best way that I know how, and that's in great part to the wonderful people we've met here."

"Shiloh," Ryan said, drawing her attention to Joseph's boss. "Your story has absolutely floored me, but there's only one thing that keeps hitting my mind. You've got to be one of the bravest people I've ever met. So don't ever beat yourself up for falling under the spell of someone unscrupulous. Because when push came to shove, you did everything you could to protect yourself and Rachel."

"And that's what makes you a hero," Joseph said, his lips near her ear.

She turned, and their faces were so close she stared into his eyes. "I'll do anything to protect Rachel. Even if I have to take her away and move again."

"You are not going to have to do that, babe," he said.

"You are never going to have to run away again. I'm going to make sure of that. Every person in this room is going to make sure of that. Your days of taking care of everything, and being afraid, are over."

27

Joseph had been sitting next to Shiloh, trying to offer quiet strength while she went through her story. He'd heard much of it when they'd started getting to know each other and then the rest right before he called in the others. Just today, he'd gone through fear, rage, incredulity, and then right back to rage. Now, listening to her go through the events she'd lived through, he was filled with admiration. He couldn't imagine the life she'd experienced in the past six years before coming to Baytown. But he was awed with her strength of character.

Looking around the table, he wasn't surprised at the expressions he saw on his friends' faces. They mirrored his own. Jumping in, hoping to spare her more questions, he said, "Just so you know, I had her bring all the paperwork with her. I've looked at it, but it's also here for you."

She pulled a folder out of her bag and handed it to him. He removed each item and placed them on the table. "This is the deed to the land that had Edward and Shiloh Wallen's name as owners. This is the bill of sale where Shiloh sold it to Mr. Kendall. Here are the receipts for what he paid for it upfront and then the rest just before she left. Mr. Kendall had the deed recorded, and she also has a copy of it here. Shiloh and Edward were Rachel's legal guardians, and she has the paperwork from the court that states that. And here are the papers that Edward had written after he and his father talked that night."

Leaning back, he wrapped his arm around Shiloh, giving the other law enforcement leaders a chance to look at the paperwork. Her body no longer felt tense, but he could feel waves of exhaustion pouring off her.

Mitch looked toward him and nodded before looking toward Shiloh. "You've got everything in order, Shiloh. You don't need to be afraid from a legal standpoint about the land you sold or Rachel. But Joseph is right. You need to be very careful of Isaiah. Everyone here knows that desperate men can be very dangerous and unpredictable. But I'll be damned if someone who lives in my town is going to be threatened. We need you to be vigilant while we investigate." Turning toward Joseph, he said, "I have a feeling you've already started an informal investigation."

Her head whipped around to the side, and he felt her gaze on him, but keeping his eyes forward, he nodded. "I'll tell you everything I know." He shifted slightly to face Shiloh, a grimace slipping across his face. "I don't know much. But initially, I did a little research because I just wanted to understand more about where you came from."

Hoping she wasn't upset at his admission, she offered a little smile and squeezed his hand.

"As she said, Plineyville started out as a commune in the 1800s. Not that uncommon and not tied to any particular religious group. It was just like-minded people who wanted to share the burden of living and share the land. Eventually, the residents there decided to maintain the community feel while owning their own property. The land was bought, deeds were filed, and it simply became a bit of small-town America that never let in all the modern trappings. Of course, as Shiloh said, that was probably due more to the geographic isolation. I couldn't find anything on Isaiah until about two years ago when a woman did a magazine article on some of the various communities in Pennsylvania. The gist of the article was not very flattering. She met Isaiah and considered him to be a pompous ass who ruled the community with an iron fist. But in her article, she figured if that's how people wanted to live, that was their business."

Shiloh heaved a sigh and shook her head. "It's so hard for others to imagine how ripe we were for his edicts when grief threatened to swallow so many of us whole."

Joseph pulled her in for a side hug and continued, "I would typically think that Isaiah's more talk than anything else if it hadn't been for the letter that came today. That shows me that he can't deal with the fact that someone outsmarted him, or he has something to lose. I fear he knows you suspect that he had something to do with the accidents." Looking back at her, he added, "The first thing we need to do is get you out of the inn. I want you and Rachel to move in with me."

Shiloh's mouth dropped open as her head gave a little shake. "What? You're kidding!"

"Obviously, he knows where you work and live since that's where the note was delivered. I don't want you to stay there."

"But, Joseph, I have to be there."

"Actually, Shiloh, you don't," Mitch said. "Tori has had other help at the inn who didn't live there. That's not a requirement for the job."

"But I still don't understand why. We live on the third floor, Joseph. I'm very safe—"

"Come on, Shiloh. Sometimes the back door stays unlocked. And if they know you're there, they can get to you. This time of year, you don't have guests staying every night."

"But Rachel?"

Colt spoke up. "I'll talk to the school to make sure they know that no one is to get to Rachel other than you, Joseph, or me."

"Me, too," Wyatt, Mitch, and Ryan all said at the same time.

Joseph's chest eased at the show of solidarity amongst the law enforcement friends in the room.

Colt continued, "She'll be perfectly safe there during the school day, and we'll make sure she knows she's not to leave the grounds or be alone."

Shiloh lifted her hand to her head and rubbed her

forehead, and Joseph wanted to take away all her fear and pain. "Shiloh, I work a day shift unless there's an emergency in the evening. We'll take Rachel to school in the mornings, and then you can pick her up in the afternoons. I can make sure you get to the inn on the days you have guests to make breakfast early. You stay locked in for cleaning, and then I'll be at the harbor. You'll have all of us on speed dial. Then you, me, and Rachel will be at my place in the evenings. Hopefully, we'll eliminate this threat before long." What he didn't say at this moment was that while the idea was for security, he was ready. He wanted Shiloh and Rachel in his life and couldn't see any reason not to make this next step.

"Please, Shiloh. We all want to help you, but we need your cooperation, too." Joseph knew he was pulling out the big guns and doing it in front of the others but didn't care.

"I thought I had Isaiah figured out when I lived there, but I never dreamed he would do this." She looked around the table. "What can you all do?"

"Colt and I will alert the deputies and my police officers about what's going on and who we need to look for," Mitch said. "I'm also going to call the detective in Pennsylvania who worked the accident case and talk to them."

"As I said, I'll talk to the high school to make sure Rachel is safe during the day," Colt added.

Joseph spoke next. "I'm going to make sure Mark knows what's happening in case Isaiah or one of the other men with him comes into the restaurant."

Shiloh heaved another sigh and then nodded. Standing, she leaned across the table and offered her sweet smile and hand out to each of the other men. As a few of them started to leave, she asked to speak to Colt and Ryan, who both stayed back with Joseph and Wyatt. "I feel bad that Cindy and Jack are here with Rachel." She winced, shaking her head. "That's not really what I meant to say. I'm glad they're here with her, but I don't want them to be in danger. I'm just not sure how to—"

"Shiloh, I understand what you're saying," Ryan interrupted. "I don't want my daughter in danger either, but the best thing you can do is have Rachel with other people. Isaiah is not likely to go after someone who's surrounded by others. I'll make sure that Cindy is aware and that the two girls are never off alone. My son, Trevor, will help with that."

"Jack may be young, but he's smart," Colt said. "And I don't suppose I have to tell you that he really likes Rachel. He'll also know what's going on, and I'll make sure that they all move around in groups. She'll be well protected."

Colt and Ryan walked out of the room, and Joseph looked over his shoulder as Wyatt clapped him on the back. "I'm here for you, bro," Wyatt said. He then walked over and pulled Shiloh in for a hug. "Whatever you need, Shiloh, we're all here for you."

Wyatt walked out, leaving just Joseph standing with her. He wrapped his arms around her, and they pressed together, her cheek resting against his heartbeat. "I know we need to get down the hall to Rachel, but I just want you to know how proud I am of you. I promise, babe, I'm going to do everything to keep you both safe."

For a moment, he thought she was going to cry, and he tightened his embrace. She sucked in a breath that hitched several times, then let it out slowly. When she leaned back and held his gaze, he could see that she was calm and resolute. *That's my girl.*

"Okay, Joseph. Let's get Rachel and tell her we need to pack to go to your place." She started to pull away, then stopped. "She'll be glad. She doesn't want to leave Baytown."

"And you? Do you want to leave, Shiloh?"

She continued to hold his gaze and shook her head slowly. The storm clouds in her blue-gray eyes lifted ever so slightly. "No, I don't want to leave Baytown. I don't want to leave you."

If his heart had wings, it would have taken flight. Instead, it simply pounded with the beat that made him smile.

28

Joseph turned onto his street and glanced into the rearview mirror, seeing Rachel's pale face. Twisting his neck slightly, he caught a glimpse of the side of Shiloh's equally pale face before she turned away to stare out the passenger window. She had wanted to protect Rachel, thinking it best if the final threat that Isaiah had made to Shiloh before they left Pennsylvania stayed secret. But he and the other LELs felt that Rachel was old enough to handle the information, and it would assist in heightening her awareness of the danger that might be around.

He shifted slightly, cracking his neck from side to side. Uncertain what to say, Rachel broke the silence.

"You don't live too far from Cindy."

"No, I don't. Like the Coates, I back to one of the inlets, although my house is smaller."

"Have you lived here long?" Rachel asked.

"No, I haven't." With one hand still on the steering

wheel as he turned into his drive, the other hand reached behind and squeezed the back of his neck, willing the tension to ease. "I'm going to go ahead and apologize right now. It's not completely furnished and isn't nearly as nice as the inn."

At that, Shiloh's head whipped around, her ponytail bouncing over her shoulder. "Joseph, you don't have to apologize for anything. We're the ones who are crashing into your life. Believe me, anything is fine."

As much as he hated the reason she broke her silence, he was still glad she had. He held her gaze for a few seconds, not happy to see the exhaustion in her eyes but pleased that he didn't see condemnation.

"Are you having a party?" Rachel called out from the back seat.

He jerked his attention out the windshield, surprised at the cars parked near his house. The air rushed out, and he chuckled. "I recognize most of these vehicles. Looks like Wyatt put in a call to my parents and a few others." When he left work that morning, it wasn't as though he'd left his house in a state of disarray. It wasn't a typical bachelor pad, but it was starkly furnished, and he wasn't sure what food was in his refrigerator.

He pulled up and parked next to a new SUV that he recognized as Luke's. A few weeks ago, he'd helped Luke move into Allie's house along with his niece and nephew. Chuckling, he realized the favor was being returned. Rachel hopped out of the back seat to greet his nephews, who were running around with Luke's kids. Looking toward Shiloh, he said, "Sweetheart, are you okay?" She was never very talkative, but the quiet trip from town had him worried.

She nodded, seeming distracted. He reached over and slid his fingers underneath her ponytail to cup the back of her neck. "Talk to me."

"Why have you never brought me here before?"

Her question caught him off guard, and a sigh whistled through his teeth as he thought of the reason. "To be honest, it was only partially furnished, sure as hell not decorated, and not really all that nice to bring you to. You always seem so comfortable at the inn, and with me working in town, I guess it just made sense for us to spend more time there. It's not that I was trying to keep you from this part of my life. I just wasn't sure you were ready." He winced, uncertain what the place would look like even now that his mother and sister had obviously been called in. "But I want you safe, and I promise it's clean."

"Oh, no, Joseph, that's not what I meant to imply at all!"

Holding her gaze, he asked, "Is that really what you've been thinking about on the drive?"

"I guess I'm just overwhelmed," she admitted. "Overwhelmed and really tired, although I don't know why."

"Your body is starting to shut down after the earlier adrenaline rush and the long afternoon you've had. Look," he continued, "We'll go in and get the lay of the land to see what's been done. And then, as soon as we can, I'll move everybody out."

She looked over at him and shook her head. "No,

that wouldn't be right. Everyone has been great, and it would be rude for me to pull a pity party and have people leave early."

She offered a little smile, and he applied gentle pressure on her neck, bringing her forward as he leaned toward her, planting a swift kiss on her lips. "Love the way you taste," he mumbled, earning a little giggle along with an eye roll, both he'd take easily. "Okay, let's see what we've got."

Entering the house, he wasn't sure he was in his home. It certainly wasn't the same place he'd left this morning. With a glance at the living room on the left and the dining room on the right, he spied his old sofa and a small table with two chairs, giving evidence that he had indeed brought her to his house. But now, there was a coffee table, an end table, another comfy chair in the living room, two more chairs in the dining room, and a couple of lamps he remembered seeing in Betsy's house at one time.

Coming down the stairs were Wyatt, his dad, and Luke. Wyatt moved directly to him and said, "Millie and I had an extra twin bed when she moved into my house, so we put that in the smaller bedroom upstairs for Rachel. Loretta and Grandpa had a small dresser in there, too."

He clasped his brother's hand, and they held tight for a moment as he offered his thanks. His small house had a main bedroom with an en suite bathroom that the former owners had enlarged and made very comfortable, but the other two upstairs bedrooms were not very large but shared a bathroom. Having had no time to plan for the contingency of Shiloh and Rachel moving in suddenly, he knew there was no way he could have pulled this off without help.

Luke moved to him as well. "Allie had a daybed. It's a twin bed that can double as a sofa. We put it in the other bedroom if that's needed for Shiloh." He shrugged and added, "If she's with you, then it can be a place to sit in an extra room."

That was another thing Joseph hadn't even considered— how the sleeping arrangements would play out. He wanted Shiloh in his bed, but since they'd only managed to squeeze intimate times together when Rachel was spending the night with someone else, he had no clue what she'd want to do. Grateful that his friends and family had thought through the situation quickly, he nodded. "I appreciate this more than you can know."

Glancing to the side, he noticed that Shiloh had moved into the kitchen, and he followed her, observing his mom, Allie, Millie, and Betsy stuffing the refrigerator and freezer full of pre-cooked meals and groceries.

At first, Joseph had been afraid that their company would stay longer than he thought Shiloh could handle. Still, he should have known how sensitive everyone was to what was happening. After hugging Shiloh, Allie and Luke rounded up their little ones, and with promises to keep an eye on everything since they lived close by, they left. Betsy and her husband also gathered their kids and, with more hugs, climbed into their SUV and backed out of the drive as well. They were soon followed by Wyatt and Millie.

Now, with only Joseph's parents left, Shiloh's shoulders seemed less tense. His mom walked directly to her and pulled her in for a hug. "Oh, Shiloh, I'm so sorry for everything that's happening. I don't know the details, but Wyatt called to say that you and Rachel might be in danger, and you'd be staying here. I couldn't imagine what Joseph's house looked like, but I certainly knew it wasn't ready for the unexpected. I hope you don't mind, but as soon as Wyatt called, we put our heads together to see what we could do to make it more comfortable."

As his mom hugged Shiloh again, she caught Joseph's eyes and winked. He winked in return, smiling his thanks.

Shiloh leaned back, shaking her head. "I hate that you all have gone to so much trouble."

Sherrie waved away her concerns. "It's no problem at all." She led Shiloh toward the kitchen. "Now, let's have a little bite before William and I head home."

After they ate, Joseph gave Rachel the grand tour of the small house, making sure she felt comfortable putting her things in one of the guest bedrooms. "I want to make sure you're doing okay with all of this," he said, seeing her peek into the small closet.

She nodded slowly, but her face scrunched into an open expression of concern. "To be honest, it all feels surreal. I surely didn't like the way I felt when Isaiah was near us. I don't want to see him again. And even though she and I didn't talk about it, I think I always knew that we'd leave one day."

"You're very smart, Rachel. And you've been a big

help to her. She wouldn't have been able to protect you as well as she did if you hadn't followed her lead."

She nodded again, then lifted her head and held his gaze. "Can I ask you a question? It's kind of personal."

Uncertainty speared through him again, but he plowed ahead. "You can ask me anything you want. If it's something I can answer, I will. But what I won't do is lie to you."

She continued to hold his gaze, and he assumed he passed whatever consideration she was giving when she finally nodded again. "I know you really care about Shiloh. I just don't want any of this to mess up what you two were building. And if my being here makes things uncomfortable—"

"Absolutely not!" He realized his words came out harsher than he meant, and she jerked slightly. "I'm sorry, Rachel. It's just that I don't ever want you to think that you shouldn't be here. Shiloh and I do care a great deal about each other, but we've been taking things slow. I wanted to make sure I was doing the right thing both for myself and for her. Having you two move in now wasn't planned, but it's fine. It's more than fine. It's good."

He saw doubt move through her blue-gray eyes that were so much like her aunt's and, for the first time, wondered if her mother had the same color eyes. "Look, Rachel. You're not a third wheel here. That's not how families work. You're not extra baggage I have to deal with because you're with Shiloh. You're the special bonus family that Shiloh has. I know I'm not like your Uncle Edward, and I can only just be me, but I want you here, protected and safe. And since you're part of Shiloh, you're part of what we're building, too. That's how family works."

She burst into tears, and his body locked as his eyes widened for a second before he did the only thing he could remember his dad doing when Betsy got upset when she was a teenager. He opened his arms, and she clung tightly. He patted her back and let her cry.

After a moment, she shifted away and swiped at her tears. He wasn't sure if she was going to be embarrassed but breathed a sigh of relief when she offered a little smile. "Thanks for that, Joseph. It feels weird to break down in front of you, but I didn't want to do that in front of Shiloh. She's been through so much, and I don't want her to worry any more than she has to."

Heart warming, he smiled in return. "As much as I want to protect her, I think she's strong enough to handle your feelings."

She chuckled and nodded. "I think you're right."

"Let's head back downstairs since I think my parents are about ready to leave. I know we've gone over the situation and safety measures for you when we were at the station, but I want to make sure you don't have any questions."

She swiped her face again, and then he led her downstairs. Shiloh's razor-sharp gaze landed on Rachel's face before darting up to his. He gave an almost imperceptible shake of his head, hoping to indicate to her that she didn't need to make a big deal about noticing that Rachel had cried. He watched as Shiloh steeled her expression, keeping a smile on her face.

It didn't take long after the house was empty for the three of them to settle in the living room. Rachel curled up in one of the comfy chairs while Shiloh and Joseph sat on the sofa, close together with his arm around her shoulders. He could see the dark circles under both of their eyes and the drooping shoulders from exhaustion. It was only eight o'clock, but he figured Rachel was ready to drop, and Shiloh wasn't far behind.

"Okay, let's do a quick review without making this day last any longer than it already has," he began, drawing both sets of blue-gray eyes to him. "No one has seen Isaiah, so we don't know if he is in the area or if he had someone else deliver the letter. You two know what he looks like and some of the men who work with him, but he could've always hired an outsider. Stay with other people, no matter what you're doing. Being alone is the most dangerous thing that you can do. So Rachel, Shiloh, and I will drop you off at school in the mornings, and the school officials will know that no one is to take you out of school except for those on your official list. At the end of the day, Cindy or Jack will wait with you until you're picked up, but even then, you'll stay in the school. I'll drop Shiloh off at the inn where the Baytown police and sheriff's department will do drive-bys. Tori and some of the other women will also have a visible presence there."

"And the Seafood Shack?" she asked.

"I've already called Mark, and he's going to have you only work the lunch crowd during the week, and you'll be off on weekends. While there, you'll always be around others, also. You'll pick Rachel up from school at the end of your shift, and the two of you can spend time at the Baytown library until I get off. Then we'll all come back here together."

Shiloh nodded, but her brow was still scrunched. "But how long will this go on? I need the money that comes from some of the weekend crowds."

The last thing he wanted was for her to worry about money. He started to tell her that but sensed that would be a topic for another day, deciding to stick to the most important matter at hand. "The police and sheriff's department are actively investigating this threat and working with the sheriff's department in Pennsylvania. We are hoping that Isaiah is making mistakes that will soon cost him his freedom."

Rachel jerked, her gaze shooting over to Shiloh. "I just thought he was mean and vindictive. I didn't know he was doing illegal things, as well."

Shiloh leaned forward and took Rachel's hand in her own. "I had no evidence, but going on Edward's suspicions about Isaiah causing the accidents made me know that he could possibly be dangerous. We have to be very careful, sweetheart."

After a few more minutes of chatting, Rachel stood and yawned widely. "I'm heading to bed. It's been a crazy day, and I don't want to fall asleep in algebra tomorrow." She leaned over and kissed Shiloh, then smiled shyly at Joseph and gave a little wave. "Good night."

"I'll be up in a little bit," Shiloh said as Rachel jogged up the stairs.

Now that they were alone, he leaned back against

the sofa cushions, glad that the tumultuous day was coming to an end. She shifted slightly and faced him, then lifted her brows. "So what now?"

"Um... um..." he stammered, eyes wide, no longer sure.

29

Shiloh hated to put him on the spot, but she'd spent the day being terrified, then hustled into the police station where she was faced with law enforcement leaders, and while they were known to her, they were still working in their official capacity. Going through her explanation of who she'd been and what had happened to her before she came to Baytown had been exhausting. So was reliving her decisions, revisiting grief, and trying to explain her thought processes, knowing that no one in that room could possibly understand what her life had been like.

Granted, it had been nice to lay the burden down, letting someone else worry about the threat. *Joseph had undoubtedly taken care of that for Rachel and me.* She'd once again been so worried about Rachel's reaction to another change in her life that she was stunned by how resilient the teenager was.

When they'd first walked into Joseph's house, she was surprised because he'd told her that he'd need to get furniture, but obviously, his family had already taken care of that, which warmed her heart. Now, after a full belly, everyone's assurances that she and Rachel were safe, and plans in place, she still couldn't help but wonder what was next for them. After all, before the letter had arrived, she and Joseph were just enjoying becoming a couple. Dinners with Rachel. Get-togethers with friends. Long kisses that left her hot and needy. And sex when the few opportunities arose.

Now, she and Rachel were living in his house.

He twisted on the sofa as well, and his brow scrunched as he asked, "I think you're going to have to be a bit more specific when you ask 'what now.'"

"I guess I'm not sure of the rules."

His brow continued to scrunch, and she rubbed her forehead for the millionth time that day. "I'm sorry for being vague. You and me, that's what I'm talking about. We've gone from being a new couple enjoying moments when we could. I guess I don't know what's expected now that we're here."

His brow eased, and he nodded as understanding dawned. She was glad, not sure she was up for asking the questions running through her mind. *Are we still a couple? Does this change everything? Is this going to be too much too soon for you? Does protection take precedence over a relationship? How do we navigate the situation?*

His hand was no longer on her shoulder, but he reached out and linked fingers with her. "I can't pretend to have all the answers because none of us expected this. But all I can do is promise to be honest with you." A little snort erupted, and he added, "That's what I told

Rachel earlier. I might not be able to answer all her questions, but I wouldn't lie to her."

"That's all I can ask of you, too," she sighed, hoping the truth wouldn't hurt.

"There's no playbook here, Shiloh. When I bought this house, I wanted to have a place to start a family when I met the right person. The first time I looked into your eyes, I knew I'd met the right person. Your past, the situation you're in now, being Rachel's guardian. None of that changes how I feel. I allowed myself to be the man who joked and flirted because I'd never found anyone to be serious about until you. It's true, we're still a new couple, and while we haven't been together all that long, I know beyond a shadow of a doubt that you're the person I want in my life. So this has moved up our time schedule, but I don't see any reason it has to change anything between us."

She stared into his eyes, not seeing the cocky Joseph but a glimpse of a young boy who wanted to be enough. *You are more than enough!*

He blinked, a light flickering in his clear blue eyes. "More than enough? For you? For us?"

Heat streaked across her cheeks as she realized she'd spoken aloud, but there was no turning back. And she didn't really want to. "You are more than I ever dreamed of. Ever hoped for."

He leaned closer and cupped her face, his thumbs sweeping over her cheeks. Kissing her lightly, she melted into the feel of his lips on hers. As he pulled back, she continued to hold his gaze.

"So we stay *us*," he whispered, his breath warm

against her mouth. "We're just like any other blended family."

While their situation was unique, it wasn't unusual. His words hit her, and a little gasp left her lungs. Colt with Carrie and Jack. Allie with Luke and his kids. Judith with Ryan, Cindy, and Trevor. Even Aiden MacFarlane from the pub was now married to a woman with a little girl.

He grinned slowly. "You're getting it now, aren't you?"

She nodded, smiling in return. "Yeah." She drew in a breath that shuddered her ribs and hitched a couple of times. But she still felt lighter than she had in hours. Her mind turned to Rachel, and she pressed her lips together before adding, "I get that we're an 'us.' But I'd like to talk to Rachel tomorrow to make sure she's good. So… um… tonight…"

He tucked a wayward strand of hair behind her ear, his grin still in place. "So tonight, you sleep in the guest room. And you keep sleeping in the guest room as long as that's where you're the most comfortable. We take this at your pace, Shiloh. You're already in my heart, and you're welcome in my bed whenever you're ready."

A nervous giggle erupted. "I'm ready, but I don't want to rush Rachel."

"Agreed."

He stood and offered his hand, and she gratefully allowed him to pull her up. Their arms encircled each other as she snuggled her cheek against his chest. They remained still for a moment, reveling in the silence. He left her embrace as he checked the doors downstairs, then linked fingers with her again as he led her upstairs.

Worried about Rachel, she gently turned the knob and peeked in, letting out a sigh of relief at the sight of the teen sound asleep in bed. She closed the door, looked over her shoulder, and smiled, offering a little nod.

"It was a busy day for her," he said. "I'm glad she found sleep."

"Me too," she whispered.

He walked to the doorway of the guest room and stood. "It's not very large, but I hope you'll be able to sleep, as well."

She glanced into the room and saw the twin daybed with mauve covers and bolster pillows. A decorative floor lamp offered a soft glow, and a small dresser graced another wall. Turning back, she squeezed his fingers and nodded. "It's absolutely lovely, Joseph."

He opened his mouth as though to speak, then, with a little shake of his head, remained silent. Bending, he kissed her lightly, although his tongue swept gently through her mouth before he pulled back. "Sleep tight, babe."

He turned and moved to the bedroom across the hall as she entered what was now her room. She sat on the edge of the bed, her gaze drifting about the room. He'd apologized for it being small, but in truth, it was no smaller than the room she used to share with Edward and lived in alone after he died. And for the past months, she'd shared a room with Rachel.

She stood and walked to the window, pulling back

the curtains and staring out into the backyard. The full moon cast its reflection over the water of the inlet, giving her the opportunity to see the small pier. She was filled with peace, something she wasn't sure she'd felt since losing her parents. Peace at knowing that she couldn't be bullied by Isaiah into giving back the land she had legally sold. Dealing with him was unpleasant, but knowing she had others at her back to keep her and Rachel safe, lifted the weight she'd felt on her chest. Maybe, if she was lucky, Joseph or one of the others would be able to tell Isaiah to leave her alone, and she'd never have to deal with him again. Although, she'd love for him to be able to lose his hold on the others in the community, shaking loose the cult-like authority he declaimed.

Hating to spend any more time thinking about him, she opened her small bag and pulled out her pajamas and toiletries, heading into the bathroom between the two guest rooms. Washing away the sweat and worry, she dressed, moisturized, and brushed her teeth. Flipping off the light, she walked back to her room, then stopped. Closing her eyes, she calmed her thoughts and centered her mind. Her lips curved slowly as certainty filled her.

Walking back into the hall, she moved to Joseph's room, tapping lightly on his door. Uncertain if he was already asleep, she jumped when the door swung open instantly. Her gaze dropped to the loose, drawstring sweatpants that hung precariously on his hips. Then sweeping upward, her attention snagged on his washboard abs and a light sprinkling of hair over his chest.

With one arm resting on the doorframe, his biceps bulged, and she couldn't help but drag her tongue over her bottom lip, which suddenly felt dry. As she continued to take him in, his expression moved from questioning to a boyish grin curving his lips.

"You okay?" he asked.

"Yeah," she breathed.

"Um... you want to come in?"

Her chest heaved as she nodded. "Yeah."

He stepped back, and she entered his bedroom. It wasn't huge, but it was large enough for a king-size bed, chest of drawers, and a small bookcase next to an overstuffed chair and lamp in one corner. The wooden floor was covered in a handmade braided rug, the blues, grays, and burgundy colors swirling together, complementing the blue comforter on his bed. A glance through an open door gave evidence of a large bathroom.

Turning toward him, she watched as he rocked back on his heels, one hand squeezing the back of his neck. He shrugged. "It's not much, but this was the only upstairs room I'd taken the time to fix up."

"It's nice." Rolling her eyes at the plain description she'd offered, she amended, "It's a lot more than nice. It's warm. Comfortable. The type of place where you could really relax. It looks like you."

He hesitated for a second, then tilted his head to the side, his gaze boring into hers. "Could you not sleep?"

She swallowed, then dropped her gaze, suddenly nervous. "I didn't try."

He stepped closer, his bare feet peeking out from

under his sweatpants as they stopped right in front of hers. His hand lifted, his knuckle tucking under her chin to raise her head. "What do you need?"

"You." The word slipped out before she had a chance to think of something more sophisticated to say, but it must have been the right thing, based on the smile on his face.

"Me?"

Emboldened, she nodded. "You. Us. Together. Now. Not waiting." His fingers danced along her chin, but he remained quiet. She hefted her shoulders in a little shrug. "I don't want to be right across the hall and filled with regret. I'm not ready for Rachel to have everything thrown into her face yet, but I can slip back into my room in the morning." She waited, feeling the seconds tick by as though each one was an hour. He remained still, and she wondered if she'd overstepped her bounds. Before she had a chance to melt down in embarrassment, he cupped her jaw and angled her head, sealing his mouth over hers.

She leaned closer, wrapping her arms around his neck, pressing her front tightly against him. His tongue was creating such delectable sensations that she was barely aware his hands on her back had separated. One snaked up to the back of her head, his fingers tangling in her tresses. His other hand slid down her ass, pressing his erection against her. Thrilled that he wanted this as much as she did, she let go of all reservations and kissed him back, her tongue dancing over with his. Electricity shot along her nerves, and she was amazed at how her body felt so connected. From her mouth to her breasts. From her nipples to her womb.

The desire to squeeze her legs together, searching for friction that he provided as he slid one thigh between her legs, and she rubbed her core over the rough material of his sweatpants. His hand on her ass shifted so that his fingers dove underneath the waistband of her pajama bottoms, squeezing her flesh.

A groan erupted, swallowed by their kiss, and she wasn't sure if it came from him or her, then decided it didn't matter. Giving up all pretense of slow and easy, her fingers clutched his shoulders as she began to walk backward toward the bed.

He halted, shifting them in the other direction. She nearly wept with frustration until she heard the click of the lock on his bedroom door. Embarrassed that she hadn't thought of that herself, she was glad for the reminder so that she would keep her noise to a minimum.

Now, having moved back toward the bed, he lifted her before gently tossing her so that she bounced on the mattress, a giggle jolting from her lungs. He leaned over and snagged her pajama bottoms, dragging them downward along with her panties. He tossed them behind him and then knelt, pulling her legs to rest over his shoulders. Diving in like a man starved, she gasped, and her fingers dug into the comforter as he licked and sucked. Another groan was heard, definitely from him, as she felt it vibrate deep inside. As he sucked on her nub, he inserted a finger, hooking it in just the right way to have her crashing over the edge like waves on the rocky shore, splitting her into a thousand pieces.

Panting, she was barely aware as he stood and kissed over her mound and up her belly. His hands dragged her pajama top over her head, and a sloppy smile covered her face as she looked down at him standing between her legs. "I'm naked, and you're not. What's wrong with this picture?"

He laughed softly and wiggled his eyebrows, dragging his gaze over her naked body. "From where I'm standing, babe, there's not one damn thing wrong with this picture." Still grinning, he hooked his thumbs into the waistband of his sweatpants and jerked them down, freeing his thick erection. "Your point is well taken, though, because what I want to do, we both need to be very naked."

Joseph loomed over her, and she quickly shifted so she was on her knees and patted the mattress next to her. He lifted a brow, and she grinned. "You've done so much for me, and I want to take care of you."

After the first time they'd been together, she'd admitted to Joseph that she and Edward had only ever tried missionary sex, but she had been more than willing to experiment with Joseph. So far, she loved discovering multiple positions, but she'd never gone down on him. Now, with his erection bobbing right in front of her, she wanted that more than anything.

"Are you sure?"

Adopting a stern expression, she whispered, "What's the matter? Afraid my inexperience might be dangerous to your, um… manhood?"

He faked a scowl and shook his head as he climbed onto the mattress and rolled onto his back. Lifting his hands, he placed them under his head as he inclined his head toward his cock. "Shiloh, babe, I trust you with my life, so I sure as hell will trust you with my... manhood."

She tried to stifle a giggle, but it slipped out nonetheless. Eagerly, she straddled his shins and leaned forward. Hoping what she'd read in romance novels was enough of a tutorial that she wouldn't embarrass herself, she took him in her hand. Fisting him gently several times, she loved the feel of satin over steel. Then slowly, she licked him from root to tip, her tongue swirling around the pre-cum. Lowering her mouth, she glided her lips around him, loving the hiss he emitted. Knowing she couldn't take all of him in, she kept her fist at the base so that between her mouth and hand, every inch of him was surrounded.

He twitched and groaned, his hips lifting slightly. "Oh God, Shiloh. Damn..."

She wasn't sure how long she would be able to suck him off, afraid she might tire before he came. But once she got going, she quickly fell into the rhythm, loving the power she'd discovered while giving him pleasure.

His hips continued to buck upward, and he finally groaned, "You gotta stop, babe. I come, I want to come buried inside you."

She slowly slid him from her mouth, then quickly shimmied up his thighs and lifted so that the tip was right at her sex. Her hair fell forward, creating a curtain around them as she slowly settled onto his cock. She eased him in until he was fully seated. His hands wrapped around her waist, pressing his fingertips into her ass. His breath was coming in shallow pants, and she was suddenly uncertain of what she was doing.

"You're perfect, babe," he said, seeming to know that she needed assurance. "Just keep moving. We'll find a rhythm together. And if you get tired, just lift slightly, and I'll do the work."

Nodding, she began to raise and lower on him, faltering a bit, clutching his shoulders to keep her steady. He was right. It didn't take long for them to find their rhythm. He undulated his hips in time to her movements, and soon she stopped worrying about the mechanics of on-top sex and just felt his cock dragging inside her core. Her muscles began to tighten, and she squeezed her eyes shut, blocking out everything but the sensations rocketing through her.

"I want to see your eyes," he whispered.

She blinked her eyes open, then kept them on his face as she moved faster. Suddenly with her gaze not wavering, she shattered from deep inside, feeling her muscles squeeze his cock. Riding the high for a moment, she wasn't sure she could keep from collapsing on top of his chest. With his upper body strength, he lifted her slightly and thrust his hips at a fast pace that soon had him roaring through his own release. She watched, fascinated as his neck muscles tightened and his face grew red until every drop was wrung from his body.

She'd managed to keep her eyes on him the whole time, thrilled with the way the light from the lamp next to the bed reflected in his blue eyes. As his fingers relaxed, she gently lowered her body onto his, wondering if she should roll to the side. His arms banded around her, holding her tight as she stretched out on top of him. They lay for long moments, his cock finally softening and sliding from her.

A multitude of emotions moved through her. Empowered. Sexy. Desirable. She finally lifted her head and stared down at his smiling face, then erased the distance between them and kissed him. Emotions crashed into her, and she squeezed her eyes shut to stop the prickly burn she felt behind her eyelids.

His hands were cupping her cheeks, then suddenly he jerked, pushing her up slightly, his gaze moving over her face, and his thumbs wiped away the moisture. "Shiloh, honey, did I hurt you?"

She shook her head, pressing her lips together. *God, I cry after fantastic sex. He's going to think I'm such a loser or hopeless head case.*

"Whatever you're thinking, babe, get it out of your mind. Just talk to me."

"I just suddenly felt overwhelmed—"

"I'm not surprised. Christ, I'm sorry. I should've never had us do this tonight. Today's just been too much for you—"

"No, I loved what we did." She held him tight, praying she could find the words to make him understand. "It's just that…"

"It's what, babe? Please. You can tell me anything."

As she stared at him, she realized he meant precisely what he said. She knew she could tell him anything, and he'd always make her feel treasured. Sucking in a deep breath, she nodded. "I feel like I've spent so many years waiting for something… a spark. A flame to ignite. I thought I had to give up that dream when it just wouldn't happen with Edward. Then later— I knew if I didn't escape, I'd never have a chance to experience the kind of relationship that moves mountains. Soars to the heavens. Eclipses everything else in life. But here, with you, I have that."

She barely got the words out before his arms tightened, and he rolled them so he was on top, his hips settled between her thighs, his strong body surrounding her.

"Shiloh, what I feel for you, I've never felt for anyone. And I don't want to wait one more second before telling you that I love you."

Her heart pounded as she sucked in a deep breath, tears leaking from her eyes and sliding down to the pillow underneath her head. "I'm afraid."

His eyes narrowed slightly. "Afraid of what?"

"I'm afraid of telling you that I love you, too. Love seems to be followed by bad things."

His lips curved into the most beautiful smile. "Never be afraid of love, babe. I promise I'll never let anything hurt you."

She wasn't sure if that was a promise he could keep, but at the moment, she'd give him anything, including the words she felt. With her hands cupping his face, her thumbs moving across his trimmed beard, she smiled as her heart sang. "I love you, too."

30

Rachel finished her sandwich, then shoved the plastic bag back into her paper sack. Her mind had been racing all during lunch, and she'd barely paid attention to what her friends were saying. Shoulder bumped from the side, she startled, looking around to see Jack's attention focused on her. Blushing, she grabbed her napkin and wiped her lips, hoping she didn't have crumbs on her face. Then rolling her eyes, she huffed.

"Hey, what's wrong?" Jack asked.

She didn't want to tell him that worrying about crumbs seemed ridiculous in light of everything that had happened the day before, so she just shrugged. "Sorry, I've got a lot on my mind."

"I'm not surprised," Cindy said from across the table. "Yesterday was crazy, and I'm so sorry this is happening to you."

To be honest," she confessed. "I was surprised that your dad didn't want to tell you to stay away from me,"

Jack snorted, shaking his head. "Are you kidding? Dad told me to stick with you like glue!"

"Me, too," Cindy agreed.

Just then, Trevor walked by with a couple of his senior football friends and stopped by their table. Rachel blushed, knowing everyone in the cafeteria was probably staring. Jack was firmly settled in her heart, but she'd have to be dead not to notice the handsome Trevor Coates.

He looked around the table, offering chin lifts to Jack and Brian, winked at his sister, then zeroed in on Rachel. "You doing okay?"

At that moment, he sounded so much like his dad that it was hard not to grin. Nodding, she replied, "Yeah, thanks."

"You see anything weird... anything that freaks you out... you let me know." With that, he offered another chin lift and walked away.

She now knew how Alice in Wonderland must've felt when falling down the rabbit hole. Her life had taken so many twists and turns, yet she'd been surrounded by people who always tried to soften the blows. Her parents and grandparents. Shiloh and Edward. Then Shiloh by herself. And now friends, and Joseph along with Shiloh. Many would say her life was not lucky, but she'd already learned that as long as someone was in her corner ready to fight with her, she could face almost anything.

"I want Shiloh and Joseph to stay together," she blurted out to her friends. She realized the statement made little sense, considering she hadn't prefaced it with anything else. Seeing their gazes locked on her, she shook her head. "I just mean that they were dating and getting closer, and I think they were falling in love when all this happened. And now we're staying with him, and I'm afraid it might make everything weird." She couldn't believe she was implying an intimacy between Joseph and Shiloh, but she desperately needed advice.

"You think they won't sleep together if you're around?" Brian asked.

She jerked her head around to see Brian's expression, but it was guileless. The heat still filled her cheeks, and she didn't miss how Cindy elbowed him in the ribs, eliciting a comical "umph."

"Jesus, Brian. A little discretion, please," Jack said, shooting a glare toward his friend before turning toward Rachel.

"It's okay, really," she said, offering a little smile. "I suppose it's better than beating around the bush and stumbling over my words."

Cindy's cheeks were red also, but she held Rachel's gaze and shrugged. "Judith moved in with us. There was a threat, and Dad didn't want her to be alone. I mean, they were together. You know, a couple. So it made sense for her to go ahead and move in with us."

"Mom and I moved in with Colt," Jack added.

She knew Colt was his stepdad but hearing that tidbit caused her attention to swing from Cindy to him. Twisting around on the cafeteria bench, she wanted to hear more.

"There was some stuff going on, and the townhouse

we lived in had water damage when the one next to us caught on fire. She and Colt liked each other, and he moved us into his house, along with our older neighbor. Even when the danger passed, we just stayed because by then, we were already becoming a family. Mom and Colt hadn't been dating very long before all that happened."

She nodded slowly. "I hadn't thought about it that way. I just want to make sure they have time for them."

"Rachel, you and Shiloh are super close," Cindy interjected. "Think of it this way… at some point, you and she were probably going to be moving into his house anyway. I mean, if they stay together, it's not like all three of you would be living on the third floor of the Sea Glass Inn. Maybe this just moves the timeframe up a little bit, but the three of you would have to figure out how to be a family sometime."

Nodding, she felt lighter than she had and smiled. The bell rang, and the quartet quickly stood and dumped their trash before heading out of the cafeteria. Cindy and Brian waved as they walked in the opposite direction.

Outside her classroom, Jack and she stepped to the side, letting the other teens rush by. He moved closer, talking just to her. "Joseph wants you safe. But you have to know, Rachel, that I want you safe, too. Promise me that you won't go anywhere without people around you. Me, if at all possible."

She looked into his eyes, butterflies swarming in her stomach. He was one of the most popular boys in ninth grade yet had chosen to hang out with her. She didn't have enough life experience to know what that meant, but she was glad he did.

He reached out and took her hand, squeezing gently as he stepped to the side, making sure the others walking in the hall didn't bump her. She stared up at his face, noticing that his attention was riveted on her and not the other girls walking past.

He jiggled her hand. "Promise me."

She nodded. "Okay, I promise. I'll wait on you at the end of the day."

He leaned closer, and her breath caught in her lungs, wondering if he was going to kiss her right next to her algebra classroom. Instead, he veered to the side, his breath puffing against her skin as his lips brushed against her cheek. Then winking, he watched as she scurried into the classroom, a wide smile on her lips.

31

Joseph was out with Callan and Jarod on routine sweeps up and down the coast around Baytown, including the inlets. Glancing at the time, he was glad to see that Jarod was heading them back toward the station. It had been a quiet morning for which he was glad, considering his mind was filled with Isaiah, keeping Shiloh and Rachel safe and wanting to end the threat while being thrilled that they were in his house. Moving to the wheel, he and Callan stood near Jarod, their eyes sweeping over the area but seeing nothing untoward.

"Anything new going on?" Callan asked.

Shaking his head, he replied, "No. It's been three days since Shiloh got the letter, and I've dropped Rachel off at school each morning, Shiloh off at the inn, and made sure they were both with others until I could get them at the end of the day and would go home."

"How's it working out having them with you?" Jarod asked.

"It's good." Those two words hardly describe what

he felt, which would have been more accurately described as fuckin' fantastic.

Jarod lifted his brow. "It doesn't feel too crowded?"

"Well, I know my house is kind of small, but it's fine. Shiloh and Rachel had been sharing the attic bedroom at the Sea Glass Inn. Granted, it's a big room, but it was never going to be permanent. And with the kitchen on the first floor, there was only so long before they would start needing to look for their own place, anyway."

"Yeah, but you two haven't been dating that long. Usually, people date for a while before they move in together," Jarod continued.

Before he or Callan had a chance to comment, Jarod shook his head and added, "Although, for around here, I don't suppose it's that odd. Seems like just about everybody we know has ended up moving in with people when shit happened." He shook his head and laughed. "I'd better hope I don't meet anyone who needs help. The last thing I want to do is share my space with someone until I'm ready to put a ring on it. Even then, it might feel too soon."

Callan barked out a laugh and clapped Jarod on the shoulder. "It'll hit you, man." He glanced over toward Joseph. "We gotta take bets at the station on how fast it happens to him."

Jarod jerked slightly. "Bets? On what?"

Feeling lighter than he had in several days, Joseph laughed. "We can take bets to see how long it is from the time Jarod meets someone to the time they're living with him. My guess? Less than a week!"

"Fuck that!" Jarod said.

As he pulled into the station, Ryan called over the radio. "Joseph? As soon as you secure the vessel, meet me in my office."

The smile fled his face, the weight of worry about Shiloh hanging on his shoulders.

"Go on," Jarod said. "Callan and I will take care of everything here."

Thanking them, he stepped onto the pier and jogged into the building, heading straight to Ryan's office. Stepping in, he spied Mitch and Colt, and his heart dropped. Before he could ask, Ryan hurried to say, "Shiloh and Rachel are fine. This is about the investigation."

Glad there was a chair nearby, he plopped into it, uncertain his legs would hold him up. "Thank God." Turning to Mitch, he asked, "What did you find out?"

"I took the information you had given me and ran with it. Thanks to you, the first leg of the investigation was already done." Mitch flipped open the folder and continued, "I tracked down the original deputy who came across the van accident. The five occupants, Shiloh's parents, her sister and brother-in-law, and the community pastor, were all pronounced deceased by the medical examiner who came out. Their injuries were consistent with severe trauma from an automobile accident. Without any question of foul play, their bodies were released to Isaiah Tolson and Shiloh Wallen. The sheriff faxed the report to me. I also contacted the local hospital that received the bodies from the accident. Shiloh signed a release form for Isaiah to identify the bodies and have a funeral home bring the five bodies back to Plineyville."

"So the body identification was done by Isaiah?" Joseph asked, leaning forward.

"I know what you're thinking, but Edward was the one who signed for the identification of Shiloh's family. Now, when the van was hauled out of the ravine, it ended up with Edward's father after the sheriff talked to him. That was where he looked at it, getting the idea that the brake line had been tampered with. I also followed up on questions about the community. The deputy told me that they were a peace-loving group. Never filed reports and never called the police. I asked him if he didn't think that was unusual, considering nobody is that *peaceful*. He agreed but said there was never a reason to check into them. He knew some people moved away after Isaiah took over as community leader, but again, no one ever filed a complaint."

"So someone can just do what they want, bully, threaten, coerce, and get away with it?" Joseph growled, leaning back in his chair with a huff. Grimacing, he shook his head. "I know that's how cults work, but that's why they're hard to shut down."

"I sent the deputy a copy of the letter from Isaiah, and he was interested. He noticed how more and more land was being acquired under Isaiah's name. Again, without anyone complaining, there was no reason to think that Isaiah wasn't doing anything more than what a lot of other people do, and that's to buy up real estate. And with a copy of the note he'd sent Shiloh, the sheriff said that it made a little bit more sense."

Leaning forward, he placed his forearms on the table and held Mitch's gaze with intensity. "What makes sense?"

"The county this sheriff is in has been growing because land developers have put in a small ski resort and lodge. He says they are looking to buy up more and more of the surrounding lands, wanting to expand."

Joseph gasped, a sharp pain hitting his chest as the air rushed out. "Isaiah's getting everyone to sign their land over to him so he can turn around and sell it. Christ, he'd make millions!"

"I've got an old military bud in that area," Colt added. "After Mitch talked to me, I gave them a call. He said that land is starting to go for a premium, and the price will only go up. Isaiah's edicts have been taking effect where the women have to turn their land over to him. If anyone can't farm it, such as the elderly, they have to turn it over to him. If anyone wants to sell and leave the area, it appears they are *convinced* to sign it over to him. He hasn't been able to gather it all. The land that Shiloh and Edward had from their parents bordered the area between Plineyville and the county where the development has already occurred."

"And she sold it to someone outside the community. Someone Isaiah had no power or control over."

Suddenly jolting, he rushed, "That older couple she sold it to. They could be in danger!" Shiloh had spoken of the couple helping her, giving her a new lease on life. If anything happened to them because of her, she'd be distraught.

Mitch lifted his hand and nodded. "I thought of that.

The sheriff made a trip out, and it seems the couple wanted to make sure nothing could happen, so their land is already in a trust. If anything happens to them, it's split among their children and grandchildren, who are spread out all over the country. In other words, Isaiah would not be able to get his hands on it."

Colt added, "Based on the letter he sent Shiloh, the sheriff will consider that as cause to go in and start an investigation in the finances. I talked to him again this morning, and the wheels are already in motion. As it turns out, Isaiah had already garnered the attention of the IRS, and they've been looking into him for the past six months. His funds have been frozen."

The four men remained quiet for a moment, and Joseph turned all the information over in his head. "Okay, so we understand Isaiah's motivation. We know that he needs to turn his attention away from Shiloh and focus on what's happening to him. But do you think he's left the area? Do you think he's realized he's got nothing to gain by coming after her?"

"I don't know, but I wouldn't let my guard down yet," Ryan said, shaking his head. "With what happened to Judith and my kids, I can tell you, don't assume anything."

Joseph looked at his boss, knowing he'd almost lost his whole family to an assassin. *Christ, if anything happened to Shiloh or Rachel...*

"Stay focused and make sure they still travel with others," Mitch agreed. "As soon as the sheriff in Pennsylvania has Isaiah under their thumb, he'll call."

The men all pushed themselves to stand, and as

Joseph walked to the door, he stopped and clasped hands with the other three. His shift was over, and he wanted to get to the library to pick up Shiloh and Rachel, knowing he wouldn't rest easy until he had them with him.

It only took a few minutes to drive, and when he walked through the library doors, it didn't take any effort to find them. Rachel and Shiloh were sitting at a table to the side. Pastor Parton and George MacElvey were sitting across from them, listening with rapt attention as Rachel described their situation. As he walked closer, Shiloh caught sight of him first and grinned. Breathing easier to see that they were safe and in good company, he walked straight over to her and bent, taking her lips in a quick kiss.

"So that's the way the wind blows, is it?" George said, his eyes twinkling.

"I told you that," Pastor Parton said, his head twisted toward George. "They've been dating for a while now."

"Well, I might not know the first gossip," George huffed, "but I will say I'm pleased. I think the three of you make a mighty fine-looking family."

Joseph jerked slightly, his gaze shooting down toward Shiloh and Rachel, finding the teenager grinning from ear to ear. Shiloh's gentle smile curved her lips, and her cheeks tinged pink.

"I hate to break up the gathering, but I need to get these two home," he said. George and the pastor hugged both women and shook his hand before he managed to get them into his SUV. It didn't take long before they pulled into the driveway.

Glad that dinner wouldn't take long, considering they just had to reheat one of the casseroles his mom had made, he filled them in on the information he'd gotten from Mitch and Colt. He skimmed over the discussion about the accident, focusing on why Isaiah wanted the land. Nothing seemed to surprise Shiloh other than Isaiah's apparent interest in selling the land for a profit after having been under his thumb for years as he preached the evils of money.

Tears welled in both women's eyes at the idea that Isaiah might have had a hand in their parents' deaths. If he could have spared them more heartache, he would have, but he needed them to understand what the man was capable of.

Shiloh clutched Rachel's hand as they continued to listen, seeming to accept the new information with a mixture of sadness at what had occurred and hope that Isaiah would soon be taken down.

As soon as they'd eaten, Rachel hopped up to wash the dishes, having grown quiet. Joseph knew something was up but wasn't sure how Shiloh wanted to play this. Leaning closer, he whispered, "What's going on with Rachel?"

She nibbled on her bottom lip and shook her head. "I'm not sure, but I'll talk to her."

"Let's talk to her together," he said.

She stopped nibbling, but her teeth still pressed against her bottom lip as though uncertain. He reached up and gently slid his thumb over the abraded flesh. "We're together, right?"

Her eyes shone as she nodded. "Yes, we are."

"Okay, look, Shiloh. All of this is new to us, but even if Isaiah pushed our timeline up, you and I wanted to get to this place in our relationship. We love each other. So we're a family."

Her shoulders lifted as she sucked in a deep breath and nodded again. "I know what you're going to say. Whatever we face, we need to do it together."

"I'm not gonna pretend I know everything about helping raise a teenage girl, but Betsy was two years younger than me, so I'm not completely without experience."

Rachel walked back into the room with a wet cloth to wipe off the table. Joseph reached out and stilled her hand. "Have a seat, Rachel. Shiloh and I would like to talk to you."

Rachel sat, her gaze darting back and forth between the two adults. He looked toward Shiloh, who suddenly appeared very unsure. Jumping in, praying he was using the right words, he said, "I know that I dumped a lot of information on you, and I want to make sure that you feel you can ask questions. I might not know the answer, but I'll find out."

Her face scrunched for a few seconds before blurting, "Will Isaiah go to jail?"

"Well, I don't know. And if he does, I don't know what the charges will be. It would be up to the county sheriff in Pennsylvania to decide if he wants to try to open a case for the brake tampering, but as someone in law enforcement, I'd have to say that might be hard to prove."

Rachel's face fell, and he shot a look toward Shiloh.

"But as far as what he's doing with the money, tax evasion, coercion… all of those things, then I'd say yes, he has a good chance of being arrested."

Her eyes widened as she nodded. "Is it wrong of me to hope he does go to jail?"

"I hope he rots in there!" Shiloh growled, causing Rachel and Joseph to swing their gazes toward her in surprise. Rachel bit back a grin, but he pulled Shiloh closer to him with his arm around her waist.

After a moment, Rachel hesitantly asked, "So what happens when the threat is over?"

"Well, um… I…" Shiloh looked toward Joseph, her gaze searching his.

"What do you want to happen, Rachel?" he asked, his heart in his throat, afraid that she wanted to leave.

Rachel's brow lowered, and she blinked several times, a tear escaping down her cheek. "I like it here."

Joseph and Shiloh sat up straighter at the same time, their gazes moving from each other back to her. The air fled his chest, and he dipped his chin. "Well, good. I like you here, too."

Rachel rushed, "I'm not a child. I know you two need privacy. You need to grow as a couple and have time… you know… just for you. I don't want to be the burden that makes you think it's too hard for this to work."

Shiloh sighed, her shoulders slumping. "Rachel," she said softly. "You've been through a lot of changes in the last months as well as years. Joseph and I want to ensure you're taken care of because we love you."

"Don't you remember what I told you before?" he

asked. "You're our bonus, not a burden. So get that idea out of your head."

She jumped up and threw her arms around him, hugging him tightly. "Oh, Joseph, thank you."

He patted her back and grinned at Shiloh over Rachel's shoulder. As she shifted away, he stood and said, "I'm gonna let you two have some time to talk while I catch a game on TV." With that, he leaned over and kissed Shiloh, chucked Rachel under the chin, and walked into the living room.

Hours later, he was surprised when Shiloh came into his room right after saying good night to Rachel. Brow lifted, he grinned as he watched her approach the bed. "Hey."

She climbed under the covers with him and cuddled close. "Hey, yourself."

"So… um… you're coming in kind of early. Not that I'm complaining, but… um…"

She giggled softly. "Well, Rachel told me tonight that she knew we were intimate and didn't want us to feel like we had to sneak around."

He shifted on his side so that he could see her face. "Seriously?"

"She said Cindy talked about Judith moving into their house. Jack talked about how he and Carrie moved in with Colt. She said it wasn't right for us to feel like we couldn't be who we were around her."

"What do you think?"

She smiled up at him, and warmth moved through his veins as he cupped her face.

"I think she's right. What we have feels solid, Joseph.

And real. And I don't want her to think that what we're building is wrong or something to be ashamed of. My parents were affectionate with each other. So were Rebecca and Thomas. And while what Edward and I had wasn't great passion, we were affectionate. So she told me I should stay here with you." She pressed her lips together and hastily added, "Not that I'm moving my things in—"

"Yes, you are."

He loved the owl-like blink she offered. Chuckling, he repeated, "Yes, you're moving your things in here. With Rachel's blessing, this is now *our* room."

Her beautiful smile spread so that her whole face glowed in the lamp's soft light. He leaned forward as he pulled her close and kissed her in the middle of her smile. Rachel was across the hall, safe and secure. Shiloh was in his bed and moving into his room. He couldn't imagine what he'd done to deserve such a bounty but was determined to show her how much he loved her.

Staying quiet, he made love to the woman who held his heart.

32

Rachel slid her backpack off and set it at her feet as she sat on the low brick wall near the steps leading to the football practice field. Jack settled next to her, sitting close enough that his arm touched hers from shoulder to elbow. The butterflies started fluttering again, and even though she wanted to twist her body to stare into his face, she didn't dare move, afraid his arm would no longer be touching hers.

"I don't want you to get in trouble with the coach while sitting here with me," she said. "I could go wait in the office until Shiloh gets here."

He ducked his head slightly and grinned. "Nah, the coach likes me. Anyway, we always have some time before practice. He looks over some of the homework and grades of some of the guys who are struggling first."

She leaned in slightly and teased, "Isn't that reason you should be down there?"

He moved his arm from next to hers, and for a second, she feared he'd been offended. But his arm slid around her back, and his hand cupped her shoulder. He pulled her in slightly to his side. "I'll have you know I've got straight A's so far. And that includes an A in English because you're studying with me."

Her brain short-circuited at the feel of his arm around her, and she couldn't think of anything to say. The butterflies in her stomach were now in full flight, and as she turned her head, it became evident how close they were. She stared straight into his eyes, their faces only a few inches apart. The always-sure-of-himself Jack suddenly appeared uncertain.

"I'm glad you moved here," he rushed.

At the same time, she spoke, "I'm glad we moved here."

They both grinned, and a nervous giggle slipped from her lips. His arm tightened slightly, and she loved the feel of being so close to him. She wanted to say more, but she really wanted to hear what he had to say.

He hesitated, his brow crinkling. "I'm not glad for the reason that you and your aunt had to move, and I'm really sorry about your parents. But it's just that I really like you, Rachel."

She couldn't imagine hearing sweeter words and continued to hold his gaze. She wanted to say so much. But for someone who'd lost and rebuilt their world several times, wanting something too much was terrifying. His fingers gripped her shoulder, just enough that she felt his steady presence. Emboldened, she gave voice to the feelings inside. "I really like you, too."

He leaned forward, and her breath halted in her lungs as longing and uncertainty battled for supremacy.

His lips brushed against hers, featherlight and soft. As they separated, her gaze never left his. That was when she knew she could see her future looking back at her. And her lips curved gently.

The sound of a vehicle approaching broke the moment, and she looked up to see Shiloh turning into the parking lot. She and Jack stood up at the same time, and as his hand dropped from her shoulder, she instantly felt the loss. While she knew she would have blushed bright red if his arm had stayed around her as her aunt drove closer, she still would've loved the affectionate and claiming gesture. Her smile felt slightly brittle until she felt his hand reach out and his fingers link with hers. As Shiloh parked nearby, she glanced into Jack's smiling face and hopeful eyes and realized she'd never forget that moment.

He reached down and snagged her backpack, and with their hands still linked, they walked over to Shiloh's car. "Hey, Ms. Wallen."

"Hi, guys," Shiloh said, smiling wide, as she stepped out of her car, still wearing her Seafood Shack T-shirt and jeans.

"Well, I'll get down to practice," Jack said.

He turned to Rachel, and she wondered if he'd kiss her again. Instead, he just squeezed her hand and winked. Then with a wave, he turned to grab his own backpack and headed down the stairs toward the practice field.

Cooped up all day, Shiloh longed for some fresh air and sunshine. Constantly vigilant, she'd spied Rachel and Jack sitting on the brick wall as soon as she pulled into the parking lot. And she'd witnessed their sweet kiss.

She walked over and hugged Rachel, then inclined her head toward the same wall she and Jack had been sitting on. "I've been indoors all day and would love some fresh air. Want to sit for a few minutes with me?" Bumping shoulders with her niece, she teased, "Although I'm not as much fun as your previous companion…"

Rachel blushed bright red as they sat on the wall, facing away from the parking lot and gazing down toward the practice field.

Shiloh's thoughts swirled around her head, tangling and untangling as the warm, late fall sun beamed down on them. "I remember the day you were born."

Rachel's surprise at Shiloh's words was evident as she jerked slightly, her head twisting around to stare at her aunt. "Really?"

"Rebecca was the picture of health all during her pregnancy. She went into the other town to see the doctor, but you were born at home with the community midwife. You were red and wrinkly and squalling. I thought you were the most beautiful thing I'd ever seen in my life." She smiled at Rachel, whose grin was equally as wide.

After another moment of silence, she continued, "I always thought I'd have a child of my own, but that was never to be with Edward and me."

Rachel's hand reached out to grasp hers. "Oh, Shiloh, I'm so sorry."

"Life is a journey full of twists and turns, Rachel. Paths that lead us through the darkest nights, the brightest sunlight, highs and lows, agony, and ecstasy. I can't give you any reasons for anything that happened in our past." She held tight to their clasped hands. "But I can tell you that you've grown into a beautiful, sweet, smart, amazing young woman. I knew the day you were born, and I held you in my arms that I was blessed to have you in my life. I am still blessed to have you in my life."

A tear slid down Rachel's face, and she leaned her head over, resting it on Shiloh's shoulder. "I'm blessed, too," she whispered in return.

Shiloh squeezed her eyes shut and leaned her head back, the sun casting its brightness over her closed eyelids, making everything feel warm and light. Kissing the top of Rachel's head, she smiled. "So, tell me about your first kiss."

Rachel sat up quickly, unable to keep the grin from her face. "Oh, Shiloh, I like him so much. I know we're young. And I know he's the first boy who ever kissed me. And I know the butterflies in my stomach, and the shooting stars I felt are just part of being so young, but… oh, I don't know. I just really, really like him. And he told me that he was so sorry about my parents and so sorry for the reason I had to move here, but that he also really liked me, too."

Shiloh's heart felt as warm as the sun on her face at the idea of Rachel's first love with someone as sweet as

Jack. She still remembered the first blush of love when Edward kissed her for the first time. And she very much remembered the burst of passion she felt the first time she kissed Joseph. "I'm glad, sweetheart. I'm so glad."

After another moment, she squeezed Rachel and said, "Let's head home. I want to cook dinner tonight."

Rachel giggled. "Joseph's mom did bring an awful lot of casseroles, didn't she?"

"She's an amazing cook, but yes... I feel like we've done nothing but eat casseroles lately. What would you say to some fried pork chops?"

"Yes!" Rachel enthused.

Turning toward the parking lot, their attention was diverted by a car pulling in closely. Most of the parking lot was empty, the students having been picked up by parents or buses. She didn't recognize the man behind the wheel, but a strange prickling moved down her spine. Shoving her hand into her pocket, she curled her fingers around her phone, whispering, "Have your phone in your hand."

Feeling Rachel stiffen next to her, she knew her niece understood. And when the man stepped out from the back seat, she was glad she'd listened to her intuition. Isaiah.

His black hair was slicked back, and his dark eyes narrowed. Wearing his typical black pants and black coat, he stalked forward. Another man climbed from the back seat, one of his minions she recognized.

Yet as he moved closer, she was struck by how much smaller he appeared than she'd remembered. He had never been a large man, yet his presence had always seemed so frightening, so in control. Now, he simply looked like an average man with an unpleasant countenance.

"Mistress Wallen," he said, stopping about five feet in front of her, his lips forming a sneer that seemed more comical than sure.

"Isaiah," she said, pressing Joseph's number on her phone, still in her pocket.

His hawkish eyes narrowed, raking over her as he leaned forward. "Besides dressing like a common woman, I see you've forgotten my title."

"I assure you, I haven't forgotten a thing. Not. One. Thing. And right now, you're trespassing on school property. So I advise you to climb back into your vehicle and leave, preferably back to Pennsylvania, since we have nothing to discuss."

Spittle flew from his mouth, and she was glad he wasn't close enough for his poison to land on her. "I was willing to give you my name! I was willing to make you Mistress of the community. Now, you're nothing but a fallen woman. But no matter." His gaze slid to the side. "Rachel will do well."

Her hand shot out, reaching toward Rachel, and Shiloh pulled Rachel behind her. "You'll touch her over my dead body."

His lips curved in a Grinch-like smile. "That can be arranged."

Her stomach curdled, and she fought back the urge to hurl. "Like you had my parents killed? Rachel's parents? Your own uncle?" Seeing his surprise, she continued, "I know what you did. I know you tampered with their brakes. I also know you had a hand in Edward's death."

"You are a simple woman and know nothing."

"I knew enough to escape you, didn't I? Escape, and make sure you never got your hands on the family land."

"I have no problem convincing the Kendalls to sell it back to me very cheaply once Rachel is my wife."

Rachel gasped behind her, which only served to steel Shiloh's spine. "You're not very smart, are you? You're being investigated for the murders you had a hand in. The IRS is also investigating you."

He waved his hand dismissively, although she saw the nervous twitch on his face. "The IRS can't touch me. God will give me his protection."

"You'll be lucky if God doesn't strike you down by lightning," she said. "But if you're really that stupid, keep going, and you'll find out what life in prison is like."

"God instructed me to get rid of those in my way."

Blinking, she shook her head as her heart threatened to pound out of her chest. "What do you mean?"

He snorted, straightening to his full height, the expression on his face giving evidence that he thought she'd be awed by his explanation. "My uncle had no vision. My uncle was willing to keep living the way he'd been raised. Simple. Poor. Relying on the goodwill of those in the community to help. But I knew the land God had placed us on gave me a vision. I tried to get him to understand that we could further God's work if we collectively gathered the land in our name."

"Further God's work? By selling it to a developer who wanted to extend his ski resort?"

"The money we would have made would've been a fortune." His voice was condescending, as though she were too ignorant to understand the concept.

"And how is a fortune godly?"

"Just like my uncle thought being poor was more godly, I knew God had no problem with us being rich. But no… he refused to listen. I approached your parents and Thomas, hoping to convince them they would follow God's will if they turned over their land to the community."

"And when they didn't, you had them killed," she said, her chest spasmed, caught between grief and rage.

His face darkened. "Making sure they were dead was simple. Insisting my uncle take the mountain road. A cut brake line." He shrugged, adding, "So much easier than I thought. I thought your weak husband would be easy. I couldn't believe it when he dug in his heels. But I was willing to wait as I made sure I gathered more land from the others. When he was the last holdout, I knew God wanted me to get rid of him, too."

Her body shivered, but she felt no fear. "I don't know if you're just pure evil or insane. Maybe a combination of both. But you've lost. You don't have the land. While you've been down here stalking Rachel and me, the authorities have stepped into Plineyville and taken over. From what I understand, plenty of people are ready to crawl out from underneath your oppressive thumb and tell them everything they want to know. Have you checked your bank lately? Your assets are frozen. And the developer you wanted to sell land to?

They already know the trouble you're in. So, Isaiah... you lose."

"Whore!" he screamed, his arm flying out as he backhanded her across the cheek. His face contorted into a maniacal expression as he reached out and grabbed her arm, jerking her to the side.

She and Rachel still had clasped hands, but this only served to bring Rachel closer to him. With his other hand, he grabbed Rachel by the arm. "She'll be mine!"

The man with Isaiah rushed forward, but Shiloh caught him by surprise when she kicked out, her foot catching him in the groin. He dropped to his knees on the pavement, and the man behind the steering wheel climbed out of the car, rushing forward. Wondering how she could take all three, she watched as Rachel kicked Isaiah in the shins.

An SUV squealed to a stop next to her car. "Get your hands off her!" A yell came from the side as a blur rushed past Shiloh and barreled into Isaiah.

She whipped her head around to see Joseph straddling Isaiah, and his fist cocked just before he sent it flying into Isaiah's face. Isaiah grunted, then tried to cover his head, pleading for mercy. She raced to Rachel and pulled her back away from the entangled limbs as the sound of sirens filled the air.

"Rachel!"

Jack vaulted over the low brick wall, not stopping until he had Rachel wrapped in his embrace with another hand around Shiloh. The sound of sirens filled the air. Colt leaped from the sheriff's SUV, and other deputies swarmed from their vehicles. Ignoring the man still clutching his crotch, he pointed his finger toward the driver and barked, "Move one fuckin' muscle, and I'll shoot." He got to Isaiah just as Joseph shoved his hands down on Isaiah's chest to push him up to a stand.

As Colt hauled Isaiah to his feet and cuffed him, Joseph followed Jack and headed straight to Shiloh. His gaze raked over her, settling on her stinging cheek. The blue of his eyes darkened, thunder clouds billowing in their depths. Wrapping his arms around her back, he enveloped her in his embrace.

Colt moved to the others as the deputies led the three men away. Her gaze shot up, and she said, "He confessed. He confessed to all the murders as well as trying to take everyone's land—"

"I know, I know, we got it."

She blinked. "But how?"

Joseph looked down and gently cupped her uninjured cheek. "When you dialed me, I was able to hear everything. At the same time, Rachel dialed 911 from her phone, so the dispatcher has it, too."

Colt looked at Jack and grinned. "Good work, son." Turning to the others, he explained, "Jack looked up from the field and saw a man talking to the two of you. As he raced up, he had his phone on video, so we've got him hitting you as well as grabbing Rachel."

Shivers raced through her body, and Joseph's arms tightened. "So that's it? Is he really gone from our lives? And from the community?"

"I was on the phone earlier this afternoon, and the detective was already opening up a new case. At this point, Isaiah is in a shit load of trouble and will most definitely spend time in prison. As for right now, he's going to our jail."

"It's over, baby," Joseph whispered in her ear. "You did great. You and Rachel were great."

She leaned back, her lips pressed together, her insides still shaking with adrenaline. "You know... he seemed... smaller."

Joseph cocked his head to the side. "Smaller?"

"I remember him as being so much larger than he really is. Why is that?"

"Before, you were frightened. He held power. He held control over you, making you feel small. But now, you've learned what all you can do on your own. What you're willing to fight for. That gives the power back to you." His arms tightened slightly, still holding her close. "And now you can see clearly what he really was."

She placed her cheek against his chest and observed the deputies putting the handcuffed Isaiah into their cruiser. His companions were also being escorted to other cruisers.

"Smooth sailing from now on."

She lifted her gaze to him and smiled. "I love you."

"Love you, too."

She heard footsteps and glanced to the other side toward Rachel, whose gaze was on her. As though Joseph and Jack recognized their need at the same time, they loosened their arms, and the two women clung together, tears flowing freely. Her heart ached for the destruction Isaiah had left in his wake, but she thanked God for Rachel in her arms and the new friends and loves surrounding them.

33

Shiloh stood at the kitchen window of the inn, rinsing off the breakfast dishes. It was two weeks after Isaiah's arrest. Joseph had stuck close for several days until he was finally convinced of what she knew—she and Rachel were fine.

Now, Joseph was at work, out on the water. It was a teacher workday, and Rachel was at home getting ready to have Jack over once Shiloh finished work and returned home. A smile curved her lips. Home. Technically, it was Joseph's house, but considering he didn't want her and Rachel to move out, they were still there, building a home and a family.

Hearing women's voices from the front, she wiped her hands and started out of the kitchen, smiling as she spied Tori, followed by Judith and Carrie. Tori had told her she was bringing the other two women for a visit. Through their husbands or children, they'd been involved in Isaiah's investigation and takedown, and all wanted to assure themselves that she and Rachel were fine.

She'd offered them tea, and the four sat and shared their stories. While hating that many of her friends in Baytown had harrowing experiences, she realized how it gave them a unique perception.

"I'm just so glad Isaiah is out of the picture, and you and Rachel can continue to build your life here," Tori said.

She nodded and pressed her lips together.

"That's the look of someone who wants to ask a question but isn't sure if she should," Judith said, smiling her way.

Laughing, Shiloh nodded. "I can't even pretend that you're not right." Gathering her thoughts, she cast her gaze among the other three, then said, "Joseph wants us to stay at his place."

"And what do you want?" Carrie asked.

Looking toward the statuesque, dark-haired beauty, she quickly replied, "That's what I want, too. But I don't know how it's supposed to work."

All three women smiled, nodding, and she realized they knew what she was talking about.

"Do I dare ask if you two had the money conversation?" Carrie laughed. "I remember when Colt and I had that particular discussion. I told him I wanted to help pay for the household expenses since Jack and I were living there, and he informed me that he took care of the money issues."

Judith leaned back in her seat and grinned. "How did that go over?"

"Probably about as well as it did for Mitch and me," Tori announced. "Not well."

"So, how do you make it work?" Shiloh asked. "I don't want to feel like a burden. I guess I'm trying to figure out the rules, and there aren't any."

"Honey," Carrie said, nodding. "You just hit the nail on the head. There are no rules to follow in relationships, so you and Joseph have to figure out what works for you. I don't want to be insensitive, but you were married before. So just like you and Edward had to discover how to build a home together, that's what you and Joseph must do. Just remember that the rules for you and Edward will be different than for you and Joseph."

"So if there are things he wants to pay for, I just let him?"

"It's called compromise," Judith added. "Let him know what you're willing to concede on, what you're willing to offer, and what you feel is an absolute. Believe me, that conversation will be a lot easier than trying to make an alpha male let you pay for things that he'd already planned on paying for."

Shaking her head, Shiloh snorted. "I guess I'd better try that compromise. It certainly has to go better than the argument we had the other day."

Tori lifted a brow and grinned. "Not all arguments are bad. Let's face it, makeup sex can be amazing."

Laughing, the women lifted their cups of tea and tapped them together. Later, as she stood at the door and waved goodbye, she cast her mind back and couldn't remember ever having so many genuine friends. Not even back in her easy childhood, laid-back adolescence, or early married days. She had been happy, and if Isaiah had never taken control, she could have spent the rest of her life in Plineyville, satisfied with her life. But there was no going back to days gone by. No undoing what had been done. All she had were the good memories she wanted to cling to, make today the best she could, and build a life of tomorrows with Rachel and the man she loved.

Leaving the inn, she picked up pizza on her way home. Once Jack came over, she was glad she'd gotten extra pizza, considering how much he had eaten. She'd managed to squirrel away several slices so Joseph could have some when he got off work. Now, she looked out toward the backyard, seeing Jack assist Rachel into the canoe. They were dressed for warmth underneath their life jackets.

Closing her eyes for a moment, she allowed the peace of the day to fill her. Her phone vibrated, jolting her from her reverie. Pulling it out, she grinned. "Hey, sweetie. What's up?"

"I'm actually not too far from the inlet near our house. Someone reported an asshole on a jet ski, and I'm trying to locate them. Anyway, how would you and Rachel like to go to Callan and Sophie's for dinner? Some others are going to be there, as well."

She laughed. "We had pizza for lunch, but I know she'd love to go out. Jack is here. Can he come, too, if Carrie says it's okay?"

"Of course. He's a good kid, and if I have to watch

someone with Rachel, I'd rather know it was someone who knows how to treat her."

"Hang on, and I'll go ask. They're just in the inlet in the canoe, but I can see them from here." Walking through the backyard, she breathed in the now-familiar scent of the bay. Hearing a motor nearby, she wondered if Joseph was already close.

Jack paddled away from the pier, grinning as Rachel leaned back and allowed her fingertips to drift through the water of the inlet. He rowed the canoe toward the bay. They weren't going all the way to the shore but just wanted to be alone for a little while on the water. They'd lucked out that even though it was late fall, the day was warm enough for her to be comfortable in the canoe.

She'd scooted close after he first helped her in, and he leaned forward, kissing her lips gently. After their first kiss, they'd snuck in several more over the past couple of weeks. Little kisses. Sweet kisses. He hadn't pressed for more, knowing she needed to take things slow.

He'd only kissed one other girl before, and that was in eighth grade. He'd liked her but hadn't felt anything special. He'd kissed her under the twinkling lights of the football stadium more because he was curious than had the desire. Plus, he assumed he was supposed to want to kiss her. Most of his friends had already kissed someone or said they had. He thought he would enjoy it more than he had but trying to figure out where to put his arms, his hands, and turn his head so that their noses wouldn't bump, had made it seem a lot more complicated than in the movies. They'd continue to kiss while they were girlfriend and boyfriend for several more months, but other than the sexual excitement, the kissing did very little for him.

Kissing Rachel had been completely different. Kissing her was like searching for the missing piece of the jigsaw puzzle, realizing that you had it in your hand all along, and it just fit. She was shy, and he didn't mind that. She let him lead, and he didn't mind that, either. Not that he felt like he had to be in control, but he liked the idea that she trusted him. And after having watched Colt for years, he wanted to treat a girl the way Colt treated his mom. He figured he'd learned from the best.

His mind cast back to a couple of weeks ago when he'd looked up and seen Shiloh trying to push Rachel behind her as a dark-haired man reached out to grab his girl. He'd seen red as he raced up the stairs, ready to cut loose on anyone who dared to touch a woman who didn't want to be touched, especially one he cared about. By the time he'd reached the top, he had watched as Shiloh took out one of the men, and Rachel kicked Isaiah's shin. He'd never been so proud.

"Are you lost in thought?" a soft voice came toward him.

He smiled, catching Rachel's blue-gray eyes staring at him, the sun's reflection making them appear lighter.

He'd noticed that about her eyes. Some days they were bluer, like a cloudless day over the bay. Other days, the gray darkened, making him want to chase the storms away. "Just enjoying the day with you," he replied honestly.

Her smile widened, and his breath caught, once again realizing how beautiful she was. A breeze moved across the water, and she shivered slightly. He rowed them around, heading them back toward Joseph's pier. "Going to take you back now, Rachel. I don't want you to get chilled out here."

Her expression fell slightly, then she asked, "Can you stay for the rest of the afternoon?"

"Wouldn't want to be anywhere else."

Her eyes brightened, and her smile curved her lips once again. It was a crazy feeling that moved through him, just knowing that his being with her made her happy.

The sound of a jet ski engine coming closer had him swing his head around, looking over his shoulder. Recognizing the driver, he cursed, "Shit!" as he dipped the paddle into the water and tried to maneuver them to the pier.

"What is it?" Rachel cried.

"Paul. Fuckin' Paul!" he yelled over the sound of the motor.

Paul cut back on the throttle and slowly circled the canoe, cutting off their attempt to make it to the pier. "Hey, look. It's asshole and his bitch." He dropped his gaze to Rachel, his eyes narrowing.

"Paul," Jack called out. "Back the fuck up, man. Whatever your problem is, don't make it worse."

"Worse?" Paul shouted. "Worse? What the fuck is worse than having to go to juvie on a trumped-up charge you caused, asshole?"

"I had nothing to do with that, and you know it. You had the pills. Your buds said you were going to distribute. Man, you gotta look into the mirror if you want someone to blame."

"Fuck you!"

Now that he was closer, he could see that Paul was weaving, and his words slurred slightly. Biting back what he wanted to say, he needed to get Rachel close enough to the pier to be out of danger's way. He wanted to believe that Paul wouldn't do anything to hurt her, but if he'd been drinking and was desperate, anything could happen.

Looking toward her, he could see Rachel's eyes now wide and her breath shallow. Keeping his voice low, he said, "Babe. Rachel." When her eyes cut over to him, he said, "I'm going to try to get you close. When I do, get to the pier." She jerked her head in a nod, but she appeared more focused on Paul.

A sudden movement on the pier caught his eye, and he looked up to see Shiloh walking toward them, her phone in her hand and a questioning expression on her face.

"What's going on?" she called out. Then as though she recognized Paul, her entire body jerked before her face contorted in a snarl. "What the hell are you doing here?"

"You're the bitch shacking up with the man who arrested me!"

While Paul focused on her, he slowly moved them closer to the pier. He watched as Shiloh whispered into her phone, knowing whoever she was talking to would send help their way. He just hoped they got there in time.

Suddenly, Paul swung his gaze back toward the canoe, his lips curled in a snarl. Gunning his jet ski, he roared toward them. Jack grabbed Rachel and tossed her overboard, yelling for her to swim. He had just enough time to jump into the water before Paul rammed his jet ski into the canoe, splintering it into pieces.

Breaking the surface, Jack started toward Rachel, who still hadn't made it to the pier. A sharp pain moved through his head, and he swiped his forehead, his fingers coming away bright red with blood. Hearing the motor coming closer, he realized Paul had turned around. With strong strokes, he made it to Rachel.

"Oh God! You're bleeding!" she sputtered, swallowing some water as she tried to swim and reached out for him at the same time.

"Go, Rachel, go!" A wave of dizziness hit him, but he pushed it down as they managed to assist each other to the wooden ladder. Just as Shiloh was kneeling, leaning down to help, he pushed Rachel upward. He grabbed the ladder and tried to climb up after her. Paul cut sharply, barely missing Jack's legs. "Goddammit! Paul! What are you doing?"

"Joseph is on his way!" Shiloh cried out.

Paul gunned the engine again, doing another circle, shouting cursing threats.

He whipped his head around, the wild-eyed expression on Paul's face giving evidence that the young man was bent on destruction and incapable of rational thinking. Jack spied as Paul slowed his vessel. He pulled out a gun from the back of his waistband. Slowly lifting the weapon, he aimed it at them.

Rachel gasped, pointing at Paul. "Oh God!"

He shoved Rachel and Shiloh behind him, holding his arms away from his sides, glad for his latest growth spurt, which had him much taller than either of the two women.

A shout from an approaching vessel had them all looking up to see two VMP boats. Joseph stood on the deck of one and Jarod on the other. With weapons drawn, they ordered Paul to lower his.

Paul shifted his weapon away from those on the pier but then slowly bent his arm, bringing the gun toward himself. Jack heard the sound of boots running from the yard and spied his dad and several deputies racing toward them but knew they'd never get there in time.

Heart in his throat, while Paul's attention was facing away, Jack raced to the end of the pier and flung himself forward, catching Paul off guard, knocking them both into the water, the gun flying from Paul's hand.

His head pounded, but at least the heavier teen had little fight left in him. Jack wrapped his arm around Paul and held his head above the water. The closest VMP boat made it to them, and Joseph pulled Paul onto their vessel.

"Jack!" Rachel screamed, tears running down her face.

He turned to see her on the edge of the pier with her arm extended and her hand reaching for him. His dad's face was hard as he knelt by Rachel's side, gently moving her over so that his much longer arm was easy for Jack to grasp. Hefted onto the pier, he barely had time to breathe before Rachel's body slammed into him, burrowing close.

"That was a helluva chance you took, son," Colt said.

Chest heaving, he kept his arms around Rachel, assuring himself that she was okay as he held his dad's gaze. "It was a helluva situation, dad."

The pier jolted slightly, and he turned around to see Joseph having leaped from the VMP boat, barely catching Shiloh as she raced to him. Joseph's face was as full of fury as his dad's, and Jack figured if he looked into a mirror, his would've been the same. Ryan soon joined them, and Shiloh ushered everyone inside as their statements were taken. Carrie soon arrived, running into the house to ensure Jack was okay. The rescue squad arrived, and Zac checked out Jack's head. The cut was small, requiring no stitches, but his mom fussed over him until his dad pulled her away, giving Rachel a chance to come closer.

After a while, Colt left to head to the jail to oversee Paul's processing, and Ryan went back to the station with two VMP boats.

As his mom stood and talked with Joseph and Shiloh, Jack linked hands with Rachel and walked over to the side of the yard. He stood facing her, her eyes slightly puffy from crying and her thick hair still wet even though she had changed into dry clothes. The first time he saw her, he thought she was beautiful. Now, she was even more so. Tucking a strand of hair behind her ear, he said, "You shouldn't have come back for me. You should have gone ahead and gotten to safety."

She wrapped her arms around his waist and blinked her blue-gray eyes up at him. "You were hurt. I didn't really think... I just knew I needed to get to you."

"I'm glad you learned how to swim."

Her lips curved upward, and a little giggle slipped out. "Thank you for teaching me."

"I guess that makes you my hero," he added, cupping her cheeks with his palms.

"You already were mine," she replied softly.

He glanced behind her and saw that his mom was heading toward their car. Looking back down at Rachel, he said, "It looks like I'm going to have to go."

"I'll see you tomorrow at school?"

"I'll be waiting on you when you get there."

Not caring if the adults were still watching, he bent and kissed her lightly, his heart thumping in his chest.

Joseph lay in bed that night, his arms wrapped around Shiloh after they'd both peeked into Rachel's room, assuring themselves that she was fast asleep after the horrifying events of the afternoon. They'd fielded concerned phone calls from friends and family, all wanting to make sure they were safe.

His fingers drifted over Shiloh's soft skin, hoping she could sleep but knowing he probably wouldn't with the image of Paul pointing a gun toward her and Rachel. If it had been possible for his heart to beat out of his chest, it would have. And he prayed he'd never have to face seeing someone threaten his family again.

"Joseph?"

"Yeah, babe."

"What did you say to Jack before he left?"

"Just man talk."

She shifted up, planting an elbow into the mattress and staring down at him. In the moonlight, he could see her brow lift. She speared him with a glare and repeated, "Man talk?"

Trying to hold back a chuckle, he lost the battle and felt her move as his chest rose up and down. "I told him that I was proud of him. I told him that he'd shown great courage and fast thinking to protect you and Rachel and then even to attempt to protect Paul from himself."

She smiled and then lay her head back on his shoulder.

He continued, "And after hearing how everything went down, I also told Rachel that I was proud of her, too. How she handled being frightened yet turning back to assist Jack when he was injured."

He wondered if she would keep talking, but she grew quiet as her breathing slowed. Finally, just when he thought she was asleep, he whispered into the night, "As soon as I think you're ready, baby, I'm buying you a ring."

Her arms tightened around his waist, and her soft voice whispered in reply. "I'm ready."

Grinning, he rolled over, holding his body above her with his forearms, staring into her shining eyes, his hips pressing into hers. Erasing the distance between their faces, he kissed her. And then he made love to her.

34

FOUR MONTHS LATER

Shiloh and Rachel walked over the grass of the cemetery, easily finding the headstones they were searching for while passing the graves of others they remembered fondly from years ago. Standing side by side, with arms around each other, they looked down at the five close together.

Carl Smithers. Karen Smithers. Rebecca Ayers. Thomas Ayers. Edward Wallen.

Joseph stood off to the side while she and Rachel carried an armload of flowers that they placed on each grave, kneeling before each one individually. She privately talked for a moment as she lay the flowers down, her memories flooding her mind and heart. She thought of her father on his tractor, waving his hat when he saw her walking down the road from school. She remembered her mother baking bread and the scent that filled the house and floated out through the open windows. She and Rebecca would lie in bed at night and talk about the men they'd like to marry one day. They wanted to have houses next to each other and raise their children together. She remembered the look on Thomas' face the first time he held Rachel in his arms.

At Edward's gravesite, she knelt and placed her hand on the warm stone, tracing his name with her fingers. "I loved you, Edward, and was proud to be your wife. And I hope you'd be proud of me for doing what I had to do. But I could never have escaped without your forethought and plans. So you'll always be a hero to me."

Lifting her face to the sun, she sucked in a deep breath of mountain air before letting it out slowly. "You'll always be in my heart, Edward, but I know you'd like Joseph for me. He's a good man. He's the right man for me now. So rest in peace, knowing that I've found another hero."

A gentle breeze blew over her, and she smiled. Standing, she whispered a last goodbye and walked over to Joseph and Rachel. All three clasping hands, they walked away from the past and toward their future.

Six Months Later

Joseph stood in the back of the Baytown Methodist Church, his gaze riveted on Shiloh standing at his side.

She turned to look up at him, and he stared into her blue-gray eyes, seeing light reflected at him. No storm clouds. Just light. "Are you ready?"

Her lips curved in a delicate smile, and she nodded. "Without a doubt."

When he'd asked her to marry him, she agreed readily. But when it came time to plan the wedding, she grew tentative. Every time his mother tried to talk to her about plans, she'd shut down, becoming quiet. Even Rachel had no idea what was going through her aunt's mind. Finally, he'd taken her for a long walk on the town pier, and holding her tightly, she'd managed to tell him what had been on her mind. She'd had the church wedding with family and friends all around. She'd walked down the aisle in a white dress that her mother had made for Rebecca and altered for Shiloh. She'd had her father give her away. And as much as she wanted to marry Joseph, she was struggling with doing a wedding the same way again. But she was in agony at the idea that he would be disappointed in her.

With her in his arms as they stood in the sunset, he'd breathed easier knowing she wasn't getting cold feet about marrying him… just the trappings of a traditional wedding. He'd looked her in the eyes, and said, "All I want is you. You and Rachel in my life. We can get married any way you want."

She'd also expressed fear that his mother would be disappointed, but it only took one conversation with Sherrie to discover that she'd done the mother of the bride with Betsy and the mother of the groom with

Wyatt. She was more than happy to accommodate whatever Shiloh wanted to have.

So here they were— he in dark pants and a white shirt with no tie and his sleeves rolled up over his forearms and she in an ivory sundress that came to her knees and her hair hanging down her back in waves, standing in the back of the church. Rachel and Wyatt stood at the front with Pastor Parton. Joseph's family and Mitch and Tori were in the front pews. Walking together toward the front, they stopped, faced each other, and grinned widely.

The simple ceremony with their written vows was soon over, and the small gathering headed down the street to the Sea Glass Inn, which had been closed for the day so a wedding reception with all their friends could attend. Guests mingled between the living room, dining room, sunroom, kitchen, back patio, yard, and gardens. Children ran and played. Friends had continuous platters of food circulating, and the MacFarlanes kept the alcohol flowing.

Joseph and Shiloh managed to greet everyone and enjoy the party all at the same time. As the evening sun descended, the entire gathering crossed the road and walked to the Baytown beach, their arms full of blankets and chairs. The massive group settled in to watch the sunset sky over the bay they all loved.

Joseph sat on a blanket with Shiloh's back pressed to his front, his arms wrapped around her. A glance to the side showed Jack sitting in a similar position with Rachel in his arms. He grinned, thinking that what Jack and Rachel shared was a hell of a lot more than what he thought he'd had in high school.

Hearing oohs and aahs, he turned his attention back to the sunset and the woman in his arms. Shiloh. His wife. He liked the sound of that.

Bending so that his lips were at her ear, he whispered, "You are everything I ever wanted." She twisted so that they were staring at each other. "And I knew it the first time I looked into your eyes."

She lifted her hand and cupped his cheek. "I love you, my hero."

Grinning, he kissed her and missed the sun dropping beyond the horizon. That was okay... they had a lifetime of sunsets to see.

Ten Years Later

Rachel stood in the small room off the vestibule of the Baytown Methodist Church. Her bridesmaids had fussed over her, oohing and ahhing over her wedding dress, and taking pictures. The wedding coordinator finally herded them out of the room, leaving only her and Shiloh. She stared into the mirror, her hands smoothing over the simple wedding dress, in awe that the seamstress had created such a beautiful gown from the wedding dress that had been passed down through the years.

Her gaze moved from her own reflection to the woman who came to stand next to her. The woman whose blue-gray eyes looked so much like her own. "It's beautiful, isn't it?"

"Yes, you are," Shiloh said, a gentle smile on her face.

"I was talking about the dress."

Shiloh's smile widened and she nodded. "I know you were. But it's the woman inside the dress that holds my heart." She sighed, her eyes bright. "But, yes, seeing you in your mother's dress, the one that I wore when I married Edward, makes me realize how we've come full circle."

"Would they be proud of me?" she asked, her voice now shaking.

"Oh, my beautiful girl. You're smart, kind, and now a teacher. Your parents would be beside themselves with pride and awe at all that you have done and all that you are. Just like I am."

Rachel turned and faced Shiloh, throwing her arms around her and battling the tears that threatened to ruin her makeup. From the moment her parents had died, Shiloh had become her surrogate mother, her champion, her hero. "You've given me everything."

"And you've given everything to me, as well," Shiloh said. Leaning back, she held Rachel's gaze then leaned in to kiss Rachel's cheek.

A knock on the door drew their attention, and the wedding coordinator popped her head inside. "Okay, mother of the bride. It's time for you to be escorted into the sanctuary."

With their gazes locked and their smiles in place, hasty words of love passed between Rachel and Shiloh. Then, watching Shiloh turn and walk gracefully out the door, she took a deep breath and let it out slowly.

Another knock on the door sounded, and she turned to see Joseph walking in. Handsome in his dark suit and tie, his light brown hair now tinged with a touch of gray at the temples was trimmed neatly, and wearing the easy smile he always bestowed upon her.

He walked straight to her, and she reached out her hands, clutching his.

"My God, Rachel. You are an absolute beauty. You remind me so much of Shiloh when we got married."

She'd remembered that day ten years ago when they stood in this very church, and she'd watched as Shiloh walked down the aisle toward Joseph. As all of her dreams and wishes had come true at the time, she now knew that this day eclipsed all other happy times before.

"Joseph," she began, squeezing his hands.

He shook his head in haste. "No—"

"I have to say this, Joseph—"

"No you don't, sweetheart."

"Yes, you need to let me say this." She gave him a moment to pull himself together, then plunged ahead, continuing to hold his hands. "I still have memories of my parents, and every little girl wants to have her daddy walk her down the aisle. And even though I don't have that today, I want you to know that I consider myself so lucky and so blessed that it's you who has the honor."

Her words faltered as she saw tears spring to his

eyes, but she kept going, determined to say what was in her heart. "I was lucky to have a wonderful father, and then when he was gone, I was so lucky to have Edward as my next father figure. It's hard to believe that my blessings could have happened again when you came into our lives. But having you as my father for the last ten years has been even more of a blessing. So while my real father and Edward are not here, I can't think of a better man to give me away today."

He pulled a handkerchief from his pocket and dabbed his eyes before shoving it away and holding her hands again. "I was a man searching but not really knowing what I was looking for until you and Shiloh came into my life. With her as my wife and you as the daughter of my heart, I consider myself to be the luckiest man alive. And while I hate like hell to be giving you away today, I can do it because the man you're marrying is a man that I trust and respect as much as anyone I've ever met. So while today is exciting, just know that a little part of my heart breaks."

Now it was her time to dab under her eyes, but then to lighten the mood, she smiled. "Yes, and then you get to do this again with Rebecca."

Joseph and Shiloh had not wasted any time after they got married to expand their family. First their son, Alex, and then their daughter, Rebecca. Rolling his eyes, he shook his head. "Oh, don't remind me."

The wedding coordinator popped her head into the room once again, and said, "It's time."

With a final hug, she accepted Joseph's outstretched arm, and they walked through the vestibule to the back of the chapel. Her bridesmaids had walked through, little Rebecca had gone next, and keeping her eyes on the man standing at the front with the minister, she smiled as Joseph escorted her down the aisle.

Jack stood in the front of the chapel, resplendent in his Naval officer uniform, hoping no one could see the sweat rolling down his back. The uniform had never felt so constricting. He'd graduated from the Naval Academy, and now was an officer stationed at Norfolk Naval Station. He wasn't sure how long he'd stay on active duty. He loved the Navy, loved the ships he served on, loved his career. But, the Chesapeake Bay always called when he was away.

Glancing to the side, he grinned nervously at his groomsmen, most who were also in uniforms, friends of his from the Navy. His younger brother stood next to them, along with Rachel's younger brother. But his best man, truly the *best* man he'd ever known, stood next to him. His stepfather, Colt.

He'd already endured the moments with his mom in tears, telling him how handsome he was and how proud she was, before she'd been escorted into the chapel. His groomsmen had stepped to the side to allow him and Colt to have their moment. A moment where he'd taken the opportunity to tell his stepfather that there was no one else he'd rather have at his side. Seeing tears well in Colt's eyes had stunned him, and when the big man told him that he could not love him more if he'd been his own flesh and blood, Jack was forced to blink his own tears back.

Now, he watched as Shiloh had been escorted and was sitting just across the aisle from his mom, Carrie. The bridesmaids had entered including his sister and Rachel's sister. And all that was left was for him to lay eyes on his bride. The music changed, the doors opened, and suddenly she was there.

His heart threatened to pound out of his chest at the sight of his beautiful woman, unable to believe this day had finally come.

They stayed together until the end of high school, then agreed to take a break when he went to the Naval Academy and she went to Old Dominion. They both dated others occasionally, but always found their way back to each other. Sometimes he hated the idea that he'd wasted any time and couldn't stand the thought of her having been with anyone else. But he knew that they were stronger, more mature, and ready to make the commitment that, in truth, they'd always known was right for them. There was no one else in his life he wanted to be with other than Rachel. And as she walked down the aisle in a beautiful, timeless white dress, he knew she was giving all her love to him as well.

Joseph gave her away, then stepped back to sit with Shiloh, but everyone else in the chapel fell away as Jack only had eyes for Rachel.

Shiloh clasped Joseph's hand as they sat next to each other, their eight-year-old son standing next to Colt and Jack's brother, and their six-year-old daughter, Rebecca preened in her dress, standing next to the other bridesmaids.

When Shiloh had been escorted down the aisle by one of the groomsmen, she looked around the packed chapel, seeing all their friends and family.

Her life had not turned out the way she thought it would when she was a little girl, or even a very young woman. But life has a way of taking twists and turns that none of us can imagine. And when the storms come, sometimes the best we can do is bend with the wind but not break. Because after the greatest storms, the sun will always come out again.

Her husband was her hero. But then, she'd come to learn that we are all heroes. When we take a stand. When we fight. When we protect. When we're afraid but push through those fears. When we become what we were meant to be.

Now, sitting in this church next to her greatest love, listening to the beloved minister officiate the wedding between the daughter of her heart and Jack, a man who was truly worthy of Rachel, she knew her family who had gone on before was looking down smiling.

Glancing to the side, she spied Joseph holding her gaze, a questioning expression on his face. She squeezed his hand and smiled. Mouthing *I love you*, he repeated the sentiment, then wrapped his free arm around her shoulders.

The service was soon over and as they all walked out

of the church, the Baytown sun beamed down on the gathering. Lifting her face to the warmth, she smiled.

> Don't miss the next Baytown Hero!
> A Hero for Her

> Visit my website for all my books!
> http://maryannjordanauthor.com

ALSO BY MARYANN JORDAN

Don't miss other Maryann Jordan books!

Baytown Boys (small town, military romantic suspense)
Coming Home
Just One More Chance
Clues of the Heart
Finding Peace
Picking Up the Pieces
Sunset Flames
Waiting for Sunrise
Hear My Heart
Guarding Your Heart
Sweet Rose
Our Time
Count On Me
Shielding You
To Love Someone
Sea Glass Hearts
Protecting Her Heart
Sunset Kiss

Baytown Heroes - A Baytown Boys subseries
A Hero's Chance

Finding a Hero

For all of Miss Ethel's boys:

Heroes at Heart (Military Romance)

Zander

Rafe

Cael

Jaxon

Jayden

Asher

Zeke

Cas

Lighthouse Security Investigations

Mace

Rank

Walker

Drew

Blake

Tate

Levi

Clay

Cobb

Bray

Josh

Knox

Lighthouse Security Investigations West Coast

Carson

Leo

Rick

Hop

Hope City (romantic suspense series co-developed with Kris Michaels

Brock book 1

Sean book 2

Carter book 3

Brody book 4

Kyle book 5

Ryker book 6

Rory book 7

Killian book 8

Torin book 9

Blayze book 10

Griffin book 11

Saints Protection & Investigations

(an elite group, assigned to the cases no one else wants…or can solve)

Serial Love

Healing Love

Revealing Love

Seeing Love

Honor Love

Sacrifice Love

Protecting Love

Remember Love

Discover Love

Surviving Love

Celebrating Love

Searching Love

Follow the exciting spin-off series:

Alvarez Security (military romantic suspense)

Gabe

Tony

Vinny

Jobe

SEALs

Thin Ice (Sleeper SEAL)

SEAL Together (Silver SEAL)

Undercover Groom (Hot SEAL)

Also for a Hope City Crossover Novel / Hot SEAL…

A Forever Dad

Long Road Home

Military Romantic Suspense

Home to Stay (a Lighthouse Security Investigation crossover novel)

Home Port (an LSI West Coast crossover novel)

Letters From Home (military romance)

Class of Love

Freedom of Love

Bond of Love

The Love's Series (detectives)

Love's Taming

Love's Tempting

Love's Trusting

The Fairfield Series (small town detectives)

Emma's Home

Laurie's Time

Carol's Image

Fireworks Over Fairfield

Please take the time to leave a review of this book. Feel free to contact me, especially if you enjoyed my book. I love to hear from readers!

Facebook

Email

Website

ABOUT THE AUTHOR

I am an avid reader of romance novels, often joking that I cut my teeth on the historical romances. I have been reading and reviewing for years. In 2013, I finally gave into the characters in my head, screaming for their story to be told. From these musings, my first novel, Emma's Home, The Fairfield Series was born.

I was a high school counselor having worked in education for thirty years. I live in Virginia, having also lived in four states and two foreign countries. I have been married to a wonderfully patient man for forty-one years. When writing, my dog or one of my four cats can generally be found in the same room if not on my lap.

Please take the time to leave a review of this book. Feel free to contact me, especially if you enjoyed my book. I love to hear from readers!

Facebook
Email
Website

Made in the USA
Monee, IL
20 October 2022